SAY THE WORD

JULIE JOHNSON

johnson

COPYRIGHT © 2014 JULIE JOHNSON
ALL RIGHTS RESERVED.

No part of this book may be used or reproduced in any manner whatsoever,
including Internet usage, without written permission of the author.

This is a work of fiction. Names, places, characters, and events are fictitious in
every regard. Any similarities to actual events and persons, living or dead, are
purely coincidental. Any trademarks, product names, or named features are only
used for reference, and are assumed to be property of their respective owners.

❧

COVER DESIGN BY **ONE CLICK COVERS**
www.oneclickcovers.com

__This one's for Buffy.__
For Veronica Mars.
For Elizabeth Bennet and Hermione Granger,
MacKayla Lane and Katniss Everdeen.
For all of my favorite fictional ladies,
who've always been there for me.

And, of course, for their wonderful creators.

❦

"I shall either find a way or make one."

HANNIBAL THE CONQUEROR

Prologue

I'VE ALWAYS THOUGHT that relationships are kind of like stars. The majority of them burn brightly for a time and then slowly die out, leaving a luminous legacy in their wake. Their residual light shines brightly for years after their dissipation – a dazzling imprint of what once was, that lingers even in the absence of the star itself.

Normal relationships, like normal stars, are no less beautiful in their ordinariness. They light the sky, weaving an infinite constellation of love, trust, and commitment. In fact, I'd always gazed rather enviously at that galaxy of wonderfully mundane relationships.

So, from what little I could tell from my view on the ground, there were these ordinary, healthy stars – glowing with a serenity that could only be indicative of domestic bliss.

And then, in another solar system entirely, there was my relationship with Sebastian.

We weren't a normal star. We were a supernova, a red-hot sun – the kind that blazes so strongly it eviscerates life on any planet foolish enough to orbit too close. And we didn't burn out. No, we imploded, leaving behind nothing but a gaping black hole so dark and so fathomless that not a trace of our light existed anymore.

So black, we didn't just repel the light...
We absorbed it.

I guess, in simpler terms, it'd be safe to say our breakup didn't go very well.

Chapter One

THEN

"D oɴ'ᴛ ᴅᴏ ᴛʜɪs, Lᴜx," ʜᴇ ᴘʟᴇᴀᴅᴇᴅ, ʜɪs ᴇʏᴇs ꜰᴜʟʟ ᴏꜰ anguished incomprehension.

I don't want to do this, believe me. I would give anything to not be doing this right now. But I don't have a choice in the matter.

Not anymore.

I schooled my face into a mask of callous indifference and forced myself to say the words in the flat, cold tone I typically reserved for the bitchy cheerleaders who ran in the popular cliques of our senior class, and who'd never approved of their perfect Sebastian dating the trailer trash girl on welfare.

"I don't want to be together anymore, Bash," I bit out. "We're going to college in a few months and I think the long-distance will be too hard."

Lies, lies, lies. Falling from my lips like raindrops in a storm.

"We've talked about this," Sebastian said in a steady voice, as though he thought by remaining calm he might somehow change my mind or force me to see reason. "I don't have to go to Princeton. I don't even want to go there, Lux... It's just my dad – you know," he broke off.

Yeah. I knew all about his father and the big dreams he had for Bash, his only son. The golden boy who was destined to carry on the Covington legacy.

"I'll go to State with you," Bash continued, moving closer to me. "We don't have to be apart, Lux. Not ever."

"It's college," I shrugged in what I hoped was a casual *my-heart-isn't-splintering-into-itty-bitty-pieces-at-this-very-moment*   gesture, moving a step backward so he couldn't enter my space. I knew if he touched me, I'd either shatter to pieces or breakdown crying in his arms, unable to conceal the true reason I was doing this.

I forged on, determined. "There'll be tons of other girls at Princeton. It's not fair for either of us to be tied down."

He shook his head, taking another step toward me. "I don't want anybody els–" he began.

I cut him off before he could finish the thought.

"I don't love you anymore," I said.

I love you more than anything, I thought.

"You're lying," he denied, his eyes fierce.

He was resolute in the belief that I loved him. He thought our love was stronger than anything.

I had to shatter that belief, wreck it so completely that he had no choice but to walk away. Sure, I'd be ripping out my own heart in the process, but that was just collateral damage. All that mattered in this moment was that he believed me.

"I never loved you, Sebastian." My sharp peal of laughter rang out harshly in the empty space between us, as though the very idea was ludicrous. I tried to ignore the note of hysteria that had crept into my voice, instead forcing my lips into a malicious smirk.

"How could I love someone like you?" I asked him, sidling closer like a rattlesnake moving in for the kill strike. "Someone so entitled and egotistical? Poor little rich boy, up in his mansion," I singsonged in a patronizing tone that made me sick to my stomach. I'd gone for the jugular, pushing the exact buttons I knew would inflict ultimate damage. His eyes flashed with pain and disbelief — it almost leveled me. Still, I forged on.

I took a step toward him, my gray-blue eyes flinty and devoid of feeling. My voice was scornful, my tone mocking. "It was fun, you see. Kind of like a game, only better because you fell for it and played along, even though you didn't understand the rules. It was simple enough – make the prince of the county fall for the girl from the wrong side of town." I pushed the words from my mouth, each traitorous syllable stabbing at my heart like a dagger. Getting right up in his face, my voice dropped to a belittling whisper. "Did you honestly believe that someone like me would ever fall for someone like you? That I'd feel anything but resentment for the life you lead? That I could ever actually *love* you?"

His eyes were swimming with ghosts, unfocused and far-seeing as he played back memories of our time together. He flinched as the new lens created by my words slipped over his mind's eye, casting a dark shade on every touch, every kiss, every smile we'd ever shared. His mouth gulped open as if to respond but no sound escaped, and I knew I was dangerously close to the point of no return – a hairsbreadth away from complete and total wreckage.

If I stopped now, if I took it all back, maybe there was still a chance for us. Maybe I could laugh and punch him lightly on the arm and say, *You big dummy, don't you know how much I love you? Don't you know nothing could ever make me stop?*

I kept going.

"Ah, yes, I can see by that wounded puppy-dog look in your eyes that you did believe it." I forced out another painful laugh. "Well, *checkmate*, baby. Game over. I win."

The memory of his face at that moment will haunt me until the day I leave this earth. I'll never forget the look in his eyes when I said the words that destroyed us – shock, rage, betrayal, grief. The blood drained from his face and he recoiled from me, as though I'd dealt him a physical blow.

I'd heard stories about racehorses who are pushed to their

limits, running so fast and so far that their hearts literally burst within their chests mid-race, killing them instantly. At that moment, I wondered vaguely if my own heart might explode — not from physical exertion, but emotional. It beat so fast I could feel my blood pulsing beneath the skin, hear the hollowed out thumping that echoed in my empty chest. My fingernails dug harshly into my palms as I prayed the tears gathering behind my eyes wouldn't escape down my cheeks.

"You don't mean that," he whispered, his voice broken, hollow with disbelief.

"Life isn't so easy outside your mansion, is it?" I plowed on, headfirst into heartbreak. I felt my heart splinter and dissolve into pieces, the void left in its place quickly filled by a sense of self-loathing stronger than anything I'd ever felt before.

I watched as the lies sunk in and he accepted my words for truth. Saw the hard glint of hatred and distrust cloud over his normally warm hazel eyes. Witnessed the change in his demeanor from welcoming to foreboding, as his shoulders straightened and his chin lifted. He looked down at me with an arrogant frigidity I'd only ever seen him adopt in his father's presence.

He despises me. The thought nearly brought me to my knees.

You see, the thing about Bash and me was that we didn't lie to one another. Not ever. So even that day, when I was lying through my teeth for the first time since he'd come into my life, he believed me. He trusted me to tell him the truth.

And I used it to destroy him.

Worse, even though he might hate me, I knew he would never lash out with cruelty or disrespect. In a twisted, backwards kind of way, it might've made me feel better to hear him yell and rage against my cruel words, to put up a fight when I broke his heart. But it simply wasn't in his nature to lose control in front of other people – especially not those who'd hurt him. He accepted my words with grim resolve and, true to his blue-blooded upbringing, banished any pain deep down, where no one could see. His expression was calm – an unrippled lake on a windless day – but his eyes were a turbulent sea, offering the only glimpse of his devastation.

"Goodbye, Lux," he said in a strangled voice, stuffing his hands into his pockets and staring at me with that quiet intensity he constantly radiated. The look in his eyes undid me.

I drank him in, knowing full well it was the last time I'd ever see him.

"Goodbye, Sebastian," I choked out, my voice catching as I said his name.

I turned quickly so he wouldn't see the tears that had finally broken free and walked away from the love of my life, leaving my heart behind.

I never let myself look back. Not even when I heard the unmistakable sound of a fist repeatedly hitting the trunk of our oak tree with enough force to strip away a layer of bark.

Chapter Two

NOW

I'M NOT A BAD PERSON.

I vote, I pay my taxes on time, and I make funny faces at babies in the supermarket to make them laugh. I tear up at those awful animal cruelty commercials Sarah McLaughlin is always singing on, and I shower on a regular basis. I donate to charities even though I'm still juggling monthly student loan and car payments on top of my rent and grocery expenses. I stay out of the drama at work because work is hard enough to get through without wondering which of my catty coworkers is going to stab me in the back with a knife clutched in her perfectly manicured fingers. I don't smoke or drink excessively – fine, I admit, *occasionally* I may indulge in a few too many glasses of Merlot, but nobody's perfect – and I force myself to go running in Central Park at least three times a week. By anyone's standards, I'm normal. A girl with her act together. Some might even call me "nice" and, for the most part, they'd be right.

I'm not a bad person.

I'm just not a particularly good one either.

To be fair, you can't ever really consider yourself a good person when you've been singlehandedly responsible for the utter destruction of another person's happiness. And that's really the only term you can use to describe what I did to Sebastian Covington all those years ago – I *destroyed* him. I watched unflinchingly as the life and love drained out of his eyes, and walked away without a backward glance.

It's kind of funny how a decision you make when you're eighteen can change your life forever. And by *funny* I mostly mean *absolutely fucking terrible*. When I broke off our relationship, I knew I was hurting him worse than he'd ever been hurt. Harder, though, was the knowledge that I was putting myself through unimaginable pain from which I would never recover.

I still remember that evening so clearly; I don't think I'll ever forget it. Two eighteen-year-old kids, standing at our spot by the old oak behind his house. The hot summer sun was setting and a slight breeze chilled the air as we stood a few paces apart staring at one another. Bash could read me better than anyone – even before I'd spoken, I think he knew what was coming. His eyes had changed, an unfamiliar wariness filling them as soon as my lips parted.

I'd taken a deep breath and forced myself to say the words that would tear us apart forever. And when I'd turned my back and walked away, haunted by the look of betrayal and incomprehension in his eyes, I'd known we'd never speak again. The damage I'd inflicted with my words had cut too deep to ever really heal. I didn't let myself cry then – that would come later, when I was alone in my bedroom and could finally allow the dull ache of my shattered heart to spread through my system like a lethal paralytic.

I'd known then, at eighteen, that my case of heartbreak was terminal, incurable. It wasn't "puppy love" or "first love" or any of the loves that supposedly fade with time and large quantities of ice cream. Because when you walk away from your soul mate – when you take real, true love and throw it in the fire and watch as it burns down to ashes – you know you'll never be the same again. The heart isn't like the liver; it doesn't regenerate, no matter how much time passes. Once it's gone, it's gone for good.

I'd left mine with Sebastian when I walked away that day, and I hadn't seen it in the seven years since.

I should've been thrilled; I'd played my part flawlessly. *And the Oscar for Coldhearted Bitch of the Century goes to...* me, Lux Kincaid. I hadn't had a choice about the plot. Sure, the script could vary here or there, interspersed with improvised lines of my own – but the endgame would always be the same. Our story ended with me walking away, leaving him to a star-studded future.

Roll credits.

Maybe I should back up a bit – start at the beginning, before everything became so complicated and convoluted I didn't even know which way was up anymore.

You know those stories about the good girl, from the perfect family, with the perfect freaking Rapunzel-like hair, who falls for the boy from the wrong side of the tracks? You know the one – that guy with the gruff exterior who, beneath all those tattoos and piercings and slutty man-whorish tendencies, actually possesses a heart of gold and a capacity for love and commitment rivaling that of a Golden Retriever?

That wasn't my story. In fact, you could probably say that was the exact *opposite* of my story.

I wasn't the good girl, with the perfect hair, and a Stepford Wife for a mother. And Bash? Well, he hated needles and he'd never been too girl-crazy – even though, with looks like his, he could've had anyone he wanted. As the son of a U.S. Senator, he'd been raised with a constant awareness of the press. His father had drilled the importance of looking the part into Bash's head from the time he could walk. We used to joke that in lieu of bedtime stories, his father had lectured on the merits of platinum cufflinks over gold in painstaking detail when he'd tucked his young son into bed at night.

Sebastian always looked like he'd just stepped off the glossy pages of a Ralph Lauren advertisement. With his longish dark blond hair pushed back from his face and each strand perfectly in place – not in a purposeful way that told you he'd spent hours in front of his bathroom mirror, but in that effortless way that only naturally beautiful people possess – his clean-cut looks instantly captured the attention of every girl in the room. And, as if to put him even further out of reach of us mere mortals, his warm nature and outgoing personality matched his appearance in every way. His heart was bigger than the county we lived in, which just so happened to be the largest in Georgia.

And me? Well, I wasn't just from the wrong side of the tracks. I was about fifteen blocks and three bus transfers away from even approaching the railway, let alone crossing over those damn tracks to Bash's side. Put in the plainest terms possible, I was white trash.

Dirt poor. Gutter scum. Lower class. It didn't matter how you said it – euphemisms wouldn't lift my family up above the poverty line or put more food on the table.

My childhood house, with its sagging roof, chipped shingles, and termite-eaten porch stoop, had been a laughable excuse for a residence. The blown-out tires on the front lawn and the rusted, ancient red pickup truck that had sat in the driveway unmoving for as long as I could remember didn't do much to improve our shabby-chic aesthetic, either. My home was such a cliché of American impoverishment that it was almost funny – although, the fact that I had to live in such a dump was sobering enough to leech any humor from the situation.

Moving on.

You know those stories where the family is incredibly poor, but the strength of their love for one another overcomes even the toughest economic obstacles? Those people who, despite having nothing, also have *everything* because they have each other?

Yeah, that's not my story either.

My parents were drunks. I don't say that to be mean, it's just a plain fact. They may have loved their children, but they'd always loved their vodka and gin just a little bit more.

When most people hear the words "child abuse" they immediately think of physical violence – fists flying and blood gushing. Some automatically assume that domestic violence is sexual. A smaller percentage of people think of emotional trauma – ugly words and the undeserved, often misplaced, destruction of a child's self-confidence.

My parents did none of those things. They weren't bad people. They weren't abusive. They were simply absent.

The official term is "neglect." That's how the lawyers and judges label it in courtrooms, anyway, right before they take you away from your parents and stick you into foster care. And maybe, if it had been just me, I'd have rolled the dice and tried out a fresh set of state-appointed guardians. But it wasn't just me. There was Jamie to think about.

James Arthur Kincaid, better known as "Jamie" to those of us who'd shared a womb with him for nine months, was my brother and my best friend.

Jamie was a lot of things besides my fraternal twin. He was the only person who could make me smile when I wanted to cry. He was the distraction I needed whenever looking at my parents passed out on the couch, or the empty vodka bottles scattered across the stained beige living room rug became unbearably depressing. Always cracking jokes or making inappropriate comments, Jamie was the goofy, hilarious, ever-cheerful part of my day. He was the reason I got out of bed every morning.

He was also a cancer patient.

When Jamie was diagnosed with osteosarcoma, we were fifteen and I couldn't even spell the name of the disease to type it into a damn Wikipedia search, let alone comprehend how much his diagnosis would alter the course of our lives. In fact, at that point I didn't know much of anything. The only thing I *did* understand with absolute certainty was that my parents could barely pay the mortgage each month, let alone afford all the expensive tests and treatments Jamie's illness would require.

MRI. Chemotherapy. Radiation. Surgery. Drug therapies. Hospital stays.

I wasn't a doctor – I wasn't even a legal adult – but I'd still known that treatments like that came with a hefty price tag. And whether thirty thousand or thirty million, any amount of money was light-years beyond our budget.

By the time we were seventeen – the year I met Sebastian and everything changed forever – we were so far in debt that most days I skipped lunch, and I was on a first name basis with Shelby over at the collection agency. She called every few months or so, when the phone or electricity bills were inevitably late, to let me know they'd be shutting off our power again.

Some people aren't built for struggle or hardship. My parents did the best they could, I honestly believe that. But they just weren't able to overcome their own demons, to pull themselves out of the depths of the bottle long enough to sort out the lives of their children, which were rapidly falling into chaos.

Someone had to take responsibility – even if that someone was a seventeen-year-old girl with five dollars in her pocket and a long-overgrown haircut.

Chapter Three

NOW

"Lux? You alive down there, girl?" The voice startled me out of my reverie. "Aren't you meeting with Jeanine in a half hour?"

My eyes flew open, taking in the sight of my wireless computer mouse and a mason jar full of multicolored sharpies. If the discomfort radiating from my left cheekbone was any indication, I'd nodded off with my face resting on my keyboard. With my luck, my stolen ten minutes of daydreaming would result in a permanent *ASDF* imprint across my face.

So professional.

Pushing strands of long blonde hair that had escaped the once-elegant chignon out of my eyes, I propped my chin in my hands and looked up at the face hovering above the wall of my cubicle. Fae, who occupied the desk space adjacent to mine, was peering down at me, her long mahogany brown hair perfectly styled into a French twist that would've taken me several hours and an industrial sized bottle of hairspray to pin up. Knowing Fae, who could've doubled as an Herbal Essences model, the sleekly sophisticated up-do had taken her ten seconds flat to accomplish.

"Sorry," I muttered, lifting my coffee cup for a hefty swig and attempting to rub feeling back into my left cheek. "Late night. I only got about four hours of sleep."

"I can tell. You look like crap," she informed me cheerily, skirting around the partition that divided our cubicles to lean against my desk.

I glared at her, but couldn't object because I knew her words were true. I'd spent most of the night tossing and turning, worried about the pitch I was giving today. There were bags beneath my eyes and my hair had definitely seen better days. I could only hope that Jeanine would be more focused on the quality of my research and the hard work I'd put into this proposal than she was on my looks.

Hah, who was I kidding?

Fae and I worked at *Luster*, the largest women's magazine in the United States. Our issues showed up on every newsstand, magazine rack, and waiting room coffee table in the nation, and circulated to more than 20 million regular subscribers each month – making us the go-to source for every feminine question you probably never wanted to know the answers to.

From sex tips to fashion, from the trashiest celebrity gossip to the latest and greatest diets and workout regimens... we specialized in it all. Complete with pictures of emaciated models in skimpy lingerie, of course.

If you'd asked me five years ago where I'd be working, *Luster* wouldn't have been in my top five. Hell, it wouldn't have made the top hundred. Most likely, it would have ranked right above "garbage collector" and just below "competitive hot-dog eating champion" on my long list of dream professions.

Fresh out of college, I'd had big-city dreams – aspirations of working at *The New York Times* or *The Washington Post*, rubbing elbows with the best journalists in the nation. Reporting on issues that mattered, like politics, religion, warfare, and finance. Heck, even covering the sports circuit would've been an all right gig. Instead, the economy went to shit and I was thrust into a rapidly shrinking workforce with few opportunities and even fewer job openings.

So now, here at *Luster* – which happened to be the only place I could land something even remotely related to my degree in journalism that also included a decent salary and health benefits – I write about really, truly, deeply important issues. You know, topics like *"How to Zumba Your Way to a Better Butt!"* and *"The Orgasm-Guaranteed Sex Positions You MUST Try Tonight!"*

Changing the world, one bimbo at a time. Go me.

But today was the day all that was going to change. I'd slaved over this pitch for weeks, doing research on my own time after work and compiling enough facts to make for a compelling piece in any publication – *Luster* included. If I could just peak Jeanine's interest, I was sure she'd let me use it as the topic of my monthly column or, at the very least, as a small feature story.

"Stop worrying," Fae scolded, thumping me lightly on the head with a stack of glossy proofs for an upcoming edition. "I'll fix your hair and even let you practice your pitch on me, because I am a wonderful friend. And hey, if you buy me a caramel macchiato from the good coffee cart – the one in the lobby with the cute barista, not the one in the tenth floor break room – I might even lend you my concealer to get rid of those under-eye circles."

"Done," I immediately agreed, spinning around on my wheelie chair so she had access to my hair. "Do your worst."

Fifteen minutes later, I was striding down the hallway – when you're wearing Christian Louboutin heels, you can't really do anything *but* stride – toward Jeanine's office. My long honey blonde locks were swept up into a graceful bun I'd never be able to replicate, my tired eyes had disappeared with a wave of Fae's magical Sephora wand, and I was feeling confident after running through my proposal one last time.

I knocked lightly on Jeanine's opaque glass door and popped my head through the entryway. Jeanine was on the phone, arguing with someone about what sounded like a graphics issue, but she gestured for me to come in and take a seat in the chair across from her desk. Her British accent did nothing to detract from the harsh words she spoke, or her scornful tone.

"Anton, I told you last week, the photo borders have to be *teal*, not turquoise. Honestly, after seventeen years in this business, you should be able to discern basic bloody colors. Or has all that time you spend staring at that computer of yours caused permanent damage to your brain?" Jeanine's lips curled into a condescending smirk. "You know, my five-year-old niece has a Crayola set – perhaps I can arrange for her to give you lessons."

I'm calm. I'm collected. I'm prepared. Just because she's an epic bitch to everyone else on the planet doesn't mean she'll shoot down my proposal.

Call me Cleopatra: The Queen of Denial.

I sat and tried not to fidget for the next five minutes as Jeanine tore poor Anton a new one. Smoothing my hands over my skirt too many times to count, I ironed out invisible wrinkles so I didn't have to meet her icy stare head-on. When she finally disconnected her call, I was nearly ready to run for the hills rather than pitch my story to her. *Nearly*, but not quite – I'd spent far too many hours working on this proposal to back out without even taking my shot.

"Lex, what can I do for you?" Jeanine asked impatiently, her tone immediately conveying that I was wasting her time simply by occupying space in her office.

"It's Lux," I corrected quietly. I'd worked here for almost three years, and she couldn't get my freaking name right? Typical Jeanine.

"Right, of course," she agreed. "Well?"

"I have an idea for a story," I began, forcing myself to meet her stare. I imagined it felt similar to looking into the eyes of one of the Dementors from *Harry Potter* – her gaze radiated frost and seemed vaguely life-threatening, as though if I said the wrong thing she'd lean across the desk and suck the life right out of me.

God, I was such a nerd.

"Alessandra Rodriguez is coming to the city next month. She's a bestselling author and Nobel Prize winner. Her awareness campaigns to put an end to violence against women have shaped global policy and helped thousands of victims." I took a calming breath. "But there has been some speculation that her nonprofit is actually embezzling some of the donated funds, artificially inflating the company's value while giving very little aid to the women they've promised to help." I heard the excitement build in my own voice and hoped Jeanine was listening. "As you know, I have a background in investigative journalism. While I was in college, I had bylines in two national papers when my story about corruption and fraud by university officials hit the circuit. If you'd just let me interview her, ask some questions, and dig around a little bit, I think I might find something. I know *Luster* isn't a newspaper, but an investigative piece would be a really great addi—"

The shrill ringing of Jeanine's antique gold-gilded desk phone abruptly cut off my words. Without a word to me, she leaned forward and snatched the receiver from its cradle.

"What is it Anna?" she clipped into the phone, likely causing her secretary to flinch on the other end. "Oh? And why is that?" Jeanine cast her eyes heavenward, clearly exasperated by whatever Anna was saying. "Fine, I'll take care of it."

She hung up without saying goodbye and returned her gaze to me. Her eyes were no longer chilly, but speculative.

"You've worked here for almost three years now, correct?" she asked, steepling her fingers in a contemplative gesture. Her out-of-left-field question took my by surprise.

"Yes?" I winced internally at the tentativeness in my voice.

"So you know where they do the photo shoots? At the ArtLust studio on Fifth?"

I nodded, confused about how this related to my pitch.

"I need you to go there for me. Right now. The assistant who normally coordinates the lunch deliveries for the models and production staff has apparently called out sick today, and evidently all of our interns are at some kind of rubbish career-building work-shop," Jeanine seethed. I think she would've rolled her eyes or frowned, if she weren't so afraid of developing crow's feet. "You'll need to pick up the lunch order from Gemelli's and bring it to the studio by noon."

My mouth dropped open in surprise. She was assigning me a task typically reserved for unpaid interns or personal assistants — so far outside my job description it was almost laughable.

I'd already paid my dues. I'd worked my ass off, despite the frivolous and often unfulfilling nature of my job. This was bullshit.

"Jeanine," I protested. "This really isn't in my job desc—"

"If you want me to consider your pitch on Alessandra Rodriguez – not to mention keep your position here – you will do this," she snapped, cutting me off. She leaned forward slightly with her eyes locked on mine, her coiled posture reminding me of some wild jungle cat about to take down an innocent grazing gazelle. "*Without* complaint."

Bitch.

She had me cornered and she knew it. After a casual glance at her Rolex, Jeanine looked pointedly from me to the door. "It's past eleven already. You'd better get moving, Lex. We can discuss your article tomorrow."

It's Lux, you narcissistic cow.

Cow or not, unfortunately she was right – the walk from our main office on West 57th to the ArtLust building on 5th took at least twenty minutes, not including the extra stop I'd have to make at Gemelli's to pick up the food. And Gemelli's was always packed during the lunch and dinner rush, with lines of hungry New Yorkers extending out onto the street as they waited for a variety of salad, soup, and deli creations that were some of the best Midtown had to offer.

"Thank you, Jeanine." I almost choked on the words, but managed to paste an acquiescent smile on my face. "I look forward to speaking with you again about my pitch."

I rose and walked out of her office, defeated and reeling. I'd prepared for the possibility that she'd shut down my proposal, but I'd never anticipated her assigning me to be her personal errand-girl for the day.

As I headed for my desk, lamenting the fact that I hadn't packed a pair of flats in my purse and would thus be forced to run around the city in heels, I thought my day couldn't possibly get any worse.

Little did I know.

⚅⚅

By the time I made it across town from Gemelli's — which was just as jammed as I'd thought it would be — to the studio, my formerly pristine blue blouse was wrinkled from the relentless late August humidity, I'd stepped in a disgusting wad of pink bubblegum someone had been kind enough to spit out on the sidewalk, and I was running late. Juggling the flimsy handles of two massive paper bags containing a spread of salads and sandwiches, I glanced down at my cellphone as I pushed through the crush of workers on their lunch breaks and winced as I saw that it was already quarter past noon.

I was late. Jeanine was going to skin me alive.

I startled as the phone rang in my hand, Desmond's name flashing across the screen. Adjusting my grip on the bags so they were both clutched in my right fist, I lifted the phone to my ear.

"Hello?" I asked, breathless from my efforts.

"Hey babe," Desmond drawled.

"Do you need something?" I clipped, my tone sharper than I'd intended.

Desmond and I had been out on a few casual dates, but I could tell he wanted more. He was a nice guy – perfect for me, really. He was a physical trainer at the gym I sometimes worked out at, and when he'd asked me out a few weeks ago I was in no position to turn him down. I hadn't been out on a date in three months and I hadn't had a real boyfriend for at least double that period. Fae was threatening to sign me up for eHarmony if I didn't break from my streak of solitude, and it was only a matter of time before she tricked me into another horrendous blind date with some poor soul from her seemingly endless stream of male acquaintances.

The last time this had happened, she'd told me we were going to get lattes at a funky, yet-undiscovered — and thus trendy in the eyes of every hipster in a five mile radius — coffee shop downtown that smelled vaguely like patchouli oil, was littered with beat up furniture that didn't match, and had purposely left its street windows too grimy for passerby to peer through. This in itself was troubling enough, though not half as concerning as what Fae did next.

Upon our arrival she'd immediately feigned a headache and excused herself, forcing me into an awkward coffee date with a poet named Lucien, who wore exclusively red flannel and donned thick-framed black glasses with nonprescription lenses. He'd read his angst-filled poetry to me for three painful hours, was offended on a fundamental level because I worked for the — *and I quote* — "materialistic magazine-industry machine," and didn't even pay for my chai tea latte afterwards.

Obviously, it was a match made in heaven.

So by the time Desmond asked me out, I figured he was the lesser of two evils and, at the very least, he always paid for coffee. Not to mention he was funny, laid-back, and good-looking – well-built, with dreamy blue eyes, a buzz cut, and a dimpled smile.

I wanted to like him, I really did. My heart just wasn't in it, I guess.

Not that it was ever fully in it, but I knew I could at least try a little harder to like the poor guy. Especially because, for some unknown reason, he seemed to like me.

"I was just thinking about you," he said, hurt evident in his voice. "Wondering how your pitch with Jeanine went this morning."

Face, meet palm. I was such a bitch sometimes.

"I'm sorry, Des," I said, picking up my pace as I spotted the

ArtLust building up ahead. "Jeanine was a total pit-bull as usual and now she has me out delivering lunches to the models at some photo shoot. Which, when you think about it, is pretty ridiculous because it's not like they're going to violate their air-diets and actually consume solid food anyway."

He snorted. "Sorry babe, that sucks. How 'bout you come over to my place tonight and I make you dinner?"

I knew very well that by *dinner* he really meant *sex*.

"Um, maybe, I don't know," I evaded, unsure whether I wanted to take things to the next level with him yet – or at all. "Hey can we talk about it later? I'm at the studio now."

"'Kay babe, let me know. I make a mean macaroni and cheese."

"Kraft?" I asked, knowing full well that he couldn't cook anything that didn't come either frozen or canned.

"Of course," he said, a smile in his voice. "It tastes better when it's from a box. Everyone knows that."

I laughed and hung up, just as I reached the front doors of the looming skyscraper before me. The studio was on the fifteenth floor – I'd only been there once before, more than two years ago when I'd had to have my photo taken for the magazine website. A thumbnail of my washed out portrait from that day accompanied every column I wrote and I still cringed whenever I saw it in print. Hopefully the photographer they'd hired for today's shoot was more skillful. Then again, how hard could it possibly be to take good pictures of practically naked, anatomically flawless women in lingerie? Unlike some of us, they didn't have any bad angles.

I crossed the gleaming black marble lobby floor and boarded the elevator, praying that nothing had changed in the months since I'd last been here. I was seriously late and couldn't afford to waste time wandering the hallways like a lost intern.

Thankfully, the elevator made relatively few stops as it climbed to my floor, and within minutes the doors were sliding open with a low chime. Entering the studio, which was essentially a large open plan with floor to ceiling windows, I saw that the right side of the room was set up for a photo shoot, cordoned off with large shades to block out any unwanted natural light. Numerous spotlights, tripods, reflective umbrellas, softboxes, and strobes surrounded the photographer, whose back was to me as he snapped photo after photo of next month's cover girl, Cara Stein.

A slender brunette whose plastic surgeries had ensured that she was abnormally well endowed, Cara was posing in a mock kitchen set, nude except for a flimsy red apron. Covered artfully in flour, she gripped a rolling pin suggestively in one hand and a cake-battered spoon in the other. As she slowly licked it clean, her seductive gaze trained on the camera, I averted my eyes so as not to gag and headed for the other side of the room.

There were three long rolling racks of garments for the models – apparently they occasionally wore more than baking ingredients – along with a hair and makeup station, where several beauty technicians hovered among their vast array of brushes and powders. Two models wearing silk bathrobes sat at the vanities, pecking feverishly at the screens of their cellphones. No doubt keeping their Twitter and Instagram followers interested with minute-by-minute updates about their *like, totally, like, glamorous* lives, while waiting for a turn in front of the camera. In the back corner, I finally spotted what I'd been searching for: a long, empty buffet table upon which I promptly dumped the heavy Gemelli's bags.

Flexing my hands, I winced as pins and needles shot through my fingertips. I was tempted to slip off my heels and rub feeling back into my arches – feet were not designed to walk ten blocks in stilettos, it's a scientific fact – but I refrained. I was about to touch people's food, after all.

When feeling had fully returned to my hands, I reached into the bags and unloaded the boxed salads and sandwiches. I heard Cara's whiney voice distantly responding to some of the photographer's directions, and tried to tune her out – she might be gorgeous, but she sounded like a feral cat caught in a rainstorm whenever she opened that million-dollar set of collagen treated lips. The studio was surprisingly quiet, the atmosphere saturated only by the hushed whispers of the makeup artists and the faint yet familiar refrains of classical music drifting through the overhead speakers.

Vitali's *Chaconne*, if I wasn't mistaken – one of my favorite classical pieces. I'd heard it for the first time on a rainy afternoon eight years ago, and in the many years since I hadn't been able to listen to it — or any other classical music, for that matter — because it was irrevocably tied to too many painful memories. And yet, as I began to arrange the containers on the tabletop, I found that no matter how much time had passed, I still knew each mournful note by heart. The violin was mesmerizing, heart-wrenching as it climbed effortlessly through the scales. As I listened to its defiantly beautiful strains, I had to fight the urge to weep.

Jesus, Lux, it's just a song. Let it go, already.

I quelled the gathering mist in my eyes and let the music wash over me. I couldn't help but think that it was a strange soundtrack choice for such a sexy photo shoot, but I was just a lowly columnist – the artistic process wasn't something I had any right to question.

I'd just lifted the last salad from the bag when I heard something far more upsetting than the tinny speaker music. Something that caused the container to slip from my fingertips and thud against the floor in an explosion of lettuce and croutons.

Or, to be more specific, *someone*.

Someone whose voice I hadn't heard for seven years – whose voice I'd never expected to hear again. That same someone who'd first played Vitali for me all those years ago.

Sebastian Covington.

Chapter Four

THEN

I T   W A S   A   B I T T E R   J A N U A R Y   A F T E R N O O N – T H E   K I N D   W H E R E   T H E
wind whips icy rain into your face and the crisp air bites against
your exposed skin like it has actual teeth. My jacket was from two
seasons ago, so worn out it barely shielded me from the elements
or retained any warmth. The ripped-out knees of my skinny jeans
sent chills racing up my legs.

I always laughed lightly to myself whenever I saw the wealthy
girls at my school wearing pairs of $150 designer jeans that had
been purposefully ripped to shreds with the help of a manufacturer. They were paying good money to look like war-refugees,
while I would've just liked to own set of pants I didn't have to
patch or turn into cut-off shorts when I grew too tall for them –
ironic, wasn't it?

I kept my head down against the spitting rain as I walked along
the side of the road. I'd missed my bus again, which meant I was in
for either a long wait in the rain until the next one rolled around at

five, or a lengthy, drizzly trek through muddy puddles. I opted to walk, hoping it would get me there faster.

Ms. Ingraham, my spring session advanced Latin teacher, had kept my entire class after school today because she was convinced no one had done the mandatory reading – or maybe it was just because she was a lonely old cat lady with no one to spend time with other than the students she coerced via detention sessions. Regardless of her reasons, I knew she was going to be a pain in the ass, and it was only the second day of classes.

The old bat was not only responsible for the hand cramp I had after conjugating approximately 17 million Latin verbs, but was also to blame for me missing my bus and being late to see Jamie at the hospital. He'd been there for almost three weeks this time, recovering from a particularly rigorous surgery on his left femur where more cancer had begun to grow.

He was supposed to start physical therapy any day now. The doctors were hopeful that he'd walk again within a few months of recovery, so long as the cancer didn't return. Unfortunately, their optimism was likely unrealistic. The sad fact that everyone knew but didn't say out loud was that with a cancer this aggressive, regrowth was an inevitability rather than a possibility. It was only a matter of time before Jamie was back at the hospital for another bone graft or, if things got really bad, a full amputation of his left leg.

They'd wanted to amputate this time, but Jamie had begged them to try to save his leg. It was riskier, but worth it, according to Jamie.

"No risk, no reward, Lux," he'd tell me, smiling through his pain.

I felt my numb lips twitch up into a reluctant grin, and pressed on through the downpour.

He wasn't responding to his chemotherapy drugs anymore, so the surgeons were taking a more aggressive approach. Limb-salvage surgeries weren't always effective, but since Jamie was young and relatively strong, they said it was his best option. They didn't say out loud that it was his *only* option, but I was smart enough to read between the lines of their sugar-coated prognoses, worried expressions, and hushed whispers.

So was Jamie.

He hated being at the hospital alone, cooped up in bed and unable to move, so I tried to visit as often as possible. I didn't like the thought of him lying there contemplating death or the possibility that his surgery wouldn't be a success.

My parents had picked up double shifts to pay the rapidly accumulating medical bills, so they weren't around much to visit him. Even if they hadn't been working, though, I wasn't sure their presence would've done Jamie any good. We'd never been as close to our parents as we had to one another — perhaps because they'd never seemed too interested in getting to know us. But I couldn't complain – not when they'd both been working nonstop to keep our house out of foreclosure and to cover Jamie's basic medical care.

Truthfully, it was silly for me worry about him getting lonely. With Jamie's handsome features – he pulled off the bald look really well – and sense of humor, he'd charmed the nurses within days of his first hospitalization. They all checked in on him and fussed over him like a son, bringing him extra pudding cups and sharing all the hospital gossip whenever they stopped by. It was hysterical and mildly inappropriate, but I was grateful he wasn't alone.

Caught up in my thoughts, I didn't hear the car approaching until it was far too late to move off the road. It whizzed by on my left, careening through a puddle at nearly forty miles per hour and dousing me completely with a torrent of dirty rainwater. I gasped, startled by the sudden icy downpour, and immediately began shivering as the chilly winds plastered my now-sodden coat and jeans to my body.

"Asshole!" I screamed after the car, shaking a fist in the air as it drove away.

My eyes widened when the car abruptly slammed to a halt about fifty yards up the road, its red brake lights brightly illuminated in the overcast sky. It was a nice car – a two-seater Mercedes hard top convertible, from what I could tell at this distance. I watched in horror as the white reverse lights flipped on and the car began backing down the vacant roadway, toward me.

Shit. I was so going to get beat up.

Here I was, walking alone on an empty roadway with no cellphone and no means of escape. Come to think of it, I was pretty sure this was the exact plot-line from the beginning of a horror movie I'd watched last Halloween...

Defenseless, isolated, idiot girl? Check.

Overcast, dark, stormy day? Check.

Psycho-killer in an expensive automobile? Check.

Dammit. Jamie was going to be so pissed at me when they found my body in an alligator-infested swamp somewhere in bum-fuck Florida.

When the Mercedes came to a stop next to me, I held my ground and stared menacingly at the darkly tinted passenger window. Whatever this jerk thought, I wasn't going down without a fight. I was Lux Kincaid – badass bitch extraordinaire, albeit in a five-foot-four, blonde pixie-like package.

Ha! I was so dead.

The window slid down silently, sending beads of water streaming off the shiny black passenger door and ultimately revealing the asshole's face. I had to clamp my lips together to keep them from falling open when the driver came into view.

Better than a road-ragey psycho killer, but not by much.

Sebastian Covington sat behind the wheel – honestly, the last person I'd expected to see. He was the most popular guy in the junior class, in part due to his looks – which even I had to admit were gorgeous, in an Abercrombie model sort of way – but mostly because his father was a U.S. Senator. I may have been the Typhoid Mary of my class, but even social rejects would recognize him on sight. Plus, I'd noticed today that he was in my Latin class. It had been hard to miss him, as there were only about twenty students enrolled, but since we sat on opposite sides of the room and had never previously interacted in the three years we'd both been attending Jackson County High, I very much doubted I'd crossed his radar.

"Hey," he called out the window, his eyes apologetic. "I'm so sorry about that – I took that turn a bit fast and didn't see you in time. I'm still getting the hang of driving this baby." His voice was nearly bashful as he gently stroked the leather steering wheel.

Translation: *Daddy bought me a new, expensive toy and I almost ran you down you with it... Sorry!*

Great apology, rich boy.

I rolled my eyes, turned away, and began walking again. To my utter annoyance, the car crept forward, keeping pace with my strides.

"Ouch, okay, the silent treatment. I guess I deserve that." I heard the sound of light laugher. "But why don't you ignore me from inside the car? It's warm and dry in here and I can tell you're freezing."

I cast a glance over my shoulder at him, trying to see if he was serious.

"I mean it, get in. I'll give you a ride home," he volunteered. "It's the least I can do."

I drew to a stop, considering his offer with raised brows. It was another half hour walk until I'd reach the hospital, and I was turning into a human popsicle with each passing minute. A glance up at the heavy clouds overhead assured that the rain wouldn't be letting up any time soon. I didn't want to accept a ride from him, but I also didn't want be out in the cold anymore. And, if I wanted to make it to see Jamie at all today, it was my best option.

With a martyred sigh, I reached out and grasped the door handle. Yanking it open, I smirked as I settled my sopping wet jeans onto his pristine tan leather seats. Prince Sebastian over there would probably have a conniption if I ruined his flawless interior. I set my backpack on the floor by my feet, crossed my arms over my chest, and looked up at him defiantly.

To my surprise, he didn't look even mildly fazed by moisture that was currently causing irreparable damage to his seats. His expression was open, friendly even. I quirked one eyebrow at him, wanting to ask what the heck he was staring at.

"Sebastian Covington," he prompted, holding out his hand for me to shake. Or maybe kiss. You never knew when it came to rich people and their weird rules of etiquette.

"I know who you are," I muttered, clicking my seatbelt into place and turning to face the windshield so I wouldn't stare at him. He was beautiful – easily prettier than most of the girls in our grade. His cheekbones were prominent, offsetting a pair of stunning green-gold eyes that seemed altogether too honest and warm to be genuine. They set me on edge, those fathomless eyes – the sincerity they conveyed seemed to me like a mask, put in place so no one would look too close or see the secrets they guarded. His jawline was so chiseled it was almost ridiculous. He was even better looking up close than from across a classroom – that realization made my stomach churn with nausea and brought an unstoppable flush to my cheeks.

"Not gonna return the favor?" he asked me, nodding down at his hand, which was still hanging outstretched in the air between us.

"Do you always feel the need to torture your victims with chit-chat after nearly running them down in the street?" I asked quietly, watching the rain droplets trickle in slow paths down the windshield.

"Fine, common courtesy be damned." Sebastian laughed, shifting the car into drive. "But it's all right, you don't have to tell me. I already know your name, Lux."

That had my attention. I swiveled my head around to look at him.

"Ah, now I've intrigued you." He smiled over at me. "Relax, I'm not a stalker. You're in my Latin class right?"

I nodded, my eyes still narrowed on him.

"Kind of hard to miss a name like 'Lux,'" he pointed out, shrugging. "Especially in Latin."

I didn't respond, and he fell silent. We drove for about five minutes, the rain falling on the windshield in a soothing patter that soon had me fighting off waves of drowsiness. I'd gotten only a few hours of sleep the night before, as I'd been up most of the night working a late shift at Minnie's, the local diner where I picked up a few shifts each week. By the time I'd dragged myself home, it had been past midnight, and I'd still had two hours of homework to get through before finally collapsing into bed.

"Not a big talker, huh?"

My eyes, which were drooping down to half-mast, snapped back open at the sound of his voice. "Sorry to disappoint," I mumbled, moving my hands up and down to rub warmth back into my frozen arms.

"Oh, shit, I really am an asshole," he muttered, reaching forward to flip on the heat. Hot air exploded out of the vents, immediately warming me. Before I knew what was happening, he'd pulled off onto the shoulder, put the car in park, and was shrugging out of his tan cable knit sweater, leaving only a thin t-shirt on his torso. "Here," he said, offering the sweater to me.

"Oh, no." I blushed, staring at the garment with wide eyes. "That's not necessary, really."

"Just take the damn sweater, " he ordered, clearly not used to being told *no*. "You're shivering."

I nodded, meeting his eyes fully for the first time as I reached hesitantly across the console to take the sweater. His gaze was intent as it moved over my face, studying my features as though I were a puzzle he wanted to solve.

I turned away, stripped off my waterlogged jacket and tossed it on top of my backpack, leaving me in a damp black t-shirt that was plastered to my torso like a second skin. Leaning back in my seat, I glanced over at him and caught him blatantly staring at my chest.

Boys were so predictable — and apparently boobs were boobs, regardless of social class boundaries.

Rolling my eyes, I smiled at the thought as I slipped his sweater over my head. It was still warm from his body, and it smelled like him – a heady masculine cocktail of aftershave and expensive cologne. Automatically, I inhaled deeply, committing his scent to memory. His cologne probably cost more than I made all week working at the diner, and I would've resented that fact on principle had it not smelled so goddamn good.

Plus, he'd given me his sweater. I was bitchy, but not unreasonable.

I turned to him and our eyes met, a look of understanding passing between us. "Thanks," I whispered, not knowing what else to say. Several moments passed in silence, the air between us becoming charged, electric, with each passing second. I wanted to tear my eyes from his to break the intensity of the moment, afraid he was seeing straight through me with that unwavering stare.

After a small eternity, Sebastian nodded, swallowing roughly before reaching across the center console. As his hand extended into my space, I forced myself not to flinch back from his touch. Our eyes still locked, I felt his fingers thread softly through the thick strands of hair at the base of my neck. His fingers skimmed the sensitive skin there, gently tugging my long hair up from where it was trapped beneath his bulky sweater. When his arm lifted, the damp waves tumbled free and fell midway down my back.

With unhurried fingers, he skimmed through the strands from the crown of my head down to the tips of each curl, his eyes following the movement of his hand as if mesmerized. I inhaled sharply when his fingers dropped down to brush the small of my back, but didn't pull away from his touch, entranced by the strange intimacy of a moment between strangers.

An involuntary exhale of air slipped between my lips, breaking the silence. Sebastian abruptly dropped his hand, his eyes seemed to clear of the haze, and he cleared his throat as he turned back to face the road. Pulling off the shoulder, we drove in silence for another five minutes before he spoke again. I didn't know what he was thinking – I wasn't even sure what *I* was thinking. All I knew was that my skin still tingled where his fingers had grazed, and I could still feel the weight of his eyes tracing over my features, as though their path had burned into my skin and marked me deep beneath the surface.

I tried to slow my racing heart as I watched the trees fly by outside the passenger window. Soft classical music – an intriguing choice for a high school boy – whispered through his speakers and lulled us back into safer waters.

"So are you going to tell me where I'm driving anytime soon or do I have to guess?" He laughed, trying to lighten the inexplicably heavy mood. "Not that I mind, really. Just wondering whether you had a destination, or were out walking in the rain for fun."

"Oh!" I exclaimed, slapping my forehead with an open palm. I could feel my cheeks heating as an embarrassed blush overtook my face. "I'm sorry, I'm an idiot. Can you please drop me off at Jackson Medical Center?"

He looked over at me curiously but didn't question my odd choice of destination. With a nod, he merged onto Main Street – which, in the one-horse town that was Jackson, housed every restaurant and shop on a single strip – and we wound through the streets toward the local hospital.

"What song is this?" I whispered, not wanting to break the silence but desperate to know the name of the hauntingly beautiful melody coming from his speakers.

"It's by a composer named Tomaso Vitali — it's the *Vitali Chaconne*," he said, looking over at me with raised eyebrows. "You like classical music?"

"Not particularly," I murmured, straining to listen as the violin crescendoed in an achingly sweet climax of strings. I'd never heard anything like it before. "But this is... I don't have words for what this is," I whispered, utterly overtaken by the music.

"I know what you mean. I feel the same way." Sebastian cleared his throat roughly. "Some people don't get music. How it can take you away from a place or a moment you don't want to be anymore, and transport you somewhere else entirely. Somewhere better." He blushed, as if embarrassed by his own admission or worried that he'd revealed something too personal.

"Do you play?" I asked.

"Every day," he admitted, laughing softly.

"What instrument?"

"Piano," he said, smiling to himself. "My mother would've preferred violin, but she thought I wouldn't have the discipline for it."

Somehow I doubted that. Sebastian didn't strike me as the undisciplined type, but I wasn't about to question him.

"I'd love to learn, someday," I mused softly, knowing that it wasn't a possibility. Music lessons were expensive and, even if I won the lottery and could somehow purchase a piano, the giant instrument would take up the entirety of my tiny bedroom. I grinned as the ridiculous image of me sleeping on top of a grand piano each night popped into my head – my pillow and blanket sliding against the glossy black wood as I tried to get comfortable.

"I could teach you," Sebastian offered casually, as though that was an actual possibility. I could only imagine what his popular posse would think of him hanging out with Lux Kincaid. I held in my snort and managed to nod.

"Mhm, maybe," I muttered noncommittally, looking out the window.

Was I actually having a normal conversation with the senator's son? I couldn't quite wrap my mind around that fact. I didn't look back at him until we were pulling to a stop in front of the hospital entrance.

"So... I guess this is it." Sebastian shifted the car into park and turned to face at me.

"Guess so," I said, gripping the door handle like a lifeline. I didn't know what to say to this beautiful boy, who talked about music and made me smile when nothing in my life seemed worth being happy about. "Thanks for nearly running me over. It was real fun."

"Anytime. It was my pleasure." He laughed.

"Goodbye, Sebastian," I said, getting out of the car.

"See you in class, Lux."

Sure, he'd see me. But we both knew we'd never talk like this again. We were from different worlds, and the reality was that the white-trash girl in the ripped up jeans simply didn't mix well with mansions and Mercedes. It was a shame, I thought, walking through the doors. For a moment, there, I could've sworn we'd connected on a basic human level. Sitting in his car in the rain, everything else had fallen away and we'd seemed like the only two in the world.

I knew better than to think it could last. Tomorrow in class, he'd ignore my presence and it would be as if it had never happened. All would be right in the world. I ignored the pang of loneliness in my chest, forcing a smile on my face as I thought ahead to Jamie.

I resolutely did not look back as the automatic glass doors slid shut behind me and, thus, had no way of knowing that Sebastian's watchful eyes followed my retreating form until I rounded a corner and faded from his view.

Chapter Five

NOW

WITHOUT TURNING AROUND, I KNEW HE WAS IN THE ROOM with me. I'd know that husky voice anywhere, no matter how many years passed. It still sent chills racing down my spine.

Ignoring the spilled lettuce at my feet, I promptly ducked behind the closest rack of designer clothing. The makeup artists were all staring at me like I was a crazy person – which, lets be honest, I pretty much was – but I didn't care. There was no freaking way I was coming face to face with Sebastian today. Actually, not ever. But most certainly not today, when my hair was slipping into my eyes, my blouse was wrinkled with perspiration and humidity, and I had gum on my favorite pair of heels.

I could, however, spy on him from behind this conveniently placed rack of clothing before making my escape to the elevator unnoticed. In retrospect, I should've walked away. No — I should've *run* away. I should've done the practical thing: high-tailed it for the elevator immediately and gone on with my blissfully uncomplicated life.

I've never been exceedingly practical.

And, obviously, I had to get a glimpse of him. Maybe he'd gotten fat and his hairline was receding. A girl could dream, right?

Crouched low, I reached shaky hands into the rack of hanging clothes and slid the dresses blocking my view apart to create a small opening I could peer through. And there he was.

His back was to me as he snapped photos of Cara. He was a photographer now, I gathered astutely, though I couldn't believe he was doing a shoot for *Luster*, of all places. It seemed so at odds with everything I knew about him – superficial, materialistic, girly.

Well, people change. His looks certainly had, at the very least.

When I'd last seen him, he'd been eighteen and – while not lean – he'd had the lithe, athletic build of a soccer player. That boy was gone, replaced by a man with broad shoulders and defined biceps that strained against the confines of his dark green henley as he lifted his camera to eye level. His hair was the same burnished gold color, but he wore it a little longer than he had in high school.

Damn.

Did it make me a bad person for wishing — just a little, teensy bit — that he'd let himself go? Maybe gotten a beer-belly or started wearing socks and sandals at the same time? It would make it a hell of a lot easier to look at him. Was that so much to ask, in the grand scheme of things?

Apparently.

From what I could see from his profile and build, he looked *good*. Great. Goddamn delicious. And I had to stare at him armed with the knowledge that I'd walked away from the literal embodiment of perfection.

Damn, damn, damn.

All sorts of questions raced through my mind as spied on him through the rack of designer dresses. Was he married? Did he have children? A house and a Golden Retriever in his backyard, where he played catch with a son whose mother wasn't me?

The hole where my heart used to reside ached, a seven-year-old wound made fresh. Whatever scar tissue had managed to heal over in the time since I'd last seen him was ripped off and I was eighteen once more, weeping into the pillow of my childhood bed. When I'd walked away from him that day, I'd honestly never expected to see Sebastian again. And though it nearly killed me, I'd never tried to contact him in the years since. I'd never even let myself Google him, knowing that his image would likely appear alongside his father's.

He'd never reached out to me either, which hurt irrationally. I'd ripped his heart to shreds, yet for years after our breakup some small, insistent, deranged part of my brain had expected Sebastian to come for me. To force me to see reason – hell, to at least *try* to get me back. I'd wanted him to fight for me, even knowing full well that we couldn't be together.

I was an idiot.

I also needed wine. And maybe chocolate. Lots and lots of chocolate. Possibly a marathon of Johnny Depp movies as well. Screw going back to work. I had stops to make on the way home, followed by plans which included getting very familiar with my living room sofa and not moving for at least three days.

I had no right to want him, no right to even look at him anymore, but when Cara Stein sauntered toward him and smeared a frosting-covered finger down his cheek before leaning in to lick it clean, I wanted to rip her beautiful face right off.

So, he was dating a model. Or screwing one, at the very least. How charming.

I tore my eyes away, feeling physically ill and unable to look anymore. I knew I had no claim on him – we hadn't spoken in seven freaking years. I wasn't naive in thinking that after our breakup he'd been so devastated he'd joined a monastery and taken an oath of celibacy – though that delusion was vastly preferable to the sharp, debilitating pain I felt now as I watched him with someone else.

So distressed by Sebastian's presence, I didn't put it together that the shoot was over until he began packing up his lenses and Cara turned and approached the food table, which was a few short feet away from my hiding spot. Casting a last, longing look at Sebastian's back – god, I was pathetic – I rose and started speed-walking to the elevator.

I was close to escape – so, so close to walking out of there without living one of my worst nightmares and coming face to face with the former love of my life. It was the one confrontation I'd have paid any amount of money to avoid. Keeping my eyes trained on the floor and my head ducked low, I reached the bank of elevators and lifted my hand to press the call button.

Vitali's *Chaconne* thrummed in my ears, keeping time with the blood that pounded through my veins in a relentless staccato. The illuminated numbers above the door showed the elevator was on the second floor. It might take several minutes for it to reach the fifteenth, especially if the lunch crowd were returning from their breaks and disembarking on every level.

Come on, hurry up, I pleaded with my eyes trained on the number panel.

"What the hell is this mess?!" a feminine voice shrieked. "Who did this? The salad I ordered is all over the floor!"

Shit.

I pressed the call button again, praying that whatever god was up there would take pity on me and let the elevator arrive before Cara spotted me.

"Hey! You!" her voice screeched. "Bitch by the elevators!"

Fuck. Too late.

My eyes closed and I sighed deeply, knowing a confrontation with her was unavoidable. All I could hope for at this point was that her boyfriend wouldn't get involved – because that would get really awkward, really fast. I listened as her heels clomped in my direction, unwilling to turn around to face her until it was absolutely necessary. I considered running for the stairwell, but I had a feeling that descending fifteen flights in Louboutins wouldn't end well for me, and Cara would probably have security guards swarming before I made it down two levels.

"Did you not hear me, bitch?" she snarled, her voice close now.

I turned slowly to face her.

"You spilled my salad all over the ground!" Cara stomped one heeled foot indignantly.

I hated girls like Cara on principle – perhaps unfairly, but I never claimed to be perfect. She was exactly like the girls who'd bullied and belittled me through my high school years because I didn't wear the right clothes or live in the right zip code. She called other women "bitch" and "skank" because it made her feel better about herself – it was classic mean-girl strategy, and I had zero tolerance for it after four years at Jackson High. I may have traded my ripped jeans and holey sweaters for designer shoes and a $100 haircut, but I'd never quite shaken the white-trash girl I'd grown up as. She was still there, beneath the refined veneer I'd meticulously crafted during my years of city living.

And, if provoked, she'd rise to the surface quicker than Cara could say "Botox injection."

There was also the small, insignificant fact that she was sleeping with my Sebastian. I may or may not have been holding that against her as well.

"You were just going to throw it up anyway," I muttered under my breath, low enough that she couldn't make out my words.

"What did you say? Speak up, bitch!"

My insult tolerance had just about expired for the day. I cocked one eyebrow and stared up at Cara.

"What is it about women like you, that think it's all right to call other women bitches? You're a freaking model for god's sake." I snorted. "Your legs go on for miles, you have a team of professionals to make you beautiful every day, and men all over the world whack-off to your picture every night – what could you possibly gain by putting other women down? Is it because, in spite of all the glamour and fame, you're still overcompensating for the gawky, insecure girl you were in middle school?"

I'd been guessing about her ugly-duckling complex but, judging from the way the smile dropped off her face at my words, I'd hit the nail on the head. She stopped breathing and her face began to turn purple as she stared at me, visibly shaking with rage. Her expression told me she was about three seconds away from clawing my eyes out – though I admit, it was a little hard to take her seriously when she was covered in flour and clad only in a sheer red apron.

"Breathe, sweetie, or you'll pass out." I smiled condescendingly.

"You...you bitch!" she shrieked again.

"Original. Ten points for creativity." I clapped three times to applaud her before casting a glance over my shoulder to check the elevator's progress. It was stopped on the ninth floor – close, but no cigar.

"Baby! Come over here!" Cara called in a shrill tone. She crossed her arms over her chest and glared down at me. Though we were both wearing heels, our height difference was absurd – she towered a full foot taller than me, well over six feet.

When I heard the sound of a man's approaching footsteps, I turned my back on her to face the elevators once more. I hadn't seen his face except in profile yet, and I was pretty sure I didn't want to. This way, I could pretend he'd grown a snaggletooth or maybe a really bad porn-stache in the years since I'd last seen him.

"What is it, Cara?" Sebastian asked, a note of frustration in his tone.

God, that voice. It was the same – a little huskier now, maybe. Deep and gravelly, but somehow soft at the same time. A rough caress, like melted chocolate over gravel. And, was it me, or did he sound just the teensiest bit exasperated by Cara?

It was probably me.

"This intern is a little bitch," Cara nagged. "She spilled my salad and was rude to me. I want her fired."

"Cara, cut the shit," Sebastian said, his voice closer now. Only a few feet separated us. "I'm sure it was an accident."

The elevator was on the thirteenth floor now. There was no escaping this unseen. Sighing resignedly, I braced myself for what was sure to be an utter catastrophe.

"Bitch! Don't just ignore me! Tell me your name so I can call your supervisor and report you," Cara sneered.

"Cara—" Sebastian began, clearly embarrassed by his girl-friend's actions.

I spun around before he could finish speaking.

Our eyes locked immediately, and an involuntary gasp slipped from my lips as I took in his face. He was gorgeous – more stunning than any of the male models that frequently graced *Luster*'s pages – but he wore his beauty like a disguise to conceal the harshness that lay beneath.

One glance was enough to tell me – this was a man who lived with demons.

Time had lent both maturity and hardness to his features, and I knew that Sebastian the boy was long gone. In his place was a man – one who seemed electrically charged with a caged intensity, his harsh beauty both terrifying and enthralling. As a boy, he'd been full of charm, ease, and good humor; before me now, I saw a man who rarely laughed and who chose his words with care, a man with walls so high no one could scale them to see inside his heart or mind.

When we'd first met eight years ago, he'd been somewhat guarded – it had taken months for him to really open up to me. Yet I had a distinct feeling that this older Sebastian wasn't only guarded, he was an impenetrable fortress of solitude and self-containment.

It made me instantly sad. I mourned for the boy who once was, and for the part I'd played in his destruction.

I watched as his gold-flecked irises widened in shock as he recognized me.

His gaze roamed my face, lingering on the smattering of

freckles on my nose before sweeping down my body in an almost predatory manner. Once, he'd known every curve and imperfection of my body more intimately than anyone. His hands had touched every secret part of me, unraveled me, set me on fire, and brought me to my knees begging for release more times than I cared to count. I'm not sure what expressions crossed my face at that moment – probably nothing good — but his own feelings were concealed from my view. Besides the initial shock I'd seen in his eyes, I couldn't read him at all.

The silence stretched for an uncomfortable amount of time. I could sense Cara in my peripherals, looking from me to Sebastian, but I couldn't tear my eyes from him. I was drinking him in, yearning for a flicker of understanding or recognition to appear in those bottomless eyes. But, when they finally finished their perusal of my body and his gaze returned to my face, I was discouraged to find nothing but flinty anger and indifference in their depths.

I averted my eyes, unable to bear him looking at me like I was a stranger or, worse, someone whose very presence was abhorrent to him, and turned to stare at Cara. I cleared my throat and broke the silence.

"Lux," I said in a shaky voice. "My name is Lux Kincaid."

"Well, *Lux*," she sneered. "You should pack up your desk cause you're pretty much *fucked* once I call your boss. Right, baby?" she asked Sebastian.

I turned my eyes back to him fleetingly, wary of his response. His eyes hadn't moved from me, and he didn't answer Cara. He just stared at me with that intense, scrutinizing look, as though he were trying to see inside my mind. Vitali's *Chaconne* played out its final aching notes from the overhead speakers, the violin echoing into silence as I stared back at him. When the final chord faded, to my absolute horror, I felt my eyes well up with tears.

I couldn't be here, looking at him – at what I might've had. It hurt too damn much. I was about to make a run for the stairwell when I heard the blessed sound I'd been waiting for – the chime of the arriving elevator. Dashing the tears from my eyes, I spun around and stepped into the empty car. As I pressed the button that would take me down to the lobby, I was powerless to stop my eyes from wandering back to Sebastian.

Cara was hanging on his arm, pouting and whining about me, no doubt, but his hands hung limply by his sides and he made no move to comfort her. We stared at one other, two strangers bound eternally by a shared past of lies and broken promises, and I wanted to throw myself into his arms. I wanted to bawl like a baby and take it all back – all the distance and the hurt, the deception and shattered trust. I wanted to erase the past seven years and kiss him until he forgot how I'd destroyed us.

But I didn't, and I never would.

Our gazes stayed locked, tears slipping silently down my cheeks, until the elevator doors slid closed and I collapsed back against the wall. I couldn't seem to get enough air into my lungs, couldn't quite bring the blurred elevator doors in front of my eyes into focus. Detachedly, I realized I was having a panic attack, but I was too overwhelmed to care much.

As the elevator began its descent away from Cara's shrill voice and Sebastian's inscrutable expression, my mind blanked of everything but one word, which I chanted internally like a deranged, hysterical mantra.

Fuck.

Fuck.

Fuck.

Chapter Six

NOW

I WALKED, UNSEEING, THE TWELVE BLOCKS BACK TO MY neighborhood in Hell's Kitchen.

Usually, I love where I live. It's a funky blend of recent graduates yearning to stretch their wings beyond the clutches of academia, young overworked professionals fighting to make it in the dog-eat-dog New York job force, struggling actors who give up food so they can afford to live three blocks from the Theater District, and artists who work all day as waiters or baristas so they have a paycheck barely large enough to cover the cost of new canvases and oil paints. They fill the air with their youth and exuberance for life, and the neighborhood pulses with a vitality like nowhere else I've ever been. The atmosphere is frenetic with movement; people rushing down the avenues with their feet on auto-pilot and their eyes trained on their smartphones, jay-walking with an ease only a native New Yorker can master, with one hand clutching a latte and the other casually flipping off a beeping cabbie.

It's the polar opposite of Georgia, where the only things more syrupy than the summer humidity are the sugar-coated southern manners that are laid on thicker than homemade vanilla cake frosting. The day I toured my apartment with the realtor I'd slammed into a stranger as I wandered down 46th, my tourist eyes tilted up to the sky to take in the soaring cityscape. I remember being filled with a nearly perverse sense of glee when the stranger simply glared at me and barreled by. In Jackson, such a collision would've turned into an hour-long affair of apologies and small talk about the crop season, local weather patterns, and, of course, the latest gossip about whatever man had been spotted sneaking back into his own house at three in the morning with lipstick stains on his collar.

That Georgian out-for-a-Sunday-stroll pace I'd grown up with left me unprepared for the fast clip of the city, and I fear my first few weeks living here I'd wandered around like a lost little girl without her mommy — an image aided in no small part by my short stature and wide-eyed wonderment at the sheer scope of the Big Apple in all its glory. Still, for a southern girl cut adrift from her rural roots, I figured I'd done pretty well adjusting, considering the fact that after only a few short months of living in Midtown I could stiletto-sprint and cabbie-curse with the best of them.

And yeah, maybe twenty years ago it wasn't safe to walk around my block alone at noon, let alone in the middle of the night. But now, the yuppie real estate agents who rent out space in the refurbished brick walkups describe my neighborhood as "up-and-coming" and its tree lined sidewalks and freshly paved streets are the home to some of the city's best restaurants, boutiques, and coffee shops. Young couples push strollers alongside a diverse but mostly cheerful — by New York standards, meaning no one flips you off on-sight — populace of ballet dancers, artisan crafters, and harried first-year interns.

The first time I stepped foot here I knew it was the place for me and, since I work my ass off at a shitty job all day to afford the outrageous rent for my tiny studio, I try to enjoy the atmosphere as much as possible. On the daily twenty-minute walk from my apartment in Hell's Kitchen to the *Luster* main office abutting Central Park on W 57th, I soak in all the sights and sounds of the bustling city. Maybe it's the residual tourist left within me — or, more likely, the deeply-ingrained southern manners that even city living can't quite wash out — but I know the street vendors by name, and I greet each of them as I pass.

Okay, fine, I'll admit that the main reason I know their names is because *occasionally* I may or may not indulge myself at the food carts that litter the avenues... Can you really blame me when Salim makes the best chicken cheesesteak sub in the entire city? Perhaps even the entire world?

But today, as I wandered down the busy block toward my apartment I absorbed nothing — none of the bustling crowds, the delicious smells, or the crazed, camera-toting tourists hoping to score a table at one of the exclusive bistros on Restaurant Row. I was stuck in my own head, lost in thoughts of a past life that seemed, now, dream-like and distant.

Today, there was no jaunty wave for Salim as I meandered past.

No bashful, responding smile for the group of construction workers on their lunch breaks when they whistled and catcalled at my passing form.

No chitchat or laughter with the gaggle of women who sold fresh fruits and veggies at the small farmer's market.

Nope. Today, it was straight to the liquor store: do not pass go, do not collect $200.

Who cared that it wasn't yet two in the afternoon? Today I'd adopt my mother's life motto.

It's five o'clock somewhere.

After purchasing two family-sized bottles of Merlot, I wandered into *Swagat*, the small convenience store on West 44th that served as my one-stop-shop for snacks, gum, and the occasional pint of ice cream. Owned by the Patel family, *Swagat* was located just around the corner from my small apartment on 43rd and open almost 24/7, the counter manned most frequently by the ancient, taciturn family matriarch Mrs. Patel, who had to be approaching approximately three or four hundred years old if the myriad wrinkles lining her face were any true indication of age. With a shock of thick silver hair she kept pulled back tightly from her temples with a shiny tortoise-shell clip, a wiry frail frame that belied the spirit in her dark eyes, and cheeks wrinkled like an apple long past its harvest, she was now a mere shadow of the lovely woman she'd undoubtedly been in her youth.

Though her son and daughter-in-law owned the store, both worked second jobs during the day, leaving Mrs. Patel in charge until six each evening — just about the time I usually popped in on my walk home from work. Stationed in a once-plush but now somewhat time-weathered velvet maroon chair by the cash register, Mrs. Patel moved infrequently and conversed even more rarely. She was always dressed to the nines in gorgeous antique saris and vibrant silk dresses that looked handcrafted, the colorful gowns skillfully sewn with impossibly small stitches. The only chink in her elegant facade was a heavy brown crocheted throw blanket she swaddled herself in from the waist down, which warded against the chill from the large section of refrigerated beverages abutting the counter.

She was the grumpiest woman I'd ever come across in my twenty-five years on this earth, a fact I determined without ever hearing her speak a word. Mrs. Patel's body language spoke loudly enough for her. From her constant refusal to make direct eye contact to the haughty lift of her chin, it was abundantly clear that the elderly curmudgeon hated working her post at the counter only slightly less than she hated communicating with her customers.

Namely, me.

Most often during our interactions, I'd hand her several bills as she bagged my groceries and hold a fully one-sided conversation with the old woman in hopes that, one day, she might respond.

Last year, when I'd come in for the first time and experienced her taciturnity, I'd assumed it was due to a language barrier rather than outright dislike. But now I was almost positive she spoke English — mostly because she was always watching reruns of General Hospital and Days of Our Lives on the small television she kept tucked away behind the counter — leaving me with the inescapable conclusion that she simply hated me. Most often, our "conversations" felt more like a hostage negotiation between a hostile, uncompromising insurgent and a largely ineffective but stubbornly dogged young officer of the law. I couldn't help but think I'd look fantastic in a badge — though those black ortho-pedic cop shoes were a definite deal breaker.

Take last weekend's late night snack run, for example:

"Hey Mrs. Patel, how's it going?" I'd said, approaching the counter.

Silently loading my bag — okay, you got me, *two* bags — of Cool Ranch Doritos and pint of Ben and Jerry's Half Baked ice cream into a reusable cloth grocery sack, Mrs. Patel did not deign to return my greeting.

"It looks nice in here. Something's different. Did you get a new display case for the gum? Oh, you have the green Tic-Tacs!?"

Shockingly, Mrs. Patel had no response other than to add my mints to the grocery sack.

"I like your sari today, Mrs. Patel. You look fantastic in turquoise. Where can I get one of those? Though turquoise isn't really my color. Is that hand beaded?"

As I reached out a hand to touch the gorgeous small beads dangling from the embroidered trim of her sleeve, Mrs. Patel snatched her arm out of reach and growled — yes, *growled* — at me, before unleashing a menacing glare she'd perfected over the many centuries since her birth.

Okay, so she wasn't thrilled with my existence. But hey! At least she'd *acknowledged* my existence that time. I was counting it as progress in our budding friendship.

Today, I was so wrapped up in my own mind that I didn't even attempt a conversation. I bought three — yes, three — bags of Cool Ranch Doritos because this was a real emergency and, let's face it, no one wants to face down a crisis without snacks on hand. Silently handing them to Mrs. Patel, I stared at the colorful array of lottery tickets hanging behind her head and tried not to think about Sebastian Motherfucking Covington or the facts that he was both dating a model *and* had the audacity to look like one himself. Seriously, karma was such a bitch.

Lost in my own thoughts, it took me a minute to realize that Mrs. Patel had stopped bagging my Doritos and was staring at me with a strange look on her face. Definitely not concern, but her weathered face showed, at the very least, a level of interest that I'd never seen in the year since I'd first come to *Swagat*. It took me a moment to register her expression as one of thinly-veiled confusion.

Wow, I really must've looked like shit if it was enough to catch Mrs. Patel's eye.

I guess I probably did look a bit dazed — like Jamie had that time when we were fourteen and he'd accidentally shocked himself trying to fish a bagel out of the toaster oven with a fork. The prongs hit the metal and *zap!*

Instant brain fog.

Everything felt slightly removed, out of focus, as though I were watching my own life play out on a fuzzy dark projector screen while I sat in the audience eating popcorn with only a vague interest in what was happening to the heroine or where the plot-lines were going to twist next.

I met Mrs. Patel's narrowed eyes and shrugged my shoulders at her before forcing my lips up into what I hoped could pass for smile.

From the way her face contorted in response, it wasn't hard to guess that my lackluster grimace fell short of the mark. Her eyes flickered away from my face to study the exposed wine bottle tops peeking out from the paper bag I was clutching to my chest like a safety blanket, before returning to examine my features. A beat of silence passed between us before she opened her mouth and spoke. As in formed words, made conversation, actually communicated with me for the first time ever, which, I might add, left me dumbfounded and utterly unable to string together a coherent thought.

"Are you alright, Miss Lux?" she asked in perfect, if accented, English.

I started, shocked that she was — freaking finally — speaking to me after a year of resolute silence.

"I— uh, I'm..." I stammered, at a loss. "I'm fine." I swallowed roughly, again fighting welling tears. You know those idiotic people who, when they're upset and someone is even the tiniest bit nice to them, immediately burst into tears?

Yep. That's me.

"You don't talk today," she noted, her head tipping sideways as she studied me intently. I don't think she blinked once — which would've been totally creepy if I'd had any brainpower left to dwell on things that weren't the ex-love-of-my-life.

I nodded, unable to speak.

Abruptly, her head snapped upright and she nodded briskly in return. Without further ado, she reached beneath the countertop and pulled out a bottle of top-grade, black label scotch, followed by two stout glasses. Before I could fathom what was occurring or even begin to muster a protest, Mrs. Patel had poured two fingers of amber liquor into each glass and was shoving one across the counter at me.

"I— what—" I began, feeling like a bumbling idiot.

"Drink," Mrs. Patel snapped at me, her shrewd glare back in full force, pinning my feet to the floor. Jesus, she was scary. No wonder her grandkids were so well behaved whenever they were in the store with her.

I nodded, grasping the glass with my free hand and watching as she lifted hers into the air — toasting god only knew what — before throwing back her scotch like an old pro. She didn't even wince as it went down and only when she had again trained her glare on me did I realize I'd been frozen, staring at her in open-mouthed shock.

Hastily, I threw back my own shot, gasping at the fire that burned down my throat, stole the breath from my lungs, and blasted an inferno of warmth into my empty stomach. My eyes a watery mess, I spluttered — clearly I was not in Mrs. Patel's league — and leaned over the counter, heaving in large gulps of air. When I'd finally regained my composure, I looked up at Mrs. Patel who, if it weren't such an impossibility, I would've sworn was smiling enigmatically at me from her maroon chair.

"Thanks?" I whispered through a hoarse throat. I wasn't quite sure what had just happened, or why ancient Mrs. Patel was forcing me to do shots with her at two in the afternoon, but I wasn't about to argue. I'd always been more a lover than a fighter.

Mrs. Patel eyed me speculatively once again. Seemingly satisfied with whatever she saw in my bewildered expression, she nodded sharply and snatched my empty glass from the countertop. Within an instant it had disappeared beneath the counter along with the bottle of scotch, and she'd folded her hands back in a demure grip on her lap. I stared at her in wide-eyed expectation, waiting for some wise words of Indian wisdom or, at the very least, any kind of explanation for the past five minutes.

I should've known better, honestly.

"That will be $8.99," Mrs. Patel said with her usual perfunctory disregard, one liver-spotted hand outstretched for my money.

Numbly, I handed over a ten-dollar bill and watched as she deposited it into the cash register.

"Thank you," I told her haltingly, as I accepted my change.

"Come again," she told me indifferently, as though I were a stranger rather than the girl who came in nearly every day spouting chitchat and who, at the moment, apparently looked like she could really use a good dose of high quality scotch.

Shaking my head in confusion, I walked outside with my bag of snacks and my bottles of wine, the door swinging shut with the telltale tinkling of bells at my back. And there on a busy New York sidewalk, with a shot of liquor in my bloodstream and the hot August sun beating down on me, at two thirty in the afternoon on the worst day of my life, I threw my head back and laughed and laughed until tears were streaming down my face and the passing tourists were eyeing me with a wariness generally reserved for hookers and homeless people.

My life was a freaking mess.

Chapter Seven

THEN

"DO YOU *SEE* HER OUTFIT TODAY?" THE GIRL'S HALFHEARTED attempt at a whisper carried easily across the small classroom to where I sat beside the window. With a stubborn set to my shoulders, I stared steadfastly out the pane to my left and refused to justify her slur with a reaction. Cursing the clear blue Georgia sky, I wished silently for a bizarrely-formed cloud or even a low-flying plane on which I could focus my attentions and use as a distraction from the catty words that were unquestionably about my wardrobe choices.

"Amber!" A second voice chimed in with a giggling rebuke. "Be nice! God, I hear her brother is, like, dying or something."

I knew those voices well.

They found themselves hilarious — two miniature, Botox-free versions of Joan Rivers apparently hosting their own unofficial version of *Fashion Police: Jackson High Edition*. Nicole was the

Skipper to Amber's Barbie: a less popular, less blonde, and significantly less well-endowed version of her Queen Bee counterpart.

"No shit?" I could hear the maniacal snap of Amber's gum from across the room. "That is so totally tragic. Like something out of a movie, you know?"

"I know, right? And Stacy's mom told my mom that her parents are..." Cue dramatic pause. "*Alcoholics.*"

I'd come to the conclusion early — approximately five minutes after the start of junior high, if you wanted the specifics — that while girls like Amber were catty and manipulative on an almost laughably shallow level, it was the ones like Nicole who were the worst. They were the followers, the sheep; the seconds-in-command who, beneath the bad hair, self-esteem issues, and remaining layer of baby fat, were intelligent enough to know better than to cater to frivolous high-school-peakers like Amber. Nicole had been my friend once. Back before she'd traded her glasses for contacts and fried her hair with a bottle of peroxide in a desperate ploy to gain entry into the elite circle. Evidently the lure of popularity — even if it was the JV version — was too strong to resist.

"Jeeze. Some families in this town." I heard Amber exhale sharply. "Did you catch *One Tree Hill* last night?"

It was at this point that I tuned out.

Fingernails biting harshly into my clenched fists, I pictured their words sliding around me, bouncing off my forcefield of indifference and never coming close enough to pierce my heart. Yet, like a tidal wave across the sand, the whispers left their mark each time — a dark, damp imprint that eroded the beach in infinitesimal amounts over days and decades. I could pretend they didn't wound me with their insensitivity, but the callous words crashed against me in unrelenting, inevitable strikes, slowly eating away at my unaffected facade and disturbing an already fragile foundation.

"Sit down please, everyone." Ms. Ingraham's stern voice rang out, calling for the juniors loitering in groups at the back of the classroom and in the hallway to take their seats. Fighting off a yawn, I listened to the acquiescent groans, the shuffle of unwilling feet, and the scrape of metal-legged desks against the linoleum as my peers settled in. It had been another long night for me. After Sebastian had dropped me off at the hospital, my already bad day had descended even further on the shit scale. When I'd arrived at his room, Jamie had sensed immediately that something was off. His twin-spidey-senses must've been tingling.

"What's wrong, light of my life?" he'd asked immediately, sitting up straighter in his gurneyed hospital bed. He'd called me that for years, his little nickname a play on my name's Latin origins. "And why are you all wet?" He eyed my tangled damp blonde locks curiously.

"Nothing's wrong," I said, shrugging lightly and forcing the worry lines to smooth from my forehead. "Ms. Ingraham kept the entire class late today to conjugate a million extra verb tenses. She's clearly gunning for teacher of the year."

Jamie smiled easily, but his face was too pale. His latest surgery had taken more out of him than any of his previous ones. He tired easily these days and, though still his ever-cheery self, he must've been in considerable pain.

"The lonely old bag probably just didn't want to go home to her cats," Jamie said, scooting over so I could join him on the bed. Once I'd settled in, I dropped my head on his shoulder and he slid a comforting arm around my back.

"My thoughts exactly." I sighed, letting my tired eyes droop closed. This was always the best part of my day. Though school had never been my favorite place, the last year without Jamie there with me had made it exponentially worse. "Missed you, Jamie."

"Missed you too, sis," he said, his arm tightening in a brief reassuring squeeze. "But I'll be back on my feet in no time and we'll rule Jackson High, you mark my words," he joked lightly, knowing that in all likelihood he would never again walk the halls alongside me. "Ms. Ingraham will be so infatuated with my handsome mug, she'll give both of us A's for the term. Oh, and we'll have a free pass to skip out of classes. I mean, seriously, what hall monitor is going to stop me? I can pull the cancer card. You've gotta be a real dick to turn in the kid with osteosarcoma, even if he is tardy three days in a row."

I tried to smile at his attempts to lighten the mood but I couldn't quite find the strength within myself. Squeezing my eyelids together harshly, I did my best to get control over my gathering tears. Jamie hated it when I cried — he'd much rather joke about his illness than weep about it. He didn't do self-pity and, while most days I admired that, sometimes I just needed to be sad. I needed to cry and rage against the world for its injustice. Shake my fists at whatever god was up there, for slowly draining the life from the best person I'd ever known.

We fell silent for a time. Jamie likely sensed I wasn't in the mood to joke with him and instead gave me the quiet solace I desperately needed. His very presence recharged me whenever my batteries dropped to dangerously low levels and I'd begun to fear that I couldn't go on juggling school, work, his illness, and my scatterbrained parents.

"So who do I have to beat up?" he whispered quietly, breaking the silence.

"What?" I lifted my head to look him in the eyes.

"The boy, sis. Whoever he is, brotherly duty requires that I give him a piece of my mind." Jamie lifted his hand to touch his chin in a gesture of deep contemplation. "Perhaps even a beat down is in order. Put the fear of god into him, and all that jazz." As if he could even stand, let alone give someone a *beat down*. I rolled my eyes affectionately.

"There's no boy, Jamie."

"The size large, $200 cashmere you're wearing would suggest otherwise," he said, staring pointedly at my torso. Sebastian's warm sweater was swimming on my petite form, cocooning me from neck to mid-thigh — I'd forgotten to give it back in my rush to escape both the confines of his car and the perceptive look in his eyes. "Thought we didn't lie to each other, Lux?" Jamie's voice held an unusual note of hurt.

"We don't!" I protested immediately. "This is nothing! It's nothing. I'd tell you if there was a boy."

"Well, if it's *nothing*, then explain." He looked at me expectantly.

I sighed in resignation.

"I was walking here in the rain and apparently some guy was practicing for the Indy 500 in his Mercedes. The maniac took a turn too fast and doused me with a puddle in the process. He felt bad so he gave me his sweater and a ride here. That's it. End of story."

"Who was it?"

"Does it matter?" I deflected, for the first time in my life hesitant to share something with my twin. There was something personal about the car ride, something I didn't want to share with anyone just yet. I wanted to hold it close to my heart for a little while longer, a private memory that belonged only to me and the beautiful boy in the rain.

"Clearly it does, if you're being so secretive about it."

Damn. Jamie was never one to beat around the bush and, when it came down to it, I was a pushover for anything he asked of me. I sighed again.

"It was Sebastian Covington, okay? Satisfied?" I could feel the heat of a blush rise to my cheeks and I avoided eye contact with Jamie at all costs, afraid of what my gaze might reveal.

"Oh my god," Jamie said, a note of incredulity lacing his tone. "I can't believe it."

"What?" I asked, staring pointedly at the flowers I'd brought with me last week in an attempt to brighten up the dreary hospital room. Their stems were limp now, their shriveled brown petals scattered on the particleboard tabletop. I'd have to bring some new ones with me tomorrow.

"You like him," Jamie said matter-of-factly.

"I don't." The denial came swiftly, shooting from my lips like a curse word.

"Mhmm," Jamie hummed. "Whatever you say."

"I. Don't. Like. Sebastian. Freaking. Covington," I growled out.

"Methinks the lady doth protest too much." Jamie was grinning at me irritatingly.

"Drop it, James." I only called him James when I was pissed — a fact he knew all too well, which could explain why his grin got even bigger. "You're being ridiculous."

"Really? I didn't think I was being ridiculous. But if you'd like, I could certainly be *more* ridiculous," he offered. He waited a beat, then raised his voice several octaves up into a girlish falsetto. "Lux has a cruuuuuush," he singsonged.

"What are you, seven years old?"

"Lux and Sebastian, sitting in a tree, K-I-S—"

"That's *it!*" I yelled, turning to glare at him. "Enough! I didn't tease you when you had a crush on Amber! *Amber!* Of all people."

"Actually, I think I *was* seven years old at that point."

"Like that's an excuse. That girl has been a demon-spawn since preschool. If you shaved off all her bleached blonde tresses I bet there'd be a 666 inscribed on her skull."

"Touché," Jamie allowed. His grin faded a little as he examined my flushed features. "And if it's really bothering you, I'll stop. I was only teasing."

"I know," I said, swallowing roughly and trying to regain my composure. "I don't know why I got so upset."

Except I did. I knew exactly why I was so upset by Jamie's teasing. Because, deep down, maybe I did like the hazel-eyed boy who listened to classical music and who'd given me a sweater that cost more than I made in a shift at Minnie's without blinking. Maybe I liked him a little too much. And that, I knew, was the stupidest thing I could ever allow myself to do.

After leaving Jamie at the hospital, I'd hopped a bus to the diner and taken impatient customers' orders for five straight hours. By the time I got back home to our dark empty house, it was nearly eleven and my parents were nowhere to be found. Well, actually, they'd be pretty easy to track down if I really wanted to; no doubt they were cloistered away in one of the five seedy bars

Jackson boasted, slurping down vodkas to cope with the shit hand life had dealt them.

I'd hopped into the shower, eager to wash off the smell of fry grease and coleslaw, only to find we had no hot water. The rusted old water heater in our basement must've finally bit the dust. Shampooing as quickly as possible, I shivered beneath the frigid torrents and vowed that once I had enough money for Jamie and me to cut ties and get away from Jackson, I'd never take cold showers again. I'd choose a hot shower over a hot meal every time.

Thankfully, more often than not Minnie, my boss, would force dinner on me before I left after my night shifts. She knew that things were tough at home and, despite her lack of creativity in the diner-naming process, she had a heart of gold. She eked out a measly living with her restaurant proceeds and didn't have much to spare — but what she could afford to give, she did without hesitation. She'd even hired me when there were plenty of qualified applicants who had more than my zero waitressing experience.

I owed Minnie a lot.

After toweling off, I'd forced myself to complete the workbook sheets Ms. Ingraham had assigned earlier that afternoon along with some of the required reading for my English class. We were covering the American classics — Steinbeck, Lee, Fitzgerald, Salinger — and although that proved to be a constant source of grumbling for many of my peers, who'd rather be reading *Luster* or *Vogue*, it wasn't a chore for a bookworm like me. When lines from *Cannery Row* began to blur before my eyes long past midnight, I'd finally fallen into a dead sleep, only to be jarred awake by the chirping of my cellphone alarm at 7:00 a.m.

Hence my serious case of the yawns, today — and pretty much every other day of the week.

I tried not to let my eyes drift closed as I focused on Ms. Ingraham, who was bustling around the front of the classroom, absently wiping excess chalk dust on the too-tight black pants that encased her thighs like stuffed sausages. I couldn't help but think that there should be some kind of statute of limitations on wearing legging jeans. Camel-toe on a sixty-year-old spinster was *not* something I needed to see. Ever.

She launched into her lesson, pushing smudged glasses up higher on the bridge of her nose and leaving a smear of chalk on her cheekbone in the process. She'd pulled her dark curly hair back from her face with a large clip, but it did little to tame the inch of frizz that haloed her head.

"Now, let's try not to have a repeat of yesterday. I'm assuming that you have all completed the required reading and the home-work assignment, so if you could pass your worksheets to the front we can get start—"

"Sorry I'm late, Ms. Ingraham. I had an extra stop to make on my way to class today." The voice of the arriving straggler cut through her orders, his interruption equal parts apology and authority. Polite enough to garner favor without encouraging further questioning. A smart approach, I thought, but I doubted it would be enough to stave off Ms. Ingraham's wrath. Every head in the room whipped in the direction of the voice, mine included, eager to see how the latecomer would fare against the strict tardi-ness policy. My bet was, this kid had some serious detention-time coming his way.

Thankfully, I'm not much of a gambler.

It was Sebastian, of course. He leaned casually against the doorjamb with his backpack tossed over one shoulder, a styrofoam cup of coffee held in each hand. Ms. Ingraham took one look at him and blushed like a schoolgirl. To my utter amazement, I watched as my overweight, bespectacled teacher turned beet red and said in a breathy, flustered, totally disturbing voice, "Oh, Sebastian, don't worry about it. Take a seat." She gestured loosely toward the only two empty desks — the one directly behind my chair by the window, and another by Amber, Nicole, and the other popular kids in the opposite corner.

It wasn't hard to guess where he was headed.

I rolled my eyes after catching sight of Ms. Ingraham, who was still staring at Sebastian in a bewildered stupor. I couldn't really blame her — the boy was good looking, and all the teachers had been thrilled beyond measure when the senator they'd elected chose to put his son in the public school system, rather than shipping him off to private school. But...*seriously?* Had we learned nothing from the Mary Kay Letourneau's of the world? Despite my best intentions, a mutinous giggle escaped my lips.

Sebastian heard my choked laugh and his eyes darted to mine as he entered the classroom and walked toward his friends with confident, self-assured strides. His lips lifted in a half-grin and he winked — yes, *winked* — at me, which only made it harder to control the escaping giggles. In hindsight, my mounting hysteria was probably a byproduct of the fact that Sebastian hadn't ignored me, as I'd assumed he would, but had seemed friendly.

Heck, he'd smiled at me. *Winked* at me.

A flurry of butterflies simultaneously burst from their cocoons inside my stomach, and I quickly slanted my face down toward my desk to hide the dopey grin spreading across my lips.

The smile quickly faded when I heard Nicole's whisper echo across the room.

"Ohmigod, Amber! Sebastian totally bought you a coffee. He's so gonna ask you out."

Amber's answering giggle was enough to instantly kill the swarm of butterflies. They dropped, mid-flight, to the bottom of my stomach where their once-beautiful papery wings were immediately incinerated by food-digesting acids.

"Oh my god," Nicole whispered. "Oh... my... *god.*"

I didn't look up. I didn't want to see the look on Amber's face when Sebastian handed her that freaking coffee. I hoped it was some gross flavor like crème brûlée or blueberry. It would serve her right.

My gaze downcast, I didn't notice him until he'd come to a full stop next to my desk, his form hovering at the edge of my peripherals.

"Here," he said quietly, sliding the foam coffee cup onto the corner of my desk. My wide, disbelieving eyes watched the cup's movement, captivated by the sight of his strong calloused fingers gripped lightly around its circumference. "Figured you could use this to get through seven hundred Latin verb conjugations."

He'd brought me coffee.

He'd somehow known I'd be yawning my way through final period — which meant maybe, just maybe, he'd paid me more attention in the past than I ever could've guessed.

I tipped my head back to meet his eyes, but he'd already moved beyond my chair. Frozen, I stared at the cup sitting in front of me and listened to the sound of Sebastian settling into the desk directly behind mine. A slow smile crept across my face and a furious blush spilled over my cheekbones. Shaking my head in disbelief, I accidentally locked eyes with Amber, who'd turned fully around in her desk to watch Sebastian's surprise delivery. Her furious brown eyes were narrowed in a glare that threatened to burn a hole straight through me.

Jeeze, it was just a coffee. No need to give herself a coronary.

Laughing lightly, I winked at her — at which point her face turned a dangerous shade of red — before reaching forward and taking hold of my cup. Raising it to my lips, I took a sip of liquid heaven and sighed contentedly. I'd say one thing for the boy: he'd certainly found the way to this caffeine-junkie's heart.

Turning my head so Sebastian could see my face only in profile, as I was far too nervous to make direct eye contact with him, I whispered a quiet, "Thank you," over my shoulder.

"You're welcome," he whispered back.

I didn't even bother attempting to listen to Ms. Ingraham's lesson that day. My attentions were elsewhere.

Chapter Eight

◦❧◦

NOW

I SWUNG THE DOOR OPEN WITH A FORCEFUL BUMP OF MY HIP and fell through the entryway, my bag-laden arms aching for relief. Beelining for my apartment's tiny excuse for a kitchen, I immediately dumped my wine and snack cargo before leaning back heavily against the counter's edge.

Priorities were simple: music on, heels off, pour wine, decompress in bubble bath. Not necessarily in that order.

I'd just popped the cork on my Merlot when the shrill ringing of my cellphone stilled my hand. With a trepidatious glance at the screen, I saw it was Fae and exhaled with relief. At least it wasn't Jeanine.

"Hello?"

"Girl, where are you?" she whispered, a faint acoustic echo sounding in the background. She must've been in the bathroom at work, one of the few places at *Luster* that a NSFW call could be made. "I covered for you with Jeanine, told her you were out researching something for next month's column. Are you okay?"

"I'm... I don't know what I am, actually. It's a long story."

"I'll be there after work."

"Fae, I'm not really up for comp—"

"See you at six!" she interrupted, clicking off before I had a chance to protest.

Damn.

I turned to examine the small studio I called home. There were dirty coffee mugs piled in the sink and a basket's worth of clean unfolded laundry lay in a tangled pile on the end of my low platform bed. My fluffy white down comforter was a knotted mess and there were enough high heeled shoes and boots spilling out of my closet and littering the hardwood floors to make Imelda Marcos envious.

There was no food in the kitchen, with the exception of the Doritos I'd just purchased — and I obviously wasn't about to share those babies with anyone, best friend or otherwise — and a few of those disgusting frozen microwavable "healthy" dinner alternatives that contained 300 calories worth of dried out veggies and cardboard-flavored pasta. Fae had convinced me to stock my freezer with them last January after informing me that we'd both be going on a post-holiday health kick. She'd only lasted about a week and a half — longer than the five hours *I* lasted — and I'm pretty sure the only time I'd touched the damn things since was when I threw half of them in the garbage to make room for my cartons of Ben and Jerry's.

Thankfully, I had wine.

I'd have to clean up, now that Fae was coming over. And that meant no time for a long soak in my antique claw-footed tub. Slipping off my Louboutins, I flexed the cramped arches of my feet and reached up to remove the clip Fae had wound artfully into my hair earlier that afternoon. I laced my fingers through the strands and shook them loose, the silken locks falling heavily around my shoulders and down my back. For years Fae had been trying me to get me to cut it into one of the trendier pixies or even a bob, but I'd kept it long since I was a teenager.

Never cut it. It's the first thing I noticed about you, Sebastian had once told me as we lay together on the sun-dappled grass at our spot beneath the oak tree on the edge of his property. *That first day in Latin, you walked in like you wished you were invisible. You kept your head down – you thought if you didn't make eye contact, no one would even notice you were there. But your hair was so bright, it shined like this crazy blonde beacon. Every guy in the class was watching. You were so beautiful, I couldn't keep my eyes off you.*

I closed my eyes at the memory. Sometimes I wished I could have my mind scrubbed clean of him — every touch, every trace permanently stripped from my thoughts, as though he'd never existed. But the days I wished for that were few and far between. Because, despite the pain and the bitterness that laced the edges of my time with Sebastian, for the most part I choose to live in the light.

I know a lot of people don't. Most people, in fact. They gravitate toward the shadows – the grief, the loss, the heartbreak. They dwell in it, reveling in their personal darkness. Focusing on the things they can never get back — the broken promises, the shattered dreams — and living mired in demons of the past.

Not me, though.

Not when, in the twenty-five years I'd spent on this planet, I'd known more love than most know in a lifetime. Not when I'd felt it – that moment when a person you need more than air or water or sustenance steps into your orbit and everything subtly shifts, like a camera finally sliding into focus. That person, who used to mean less than nothing, enters your life and rearranges your entire atmosphere around them, as if every atom and cell that makes you *you* isn't your property anymore. Suddenly, every part of you becomes theirs – your particles dissembled and rearranged to align perfectly with someone who you don't even know or understand yet. You cease to exist as you once were, and that person who meant nothing is suddenly, overwhelmingly, *everything.*

I'd known it well, that all-consuming sense that every fiber in your being was crafted and created specifically for another human being. And so, even after that feeling – that ridiculous, head-over-heels, transient, life-shattering feeling – was eventually lost to me, I couldn't step fully into the shadows. I couldn't be broken or even too sad about the things I'd lost.

Because, for a brief span of time, I'd been complete. I'd been his, and he'd been mine, and nothing and everything made sense all at the same time. And once you've felt that joy of breathing, of being, entirely for someone else, you can't ever really go back.

So I live in the light.

I dwell in the good memories. Revel in their happy, water-colored hues and fuzzy edges. I skim over the darkness – not out of denial or avoidance, but because in the grand scheme of things, isn't it the light that matters more? I knew, at the end of the day, that even if I were living in some *Eternal Sunshine of the Spotless Mind* universe where erasing someone from your mind was possible, I'd keep Sebastian where he belonged — etched into both my heart and my memories.

꧁꧂

BY THE TIME THE BUZZER SOUNDED, SIGNALING FAE'S ARRIVAL, my messy apartment was somewhat in order and I was several glasses into a bottle of Merlot. My hair was still damp from my bath and I hadn't bothered with makeup. The only place I was going tonight was to bed, preferably within the next two hours.

I hopped up from my couch — a sleek low-slung black IKEA unit I'd gotten for cheap from a furniture vendor at the flea market on 39th last fall — and buzzed Fae in. Her knuckles had barely grazed the door in a knock when I slid off the security chain and flipped the deadbolt.

"FAE! What's goin' on, guuuuurl?" I yelled, throwing open the door with enough force to send wine sloshing over the edge of the glass clutched in my free hand. Fae made no move to enter, staring at me from the threshold with a mix of amusement and concern.

"And how much wine have we consumed this evening?" she asked, one dark eyebrow quirked up.

"Don't worry, there's plenty left for you," I said, grabbing her arm and hauling her inside with a giggle.

"That wasn't my question."

I chose to ignore that statement, flopping onto my couch and closing my eyes with a sigh. I gestured vaguely toward the kitchen area. "Glasses are in the ca—"

"Cabinet above the stove. I know, love. I've only been here about a million times over the past two years," she reminded me. I heard the pop of the cork and the familiar gurgling sound of wine filling a glass.

"You're funny," I giggled.

"You're hammered," she countered, sitting down gently beside me and crossing her legs. "I haven't seen you this bad since last year's Christmas party when we caught Trisha and Stu doing it in the copy room. And *that* was an occasion that called for alcohol, if there ever was one."

"Trisha!" I squealed, deteriorating into giggles once more. "Totally the secret president of the Itty Bitty Titty Committee. Who would've known under all that padding? Do you think Victoria's Secret sponsors her?"

"Unlikely," Fae said, taking a sip of her wine. "Back to you. Care to share why you're shitfaced at 7:00 p.m. on a work night?"

"I saw him." I sighed.

"Saw who?"

I shook my head back and forth in slow denial. "Never thought it'd happen. Nuh uh, never in a million years," I confided, opening my eyes and turning to face Fae. "'Specially not today. I wasn't even wearing my good bra... Hey! You think I should talk to Trisha? Maybe she can get me a discount!" I snorted at my own joke, laughing so hard tears started to leak from the corners of my eyes. Fae reached over and removed the wine glass from my precarious grip. Setting it carefully on the coffee table and far out of my reach, she grabbed me by the shoulders and gave me a firm shake.

"Lux, *who* did you see today?"

"Sebastian," I told her, rolling my eyes in exasperation. "Obviously."

"Obviously," she agreed dryly. "But who, my darling little drunkard, *is* Sebastian?"

"I'm not supposed to talk about that," I said with a laugh, lifting one hand to mime zipping my mouth closed and locking it. I nearly fell off the couch when I wound up to hurl the imaginary key across the room, which set me off in another fit of giggles. "It's a secret."

"Lux, focus." Fae snapped one finger in front of my face in an attempt to capture my attention, her tone growing impatient. "Sebastian. Who is he?"

"Fae, you're my bestest best friend, you know that?"

"I do know that, but I'm beginning to doubt whether I want to keep the position," she muttered.

"What?"

"Nothing. Now tell me the big secret, otherwise I'm leaving and taking the wine with me when I go."

"Okay, but you have to *promise*." I leaned across the couch into her space, my voice dropping to a grave whisper. "*Promise* not to tell."

Fae looked like she was fighting off a grin, but somehow managed to keep her face relatively serious when she stuck out her left pinky finger. "I promise," she agreed.

I wrapped my pinky around hers and nodded solemnly. Her lips twitched.

"So who is this mystery man?"

"Oh." I shrugged, reclining against the couch cushions and curling my knees up to my chest. "He's only the love of my life."

"Excuse me?!" Fae shrieked.

"Mmm," I murmured noncommittally. The wine had worked its magic, loosening my muscles into relaxation and lulling me toward that indiscernible, transient state somewhere between consciousness and dreaming.

"What? Lux! You seriously cannot leave me hanging like this right now."

Sleep was beckoning with undeniable force, and Fae's voice was an unwelcome intrusion — a pesky mosquito buzzing around my head and demanding attention. I grumbled in response, nestling further into the cushions.

"What happened, Lux?"

"I broke him," I mumbled. "So he hates me." A solitary tear escaped from under my lashes and tracked down my cheek. "But I love him," I added in a broken whisper.

"Christ," Fae cursed under her breath, her tone softening. I felt the cushion beneath my head sink as she scooted closer to me, followed by the gentle touch of a hand on my hair, petting me in long soothing strokes a mother might use to calm an upset child. "Lux, love. Why didn't you ever say anything about him?"

A sob rattled in my chest but I forced it down, trembling with the effort.

I will not shatter. I will not break. I will get through this, just like last time.

"Shhh," Fae breathed, listening to my small hiccups of air as I fought for control. "It's okay, love. Just relax."

I listened to her quiet words, breathing in and out until my chest stopped aching and my tears had subsided. And with Fae's voice in my ears and her hand in my hair, I slipped over the line of consciousness and was dead to the world.

❦

THE LOUD RINGING WOKE ME FROM A DEEP SLUMBER.

My eyes snapped open to find my apartment cloaked in blackness. Bleary eyes yet unadjusted to the pervasive dark, I threw off the blanket Fae must've tucked around me before leaving and fumbled for my phone on the coffee table. My head was pounding and night had fallen outside my window, which meant I'd been out for several hours.

"Hello?" My voice was huskier than usual, cracking with the remnants of sleep I'd yet to shake off.

"Babe! You okay? I didn't wake you, did I?"

Desmond.

"I'm fine, just nodded off for a few minutes I guess," I fibbed, rubbing an aching temple with my free hand. Pulling the phone away from my ear, I glanced down at the screen. It was 9:57 — I'd been out for nearly three hours. More of a mini-coma than a nap, but Desmond didn't need to know that. "What's up?"

"You never called," he reminded me, his voice curious without being accusatory.

Shit. I slapped an open palm against my forehead. We'd had dinner plans.

"Oh, crap. I completely spaced. I'm sorry, Des. Really, I mean it." I cleared my throat lightly. "I just had a crap day, and came straight home after work to try and get my head together."

"And here I thought you were excited about my mac and cheese," he teased lightly, clearly unaffected by my memory slip. "Don't worry, though. Since it's the only thing I know how to cook, the statistical probability of you getting to try it at some point in the future is highly in your favor."

I smiled into the phone. This was why I liked Desmond — no guilt-trips or underhanded barbs. No manipulations or mind-fuck-ery. He was surface-level: what you saw was what you got.

"I'll look forward to that."

"Good. Can I see you tomorrow?" he asked.

"No can do," I told him, the smile slipping off my face. "Tomorrow's Friday, which means—"

"Girl's night. I know, I know. Can't fault a guy for trying though."

"Hey, take it up with Fae. She actually hacked into my Google Calendar app and programmed herself in for every Friday night for the next five years. Seriously, my iPhone screen flashes little 'Fae

Friday — Attendance Mandatory' alerts every 20 minutes in the four hours leading up to girl's night. I can't figure out how to turn the damn things off."

Des laughed. "Yeah, but babe, technology is really not your strong suit. Need I remind you of the TiVo incident?"

"Oh, of course you'd bring that up!" I rolled my eyes. "I'll have you know that *anyone* could've made that mistake. The 'delete' button should *not* be located right next to 'record.' It's just not practical. Poor planning by the manufacturer," I noted. "And, really, what man needs immediate access to every single rerun of *Sports-Center* ever broadcasted? With your ass fused permanently to your couch, all those pretty arm muscles you spend your days building would've shriveled right up. So I'm pretty sure in the long run I did you a favor."

Desmond didn't respond. He was laughing too hard.

"Good logic, babe. Really stellar," he choked out when he'd finally regained control.

"I certainly thought so. And at least you can laugh about it now," I reflected. "At the time, I thought your head might explode."

"I'll call you soon," he promised, and I could hear the smile in his voice.

"I might just answer," I teased.

"Oh, you'll answer," Desmond said, ever confident.

I smiled. "Night."

"Night, babe." He clicked off.

Desmond was a good guy. Decent and kind. Funny and hand-some. I should've been glowing after that phone call, dancing around my apartment in an unchecked display of glee because such a pretty-damn-close-to-perfect man was interested in me. And yet, the happy bubble that had formed in my chest as I'd joked and laughed with Desmond was dissipating rapidly in the face of the immense guilt I felt for leading him on.

Sure, technically I was single. There was nothing — no one — holding me back from dating Desmond. But I knew that while I could give him my body and maybe, if enough time passed and we really grew to care for one another, even a piece of my heart, he'd never get all of me. I'd given away the innermost bits of myself eight years ago, and I'd never collected the missing parts.

And Desmond was the kind of man who went all in. He gave everything — his body, his mind, his heart. He'd give me his soul in good faith, not knowing that mine had already found its mate and that I could never return the favor.

But what did you do when you'd lost your soulmate, and there was no chance of ever having him again? Did you move on, even with the knowledge that nothing would ever be quite as good? Did you try to fill the empty holes inside yourself with the misshapen parts that someone else could offer?

And, if you did these things, could you bear to look yourself in the eyes at the end of the day, knowing that you'd allowed someone to love you, to bind himself to you, in a way you could never reciprocate?

Or was it simply better to isolate yourself — to grow old alone, rather than subject an undeserving man to your own emotional inadequacies?

I didn't know the answers to these questions.

All I did know, was that no matter how much I wanted Sebastian Covington — and I *did* want him, whether it was today, yesterday, eight years ago, or eighty years from now — I couldn't ever have him again.

So for now, I'd carve out my own little slice of happiness.

I'd skip the tough questions I hadn't quite figured out the answers to yet.

I'd ignore the bleeding crater in the left side of my chest.

I'd write my column and laugh over margaritas with Fae.

I'd fill my apartment with pretty things, and maybe even get a pet.

I'd live in the light.

Chapter Nine

NOW

I GOT TO WORK AN HOUR EARLY THE FOLLOWING MORNING TO compensate, at least in part, for skipping out yesterday afternoon. The imposing steel and glass skyscraper that housed the *Luster* offices was a modern architectural gem, with fifty floors and a gorgeous asymmetrical design that sliced into the Midtown skyline like a knife. The building, known best as Harding Tower, served as the global headquarters for Harding Corporation, the largest mass media conglomerate in the United States and, consequently, the owner of *Luster* and about 300 other popular magazines. From television talk shows to magazines and newspapers, Harding Corp's combined subsidiaries alone accounted for nearly 20% of all media consumed by American citizens. *Luster* was just a small piece of that pie — namely, the piece that targeted women in the 18-35 demographic, who cared about things like cellulite, sex positions, and celebrity meltdowns.

The *Luster* offices spanned three floors of the building, with the different departments — art, photography, production design, advertising, fashion, and marketing — dispersed among them. My fellow columnists and feature writers claimed the 39th floor, which was essentially just a large open plan crammed full of sleek dark-stained wood cubicles. There were no solid walls, only floor to ceiling windows that looked out over Central Park on one side and the rest of Manhattan on the other. Screw the corner office Jeanine occupied — my lowly cubicle had arguably one of the best views in all of New York.

On the left were the editors' offices — Jeanine's included — and a large conference room, partitioned off with glass-block walls to maintain the illusion that we were suspended in the air above the city. The only windowless wall, adjacent to the bank of eleva-tors, served as a living, ever-changing storyboard for future editions — chock full of photo proofs, notes, drafts, and ideas. Placements were always shuffling as the timeline came together; I'd leave for the night with one of my columns slotted on page 27, next to makeup application tips, and return the following morning to find that same article close to centerfold, framed by the "Who Wore It Better?" and "Best Dressed" sections. Nothing was ever permanent until the entire draft was sent off to the presses, and even then things could be pulled at the last minute, if the higher-ups ordered it.

It might not have been my dream job, but I couldn't deny that working here was an adrenaline rush — the thriving atmosphere bred the feeling that things could change at a moment's notice. The fashion industry was constantly evolving; what was *in* last month could be passé within the span of a week. There was also the problem of our readers who, for the most part, possessed the attention span of goldfish. Keeping up with the demands of the masses took strategy, time, and commitment for anyone who chose a career at *Luster*.

Trend-spotting was a priority.

Daily Tweets and Facebook updates were a must.

Ferreting out the competition's material was a necessity.

Professional clout was determined by number of Instagram followers, not one's work ethic.

In the old days — also known as the pre-internet era — a columnist might've written a few stories in the span of a month, which would be sent out all at once for the next print edition. Now I wrote a few stories in a week — sometimes in a single day — to release on the *Luster* website and social media pages, with one or two larger stories set aside exclusively for print. What didn't get put into circulation via *Luster*'s outlets was posted on my personal blog, "Georgia On My Mind," where I detailed all of my hilarious, somewhat embarrassing culture-shock testimonials. The blog had amassed thousands of followers in the past year alone. Apparently, people loved to read about — and laugh at — the trials and tribulations of a country girl adapting to city life.

Point was, the workday didn't end at five or start at eight anymore. Before I'd even slurped down coffee — hell, before I'd even gotten out of bed in the morning — I'd checked my social media accounts at least once.

The world had changed. The entirety of the publishing industry had changed. And you could either adapt alongside it, or be left to the wayside — hell, it was practically the company motto. Fae and I liked to say that there was an invisible, implied contract along with the paper ones we signed before our first shifts here — a set of expectations never voiced, but harshly enforced:

You don't want to work 10-hour days?

That's fine — there's someone else who's happy to, and probably at a lower pay grade.

You don't want to come in on weekends?

Hey, that's cool — so long as you don't mind when someone else is given that promotion you've been wishing for.

You don't want to spend your entire paycheck on designer heels?

Good for you — go get a normal office job where you can wear all the comfortable shoes you want because image isn't important.

This was *Luster*. It was materialistic, catty, competitive, and trendy. Darwin would've loved to spend a day observing my coworkers: it was survival of the fittest at its very best. High school reincarnated.

There was a good reason Fae was the only girl from work I associated with.

Ever punctual, she arrived at her cubicle fifteen minutes early. She stopped abruptly as she caught sight of me at my desk, her eyes wide with surprise. For once I'd gotten to work before her. Most days, I made it in with seconds to spare before the daily morning briefing, rushing in as though the devil himself were on my heels — hair flying out of its fastenings, hastily-sipped coffee charring my tongue, and a half-done face of makeup that Fae would bully me into fixing in the bathroom at some point during the morning.

"You're here early," she noted, dumping her large Louis Vuitton hobo bag onto her desk. "Thought you'd be battling a hangover or calling in sick, after the way I left you last night."

"I'm surprisingly bright eyed and bushy tailed this morning." I smiled at her, standing up to hand her the steaming latte I'd purchased only moments before her arrival. "Here."

"You're a godsend," she muttered, taking a delicate sip so as not to ruin her flawless lipstick with unwanted foam.

"Not quite," I said. "And I've never really understood that phrase. I mean, who wants to be a god*send*? Wouldn't you rather just be a goddess?"

"So, I'm giving you thirty more seconds," she told me, completely ignoring my musings as she moved around to take a seat at her desk.

"Oh?" I asked. "What for?"

"Thirty seconds to tell me who in the hell *Sebastian* is and what happened to induce the Merlot bath you took last night." She glanced at the dainty silver watch on her wrist. "Make that twenty seconds."

"Thanks for tucking me in before you left," I said, smiling down at her.

"Fifteen."

"Really, I appreciate it."

"Ten."

"So do you think Jeanine will make us do a column on that new jazzercising techni—"

"*Lux Kincaid!* Do not make me drag you into the bathroom by your hair and torture you for information," Fae whisper-yelled at me, her eyes glaring daggers. "You know I'll do it." She crossed her arms in front of her chest menacingly.

"Oh, relax." I grinned down at her, leaning a hip against the cubicle partition.

She arched one eyebrow and cast an impatient look at her watch. I held my hands up in a gesture of surrender.

"Fine, fine. It's just..." I took a steadying breath. "This thing with Sebastian... It's complicated."

"So *un*-complicate it."

"Sebastian is—" My words cut off abruptly, drying up in my throat as I caught sight of the man stepping out of elevator banks. The tempo of my heartbeat stuttered erratically, before thundering to twice its normal rate.

"Sebastian is *what?*" Fae snapped impatiently.

"Here," I whispered, feeling the blood drain from my face. "Sebastian is here."

༺༻

IN MY PERIPHERAL, I SAW FAE'S HEAD SPIN AROUND SO FAST she'd probably have whiplash for a week. My eyes, however, were locked on the shiny gold elevator doors that were sliding shut, and the man now standing in front of them. His eyes swept the space, taking in the office layout with a shrewd composure born from his years as a politician's son. When they skimmed over me, halting for only the briefest of moments, I thought they may have narrowed in disgust or suspicion, but they moved away too quickly for me to be sure.

He was a fortress. A stony castle with walls so high no army could breach them, let alone one solitary woman. I couldn't read him at all. Yet my own expression, I feared, was unguarded; cheeks flushed, lips parted, eyes wide with surprise and maybe, if you looked a little closer, the faintest remnant of longing. I'd been caught unawares by his abrupt entrance and hadn't the time to gain composure or don any number of the schooled expressions that would be considered appropriate when one saw a distant acquaintance or a stranger. If he looked now, he'd see it shining from my eyes, radiating from my pores, and saturating the room — a yearning, a need that hadn't been filled in all our time apart.

I needn't have worried.

His eyes swept over me, through me, as though I were just another piece of the colorless office furniture littering the room. Either he was the best actor I'd ever come across, or he was sincerely unaffected by my existence. There was no emotion in his eyes, save the cool disinterest of a stranger taking in his surroundings for the first time. He looked like his mother, I realized, both startled and saddened by the thought. There was a tightness around his mouth that hadn't been there in the years of our youth — lines weathered not by laughter but something far more trying.

One look at him, and I'd known that the boy I'd loved — the one whose very essence seemed a product of light and laughter, who'd grinned freely and joked as easily as he breathed — was gone. The man before me was a hollowed out husk, his carefree soul scrubbed clean from his perfect frame, leaving a heartbreakingly foreign doppelgänger behind.

Physically he was nearly the same. His muscular frame may've filled out considerably, but those clear hazel eyes and that mop of burnished gold hair remained achingly familiar to me even after all these years of distance. And yet, at the same time, he was now a stranger.

My throat worked against the lump that had lodged itself painfully in my airway and I studiously ignored the lance of pain that shot into my heart as thoughts tumbled through my mind unchecked. I wanted to tear my eyes from him yet, being an eternal glutton for punishment, I couldn't look away as he made his way toward Jeanine's office without a backward glance at me.

"So that's him, huh?" Fae's voice snapped me out of my trance, and when I turned my eyes to face her she was looking at me with more than a little concern. "He'd be sexy if he weren't so serious."

I nodded slowly, my mind reeling with thoughts.

Why was he here?

Did Cara send him?

Was he going to report me to Jeanine?

Was I about to lose my job?

"I take it the break up didn't go well?" Fae asked.

I nodded again.

"I have a feeling this particular Fae Friday is going to call for extra tequila."

"You can say that again," I agreed, collapsing into my desk chair with a deep sigh.

Chapter Ten

THEN

"Lux! Hey, wait up!"

Crap.

I sped up my pace, weaving between clusters of people in the crowded hallway as I headed for the exit. Once the final bell rang, the halls filled with a cacophony of voices as my peers gossiped about the happenings of the day. I always made a point to visit my locker before last period so I could avoid the 3:00 p.m. corridor traffic jam and escape outside to catch my bus.

"Lux!" The voice was persistent and, if I wasn't mistaken, faintly amused by my dodging efforts.

Maybe he'd give up if I just ignored him. He'd think I hadn't heard his calls and move on. The exit was directly ahead, just ten feet away — I could make it.

"Hey!" His voice was closer now, definitely within hearing range and near enough for him to know that I'd either developed a hearing impairment overnight or was blatantly ignoring him.

Tough call.

Still intent on escape, I finally cleared the exit doors, relieved when they closed behind me to shut out the noisy hallway and my pursuer.

I hiked my backpack higher on my shoulder and started walking toward the bus stop.

"You know, I should be offended," his voice whispered in my ear. I jumped about a foot into the air, whirling around to face him. I hadn't even heard him exit the building — he must've made it outside before the door swung closed.

He stood grinning down at me, the only spot of color in the dreary, bleached out January landscape. My breath caught in my throat at the sight of him. A lock of hair had fallen in front of his eyes, and I had the sudden urge to reach up and push it back for him. Internally cursing myself, I managed to keep my hands to myself.

"Most girls run *toward* me, not away as fast as their feet can carry them," Sebastian noted.

"Did you need something?" I asked quietly, my breath puffing visibly in the crisp air.

"Need? No." He stepped closer to me, lifting one hand to rub at the light stubble on his jawline. "Want? Yes."

"Well, what do you want?" My voice practically squeaked with nerves. I moved back a step out of his space, casting my eyes down at the ground. The grass beneath my sneakers was dead and gray, flattened against the hard-packed earth.

"I want to give you a ride home."

My eyes snapped away from my shoes, up to examine his face. His teasing grin was gone, in its place a serious expression. "Why?" I asked.

"Do I need a reason?"

"You're Sebastian Covington," I said, only just managing to leave off the implied *duh* at the end of that statement.

"And you're Lux Kincaid," he replied, the beginnings of a smile forming on his lips.

"So you see the problem here." I spoke slowly, as if to a small child who wasn't quite getting the concept.

"Nope," he said, grinning full out. "I don't."

I titled my head sideways. "Are you being purposefully obtuse?"

"I'm not sure. Let me think on it. Why don't you ask me again while I'm driving you home?"

He leaned forward and grabbed my hand, lacing our fingers together as though it was the most natural thing in the world for the two of us — two strangers from completely different worlds, with nothing at all in common — to be holding hands. With a gentle tug, he pulled me in the opposite direction of the bus stop, toward the student parking lot.

"I don't understand you," I murmured quietly, the entirety of my attention riveted on the warm, unfamiliar point of contact between his palm and mine.

"See, the thing is, Lux," he said in an equally quiet voice. "I think you might be the only one who can."

I nearly laughed. What could I possibly understand about him? We had nothing in common.

No sooner had the thought entered my mind, than an image of his face from that rainy day in the car last week flashed before my eyes.

I saw the bashful flush on his cheeks as he spoke of his love for music. Heard the underlying hurt as he casually dismissed his mother's beliefs about his inadequacies. Replayed the uncertain canter of his voice as he talked about himself — as though he didn't really know who he was.

Could it be that he was lonely? That, despite the popularity, despite the media attention his family drew — he was somehow alone? Unsure of himself, of who he was beneath the photoshopped image of Sebastian Covington that the rest of the world saw on magazine covers and news footage?

If so, that was something I could understand. Obviously not the fame or the attention, but the sheer loneliness of self-containment. The isolation of never letting down your walls, never letting your happy mask slip.

I'd been alone for a year without Jamie by my side. Sure, I still had him on weekends and during our brief after-school visits at the hospital. But it wasn't the same. And a part of me was beginning to accept that it would never be the same again. Jamie was fading, slowly. Each day, each surgery, each round of chemo took him a little further away from me.

And that was a burden I shouldered all by myself.

I cast a glance up at Sebastian, who was staring down at me. Tentatively, I squeezed his hand and watched, mesmerized, as a smile bloomed across his face in response. He gave my hand a gentle squeeze in return and was opening his mouth to say something when a voice boomed across the courtyard, stopping us in our tracks.

"Sebastian! Come to The Grill with us," Amber called in a syrupy-sweet, arsenic-laced voice. Her dismissive gaze swept over me like a slap, and I tried not to let it bother me that her invitation wasn't extended in my direction.

"Not today, Amber," Sebastian called back.

"I know you don't have anything better going on." She smirked, planting one hand on her hip in a suggestive pose. "And I'll make it worth your while."

I felt my cheeks flame with embarrassment — I'd clearly misread Sebastian's intentions. I'd been foolish to assume that the coffee he'd given or the smiles we'd shared meant anything. Girls like Amber — who wore the right clothes and came from the good families — would always win. It wasn't even a contest.

Already anticipating the dejection I'd feel when he walked away, I unlaced my fingers and started to pull my hand from Sebastian's. His grip tightened immediately, locking our fingers together firmly so I had no hope of disengaging.

"Actually, Amber, I do have something better going on," he tossed out casually, and I watched as Amber's smirk became a look of shock. "You've met Lux, haven't you?" Sebastian added.

I could hear the smile in his voice, but my eyes were still trained on Amber. She'd stopped feigning sweetness and was glaring at me with the full brunt of her malice. She didn't bother to reply, instead turning around with an audible huff and storming away with a silent Nicole close on her heels. We stood in silence for a frozen moment, neither knowing quite what to say to the other.

"You didn't have to do that," I murmured. "You should go with them. They're you're friends."

"Hey," he said, reaching under my chin and tilting my face up to meet his eyes. "I already have plans. Not with a friend, because this girl I'm with – she's pretty stubborn and she hasn't agreed to be my friend just yet. But I'm not worried. I'm persistent. I'll wear her down eventually."

I cracked a smile. "You seem pretty sure of yourself."

"Well, Freckles," he whispered eying the lightly-spackled bridge of my nose. "I'm Sebastian Covington." His grin was rakish, his posture confident.

"*Freckles?*" I wrinkled my nose in distaste at the endearment. "That's not a nickname."

"Too late." He laughed boyishly.

"Seriously, there's no need dub me with a constant reminder of my imperfections."

"They aren't imperfections. They're cute," he insisted. "I have a thing for freckles."

I rolled my eyes. "Let's go, weirdo," I said, walking toward the parking lot and tugging Sebastian behind me. There was a warm feeling spreading though my system, and as I let my eyes skitter over to meet his, I couldn't help but grin — a full-out, happy, no-holds-barred grin — for the first time in months.

"Thanks," I said. "For Amber."

"Believe me, Lux — it was my pleasure."

◈

"No way," I said, crossing my arms over my chest.

"Why not?"

"You shouldn't even be in here! In fact, I specifically asked to be dropped off at the front doors!"

"Yes, and?"

"And now you're standing in front of my brother's hospital room, acting like you're coming in to visit with me!"

"Right, and?"

"And don't you see the problem with that?"

"Nope." He was grinning again. I growled in frustration. The boy was intolerable, really. In the space of thirty minutes, I'd gone from infatuated to indignant — no doubt some kind of record.

"Bash, you can't come in with me. Jamie doesn't know you. And it doesn't make any sense for you to visit!"

"So you're saying Jamie doesn't want company?"

Ugh. He had me there. Jamie was *always* looking for company. He was bored stiff in that room all day, so any novelty was welcome. Several times, I'd caught him charming the candy stripers into neglecting their shifts and staying for extended visits, but that was probably just because he liked to look at their cute little red uniforms.

"Well, no. Not exactly," I hedged.

"So you're saying you don't want to be seen with me?"

"No! That's not my point here," I whispered in a frustrated voice. He was twisting my words, muddling my argument.

"What *is* your point, then?" he asked. "Because if Jamie wants visitors, I want to visit, and you have no issues with it... I don't see the problem."

"But— Well—" I spluttered, at a loss for words. Somehow this entire conversation had been steered out of my control, and I had no idea how to get it back. I opened my mouth to protest again, but froze abruptly when I heard it.

The sudden, unmistakable sound of the heart monitor in Jamie's room as it stopped its rhythmic metronomic beeping, and instead released a horrifying, long tone that pierced the air and made every inch of my body break out in gooseflesh. I knew that sound — I spent my every waking moment dreading its arrival.

A flat line.

Jamie's heart had stopped.

My terrified gaze met Sebastian's for one suspended instant before I sprang into action, racing around the corner that concealed us from view and sprinting into Jamie's room.

"Help!" I called over my shoulder, hoping someone at the nearby nurse's station would hear my cries. "His heart's stopped!" I could feel the tears of panic gathering behind my eyes, and I sensed Sebastian's presence close behind me as we stopped short at Jamie's bedside. Distantly, I registered the sounds of nurses yelling for the crash cart, wheels and sneakers moving on the squeaky linoleum floors.

I looked at Jamie and felt my own heart stop.

"Hey, sis," he said, grinning at me from his bed. I watched, dumbfounded, as he fiddled with the heart monitor wires on his right wrist. When the electrodes slid back into place, the flat line ceased abruptly and the sound of his strong, even heartbeats filled the room.

"Sorry, Wendy!" Jamie called to the harried woman in scrubs standing in the doorway. "False alarm. These dang electrodes just won't stay on, today." My head swiveled back and forth between them and I watched as he winked at her and she smiled in return.

"Haven't you heard the story of the boy who cried wolf, James?" she asked with a disapproving *tsk* sound. "Just do me a favor and don't mess with the wires when Benita is on the floor. She's cranky enough these days." With a playful wave in my direction, Wendy left the room, shooing out the crash cart response team as she went.

"So, sis, how goes it?" Jamie asked, leaning back on his bed in a pose of full relaxation.

I stared at him, vibrating with anger. I heard Sebastian let out a snort of laughter behind me, and promptly elbowed him in the ribs.

"James Arthur Kincaid, you are in *so much trouble!*" I hissed, striding closer to the bed.

"Aw, come on sis. Don't have a heart attack," he joked. Looking around me to Sebastian, he asked, "Too soon?"

"You might want to let her cool down a little before throwing around the heart failure jokes," Bash advised with a grin. I glared icily at them both in quick succession.

"What the hell were you doing, Jamie? Trying to scare me to death?" I asked.

"Oh, relax. Without my little flat line, you two would still be out in the hall bickering about whether Sebastian here could come in and see me, and my precious visiting hours would be wasting away," he said. "Also, I want my contraband."

"Contraband?" Bash asked, his brows lifting amusedly.

"Maybe you don't deserve it," I told Jamie.

"Give it up, sis, or I tell Sebastian the fish food story."

"You wouldn't!" I cried indignantly.

"Oh, I would," he promised, a gleeful grin spreading across his face.

"I want to hear the fish food story," Sebastian chimed in.

"Fine, you devil," I said to Jamie, unzipping my backpack and handing over three Cadbury chocolate bars. "Not a *word* about fish food, or that will be the last candy you get from the outside world."

"Like you're my only source," he snorted, making light of my threat. But I knew he'd keep his mouth shut. Jamie might tease me, he might do his best to drive me up the wall with his antics and practical jokes, but he'd never do something that would genuinely hurt me.

"Chocolate?" he offered around a mouthful of candy, extending the half-wrapped bar in Sebastian's direction.

"Nah, I'm good," Bash replied, dragging one of the stiff-backed wooden chairs away from the wall and positioning it next to Jamie's bed. He promptly flopped down in it, turned to my twin, and struck up a conversation about the Bulldogs' postseason performance. Jamie's eyes lit up instantly — it'd been a long time since someone talked football with him.

While Jamie was a full-fledged Auburn-hating, UGA-loving "dawg," I shunned my Georgian roots with my total lack of interest in our state sports teams. Once terms like NCAA and SEC started floating around, I was more liable to nod off than join in the conversation — not exactly an ideal chatting partner when it came to discussing the Deep South's Oldest Rivalry.

All things considered, it was pretty remarkable we'd shared a womb for nine months.

Within minutes, as was inevitable whenever boys talked football, a heated debate had broken out concerning next season's new recruits. Sebastian was confident they'd have the sheer talent to take us all the way through the bowl games with certain victory, while Jamie contended that their inexperience would make for an uncoordinated, unsuccessful performance on the field.

I looked at the two of them, sensing already that this budding friendship did not bode well for me. Leaning back against the wall, I let my eyes drift closed and released an extended, unladylike snore loud enough that both their heads snapped in my direction and their conversation instantly came to a halt.

"Sorry," I said, lifting my hand to cover the large faux yawn splitting my face. "Fell asleep for a minute there."

"Cute," Bash commented, grinning across the room at me and throwing in a wink for good measure. I fought off a blush, but couldn't stop my answering smile.

"Dude, that's my sister," Jamie complained. "You seem like a good guy, and you hate the Crimson Tide almost as much as I do... but boundaries, my friend. *Boundaries*."

"Jamie," I protested, feeling my cheeks heat.

"Alright, alright, I'm sorry." Sebastian laughed, turning back to Jamie. "How about I get us into my father's private box next season for a game? Will all be forgiven?"

"Dude," Jamie said, eyes wide. "You make it a championship

game, you can call my sister whatever you want. Seriously. *Whatever* you want."

"Standing *right* here," I noted, glaring at my traitorous twin. "I can hear you, you know."

"I know, sis," Jamie said, laughing lightly when he caught sight of my expression. "But we're talking box seats. Prime real estate. You know I love you, but...don't make me choose between you and football." He grimaced at the thought.

"Listen to the man, Lux. That's a real *Sophie's Choice* you're giving him," Sebastian added, shaking his head in feigned sadness.

"I hate you both," I told them, trying very hard not to smile at their teasing.

In actuality, I was thrilled.

Jamie hadn't looked this happy in a long, long time. I knew a big part of that was due to Sebastian's presence. Jamie always perked up when he had visitors other than his lame, boring sister, as he so affectionately referred to me. His spirits were high, there was a healthy dose of color in his cheeks, and for a minute I let myself be overtaken by dangerous hopes.

Hopes that he'd recover fully.

Hopes that this latest surgery would also be his last.

Hopes that he'd walk again.

Hopes that he'd be well enough to enjoy those box seats next season with Sebastian.

And, finally, hopes that there'd be more afternoons like this one. That Bash wouldn't stop visiting. That he'd continue to use that inner light he carried around to ward off the shadows clinging to my life. Because I was pretty sure that Jamie liked him.

And I knew for certain that I did.

Chapter Eleven

NOW

"Lux!" Jeanine's voice clipped out, her order cutting through the air like an arrow aimed straight for my heart. "My office. Now."

My head snapped away from the computer screen on my desk, turning automatically toward the sound of her voice. The harbinger of my doom. I caught sight of her for only a brief moment before the opaque door closed at her back.

This was it — I was definitely getting fired. Cara would be so pleased.

I didn't allow myself to think about the fact that Sebastian had made a special trip down to Harding headquarters to report me to my supervisor. That would only make this harder. He'd been in there for less than fifteen minutes — more like fourteen minutes, thirty-seven seconds, but who was counting? — but I figured that was ample time to describe yesterday's incident in enough detail to justify my dismissal.

I cringed inwardly as I wove through the labyrinth of cubicles toward Jeanine's office. Outwardly, though, I kept my brow unmarred by worry lines, my shoulders back, and my head held high. I felt the weight of my coworkers' eyes on me; there was blood in the water, and the sharks were excited. They all watched my journey — some with sympathy, but most with a poorly concealed anticipatory glee at my impending demise.

"Good luck, girlie," Sasha murmured with practiced solicitude, her forced frown rendered unconvincing by the excited gleam in her eyes. My gaze shot past her to Fae, who rolled her eyes and proceeded to make ridiculous faces and inappropriate hand gestures in Sasha's direction.

I felt my lips twitch in repressed laughter as I walked the final steps toward my destiny.

The faint smile died when the glass door slid open and Sebastian stepped out of the office. I froze like a startled doe caught in someone's high-beams, unsure whether I should acknowledge him or walk past without so much as a *hi-how've-you-been-for-the-last-seven-years-since-I-ripped-your-heart-to-shreds-like-an-old-grocery-list*.

Maybe I could just do something casual.

A wave? No. Too friendly.

A smile? Definitely not. Too fake.

A wink? HA! Who was I freaking kidding?

A nod? Hmm.

Actually, a nod sounded perfect. A nod was casual. Indifferent, yet polite. Neutral but direct.

So I nodded at him — just a slight bob of my head to show that I wasn't being rude, but remained as unruffled by his presence as he evidently was mine. If only.

To my surprise, Sebastian nodded back — and he didn't even glare at me while he did it! Not that he smiled or anything. But I was going to consider Operation Nod a success.

Good call, Lux.

My mental congratulations came to a halt when, to my horror, I sidestepped right to pass by him at the exact moment he stepped left to do the same. What followed can only be described as the most awkward, uncoordinated, sidestep-shuffle ever to occur in the history of such collisions.

I immediately corrected my course, stepping left.

At the same time, Sebastian took a hasty step right.

"Sorry," I muttered, bobbing.

"Pardon me," he murmured, weaving.

This was completely ridiculous. *Why me?* I cast my eyes heavenward.

An uncontrollable, semi-hysterical laugh slipped through my lips as I admitted defeat and stopped moving altogether. At the sound, Sebastian froze and his eyes flew to my face, riveted on my lips, as though he was fascinated they'd just produced such a noise. We were face to face, frozen in time for a brief moment, and all I could do was stare at him.

There were faint shadows under his eyes, as if he hadn't been sleeping well. A light growth of blond stubble covered his chiseled jawline, which I knew meant he probably hadn't shaved this morning. He had a tan, so he either sunned regularly on his rooftop — *doubtful* — or he was still an avid fan of the outdoors, as he'd been as a teen.

I wondered what he saw when he looked at me.

In some ways, I was still the same girl I'd always been. But the stylish clothes were new, as were the expensive accessories and high profile job. I had more confidence now than I'd had as a girl, in part because of my career but also because I'd come into my own once I graduated college and moved to the city. But I was still the first to laugh at a good joke, and the first to cry at a sad movie scene. Still the girl clumsily tripping over her own feet as she rushed from one task to the next, and still in the habit of leaving dishes in the sink and laundry unfolded if it meant not missing out on something better.

Different, yet the same.

"Hi," I whispered, not knowing what else to say. I wasn't

exactly familiar with the protocol for what one said to her ex after seven years of distance.

"Ms. Kincaid," Sebastian said, nodding in acknowledgement. I felt chills break out across my skin at the sound of my name on his lips, something I thought I'd never hear again. I stared unblinking at him, in that moment utterly unconcerned with the fact that he hated me and had likely just gotten me fired. His eyes roamed my face and hair as mine drank in the sight of him in turn. The air between us grew charged, practically crackling with electricity as the seconds passed and neither of us made a move to leave.

The moment was broken when Sebastian's mind seemed to clear of whatever spell had fallen over us, his face darkening to an expression of anger — whether at himself or at me, I wasn't sure. He extended his arms into my space, each of his hands forming a light grip around my biceps, and moved me two feet to the his left so our paths were finally clear of one another. I allowed him to steer me, my befuddled feet moving at his command.

His touch was perfunctory, in no way lingering or intimate; in the space of an instant, we'd slipped back into being strangers. Before I could say another word, he'd moved past me and was headed for the elevators. I didn't care what my nosy coworkers might read on my face as I watched him go. Never had I felt more keenly the sting of regret at the way our lives had played out, at the hand we'd been dealt by fate. Wondering if I'd ever see him again, my eyes followed his departure until he boarded the elevator and its gleaming gold doors slid shut behind him. Only when he'd disappeared from view did I turn to face Jeanine's door.

With a deep inhale and a bolstering roll of my shoulders, I grasped the handle and walked inside.

◈◈◈

"YOU'RE NOT SERIOUS," I SAID, JUST SHY OF SCOFFING.

Jeanine stared impassively, her expression unchanged but for the subtle lift of her brow.

"Sorry," I recovered. "But Jeanine, that's just absurd. I can't be Sebastian Covington's... what would you even call it? Personal assistant? Errand girl? Slave?"

"Listen, Lux, I like you," Jeanine announced, crossing her arms across her chest and leaning back in her leather chair.

Could've fooled me.

"You do consistently good work, you don't make waves, and you don't bother me with inane complaints like so many of your coworkers," she continued.

I sensed the impending *but* coming.

"But," she said, confirming my prediction. "You messed up on this one. I don't know what you did to piss off Mr. Covington and frankly I don't care. The bottom line is, his shots of Cara are a huge part of the September issue — which, as you may or may not have put together at some point during your three years here, is our most important edition of the year. So I don't care if we have to jump through hoops or tame dragons or run marathons to make him happy. Mr. Covington gets *whatever* he requests. And he specifically requested you."

He was going to derail my life, just like I'd done to him all those years ago. This was it: the moment karma bit me in the ass. The ghost of boyfriends past, come back to haunt me.

I nodded, at a loss for words.

"More importantly, though, *Luster* is celebrating its 100th birthday in a few short weeks," Jeanine went on. "The Centennial. It's going to be huge. Big party, media coverage, the whole package. Mr. Harding *himself* will be attending." She leaned forward and stared at me intently, pressing her hands against the edge of her desk. "Then we have the December issue, which will be a tribute to 100 years of *Luster*. We'll be doing a slew of special features and photo shoots to commemorate and recreate the magazine's history."

I nodded again — the entire staff had been briefed on the Centennial celebration months ago, and preparations were well underway for the event. It was going to, quite literally, be the party of the century. Fae had already purchased her dress on special order — designer, of course — and was nearly incapacitated by distress when I told her I'd yet to purchase mine.

"I'm sorry Jeanine, but I just don't understand what the Centennial has to do with Sebastian Covington."

"Dear, it has *everything* to do with Sebastian Covington. He is one of the most exclusive, well-respected photographers in the industry. The projects he agrees to are few and far between, and he doesn't typically do fashion. We're lucky to have him and, if we're being candid, we probably wouldn't if Cara Stein hadn't convinced him. Apparently, they have a...personal connection."

I'll bet they do.

"He'll be doing ten different themed spreads for us, recreating famous *Luster* shoots through the ages. One shoot per decade. Cara will pose for several of them. And you'll be the *Luster* liaison assisting him," she told me. "With *whatever* he needs. I don't care if he wants you fetching dry-cleaning and coffee. You're at his disposal. Do I make myself clear?"

"Crystal." My saccharine smile was far from sincere.

"Wonderful," she said, clapping her hands twice in quick succession. "You'll report to the ArtLust studio bright and early Monday morning. Mr. Covington has your contact information." Her smile was vaguely amused as she glanced pointedly from me to the door. Apparently, I'd been dismissed; I stood to leave.

"Oh, and Lux?" Jeanine called when I'd reached the exit. "I'd suggest doing some preliminary research on Mr. Covington. Get familiar with his background, his past, his likes and dislikes...it may be useful."

His past. I turned to face her and nodded, forcing the bubbling hysteria down.

"I'll be sure to do that, Jeanine. Have a good weekend."

I exited her office in a stupor, not exactly sure how it had happened but knowing full well that in the last five minutes, every-thing had changed irrevocably. When the door closed at my back, Fae was there by my side almost instantly. She took one look at my shell-shocked expression, looped an arm through mine, and guided me through the gauntlet of curious stares and gossip back toward our desks.

"So, we're going to that new sushi place for lunch. The one with the spicy tuna roll I'd sell my soul for," Fae prattled loudly, filling the silence with a cheerful tone meant to fend off the unwanted attention of our onlookers. "I remember you said you wanted to get salads but I'm really craving sushi. I know you Georgia girls get nervous about anything that hasn't been fried or smothered with Crisco first, but just trust me on this one. You'll love it."

I kept my eyes focused forward, not meeting anyone's gaze and pretending I didn't hear the speculative murmurs about my meeting with Jeanine and my halting interaction with Sebastian. My face was carefully blank, my posture rigid with self-containment.

Once we were out of earshot, Fae dropped her ruse, falling silent with a reassuring arm squeeze.

"You gonna make it through the morning meeting? 'Cause if you need to ditch, I'll come with you. Or I can stay here and cover for you. Whatever you need, love," Fae offered quietly when we'd reached the semi-privacy of my cubicle.

"I'll be fine," I told her. "But thanks."

"Want to talk about it?" she asked. I glanced at my watch. The daily staff briefing began in five minutes — not enough time to even scratch the surface of my past with Sebastian.

"Later," I said. "Over margaritas. With double tequila."

"That bad, huh?" She grimaced in sympathy.

"You have no idea."

"Well, if what I saw earlier is any indication, there's definitely some unresolved tension between you two. I mean, Jesus, your little stare down in front of Jeanine's office? Talk about intense."

I nodded.

"Well, time to go face down the devils," Fae announced, looping her arm through mine once more.

"...in Prada," I added with a wry smile.

Fae laughed as we made our way to the conference room, the final two to straggle in behind the other twenty people in our department — nineteen catty women and one fabulous gay man named Simon who often tagged along with Fae and me for post-work cocktails or girl's night out.

After moving to the city at eighteen from a small, über-conservative town in Ohio, Simon had attended Parsons, where he liked to say he'd majored in fashion design and a minored in celebrity stalking. His talents were put to good use here at *Luster*, as he managed the "Who Wore It Better," "Hot or Not," and "Trendy Today" sections. He and Fae could talk fashion for hours on end, which would've been nauseating except they were so genuinely obsessed I couldn't help but listen in — even though I didn't have a firm opinion on whether high-waisted shorts were a *do* or a *don't*, or whether color-block maxi dresses were glam or gauche.

For the most part, my best friends were pretty awesome.

The one exception to this was when they turned their chic eyes on *my* wardrobe and decided to make what they considered "necessary" changes. Three separate times over the last two years I'd returned home from a run in Central Park or a trip to the grocery store, only to find the two of them huddled in my closet adding new items and confiscating things they considered out of vogue. And that was only counting the occasions I'd caught them in the act — god only knew how many times they'd broken in without my knowledge.

I really needed to get my spare key back from Fae.

Simon waved us over from the corner of the conference room, where he'd staked out three seats by the window. As soon as we'd settled in, he turned to me with wide, curious eyes.

"Lux, baby, who was that delicious man you were talking to earlier? I sensed a vibe." He looked at Fae. "Did you sense a vibe, or was it just me?"

"There was definitely a vibe," Fae noted.

"Very Tarzan and Jane," Simon added. "So brooding and tortured."

"No, to me it's more a forbidden Victorian romance. Stolen glances and muted conversations," Fae chimed in, adding her two cents.

"Guys!" I protested. "You don't even know the real backstory yet."

"Yes, baby, but that's what's so fun about it. We have all day to fill in the blanks with our guesses, and then all night to hear the real story," Simon explained. Apparently, he was ditching one of the posh parties he typically frequented on Fridays in favor of crashing our girl's night. "I can only hope that the reality lives up to my mental version," he said.

"Did you see the way they looked at one another?" Fae asked him. "So tormented. So angsty. It'll live up, I can tell."

I huffed. "Well, maybe I won't even tell you guys the story, since you're enjoying your own speculation so much. Maybe you don't deserve the real version."

Fae and Simon looked at each other and burst into laughter simultaneously.

"I really hate you guys," I muttered.

"No you don't, baby," Simon said, leaning in to kiss my left cheek.

"You love us," Fae added, with a light arm squeeze.

I heaved a martyred sigh, but didn't protest.

They were right.

Chapter Twelve

THEN

"You're crazy," I whispered, attempting to tug my hand from Sebastian's grip.

"Crazy for you," he countered, leading me into his kitchen through the back patio door.

"You're ridiculous." I rolled my eyes.

"Ridiculously infatuated with you," he revised, tugging me along behind him.

"Sebastian!" I protested. This was not a good idea.

"Lux!" he mimicked in a falsetto, towing me past gleaming stainless steel appliances.

"I hate you," I whispered.

He spun around so fast I didn't have time to react, and before I knew it I was pressed tightly between the countertop and Sebastian. His hard body dwarfed mine and I struggled to remain calm and collected, not wanting to reveal how much his closeness affected me. I felt my own inexperience rolling off me in waves of uncertainty, saturating the air around us. I clenched my clammy hands into fists, hoping he wouldn't see through me. Praying he couldn't tell that I'd never been this close to a guy before — besides Jamie, of course, but considering the fact that we shared nearly identical DNA, I wasn't counting him.

Sebastian leaned down into my space, catching my eyes. Abruptly, he hitched his hands around my waist and lifted me so I was sitting propped on the countertop at eye level with him. I felt my lips part on an exhale as his hands skimmed lightly from my hipbones down to my kneecaps. Gently, he nudged my legs apart and stepped between them, so our bodies were flush against each other.

"You don't hate me," he whispered, his breath warm against my neck as his head dropped forward to rest in the hollow between my chin and my shoulder blade. Acting on some deeply ingrained instinct, I arched my head back to give him better access. His lips trailed down my neck to my collarbone, and I shivered. "In fact," he continued between butterfly kisses. "I'm pretty sure you lo—"

"Sebastian Michael Covington!" The smooth southern accent did nothing to detract from the outrage in the voice that pierced the air and interrupted our moment. We instantly sprang apart, Sebastian stepping fully out of my space as I scooted forward off the counter and landed roughly on my feet with a jolt that made my arches ache.

"Hey, Mom," Sebastian said, casually lifting one hand to rub the back of his neck and grinning at the scandalized woman standing in the doorway to the kitchen. Though my fashion knowledge was limited to trips to Walmart and the local Goodwill, even I could tell that her clothing was designer. I found it strange that she was wearing both high heels and a set of pearls despite the fact that she didn't work and likely had been home alone all day, but what did I know about the glamorous life of the rich? Her platinum blonde hair was coiffed elegantly, and it was clear where Sebastian had gotten his looks — Judith Covington had bone structure any model would kill for and stunning blue eyes that nailed me to the floor with a single glance.

My cheeks were probably as red as hers, though from embarrassment rather than stark disapproval. I smoothed my hands through my hair self-consciously and forced my shoulders not to curl in on themselves, never more aware of my second hand boots and threadbare jacket than I was at that moment.

"Hello, Mrs. Covington," I said with as much grace as I could muster, stepping forward and offering her my hand. Her gaze moved away from her blatant appraisal of her son and she seemed to fully register my presence for the first time. Her eyes widened as she took me in. I wasn't what she'd expected, that much was obvious — not like Amber, or any of the other girls who came from money and would've been considered a good match for her son. Ignoring my outstretched hand altogether, her gaze swept down my form, pausing to take in each minute detail of my attire. Her lips tightened, a crosshatching of stern lines appearing in the flesh around her mouth that no amount of Botox could remove.

It couldn't be clearer that she disapproved.

"Mom, this is Lux," Sebastian offered, wrapping an arm loosely around my shoulders. I wanted to shrug off his touch, uncomfortable under his mother's hawk-like eyes. Not wanting her poisonous stare to ruin what had, until her arrival, been blossoming between us.

"It certainly is," she murmured, her sharp focus lingering on Bash's arm. Though the kitchen was warm, the air had become decidedly frosty since her arrival. "Sebastian, you know how I feel about having guests when the house isn't tidy. Greta comes on Mondays and Fridays, you know."

Tidy?

There wasn't a dirty dish to be seen, and a three-course meal could've been eaten off the floors, they were so clean. Greta, who I assumed was their housekeeper, should definitely be getting a raise if she alone was keeping the mansion in this unblemished state. But of course, Mrs. Covington's protests had nothing at all to do with the state of her home. Southern manners demanded a certain modicum of respect be paid to all houseguests, even to those one so blatantly disapproved of. And she'd been bred a political animal — as the wife of a politician, she couldn't say what she really meant, which was likely something along the lines of, *Get this trailer trash out of my house immediately.*

In politics, image was everything. Propriety always reigned supreme. And it sure as hell wouldn't be proper for a senator's wife to demand that her perfect son remove the poor girl from both her presence and her pristine household, lest she soil something.

Like the furniture. Or the family name.

"Mom—" Bash began.

"Sebastian." Her smile was arctic. I fought off a shiver. "Drive your..." Her beat of silence was timed impeccably — the work of a masterful conversationalist. "...*friend* home now, please."

I wanted to point out that adding the word "please" to the end of an order didn't detract from the fact that it was, in actuality, still an order, but I figured that would only make a bad situation worse. With her ringing endorsement hanging in the air, she glided from the room, her heels clicking sharply against the gleaming hardwood floors.

"That went well," I joked lightly, eyes averted. "I think she liked me."

"Lux," Sebastian said, sympathy threading his voice. "I'm sorry about her. I thought she'd be at Pilates or a DAR meeting or one of her afternoon activities. I had no idea she'd be here."

"No worries," I said breezily. "This is her home, she's entitled to her opinions and decisions."

"Well, her opinions are wrong," he said, leaning in to wrap his arms around me. I tensed in response, wary of his mother's disapproving eyes. "Relax," he whispered.

"We should go," I told him, feeling completely out of my

comfort zone and wanting to be anywhere on earth but in his kitchen. "Please."

"Alright, come on." He grabbed my hand and led me back through the kitchen to the patio door we'd entered through. "I want to show you something."

Despite my continual requests that he give me at least a hint about our destination, Sebastian remained stubbornly silent. He led us out onto the patio, skirted around the perimeter of the house, and cut through the yard toward the back edge of the property. The well-kept greenery of his sloping lawn eventually gave way to longer, wilder grasses and a copse of tall yellow poplar trees. As we wove through them, I stopped asking about our destination and silence descended over us. The poplars were old, soaring high above our heads with a majesty only Mother Nature can conjure. Walking beneath the shelter of their branches, we seemed miles from civilization rather than mere steps, as though we'd been transported to another world when we crossed the barrier from landscaped lawn to untamed wild.

There was serenity here, a hushed dignity it felt wrong to interrupt with words. Our footfalls were quiet against the mossy earth, and the only sounds were that of the wind whistling through the trees and the gentle trickling of a nearby stream as water flowed over the rock bed.

There was no trail — none that I could see, anyway — but Sebastian walked with purposeful strides, as though his feet had walked this path so many times he'd long since committed it to memory. After about five minutes, we broke through the dense-packed trees and came to a small clearing.

I gasped when it came into view, in awe of the mammoth sentinel before my eyes.

At the center of the glade was a huge, red oak tree. It dominated the clearing, dwarfing the surrounding trees with its thick trunk and long-reaching branches. It was so wide that had Sebastian and I stood on opposite sides and stretched our arms around its circumference, our hands wouldn't have touched. Its boughs were low-hanging, the bottom branches only about ten feet from the earth. It must've been a dream to climb as a child.

Detaching my grip from Sebastian's, I ran forward to skim my hands across the trunk, moving around it in a circle with my neck craned to catch a glimpse of the top. I felt a wondrous smile break out across my face as I made myself dizzy running in circles with my gaze trained skyward.

Giggling and breathless, I came to a halt with one hand planted firmly against the bark to steady myself. "Wow," I breathed. It must've been seventy feet tall.

"This is my favorite spot on the property," Bash revealed. I looked up to find him standing ten feet away, his eyes locked on my face. I could feel the color in my cheeks and I was warm in spite of the crisp air. My hair had slipped out of its ties during my mad dash and was hanging loose around my torso, a wind-tousled mess. "I hate that house," he added, nodding his head in the direction we'd come from.

I could see why. The plantation-style mansion he lived in was gorgeous — certainly fit for a senator's family. It looked like something off the set of *Gone With the Wind*, with its grand-scale white columns and sprawling front lawn. The circular drive leading to the house wound around a huge fountain, and the freestanding car garage was larger than my entire house. On our way to the woods, we'd passed a bean-shaped, in-ground pool in the backyard, as well as a stable which, from the soft neighing sounds and wafting fresh-hay smell, I'd bet contained more than one thoroughbred. Though I hadn't seen much beyond the kitchen, I could imagine the rest of the interior was equally extravagant.

And yet, for all its apparent wealth, the house was cold, impersonal. Like some museum exhibit where everything was warded with *look-but-don't-touch* signs, encased behind glass panels, and cordoned off with red velvet ropes. It was probably as pristine and unlived-in as the day it had been constructed.

No wonder Sebastian hated it.

"Have you ever climbed it?" I asked gesturing up at the massive red oak. I was genuinely curious but also hoping to steer his mind to happier topics.

Bash grinned. "More times than I could count," he told me.

"I'd like to see that sometime," I said, grinning back at him happily.

"Come here." His command was soft, his eyes beckoning with a gentle intensity. My feet responded instantly, drawn like the proverbial moth to his flame. When I came to a stop in front of him, he leaned forward into my space so only a hairsbreadth existed between our faces. His hands came up to cup my neck, then slid back to wind into my hair. With the lightest of pressure, he guided my mouth forward to brush against his.

His lips were softer than I'd expected, pushing against mine with gentle insistence. I bent into his frame, bringing my body flush with his. My lips parted and Sebastian deepened our kiss, the unfamiliar sensation of his tongue brushing mine nearly startling me off balance. My mind raced at twice its normal speed and I prayed I wasn't messing this up, making a fool of myself.

"Is this okay?" he asked me softly, pulling away a fraction of an inch.

"More than okay," I whispered back.

"Your heart is beating really fast," Sebastian said, his right thumb skimming over the pulse point in my throat.

"I'm nervous," I admitted.

"Don't be nervous." He leaned down to brush a featherlight kiss across my lips. "It's just me."

"That's exactly why I'm nervous," I pointed out.

He laughed lightly, wrapping his arms around me and drawing me in for a comforting hug that warmed me down to my bones. Without fully detangling our limbs, Sebastian walked me backwards until we were standing directly under the tree. Stepping out of my space, he sat with his back leaning against the thick trunk and extended one hand up to me.

"Come sit, Freckles."

I sat next to him and within seconds he'd hooked one arm

under my knees and swung them across his lap so I was settled on top of him. My head landed on his shoulder, and one of my arms curled naturally around his waist. I sighed contentedly when Bash's lips pressed against the hair on the crown of my head.

We sat for a long time, the prince and his pauper, sharing a moment beneath the most beautiful tree I'd ever seen. I could only imagine what it would be like in a few weeks, when spring arrived and it was once again full of lush green foliage.

"Lux?" Sebastian asked, his arms tightening around me slightly.

"Yeah?"

"What's wrong with Jamie?" He turned me in his arms so he could look into my eyes. "It's cancer, isn't it?"

"Yeah." I swallowed roughly.

"I'm sorry. I shouldn't have asked, it's just—" He broke off and took a deep breath that shifted my whole body. "I really like Jamie."

"He likes you too."

"Will he get better?" His question — *the* question, the one people were always terrified to ask and I was even more terrified to answer — hung in the air between us.

I was silent for a long time, trying to breathe normally.

"I don't know," I whispered eventually. "I hope so. We take it one day at a time."

Sebastian's arms hugged me tighter. "Is there anything I can do?"

"Keep visiting. Keep talking football and messing around with him. Keep treating him like he's a normal seventeen-year-old boy, who's not dyi—" My voice cracked on the word. "Who's not sick," I amended. I felt my eyes fill with unshed tears, and Sebastian leaned in to kiss my forehead gently.

"Keep being *you*," I whispered.

"I think I can do that," he whispered back.

Pushing aside all the worries that I'd screw it up or move too fast, I turned in his arms, followed my instincts, and brushed a light kiss across his lips. He kissed me back gently, as though I might shatter right there in his arms if he were to apply too much pressure.

And for a moment — for one blissful, perfect, sun-dappled moment in the arms of a boy I barely knew — I didn't feel so alone.

Chapter Thirteen

NOW

S<small>IMON AND</small> F<small>AE WERE SMASHED</small>.

Then again, after watching them down seven rounds of lemon drop martinis, I couldn't say I was surprised.

"Where in the name of Kristin Chenoweth are all the goddamn cabs?" Simon yelled, shaking his right fist at the heavens.

"In the theater district?" Fae proposed, which set them both off in an uproarious fit of laughter.

"It's two in the morning," I pointed out.

"So?" Simon said, turning incredulous eyes on me. "This is the city that, I remind you, never sleeps. Except apparently at two in the morning on Fridays in August. Not a freaking cabbie to be found for miles."

"We could always walk to Fae's," I suggested. It was only a fifteen-minute walk to the Meatpacking District from here — twenty at the most.

"I'll ruin my Manolos," Fae muttered forlornly.

"We're so not walking. Plus, I thought we'd agreed — sleepover at my loft," Simon whined.

I rolled my eyes. Simon *always* wanted to go to his loft. Not that I could blame him — it was located at the heart of SoHo, and between his own larger-than-life personality and the equally large presence of his two artistic roommates, the loft was a veritable hot spot every night of the week. Music throbbed at all hours and random strangers that had been collected by one of the loft's three residents were always filtering in and out. And, in a stroke of good fortune for Fae and me, Simon's roommates were extreme eye-candy.

Shane was a model — gorgeous, easy-going, and interesting in spite of his intellectual shortcomings. He slept almost exclusively with other models, and most weekday mornings saw a near-constant parade of women sneaking out of his room for their walks-of-shame.

Nate was an oil painter — brooding and darkly handsome, with a quiet edginess and a troubled aura that seemed to follow him around. He always smelled faintly like acetone and every article of clothing he owned was splattered with paint, but that only enhanced his appeal, judging by the harem of hippie-chic female art connoisseurs who trailed in his wake from his studio to the loft and back again.

Unfortunately, while both attractive in their own rights, they were also completely undateable — in part because they lived with one of our best friends so any potential breakups would be messy, but mostly because since adopting Simon into our fearsome twosome, Fae and I had become fixtures at the loft and thus born witness to so many farts, belches, and sleazy one-night-stand-after-maths that whatever initial attraction we'd felt had quickly died.

Now, we were standing on a street corner in the Village, outside the small hole-in-the-wall jazz lounge Simon had dragged us to after work. With fabric-draped walls and a dark, modern speakeasy atmosphere, the trendy little gem was always packed on Friday nights, with every velvet booth and candle-lit high top filled. It was a popular venue for those who wanted to escape the pounding electronica that poured from the speakers of the dance clubs, or those who aimed to avoid spending $25 for a cocktail in the more exclusive bars of Manhattan.

"Oh, shut up, you princesses. If we walk half a block west we'll have better luck," I said, gesturing toward the cross street where 10th bisected Hudson. Grumbling unhappily, they followed along after me.

It had been an interesting night, to say the least.

After work, the two of them had dragged me out and immediately plied me with drinks in hopes of getting the full backstory of my saga with Sebastian.

"Hit me," Simon had said, his eyes lit with anticipation.

"It's time," Fae had chimed in, her patience expired after two days of waiting.

"Fine, fine." I'd taken a fortifying sip of my martini before launching into the details. Or, to be more specific, the few details I could actually reveal to them. "It's not all that dramatic, honestly. We were high school sweethearts."

Simon and Fae nodded simultaneously, like two twin marionettes controlled by the same strings.

"I was dirt poor and he was ridiculously wealthy, and besides the fact that we both lived in Georgia, we had pretty much nothing in common. But somehow it worked," I told them, a faint smile pulling at the corners of my mouth as memories filtered through my mind. "His father was a U.S. Senator. Now I hear he's considering a run for the next presidential race on the Republican ticket. I don't know for sure."

Simon and Fae both stared at me expectantly, even as my words trailed off.

"What?" I asked.

"That's it?" Fae complained.

"You've barely told us anything!" Simon said. "We want the dirt, woman. The juicy details. So go ahead and spill it."

"I just told you! We were from completely different backgrounds. It never would've lasted."

"So you ended it," Fae guessed.

"Yeah," I said, sipping my drink. "I ended it."

"Even though you loved him?" Simon asked, skeptical.

Especially because I loved him, I thought.

"Listen, guys, you're not getting it. He was Princeton-bound. I was lucky to even go to college. If I hadn't gotten that academic scholarship to UGA I'd probably be barefoot and pregnant in a trailer somewhere south of the Mason-Dixon line right about now, rather than sipping martinis with you fools."

"But, Lux, baby," Simon said, shaking his head in incomprehension. "Lots of people make long distance work. You could've figured it out, or at the very least *tried*. I don't understand how you could just give up on someone you say you loved. It's not like you." His light blue eyes scanned my face, searching for answers I couldn't give him. "The girl I know is fearless. She meets challenges head on. She moved to New York City all by herself, walked into *Luster* without an appointment, and walked out with a job that pays more than mine. She haggles with street vendors and, despite her deceptively soft southern accent, can be a force of nature when someone insults her friends."

"He's right, you know," Fae added, her head tilting as she examined me. "You're not telling us everything."

"Alright," I conceded. "Maybe I'm not. But I've told you all that I can. Trust me when I say that if I could talk about it, you'd be the first to know. For now, though, can you guys do me a favor? Can you please just be my friends and not push me on this?"

"Are you in trouble?" Fae asked immediately, concern overtaking her features. "Did something illegal happen?"

"Ohmigod!" Simon exclaimed. "Are you in the Witness Protection Program? I bet that's it. You found out his dad was a mob boss or something, and he was gonna have you whacked so you had to go into hiding!"

"No one says 'whacked' anymore, Simon," Fae chided.

"What about 'sleeping with the fishes'? Can I use that one?"

"I'm pretty sure that's a Hollywood fabrication," I added. "And as for your theory... No, I am not in the Witness Protection Program. And no, Sebastian's father is not a villain — he's just a politician."

"Some would argue those are actually one and the same," Fae noted.

"Damn, I've always wanted to know someone who was in hiding. Leading a double life. On the run from her past," Simon said, his tone dramatic and his eyes distant. Strangely, his comments made Fae's cheeks flush red and she diverted her gaze abruptly, scrutinizing the cracked imperfections in our tabletop with studious intensity.

Hmmm. Curious.

She was not easily ruffled. Cool, collected, polished — that was Fae. In the nearly three years I'd known her, I'd never once seen her blush. I wanted to ask about it, but I'd have to wait until later, when we were in private. I wouldn't put her on the spot.

"Sorry to disappoint," I told Simon. "Let's get another round, shall we?"

"Definitely," he agreed, signaling the waitress over.

"Fae?" I asked. At the sound of her name, her head snapped up and she met my gaze. She'd been lost in her thoughts, and the remnants of ghosts still lingered in her eyes. "You okay?"

"Fine, fine," she said, shrugging off whatever had sent her spiraling down memory lane. She smiled reassuringly. "Just spaced out for a second. Are we getting another round?"

I nodded in confirmation, but my mind was racing.

So Fae had some secrets — didn't we all? Perhaps that's why she hadn't pushed me to reveal my past with Sebastian, whereas Simon would've gladly reenacted the Spanish Inquisition in order to get answers from me.

I'd been lucky, I knew that. Not everyone had friends who'd accept them in spite of their flaws, secrets, and shortcomings. I tried to hold onto that feeling now, as I listened to the two of them rambling drunkenly as we walked toward the busier intersection in the early hours of the morning.

"Bingo!" Fae exclaimed, pointing across the street at an oncoming cabbie. After her brief reverie earlier she'd proceeded to get hammered, sucking down martinis faster than the bartender could pour them. Simon had happily matched her pace, so I'd stopped after three rounds, figuring it was probably best if at least one of us was coherent enough to see straight.

Putting two fingers in my mouth, I whistled to signal the cab, and immediately broke into a smile when he slowed to a stop near the curb. Even after years in the city, the thrill of doing that had never worn off. I grabbed hold of Fae and Simon's hands, checked for oncoming traffic, and led them across the street to where the cabbie was waiting for us.

"Spotted!" Simon said, slipping effortlessly into a falsetto. "F and L getting into a cab in the Village after a night of debauchery."

"Okay, Gossip Girl, just get in the cab," I said, laughing.

Within seconds, we were on our way to SoHo, with me crammed into the middle seat between Fae and Simon. Not even five minutes into the ride, both of their heads dropped onto my shoulders as they nodded off. Trying not to jostle them too much, I slipped my phone from my pocket and snapped a quick picture of the three of us. I laughed when I glanced at the image: me, smiling wide; Simon, his face slackened in a drunken stupor; and Fae, her lips parted and a puddle of drool forming in the corner of her mouth.

I chuckled under my breath as I uploaded the picture to my social media pages, with the caption:

If you can't run with the big dogs, stay on the porch.

They'd both shriek in horror when they saw it online tomorrow morning, but at the moment I didn't care. I'd learned some hard lessons in my life, but perhaps the most important one was that you have to cherish the insignificant moments you have with your most significant people. To hold onto the times when you're happy. To smile often, and laugh loudly. To enjoy the ones you love, and hold them close to your heart while you still have them.

I closed my eyes and smiled as the cab wound through the bustling streets of SoHo, still vibrant with life even in the wee hours of the morning. Things weren't perfect — they'd never be perfect — but in this moment, life was good.

⚜

"Ughhh."

The noises coming from Fae's mouth were eerily similar to the sounds made by zombies on *The Walking Dead*, a sure sign she was hungover. Perched on one of the kitchen island barstools, I sipped my coffee and watched as she cracked one bleary eye open.

"Morning sunshine," I called.

"Unggh."

"Coffee?" I asked.

"Mmhh."

I'd take that as a *yes*. I hopped down from the stool, bypassed Nate — who was frying an egg shirtless and, let me tell you, his abs were nothing to shake a stick at — and fetched a mug from one of the overhead cupboards. After pouring a cup for Fae, I navigated slowly across the loft to where she was sprawled on one half of the red sectional.

The loft had a modern-industrial feel, with exposed brick walls and a ceiling crossed by painted ducts and beams. Yet, despite the minimalist architecture, the space was bursting with color. None of the furniture matched, and several of Nate's vibrant, 10x10 foot canvases leaned against each wall. The windows were huge, looking down at a street full of similar refurbished industrial warehouses, most of which housed artists and eccentrics. The amount of natural light that poured in from the large windows was incredible — a vast change from the one small pane my own apartment boasted — but always left the uninsulated loft chilly. Fae and I kept spare sweaters tucked away in Simon's closet, though, in a pinch, we'd both been known to steal a sweatshirt from Shane or Nate.

Thankfully, each of the boys had their own room, so whenever Fae and I crashed here we made good use of their large sectional. When I approached, Fae perked up and immediately reached for her steaming cup.

"So what's on the agenda for today?" she asked, after she'd taken her first sip and once again joined the world of the living.

"Nothing much," I said with a shrug. "Cyber-stalking the ex-love of my life for a few hours. After that, my schedule's pretty free."

Fae snorted with laughter, sending a line of coffee dribbling down her chin.

"Nice," Nate called from the stove. "Very ladylike."

His comments only induced more laughter from Fae, and after a few seconds I joined in with her.

"I propose we ex-boyfriend-stalk as a team, and then hit the market as a reward," Fae suggested.

"Done," I agreed instantly. The Hell's Kitchen Flea Market was a labyrinth of second-hand treasures, from furniture, to jewelry, to designer fashions that had been worn once by wealthy owners only to be cast away. We made it a habit to go every few weeks — more often in the summer months. Like a bloodhound on the trail, Fae somehow always managed to find the best deals. She'd once found a vintage Chanel jacket for a tenth of its original value. Another time, she'd bartered a Miu Miu handbag with a broken clasp down $500 from the seller's starting price.

Fae grabbed Nate's laptop off the coffee table. "Nate! Can we use your laptop?" she yelled, already powering it on.

"No!" Nate yelled back. "Last time you left about seventy-five Pinterest tabs open and you changed all my bookmarks to fashion websites."

"Okay, thanks! You're a peach!" she called, clicking the internet icon. Her fingers tapped the sides of the keyboard, impatiently waiting for the search bar to appear. I watched as she typed "Sebastian Covington" and my breath caught in my throat as her index finger hovered over the ENTER key. I had never — not once in seven years — allowed myself this weakness. Looking for him before would've been pointless and guaranteed nothing but pain and suffering on my part. And now, ironically, I was being forced into the one thing I'd never wanted to know about — how his life had turned out once I'd left him behind.

"Ready?" Fae asked, turning speculative eyes to me. I was clutching my coffee cup so tightly that my knuckles turned white and I was afraid the thin porcelain might crack beneath the strain. I swallowed roughly.

"As I'll ever be," I replied. "Just do it. Rip off the Band-Aid."

For the first time ever, I cursed Google's speediness. Within milliseconds, thousands of results poured across the screen. His personal website. Links to his most famous magazine covers. His online photo gallery. His credentials. The prestigious awards he'd won.

2009 IPA Photographer of the Year.

2011 L'Iris d'Or Award Winner.

2011 National Press Photographer of the Year.

2013 Pulitzer Prize Winner.

I wasn't a photography buff by any means, but even I recognized some of those awards by name and knew that they were a big deal. Moreover, his client list boasted some of the biggest magazines in the industry, including *National Geographic*, *TIME*, *Sports Illustrated*, *People*, *Maxim*, *Rolling Stone...*

The list went on and on.

As if I hadn't been intimidated enough whenever I was in his presence, now I knew I'd be sharing airspace with a photography god. Sebastian Covington had been hailed by even the toughest critics as a marvel. A creative genius. A breath of fresh air, who captured real human emotion with his lens.

Fae and I read in silence for nearly an hour, eyes skimming simultaneously over articles about his travels. He'd been everywhere we'd ever talked about going together as kids — and he'd done it without me.

Paris.

The Australian Outback.

Thailand.

Belize.

Cape Town.

Iceland.

Buenos Aires.

Fiji.

I felt my heart swell uncomfortably in my chest as jealousy warred with happiness. He'd done it — everything we ever wanted to do together. That made me feel overjoyed, because it meant walking away from him hadn't all been for nothing. He'd had a great life without me.

And yet, deep beneath the surface in a place I didn't want to admit existed even to myself, I was tremendously saddened by that knowledge. Irrationally jealous that he'd lived out our dream without me. He'd gone everywhere. Seen everything. And sure, I was living in the best city in the world — but I'd never left the country. Heck, I'd never left the east coast, or even been on an airplane. The most travel I'd ever done was when I rented a truck and drove for two days straight from Atlanta to New York.

There's a nonsensical dichotomy that exists within you after you break up with someone — especially if it's someone you loved deeply. A large part of you hopes they'll move on, be happy, follow their dreams to the fullest.

That's the side you show the world.

But a smaller part of you, whether you admit its existence or not, secretly and selfishly yearns for a reality in which that person would never move on. Never forget your love, or replace you with someone else; never be fully complete again, without you by their side.

That's the side we hide away, the innermost part of ourselves that we push down below the socially-acceptable responses to heartbreak.

"You okay?" Fae asked.

"I could use a shot or two of tequila, but considering it's ten in the morning I should probably wait at least a few more hours."

"Valid point."

Having finished his breakfast and gotten dressed for the day, Nate eventually joined us. The three of us spent a few more minutes scrolling through images of Sebastian — at art gallery openings, at awards dinners, in exotic locales — and I felt my stomach turn at the sight of all the women who'd graced his arm. Models, heiresses, accomplished artists — all of them beautiful, wealthy, and a better match for Sebastian than I'd ever been.

When the tears began to threaten, I knew I'd reached my limit so I asked Fae to turn off the computer. Nate slipped one comforting arm around my shoulders and Fae grabbed hold of my hand, and for a while we just sat there in the quiet. I focused on breathing in and out, lost in my thoughts until the door to Simon's bedroom was thrown open with a metallic bang, and his voice cut through the loft.

"Jeeze, who died?" he asked, walking into the room. "Or are you guys putting together an ensemble audition for a production of *Les Mis* no one told me about?"

Nate, Fae, and I all burst into laughter at the same moment.

Chapter Fourteen

NOW

THE CROWDS WERE NEARLY OPPRESSIVE, BUT THAT DIDN'T DETER
Fae from her mission.

After we left the boys at the loft, we'd headed back to my
apartment for a quick change out of our evening wear. Fae was
taller than me by a few inches, so even my largest shorts were
booty-hugging on her frame, but she pulled off the look with the
same cool confidence she exuded when wearing Prada and pearls.
We set out for the flea market not long after, and she soon become
a woman obsessed — not, unfortunately, with finding designer
deals or hunting down hidden gems amongst the many racks and
displays that made up the flea market, but with distracting me
from all thoughts of Sebastian. We wound our way through the
maze of colorful carts and tables, chatting with the street vendors
we knew and giggling at the sight of confounded tourists trying to
discern some kind of pattern from the chaos.

The first time I'd been here, I'm sure I'd worn that same shell-shocked look of astonishment as my unaccustomed eyes tried to take it all in at once. Milk crates full of vintage records were stacked along tabletops, mothball-scented mink coats hung from long racks, plastic bins brimmed with unorganized shoes of all sizes and styles, and various food carts exuded spicy, exotic smells. Though it was the first weekend of September, the day was unseasonably warm and sunny. Fae and I weren't the only shoppers milling around in cut-off shorts and tank tops.

We wandered for about an hour without purchasing anything, before the unrelenting midday sun began to bake the concrete and my skin started to glisten with a thin sheen of perspiration.

"I'm going to grab an ice cream before we go, you want one?" Fae asked. "My treat."

"Sure," I told her, wiping the beading sweat from the back of my neck. "But I have to make a pitstop at Vera's table, just to say hello."

"Tell her hi for me," Fae ordered. "What flavor do you want?"

"Mint chip, but only—"

"Only if it's the green kind. I know, I know," she said, rolling her eyes. "Don't know why I even bothered to ask."

"It doesn't taste the same when it's white!" I called after her.

I heard her answering laughter even after I'd lost sight of her in the crowd.

Turning, I made my way to the end of the row, where Vera always set up her table. We'd met last summer, on one of my many weekend trips to the market, and though our language barrier didn't allow for much communication, we'd struck up an unlikely friendship through shared smiles, a few odd phrases, and a variety of creative hand gestures. Sometimes, after our visits, I'd plug whatever Albanian words I could recall from our conversations into my iPhone in a pathetic attempt to retrospectively decode the things she'd said to me. It was safe to say, the only words I could keep track of with any kind of consistency were "*Alo!*" for *hello* and "*Mirupafshim!*" for *bye*.

Petite, with glossy brown hair and delicate features, Vera

couldn't be more than fourteen or fifteen, yet she spent every weekend sitting behind her table at the flea market, selling stunning handcrafted jewelry and colorful scarves from dawn until dusk. Rain or shine, she was always there — usually alone, sometimes in the company of her little sister, Roza — and she bore her responsibilities with a shy smile. I had no idea where her parents were, and no way to even communicate my concerns that she should be out laughing or playing with kids her own age, rather than working.

Truth be told, I'm not sure why I was so invested in her, specifically — there were many similar young girls who spent their weekends helping their families sell wares here. Perhaps it was that she was alone, and far too young to be supporting herself and her sister. Perhaps it was the warmth in her brown eyes when she'd given me a turquoise bracelet on the Fourth of July last year as a gift, and gently refused to accept any money for it. Perhaps it was because she reminded me of myself at that age — carrying the weight of the world on her shoulders, and doing it with the maturity and grace of someone with twice her years.

I didn't know. But I made it a point to stop by her table and purchase jewelry whenever I came to the flea market. Sometimes, I brought along sweets for the two girls to enjoy, understanding even without the benefit of words that they didn't have the easiest of childhoods and likely didn't receive much in the way of surprises.

So today when I came upon the spot where Vera's table had been stationed every weekend for the last year and a half, only to find it empty, I drew to an abrupt halt. My first thought was sadness that I wouldn't see her or Roza, as it had been a few weeks since our last visit and I'd been looking forward to a reunion. My second feeling was worry that something had happened to one of them that kept Vera from setting up her stand. But finally, as I stood examining the unoccupied strip of pavement before me, I felt happiness — maybe they'd finally taken a day off, and were out enjoying themselves like young girls ought to.

I smiled as I turned to go.

"Lux?" The small, uncertain voice cut through the din of the crowd and clutched around my heart like a fist. I knew that voice.

"Roza?" I called, my eyes sweeping the scene as I looked for her amidst the crowd. Finally, I spotted her crouched in the shadows behind one of the adjacent tents. Huddled close to a rack of puffy down jackets and outerwear, her tiny form was barely discernible. She was small for her age — seven or eight at the most — but she spoke more English than her older sister. Not a lot, but enough that we could get by. Whether she'd picked it up from other kids or from television, I wasn't sure. I didn't even know if she attended school.

"Come here, sweetie," I said, approaching her cautiously. I crouched down a few feet away and extended one hand toward her. "Where's Vera?"

At my words, Roza shook her head back and forth, not meeting my eyes. Her body trembled slightly. She was scared, I realized. I felt my heartbeat pick up speed in my chest.

"Roza, what's the matter? What's wrong?"

Her gaze darted up to meet mine, then quickly skittered away to focus on her threadbare sandals. Though our eyes met only briefly, it was enough time for me to see that hers were full of unshed tears.

"You can tell me, sweetheart," I murmured. "I'll help you, I promise."

"Vera," she whispered. Finally, she glanced up at me, and the look in her eyes nearly stopped my heart. Naked fear was etched into her features.

"What about Vera?" I whispered back, hearing a tremor in my own words.

"Gone," Roza said quietly, taking a step forward into my space. A tear leaked from the corner of her left eye. "She's gone."

I stretched out my hand once more and this time she took it, her small, unwashed fingers and quick-bitten nail beds a stark contrast to the bright poppy color coating my own manicured fingernails.

"Where did she go, sweetie?" I asked.

She shook her head again, and her grip tightened on mine.

"It's okay, Roza." I assured her with a comforting smile, though I was anything but calm beneath the surface. My mind reeled with worries. "You can tell me. You won't get in trouble."

Roza stared at me for a long moment, weighing my words with a solemnity I wouldn't have thought a seven-year-old capable of. Finally, she opened her small pink lips and whispered the words that brought my world to a screeching halt.

"He took her."

⚜

ROZA SAT ON A STACK OF MILK CRATES, HER THIN LEGS KICKING at the air as she licked an ice cream cone. Fae had found us a few minutes ago, and I'd immediately handed over my mint chocolate chip to Roza before filling my best friend in on what the girl had told me.

"What does she mean, 'he took her'? *Who* took her?" Fae asked, her own untended ice cream cone melting down her hand.

"I don't know," I said. "But she's pretty shaken up. Do we call someone?"

"Who? The police?" Fae lifted one eyebrow doubtfully.

"Well, we have to do *something*." I looked over at Roza. "She was waiting for me, you know. She waited all last weekend, too. She knew I'd come eventually. That's what she told me, right before you got here." I couldn't help but think about the three weeks that had passed since my last visit. If I'd come sooner, if I hadn't been so caught up in my own life...

"Lux, this isn't your fault," Fae told me.

"I know that," I muttered. "But these girls... They don't have anybody."

Fae sighed. "We don't know that for sure. And we can't call the police. Vera and Roza might not be legal citizens...the last thing we'd want is to try to help and in the process accidentally get them deported."

I nodded in agreement.

"Roza," I called, approaching the little girl slowly. "Can you do me a favor, sweetie?"

She nodded, licking the green ice cream residue from her lips and fingers as she finished off the cone.

"Can you tell me where you and Vera live?"

She stared at me blankly.

"Do you know your address?" I tried again. "Your neighborhood? The name of your street?"

"Don't know," she said, shaking her head remorsefully.

"Could you bring me there?" I asked. "You...take me....home?" I did my best to mime the question with my hands, and watched as comprehension flared in Roza's dark eyes. She nodded once, then reached out and grabbed hold of my left hand. Hopping down from her milk-crate throne, she turned and began walking, tugging me along after her.

"Where are you going, Lux?" Fae hissed, keeping pace with us. "You don't know where she's taking you. It might be a bad neighborhood. You could get in trouble."

"I know," I said, catching her eyes with mine. "That's why you should stay here. If I don't call you in an hour, you'll know something's up. Okay?"

Fae was silent for a minute. "You're serious about this?"

"Yes," I said, nodding firmly. "I have to know that Vera is okay. If something happened to her..."

"This is insane," Fae grumbled.

"That's why you're not coming," I said.

"That's exactly why I am *definitely* coming." She scoffed. "At least one of us with common sense should be going on this crazy escapade."

"I have common sense," I muttered indignantly.

"No, what you have is a soft heart and a heck of a lot of leftover southern charm. That whole 'love thy neighbor' bullshit really doesn't apply to New York," Fae explained. "Here, it's more like 'tolerate thy neighbor until they play their music too loud, then call the cops on their asses.'"

I rolled my eyes, turned my feet forward, and followed after Roza in silence.

❧

ROZA WALKED FOR FIVE BLOCKS, CUTTING ACROSS THE GARMENT District and eventually leading us down onto a subway platform on 34th Street without speaking so much as another word. Fae and I looked at each other warily for a moment, indecision warring with concern for Vera's wellbeing. I wasn't about to force Fae to come with me, but it was too late for me to turn back at this point — I'd promised Roza that I'd help her.

"I can't let her go alone," I whispered, tilting my head down at Roza. "She's only like seven. It's not safe."

Fae shrugged her shoulders in agreement and followed me onto the platform with a resigned sigh.

Within minutes, the F line arrived and we were being whisked away southbound toward the lower east side. When the train screeched to a stop at East Broadway — the last stop in Manhattan before the tracks crossed over the East River into Brooklyn — Roza hopped off her seat and entwined her sticky fingers with mine once more.

"Come," she said, looking from me to Fae before tugging us toward the car exit.

"If I die on this asinine adventure of yours before ever seeing John Mayer in concert, I swear to god I will haunt you until your dying day," Fae told me, a simpering smile crossing her face.

"No one's dying," I assured her.

Roza led us out onto the street and walked with small yet determined strides down another three blocks, deeper into a neighborhood that was visibly poorer than the sections of

Midtown I was accustomed to. Most of the restaurants and businesses we passed by were marked with colorful signs bearing intricate Asian characters, and while many different languages were spoken by the people on the streets, Fae and I were the only ones I heard speaking English. Before I'd made the move to New York, I'd spent months studying maps of the different neighborhoods and enclaves that made up the massive metropolis, but even without my cartographical obsessions I'd have known where we were — the sprawling bridges overhead were a dead giveaway.

Roza and Vera lived in Two Bridges, a neighborhood comprised mostly of low-income public housing tenements and best known for its location, sandwiched between the Brooklyn and Manhattan Bridge overpasses on the southern tip of Manhattan. It was a well-known immigrant borough and the poverty here was apparent, from the cracked sidewalks and the lack of greenery to the graffiti-sprayed buildings and the heavily-lined faces of the residents. Taking it all in, I felt guilty for ever complaining about my own tiny apartment here in the city, or my money woes as a child.

Though my family had been poor, there was a difference between growing up below the poverty line in a city like New York versus somewhere like Jackson. In Georgia, I'd always had neighbors to lend a helping hand, appearing unexpectedly at our door with "extra" casseroles they couldn't possibly finish, or pies they'd "accidentally" baked by following a double recipe. There'd been no lack of nature or room to breathe as a child, and Jamie and I had both relished the freedom of the outdoors. Here, though, I couldn't imagine Roza ever finding a space to call her own, or a minute to breathe. She probably shared a room at the very least with Vera — but I'd heard stories of entire families sharing a single space in buildings like this.

Fae and I traded apprehensive glances as Roza came to a stop in front of an ancient brick walkup.

"Home," Roza told us, pointing up at the third story window.

"Rozafa!" The woman's voice cut through the air like a whip, and Roza turned instantly toward the sound. A string of rapid

Albanian followed, and we watched as Roza's cheeks flushed in response to whatever was said. A small round woman stood on the street corner, her hands planted on her hips as she glared at the seven-year-old. She was flanked on either side by a small group of women, all of whom were staring at Fae and me with varying looks of unwelcome.

I'd bet my last bag of Cool Ranch Doritos that this was Roza and Vera's mother.

Roza walked over to the woman, who immediately grabbed hold of her shoulders and shook her hard enough to set her teeth rattling. "Mama!" Roza squealed unhappily.

I opened my mouth to protest and started forward, but Fae's hand clamped down like a vise on my arm and held me in place.

"Don't," Fae advised quietly. "Their turf, their rules." My mouth snapped closed and I cast a glance at her. Apparently, Fae was taking our street confrontation very seriously; that, or she was living out some *Outsiders*-themed fantasy leftover from her grade-school days.

"Whatever you say, Ponyboy," I whispered, barely containing my laughter.

Fae's lips twisted up into an amused smirk. "Chill out, Sodapop."

The five women, who ranged in age from a teenager around Vera's age to a stooped elderly woman who was likely a centenarian, stared at us impassively.

"I'm Lux," I called in what I hoped was a nonthreatening tone. "A friend of Roza's."

None of them responded — either they didn't speak English, or they really didn't care what I had to say.

"I just want to know if Vera is okay," I told them. "I was worried."

At the sound of Vera's name, their faces changed. The woman at the front of the pack who I assumed was her mother instantly crumpled, her face shuttering of all expression and her shoulders stooping in defeat. The other women had similar reactions —

some looked fearful, casting their gazes around the street at the passerby, while others just looked saddened by the mention of her name.

I felt my stomach clench at their reactions, and Fae squeezed my arm lightly in support. We both knew it wasn't a good sign — it meant that Vera was in some kind of serious trouble.

"Can we help?" I asked, locking eyes with the girls' mother. Her own turned from sorrowful to steely as they held my gaze.

"Go," she spat at me. "Go away."

"But—"

"We don't need your help." The words were spoken in broken English, but their meaning was inescapable. We were sticking our noses into their business, and they didn't like it.

"Time to go, Lux," Fae whispered. "There's nothing more we can do here. We tried."

"I'm sorry," I called, backing away a step. "We didn't mean to intrude on family matters."

"Go," the woman repeated, turning on her heel and walking away. Roza waved sadly at me before following her mother and the rest of the women into the building and out of sight.

"What the hell just happened?" Fae asked, turning a dumbfounded stare on me.

"I have no idea," I told her, equally confused.

"What now?"

"I guess we go hom—" I began to answer her, but my words were interrupted by a tentative voice.

"Excuse me?"

Fae and I turned our heads to find the youngest from the group of Albanian women hovering unsurely several feet from us. She looked ready to bolt at any moment, her eyes restlessly scanning the neighborhood for an unknown threat.

"You speak English?" I asked her.

"A little," she confirmed in a whisper. "You...you want to talk about Vera, yes?"

I nodded.

"I will tell you what I know, but..." Her fearful gaze met mine and held for one fleeting moment. "Not here. Meet me at this address. Tomorrow, three o'clock. Come alone." With that, she shoved a small piece of paper into my hand and was gone, vanishing into the building before I could even process her words or formulate a response.

"Well, Alice, you've done it now," Fae said, linking one arm through mine and guiding me back toward the subway entrance.

"Done what?" I asked distractedly, my mind reeling as I studied the address on the paper in my hand.

"Stumbled down the rabbit hole."

"Did you just call me Alice?"

"Yes, *Alice*. As in, Wonderland." Fae shook her head. "Bit of advice? Don't drink the tea. And definitely don't take directions from a cat."

Chapter Fifteen

❧✿❧

THEN

I PUSHED THE WHEELCHAIR FASTER AS WE MANEUVERED DOWN the sidewalk, hoping we wouldn't be spotted by a nurse peering out one of the windows.

"What's the hurry, sis?" Jamie asked.

I winced as the chair went over a particularly big bump and jostled Jamie, but I didn't slow down.

"Seriously, what's going on?" His voice was curious, but still largely unconcerned. He was always up for an adventure.

"I'm breaking you out of here," I said, smiling widely as I wheeled the chair around a bend and the beat up old pickup came into view. Sebastian saw us in the rearview and hopped out, leaving the truck idling by the curb as he jogged around to meet us.

"Are you serious?" Jamie asked, his voice excited. He'd been complaining for weeks about his incarceration — his word, not mine — and begging for more time outside the hospital walls. Initially he'd been satisfied with our afternoon walks, when Bash and I would push him around the grounds for an hour or so, but he'd quickly grown bored with them. He wanted to feel alive again — and that's exactly what we hoped to achieve with today's plan.

"Just for the afternoon," I told him, wishing I were taking him away from this place permanently. He'd been moved from the hospital about a month ago to the adjacent rehabilitation building, where he could recuperate from his surgery and do daily strength building exercises with a physical therapist. He wasn't walking yet — that wouldn't come for months — but the hospital staff were optimistic he'd get there eventually. For now, he was confined to a wheelchair if he wanted to get around, which he liked about as much as the hospital food he was forced to consume every day.

"You'll get in trouble," Jamie warned. "Loretta will be pissed."

"Loretta loves me," I told him. "I baked her a cake for her birthday last week *and* I agreed to babysit her kids next weekend so she and her husband can have a romantic night out."

Jamie winced in sympathy. Loretta's twin boys were well-known terrors — two miniature, six-year-old Tasmanian devils in human-suits. Last week on bring-your-kid-to-work day, apparently they'd ripped apart the nurse's station and had wheelchair races down the hallways of the ICU. Needless to say, volunteering to babysit them put Loretta in my debt for far more than a stolen afternoon off hospital property.

"Jamie, my man!" Sebastian yelled, a happy smile on his face as he leaned down to initiate some kind of bizarre man-hug, back-slapping ritual with Jamie. Boys were so weird. "You ready to bust out of here?" Bash asked.

"Depends," Jamie said. "Are we going to Vegas for some action on the strip?"

"Ew," I replied.

"Not today," Sebastian told him, grinning. "Don't think we'd get there and back before the night shift starts."

"Can we go to the track and bet on some ponies?" Jamie asked. "Oh! Or can we cover all the trees on Amber's property in toilet paper? I've always wanted to do that."

"I'd be surprisingly okay with that," I muttered darkly.

Sebastian cast an amused glance my way, before steering Jamie's chair closer to the truck bed. He pulled down the gate and turned to my twin, suddenly all business.

"As fun as that might be," Sebastian said, a wry grin twitching the corners of his lips up. "I've got something else in mind that I think you'll enjoy — even if it doesn't involve illegal gambling or vandalism."

Jamie made a regretful *tsk* sound but otherwise refrained from commenting.

"But first, we have to get you up here," Sebastian told him, nodding his head back toward the truck bed. "If I lift you onto the edge, think you can scoot yourself backwards?"

"Do you see these guns?" Jamie asked, flexing a pathetically underdeveloped bicep. "I'm a champion. I can do it."

I rolled my eyes, but my amusement faded and my heart flipped in my chest as I watched Sebastian with Jamie. He was so patient with my brother — his hands were gentle but not coddling, his smile was one of understanding rather than pity, and his tone was caring without being condescending. Bash had a unique ability to put Jamie at ease, and it allowed my twin to keep his pride even while accepting help.

I was trying really, really hard not to fall head over heels in love with the boy, but damned if he didn't make it the toughest thing I'd ever done in my life.

Ten minutes later, Jamie's wheelchair had been strapped down to the truck bed. Its wheels were locked in place with two separate ropes, and another strap looped around Jamie's waist to hold him securely when the truck began to move. I hopped up to stand beside his chair, and turned to watch as Sebastian slammed the gate closed behind me.

"You feeling up for some speed?" Sebastian asked, leaning against the cab and grinning at us.

"Bring it," Jamie challenged, an answering grin crossing his face.

Bash winked at me playfully before running around to the front seat and hopping in. He'd opened the cab's back window so we could talk, and he looked over his shoulder at me as he started the engine. "You ready to fly, Freckles?" he asked, leaning close to the window.

I held my arms aloft by my sides and flapped them up and down in a caricature of a bird. "Make me forget the ground exists," I whispered, tilting my head forward through the small opening and kissing him lightly on the cheek.

"Will you two get ahold of yourselves so we can get this show on the road?" Jamie yelled over his shoulder at us. "I'd like to actually leave the hospital parking lot at some point."

I grinned and moved away from the window, landing a light punch on Jamie's arm in retaliation. Sebastian laughed as he maneuvered the truck out of the parking lot and onto the main road. I settled in facing Jamie with my back pressed against the cool metal carriage, and we chatted as we rode through town. We got a few strange looks from people out walking — it wasn't every day that Jacksonians saw a boy in a wheelchair strapped down to the back of a truck bed like a bizarre, macabre parade float — but most passerby recognized us and smiled or waved.

Within minutes we'd traveled out of the town proper and were cruising down the back roads. The unpaved, dirt paths on the outskirts of Jackson were lined with towering waxy-leafed magnolia trees that blossomed in the springtime and showered the earth in pale pink petals as the seasons waned. The winding network of densely-forested roads provided local teenagers with an arena for every pastime — from parking for some private time with your special someone to dirt-biking and drag racing.

Turning onto a straightaway, Sebastian yelled that it was time. As the cab picked up speed, I wound one hand through the straps attached to the truck bed for support, and grabbed hold of Jamie's chair with the other. He smiled in anticipation — a look I hadn't seen on my brother's face in so long, it took me a minute to recognize it.

What most people don't realize is that cancer takes more than just flesh and blood — it sucks the spontaneity out of life. Because when someone you love is sick — when their very future is uncertain — it's hard to look forward to much of anything. Facing the world with a smile becomes the ultimate act of resilience.

It was late March now, and the early blooming trees had just begun to open their petals. They were beautiful, to be sure, but they couldn't hold my attention. My eyes were trained on my brother's face, which bore an expression of sheer, unadulterated joy as we barreled down the road, red dirt flying up in a cloud behind our tires, the radio cranked high to a classic Journey song, and the magnolia blossoms turning to a smeared pink tunnel as we pushed past sixty miles per hour.

Seeing that look on Jamie's face again was worth any amount of time spent with Loretta's twins.

"You okay?" I yelled at Jamie.

He nodded without looking at me, his grin never faltering. "Faster!" he yelled back over the strains of *Don't Stop Believin'* that were pounding from the truck's speakers.

I passed along his orders to Bash, and watched as the speedometer needle topped seventy.

"Faster!" Jamie yelled again.

I heard Sebastian whoop in exhilaration as we went even faster, pushing the truck to dangerous speeds. He hadn't been kidding — we were definitely flying, now. The wind roared in my ears and my hair streamed back in a blonde ribbon as we whipped down the roadway. I felt my stomach flip and held on tighter to the straps.

"I thought you promised me some speed!" Jamie yelled at the sky, his words immediately swallowed up by the wind as we hurled along.

"I don't think this rust bucket will go much faster," I screamed into the air tunnel whooshing between us. "Bash borrowed it from his gardener!" I tried to laugh, but the sound was swept away as soon as it left my mouth.

Jamie's grin widened but he didn't respond. His eyes drifted closed and he lifted his arms straight up above his head in a gesture I could only describe as one of pure, unabashed victory. My breath caught as I looked at him.

There, in that pink-smeared, dusty, wind-swept moment, he wasn't a cancer patient or a sob story whispered about at the town-wide pancake breakfast on Sunday mornings. He was just seventeen again — alive and invincible, untouched by illness or worries about whether he'd live long enough to attend his prom.

There, in that perfect, solitary sliver of time, with his hands fisted in the sky in defiance at the cruel twists fate so often seemed to take, Jamie was flying. Life held a million limitless possibilities.

And he was free.

I only met my grandmother a few times as a young girl before she died. My mother's mother was the only grandparent left by the time Jamie and I arrived in this world, and she had one foot out death's door even as we took our first steps of childhood. My memories of her are both scarce in number and dimmed by time's passing, but I do remember one thing she told me with intense clarity.

"There'll be moments in life, sweet pea, that stand out in your memories like a photograph. Scenes captured perfectly in your mind, frozen in time with each detail as colorful as it was that first time you saw it. 'Flashbulb memories,' some people call them," she'd told me, her eyes crinkling up and nearly disappearing in a face etched with too many laugh lines to count. *"Most people don't recognize those moments as they happen. They look back fifty years later, and realize that those were the most important parts of their entire life. But at the time, they're so busy looking ahead to what's coming down the line or worrying about their future, they don't enjoy their present. Don't be like them, sweet pea. Don't get so caught up in chasing your dreams that you forget to live them."*

This moment with Sebastian and Jamie was one of those moments. A flashbulb memory in the making. I knew I'd remember every detail of it for the rest of my life.

I hoped they would, too.

So, with Jamie's image burned into the backs of my eyelids, I stopped worrying about his prognosis, my family's finances, and my unlikely college prospects. I pushed the future away and embraced this moment of jubilant recklessness. Closing my eyes, I crossed my fingers and wished with everything I had in me that thirty years from now, we'd all be sitting around laughing about what dumb kids we'd been on that bright spring day when the world was as new as our dreams for a different kind of future.

One with a happy ending.

๛

"DO YOU THINK HE LIKED IT?" BASH ASKED ME, LINKING OUR fingers together as we walked through the dense foliage. We'd dropped Jamie back at the hospital about an hour earlier, before returning the gardener's truck to Sebastian's garage. I'd worried that Bash might want to go inside his house — I was definitely not looking forward to another encounter with his mother — but he'd surprised me by grabbing my hand and leading me toward the wooded path that led to the old oak.

"He loved it," I assured him. "Jamie doesn't do false enthusiasm. If he doesn't like something, he's not exactly shy about letting the world know it. Seriously, you should've seen him when the new trilogy of Star Wars movies came out — he was quite vocal. I think he even wrote a letter to George Lucas, petitioning him to recall *The Phantom Menace* from circulation worldwide."

Sebastian chuckled lightly. "Well, I'm glad he had fun today. It was good to see him laugh like that."

"He used to be like that all the time," I said, my own smile slipping as I thought of the animated boy Jamie had been before his diagnosis. "Not that he doesn't still joke around — he's just a little different. More contemplative. Maybe a little more serious."

"He's brave," Sebastian noted quietly. "I don't know if I could wake up every morning and face the reality he faces. All the chemo, the surgeries..."

"Jamie believes that everything happens for a reason," I told him.

"And you don't?"

"I'm not sure," I said, shrugging. "What do you think?"

"You can't laugh," he ordered, looking at me sternly. "Promise?"

"Promise."

"Well," he began, reaching up to rub the back of his neck in what I'd come to recognize as one of his few nervous tells. "It might sound cheesy, but I think some people are destined." He looked anxious as the words left his mouth, as though I might laugh at him after all. In truth, laughter was the farthest thing from my mind.

"Destined?" I whispered.

"Destined to cross paths. Fated to enter each other's lives, and change them in some fundamental way. Call them soulmates or star-crossed or whatever you want — the point is, I think some people are just..." he trailed off, taking a breath as our eyes locked. "...meant to be."

"Meant to be," I echoed, my breaths shallow as I stared at him. "So you think there's only one 'right' person for everyone?"

"Essentially," Bash said, nodding.

"But what if you never find that person? Or what if you meet them, and it doesn't work out? Or what if they're married to someone else with seven kids? Are you supposed to just... live the rest of your life without the other half of your heart?"

"Truthfully?" he asked.

I nodded.

"I don't think many people even find their soulmates. Most of them meet a nice boy or girl who fits a specific set of criteria — good job, good looks, good family — and they decide, 'Hey, this must be it. This must be true love.'" Sebastian looked at me, his eyes intense. "So they give up their search for the elusive 'one' and they settle for what they consider to be the next best thing. And maybe they even convince themselves that they're happy for a time — that they're living in perfect sync with the person who was designed for them — but that feeling rarely seems to last."

"So, you're saying that if you were separated from your soulmate — from the person you supposedly *knew* was the one for you — you'd never move on? Never get married, or have kids with someone else? You'd choose to be miserable and alone forever?" I asked, incredulity lacing my tone.

"I'm saying that soulmates are a reward, not a certainty. I think you have to earn them. And I believe, if you're one of the bastards lucky enough to stumble across yours, that you have to fight for them with everything you have," Bash told me. "There's this phrase that kind of sums up how I feel about life in general, but also how I feel about love — *aut viam inveniam aut faciam.*"

"I shall either find a way, or make one," I translated, my three years of high school Latin finally paying off in a real life scenario. "Ha! Take that, everyone who ever told me to take Spanish because it was more practical."

Bash smiled at me indulgently. "Legend goes that when Hannibal the Conqueror's generals told him it would be impossible to cross over the Alps during the Second Punic War, that was his reply."

"And did he do it?"

"He did." Sebastian nodded, his expression earnest. "Despite insurmountable odds, despite huge losses, he found a way. That's how I want to live. It's how I want to love."

"Epically?" I asked, equal parts teasing and serious. "Or tragically?"

"Maybe both," he said, laughing lightly. "Aren't the truly epic love stories also the most tragic?"

"That's kind of...devastatingly sad but beautiful all at the same time."

"Well, if it helps, I also think that if two people are meant to be together, nothing can ever truly separate them. Time, distance, other people — it doesn't matter. They'll circle back around to each other eventually."

"You're a closet romantic," I whispered, more than thrilled at the discovery. "I bet you like Jane Austen novels and Nicholas Sparks movies," I teased lightly, squeezing his hand in mine.

"Oh, shut up," Sebastian growled, pulling me in for a hug as we came through the final stretch of woods and entered the clearing. "And don't diss Jane."

I burst into laughter and he begrudgingly joined in after a few seconds and a coercive elbow to the stomach.

My giggles abruptly dried up as I took in the clearing before me. This was clearly not Sebastian's first trip to the glade today. Beneath the massive oak, a fluffy white blanket had been spread across the ground. Pillows were tossed artfully on top, and a picnic basket sat unobtrusively on a small mossy boulder nearby. Tall, unlit pillar candles in glass jars were scattered around the perimeter, and a string of white paper lanterns had been hung from the lowest tree branch overhead.

It was beautiful — like I'd stumbled into a scene from a fairytale.

"What is all this?" I whispered, turning to face Sebastian.

"It's our two month anniversary," he told me matter-of-factly. "I wanted to do something special."

"We have an anniversary?" I asked, unable to contain the teasing smile that was overtaking my face. "I wasn't even sure we were dating."

Sebastian glared at me playfully, then clutched one hand to his heart and fell to his knees as though my words had mortally wounded him. I giggled and grabbed his free hand, pulling him to his feet and leading him forward into the clearing.

"We met two months ago, today," he explained. "And I don't care how you label yourself — friend, girlfriend, strange blonde girl who follows me around…"

He laughed when I smacked him on the arm.

"It doesn't matter. What matters is that I'm crazy about you," he told me simply, tucking a wayward strand of hair behind my ear.

"Yeah?" I asked, eyebrows raised.

"Yeah," he echoed, leaning in to kiss me lightly.

What began as an innocent kiss quickly morphed into something more. We'd been taking things slowly — getting to know one another before rushing into the physical aspects of our relationship. And I wasn't sure how Bash felt, but the crawling pace had been killing me. The careful, chaste kisses and soft, stolen touches might have been enough at the beginning, but for weeks now a storm of sexual tension had been brewing in the air between us, apparent in each charged interaction and heated glance we exchanged.

If you walk outside before a heavy rainfall or at the start of a particularly strong lightning storm, there's a feeling in the air — a crackling intensity, like standing by a live wire letting off sparks. There's a smell — the sharp, pungent scent of ozone, as a current fills the air. The atmosphere is electrified, humming with energy and, at any moment, ready to unleash a monstrous storm on the earth below. Being near Sebastian felt that way — and I was standing in the center of a treeless field holding a metal rod up to the sky with both hands.

It was only a matter of time before lightning struck me.

The more time we spent together, the longer the charge had to build; and as that sensation got stronger, I was near ready to explode in sheer anticipation every time we were alone together.

So once our lips brushed...once his hands began to slide around my waist to the small of my back...once my arms twined up around his neck...

The storm finally broke. And there was no turning back.

Restraint wholly abandoned, we lost ourselves in the moment. Drugging kisses stole our breath and hurried touches made the rest of the world disappear. We tumbled down onto the blanket, the light filtering through the new spring leaves overheard casting our tangled limbs in a calico pattern of light and shadow. Sebastian braced himself over me with one hand, the other running through the long strands of my hair that fanned across the blanket. I craned my neck to meet his lips with my own.

I didn't allow myself to feel inexperienced or unsure — we were long past that now. Instead, for the first time in my life, I felt wanton. Passionate.

I wasn't a young girl in his arms — I was a woman, standing on the precipice of adulthood.

Emboldened, I tugged on Sebastian's lower lip with my teeth and his answering growl was more than enough to urge me on. I giggled breathlessly when he rolled and took me with him, so I landed sprawled across his chest with my legs straddling his waist. My hair fell down around us in a honey-colored curtain, and Bash's eyes roamed my face hungrily even as his fingers played with the hanging locks.

"This wasn't my intention, you know," he whispered. "I didn't set this up to get you in bed with me."

"I know," I said, brushing a kiss across his lips.

"And I don't want you to think that I don't respect you, becau—"

I silenced him with my lips, deepening our kiss and tracing my palms over the planes of his chest. His hands gripped my waist, pulling me tighter against him as his fingertips skimmed along the exposed skin between my jeans and the drapey white peasant top I was wearing. My hands trembled as I fumbled with the top button on his shirt, but it was with excitement rather than fear.

There was no one in the world I felt safer with.

We shed our clothes along with our inhibitions as we laughed and loved beneath the oak tree, a spot I knew from this moment on would be branded forever in my memories as *ours*. Hands and lips explored unfamiliar places. Passion mounted until I felt combustible, as though the superheated air we'd made with our bodies might reach a flashpoint and simply ignite, turning oxygen to flame. Maybe we'd burn up with the heat of it, so lost in each other we'd let the fire eat us alive rather than stop. And maybe someday, a man out walking in the woods might stumble across two charred skeletons, locked together in an eternal lovers' embrace beneath a tall oak tree, and our story would fade into folklore — the urban legend of a couple with a passion so intense it burned them alive.

As we moved together, the initial pain eventually gave way to pleasure and, finally, to an aching sense of completeness as our limbs turned languid and eventually stilled altogether. The crisp spring air cooled our heated skin as we lay chest to chest, our breaths mingling and labored, and disappeared for a time into one another. Sebastian pressed a kiss into my hair and nipped my earlobe gently.

"You didn't even let me light the candles," he grumbled, tilting my face so our gazes caught.

"Sorry," I said, grinning unapologetically. "I was just so turned on by the fact that you like Jane Austen, I couldn't control myself."

Sebastian glared at me. "If you reveal my secrets to anyone, I'll be forced to seek retribution," he threatened in a low voice, his fingers tickling my sides lightly.

"Oh, don't worry," I told him, rolling my eyes. "Your secret is safe with me."

"Good," he said grinning. "Because it would really suck to have to kill the girl I'm falling for."

I stared at him wide-eyed, wondering if this was just another part of his teasing, but found nothing but sincerity in the depths of his hazel gaze. "You're falling for me?" I breathed.

"Of course I am," he told me, sighing. "And of course, you'd doubt it."

"What does that mean?" I asked, growing defensive.

"Lux, It was obvious from the first moment I met you that you don't see yourself very clearly. You have no idea how beautiful you are. And, yeah, at first maybe it was that undeniable, exterior beauty that drew me to you. But once I got to know you — once I realized that your beauty wasn't just surface level, that it extended down to your soul — it was only a matter of time before I fell for you."

I opened my mouth to respond — with what, I wasn't sure,

because I didn't feel entirely confident in my abilities to formulate words at the moment — but Sebastian continued speaking.

"You're entirely selfless. You work yourself to the bone to pay off your brother's medical expenses, and you do it with a smile on your face because you love him. You go without basic necessities and have no regrets about it, if it means Jamie has better care. You give love deeply and freely without expecting a damn thing in return," he told me, his hand cupping my jaw and one thumb stroking my cheek. "You are remarkable. A gift. Completely unlike everyone I grew up surrounded by." He shook his head in disbelief. "My parents and their high society friends...they're poison. But you're my antidote."

I stared into his eyes, feeling my own fill slowly with tears.

"You idiot!" I blubbered, my voice trembling with emotion. I knew I probably sounded like a crazy person, but I didn't care. At the moment, I was full to the brim with love and fear, and the only outlet for my emotions was spilling over from beneath my lashes and tracking down my cheeks.

Sebastian's brows rose in question even as his thumbs worked to wipe the tears from my damp face. "Well, I have to admit, that wasn't the *exact* reaction I was expecting..."

"This was sup-supp-supposed," I forced out between hiccups. "To b-b-be a fling. You weren't su-supposed to *f-f-fall for me*." My tone was mournful, the tears coming faster and faster. Sebastian could no longer stem their flow down my cheeks, and his expression was completely bewildered as he watched me falling to emotional pieces.

"W-why'd you have to be so w-wond-wonderful?" I wailed, smacking him on the arm. "You made me f-f-fall for you, too, you idiot!"

I was a snotty, sniveling mess and I wasn't even sure why.

Maybe because, in all my life, I'd never expected that a boy like Sebastian could ever care for someone like me. Maybe because my intended pre-college carefree dalliance had spiraled quickly out of control, and suddenly I was head over heels for a boy so far out of my reach I feared I'd never be able to hold onto him. And maybe, just maybe, because in spite of everything he'd said, I was terrified that forces beyond our control might someday tear us apart — and with that, tear out my heart.

Bash wouldn't have understood if I'd voiced my nagging fears. Hell, I barely understood them.

"You fell for me?" he asked, his grin so bright it nearly hurt my eyes.

I nodded miserably.

He leaned forward and kissed the tears from my cheeks, before brushing my mouth with his own.

"Good," he whispered.

Chapter Sixteen

NOW

I STARED UNWAVERINGLY AT THE RED VOICEMAIL ICON ON MY cellphone screen.

The phone was sitting on my coffee table, propped against a jar candle five feet from my spot on the couch, where I sat with my arms crossed and my wary eyes narrowed in indecision. The little round alert symbol was taunting me.

Play me, it whispered. *You know you want to hear what he has to say.*

I reached out a hand to grab the phone, but pulled back at the last second. I wasn't ready for this. Maybe I needed another glass — or three — of wine. Or maybe I could get Fae to come over and hold my hand so we could listen together.

Though the number wasn't registered to any of my phone contacts, I recognized it from the business card Jeanine had handed me Friday afternoon. As to why I had a missed call from that number now, well after dinner hours on a Saturday night, I could only speculate.

You know you're curious, the phone beckoned.

Damn. I'd been locked in limbo staring at my phone for so long, I'd begun to hear the voice of an inanimate object calling out to me. When hallucinations began, it was officially time to put on my big girl panties and deal with the matters at hand.

I reached forward and grabbed the phone, took a healthy swig of my wine, and hit a button to play the queued message. It took everything in my power not to flinch when his voice filled the room, echoing loudly off the walls of my small studio and seeming to bounce back at me from all directions. I dropped my phone onto the coffee table, as if holding it might sear the flesh from my hand.

"Ms. Kincaid." There was a marked pause, as though he were weighing which words to use. "It's Sebastian...Covington," he tacked on hastily, either as an afterthought or an unnecessary reaffirmation of the formality that now existed between us. As if I wouldn't have recognized his voice from the way every hair on my body had stood at attention at the sound of it.

"This call is in regard to your new work arrangements, which I'm sure by now you've discussed with Jeanine." His tone was brisk. "I'm not sure what you're accustomed to at *Luster,* but I expect my employees to arrive at eight-thirty sharp for the morning meeting."

I rolled my eyes. Apparently, I was *his* personal employee now. And, from the sound of it, he was going to be a real pain-in-the-ass about the whole thing.

The sound of his throat clearing echoed over the line. "We meet in the offices on the fourteenth floor, directly below the studio. I'll give you your daily instructions then."

There was a long pause, then a muffled sound I couldn't quite make out. If he were anyone else, I might've thought he'd a held a hand over the receiver and cursed. But that wasn't possible with Sebastian — he'd illustrated just how unaffected he was by me.

"Well," he finally said, breaking what had become an uncomfortably long silence. "Until Monday, then."

The message clicked off.

I stared at the phone like it would offer up something else — some kind of cypher key that might decode his message and explain what it all meant. Perhaps I was reading into things a bit too much, but something didn't really add up here. On the one hand, he'd called me to issue orders and had sounded like a total jackass. That refined articulation and careful word choice reminded me of the people he'd once so strongly detested — his parents.

Yet, on the other hand, there was the fact that he'd *called*.

Not an email — which would've been the most professional form of communication.

Not a text message — even that might've better maintained his aloof conduct.

No, he'd picked up the phone and called me — at eight in the evening no less, and not even on a work night. I couldn't help but feel there was something strange about that.

One thing was certain: Monday was going to be interesting.

I wished I could say I wasn't terrified.

I also wished I could say that before the night was through, I wouldn't re-listen to his message countless times, finish my bottle of wine, and put myself to bed before midnight.

Oh, well. I never claimed to be perfect.

☙❧

SUNDAY MORNING, I AWOKE WITH A HEADACHE AND A hangover. My cellphone still clutched in one hand, I turned bleary eyes up to the ceiling and cursed myself for not just deleting the damn message. Not that it would've helped — I'd pretty much memorized it by now.

I'd tossed and turned for most of the night, unable to think of anything besides Sebastian and what Monday morning would bring. Though we'd seen one another twice now, we'd barely spoken a single word. And each time, it had taken everything in me not to reach out for his hand, or throw myself at his feet and beg forgiveness.

Not that I would — or could — ever do such a thing.

Regardless, I knew that Monday would be a test unlike any I'd yet endured. I reached up to trace an index finger over the tattooed line of script on my left breastbone. The curving letters were simple and sat just above my heart, unadorned by flourishes or inky embellishments. When I'd gotten the tattoo three years ago, just days after I'd scattered Jamie's ashes over the ocean, I'd known that the meaning behind the words was beautiful enough to stand on its own.

aut viam inveniam aut faciam

I shall either find a way or make one — that had never held truer than it did now.

I'd somehow summon the strength to work with Sebastian without falling to pieces or crossing any professional boundaries. I'd walk away with my job — and hopefully my soul — intact. My heart, I didn't even bother to factor into the equation; after all, if I were being honest, Sebastian was still in possession of it after all these years.

I couldn't blame him for any of it. He'd done nothing to me. For all intents and purposes, I was the villain here, who'd ripped out her own heart along with his all those years ago. I'd made a choice and, though I'd been living with the pain of Sebastian's absence for years now, it was an altogether different kind of torture to see him every day and interact with him, knowing I could never again have him as my own.

A glance at my cellphone screen informed me that it was already midmorning. If I wanted to get a run in before meeting

Vera's strangely secretive friend at three o'clock, I had to get a move on. After chugging down two Advil tablets with my morning coffee, I changed into sneakers and running attire and grabbed my iPod off the coffee table. Slipping on the headphones, I chose a pounding beat that I could keep pace with and turned the volume up loud enough that I couldn't hear my own thoughts.

I headed for Central Park, maneuvering around clusters of people on the sidewalk and focusing on the feeling of my rubber soles smacking against the pavement with each stride. I ran my normal three-mile loop, then pushed on — faster, further, until my lungs ached and a cramp sliced into my side like a knife wound.

Until I forgot everything, and my world dwindled down to basic elements.

Inhale. Stride. Sweat. Exhale.

I ran until I thought I might pass out, finally forced to stop and gasp for air with my hands braced on my knees by a water fountain in the park. And as I drank my fill, my spasming muscles protesting greatly, the clarity from my run slipped away and my mind once again filled with worry. Sebastian's face flashed in my thoughts and I couldn't help but think no matter how far I ran...

I'd never outrun my past.

৩১৫১

I SAT IN THE CROWDED CAFE AT AN UNOBTRUSIVE TABLE BY THE window, my fingers playing absently with the ends of my freshly showered hair. I crossed my legs beneath the table, barely suppressing a wince at my sore thigh muscles, and took a sip of the frothy latte I'd ordered.

I'd been waiting for about a half hour. The girl was now beyond what could be considered fashionably late and, at this point, I was beginning to worry she'd gotten cold feet and had decided not to come at all. What I couldn't understand was *why*. Her note had directed me to a dimly lit, off-the-beaten-track coffee shop in the

East Village — surely, none of her relatives would ever find us here. And even if they did, I still wasn't sure why it was such a cause for alarm.

But the truth was, on the subway ride out here I'd had some time to think about my trip to the tenements yesterday. It might've been the aspiring journalist within me, making me see things that weren't there, or maybe, as Fae said, it was just my inability to shed my southern roots and stop trying to take care of the people around me. Regardless of the reason, my whirling mind had eventually settled on one conclusion.

Namely, that the women who'd been so unfriendly and uncompromising were also quite obviously something else: afraid.

Their scanning eyes and flighty demeanors said, even to my untrained eyes, that they were scared of something — or someone. And while I supposed it was possible that they simply didn't want some young, American nobody interfering with family business, I had a nagging, if unsubstantiated, feeling that there was something else going on here.

My thoughts turned to Vera as I fiddled with the silver and turquoise bracelet on my wrist, remembering the girl who'd given it to me so joyously. Her warm brown eyes had seemed to glow from within — full of life and youth and hope for the future. If there were anything I could do to ensure that future didn't get snuffed out, I'd do it.

Yet, after another half hour of staring listlessly at the residual latte foam in my mug, I decided to give up for the day. This was a bust; the girl wasn't coming. With a sigh, I rose from my seat and headed for the door.

I was almost there when I heard a familiar accented voice call out.

"Wait."

I turned and spotted her in a shadowy corner on the opposite side of the cafe. There was an empty teacup sitting in front of her; evidently she'd been here a while, watching me without approaching. There was no way she'd missed me sitting by the front window.

Puzzled, I walked over to her table and stopped a few feet away.

"Please," she implored, her eyes wide and apologetic. "I'm sorry. Just...please sit."

I stared at her, my emotions wavering between confusion, sympathy, and worry. The girl was young — even younger than I'd thought yesterday, maybe thirteen or fourteen — and she was scared. That much was evident. I moved forward and sat across from her.

Down the rabbit hole, I thought, remembering Fae's words.

"I'm Lux." I held my hand out for the girl, and she hesitantly clasped her own palm against mine.

"Mirjeta," she returned, her voice soft. "You can call me Miri."

"Hi Miri," I said, offering a smile to put her at ease. "Thanks for meeting me."

She nodded, her light brown eyes scanning the perimeter of the coffee shop and her attention focused elsewhere.

"Can you tell me about Vera?" I prompted. Her eyes flew back to my face, a new solemnity filling them. "It's okay, Miri. I just want to help. I'm a friend of Vera and Roza. I visit them almost every week at the flea market. See this bracelet?" I held out my arm so Miri could see the handcrafted jewelry cuffing my wrist.

Miri's eyes locked on the thin-pounded silver and the embedded stones that marked the piece, no doubt recognizing its craftsmanship. Her fingers trembled as they reached across the table to brush against the cuff. When her eyes returned to meet mine, they were full of unshed tears.

"I can help," I told her in a gentle voice. "Please just tell me what happened. I promise you won't get into any trouble. I need to know that she's okay."

"She's gone," Miri whispered, her eyes staring through me. "She was taken."

"What do you mean?"

Miri's eyes pressed closed, and I could tell she was afraid to reveal anything else.

"Miri," I whispered, squeezing her hand in my own. "I know you're scared. But I need your help right now. *Vera* needs your help."

Her eyes opened slowly. "There's a man," she began, visibly shaken. "He watches us — the young girls. We don't know why... But he's always there. He's always watching." Her breath caught in her throat. "I told Vera not to walk by herself. I told her not to go."

I nodded, my chest beginning to ache with foreboding at the direction her words were taking. I didn't want to hear the rest of this story any more, since it likely didn't have a happy ending for Vera — but I knew that I needed to.

"She didn't listen. It was Roza's birthday, and she wanted to get ingredients for a cake. To surprise Roza, you know?" Miri's eyes filled with tears that quickly spilled over her lashes, leaving wet trails streaking down her cheekbones.

I squeezed her hand a little tighter, transfixed by her hushed words. Blood pounded in my veins as I watched tears drip from her chin onto the tabletop, polka-dotting it with tiny puddles of grief.

"She's my cousin. My best friend. We do everything together." Miri's voice was hollow, her expression one of clear self-blame. "Normally, I would've gone with her that day. I *should* have been with her. But I had the flu, so I stayed home in bed. And she never came back."

The ache in my chest began to spread through the entire cavity, as though someone had sucker-punched me in the stomach and knocked the breath from my lungs. I fought hard to keep the tears out of my eyes, looking up at the ceiling for nearly a minute to stem their flow. I had to be strong — Miri was practically a child, and she was somehow managing to maintain control.

"What—" My voice cracked, betraying my internal struggle. "What happened?"

"The man," Miri said. "The one who watches. It was him."

"How do you know?"

There was a beat of silence, as our eyes caught once again across the tabletop.

"Because," Miri whispered. "He takes all the girls."

Five words. Eighteen letters. They changed everything.

The air around me seemed to still, her words triggering within me a cataclysmic reaction that set my world atilt on its axis and blanketed my atmosphere in an overcast cloud cover that shaded everything a hue darker. When I once again found the ability to speak, my words were a study of restraint, each pushed out through my lips without emotion.

"Vera wasn't the first to disappear." It wasn't a question; it was an affirmation.

Miri nodded.

"How many gi—?" My voice broke on the last word, and I quickly reined myself in. "How many others have been taken?"

"I don't know for sure," Miri whispered. "Three or four from our neighborhood, maybe more."

Three or four. Maybe more. I clasped my hands together in my lap beneath the table where Miri couldn't see them, and felt blood well as my nails cut harshly into my palms.

"Do you know what happens to them, Miri?" I swallowed. "After they're taken?"

Miri shook her head. "Nothing good," she murmured sadly. "They never come back."

"Why aren't the police involved?" I asked, trying to reconcile what I was hearing with the world I thought I lived in. This was America - girls didn't just disappear here, without anyone noticing. If this were true, where were the news crews? Where were the human rights activists, with their picket signs and protests? Surely, this must be a mistake. Some grand misunderstanding.

My paltry reassurances sounded trivial even in my own mind.

"We can't trust the police," Miri whispered. "Can't trust anyone."

"Why not, Miri?"

"Santos," she told me. "The man who watches…"

I nodded, storing that name away in my mind.

"He *is* the police."

Chapter Seventeen

❦

NOW

"So she just left?"

"Yeah," I told Fae, shaking my head back and forth. "She dropped the bomb about Santos and then said she had to go. She was gone within minutes."

"You didn't try to stop her?" Fae asked.

"What was I supposed to do, tackle her?"

She shrugged lightly before pouring us each a glass of wine and turning to face me on the couch. "So what's next?"

"Well, Miri promised that she'd meet me again at the coffee shop on Tuesday night, after I get out of work. Hopefully she'll be able to tell me more then."

Fae was staring at me intently. "Aren't you going to talk to someone? The authorities, or maybe just someone over the age of fifteen who knows what's been going on?"

"You saw those women in Two Bridges — they didn't exactly

throw down the welcome mat or invite us in for supper. I doubt they'd be very helpful if I showed up again. And if Miri is right — if the police are involved in this — who knows how high up the corruption goes? I could end up causing more problems for these girls than I'd solve."

Fae sighed. "Well, that doesn't exactly give us many options."

"Tell me about it," I said, taking a sip of my Merlot. "All I know is, there's a story here."

"What if she's making it all up?" Fae asked. "What if Vera ran away with her boyfriend and she's jealous? Or what if she's a compulsive liar? She's young. Maybe she doesn't know what she's talking about."

"You didn't see the look in her eyes, Fae. Something terrible is happening to those girls. I might not have proof yet, but I can sense it with every fiber of my being. And I'm going to find out what it is."

"I don't like this," Fae told me.

"Neither do I." I swirled the dark red liquid in my glass, watching as light from the setting sun through the window refracted off it. "But for Vera... I have to do something."

My cellphone buzzed on the coffee table, vibrating with an incoming text message. I scanned the screen quickly and, nosy as ever, Fae peered over my shoulder to read it too.

Desmond: Babe! Dinner tomorrow?

"Shit," I muttered.

"Are you going to say yes?"

"I don't know." I stared at the screen, riddled with indecision.

"Because of Sebastian?" she asked, leaning forward to catch my eyes.

"Yes. No. Maybe." I sighed. "I don't know, okay? It just feels wrong to date someone who I feel nothing more than friendship for."

"Well, I think you should go. You've barely given him a chance," Fae said.

"Said the girl who never dates."

"I date!" Fae protested.

I snorted into my wine glass.

"I do!" she snapped. "I'm the *Luster* relationship expert for god's sake! Women from all over the country write in every month for advice after reading my column."

"No, love, you really don't," I said, patting her thigh gently. "And in the rare case that you *do*, it's with emotionally unavailable men who you know won't get attached. You might be the *Luster* relationship expert, but you haven't been in an actual relationship in all the time I've known you."

"That's so false." Fae pouted, jutting out her bottom lip like a little girl. "There was... Paul!"

"Paul was your very openly gay yoga partner," I said, shaking my head.

"Ben," Fae suggested.

"Wasn't he engaged to a girl from Jersey?"

"Well, what about Tom?" she asked, cheeks flushing.

"The security guy at your building?" I elbowed her in the arm. "Pretty sure he doesn't count either."

"Fine, so I don't date," she muttered, planting her chin in her palm. "I don't see why it's such a big deal."

"Besides the fact that you're the *Luster* relationship expert, that is?" I laughed.

"Shut up."

"Fine, maybe because you insist on setting *me* up with every available penis in the tri-state area, but never even attempt to find someone for yourself?"

Fae giggled, but didn't counter my words. She knew I was right.

"Or, maybe because you're gorgeous and could have anyone you wanted in this city?" I proposed gently. This wasn't the first time we'd discussed her lack of male companionship, but usually she just laughed me off or evaded the subject entirely. This time, though, she seemed to take my words to heart — maybe now that she knew a bit about my past, she finally felt free to talk about her own.

Fae was silent for a long time, her laughter subsiding and a sad, reflective expression overtaking her face. "There was a guy, a long time ago. He was..." she drifted off, her eyes distant with memories. "Well, we were too young, and it was too serious."

"First love?" I asked, treading carefully. I didn't want to scare her off, not when she was finally opening up to me. Fae was many things — warm, fashionable, funny, beautiful — but forthcoming wasn't one of them.

"I guess you could call him that," she said. "People say you never forget your first love, that you carry them with you in your heart for the rest of your days. And they're right. I just wish someone had warned me about that when I was eighteen."

"Tell me about it," I murmured, Sebastian's face appearing in my mind.

Fae laid her head down on my shoulder and, for a moment, we found comfort in the fact that though we may have lost our first loves, we'd found each other. I didn't press her for more details; when she was ready, she'd tell me.

"Are you nervous about tomorrow?" Fae whispered. "About seeing him?"

I nodded.

"I'll miss you at work. It won't be the same without you."

"It's temporary," I told her. "Sebastian will be gone again as soon as these shoots are done, and I'll be back on 57th in my cubicle with the rest of the Harding slaves before you know it."

I wished my heart didn't ache so much at the thought of him walking back out of my life, with nothing resolved between us. I wished the past didn't have to stay in the past. And, most of all, I wished I could live the way those two naive teenagers had aspired to all those years ago, and find a way back to him regardless of the odds stacked against us. Unfortunately, without a magic genie or a fairy godmother at my disposal, I was pretty certain my wishes would go unanswered.

When Fae left for the night, I corked the bottle of Merlot and made myself a quick dinner — otherwise known as pouring some Cool Ranch Doritos into a bowl — and texted Desmond back.

Dinner tomorrow sounds great. Call you after work.

I figured when I saw him in person again, I'd know what to do. For now, my mind was too preoccupied by thoughts of a very different man to even consider what was happening with Desmond. Between my boy issues, Miri's revelations earlier that afternoon, and the fact that I'd just reached the bottom of my final stash of Doritos and would have to restock at *Swagat* tomorrow, it was safe to say that my mind was spinning and I'd been through the emotional wringer. There was only one thing — besides copious amounts of Merlot — that might help at this point.

The Jamie Box.

I pulled it down from its spot on the top shelf of my closet, running my fingers reverently across the carved wood. Flopping down in the center of my bed, I laid the box gently on the comforter in front of me and slowly lifted it open. My eyes immediately caught on the framed photo of Jamie and me embedded on the inside of the lid, then moved down to take in the neatly ordered row of colorful envelopes that sat within the box itself.

The photo had been taken five years ago, when I was a sophomore in college. At the time, Jamie had lived with me in a small apartment near the UGA campus, and I'd planned my course schedule around driving him to treatments and appointments in Atlanta so he didn't have to be alone. We'd moved away from Jackson two short days after I'd broken Bash's heart, and we'd never looked back. I hadn't returned for a single spring break or summer vacation because I couldn't bear to see the love of my life look at me with hatred in his eyes.

Except for the memories that would always haunt us, Jamie and I were free of our past. Our parents called occasionally under the pretense of checking on us, though truthfully I think they were relieved to be rid of us and the responsibilities Jamie's illness had piled on them.

And while I'd still been heartbroken two years after leaving Sebastian, you wouldn't know it by looking at this picture. Jamie and I had been happy — staring at each other rather than the camera lens, with matching grins crossing our faces as we laughed at some ridiculous joke Jamie had cracked. A nurse had snapped the picture just after we'd received the news that his scans had come back clean. He'd been headed toward remission.

As the camera flashed and captured the frame, we didn't know just how short-lived our relief would be. We didn't know we'd have only a few blissful months of thinking he'd defy the odds, before the cancer would return with a vengeance. We didn't know the struggle that lay ahead of us. And we didn't know that two short years later, that same struggle would claim his life and take him away from me permanently.

My fingers traced the glass covering our happy faces. I missed my twin, with his endless positivity and his refusal to quit living even when he learned that his life had an expiration date a lot sooner than he'd been expecting. I missed the way he'd call me the "light of his life" when, in truth, he was really the brightest part of mine. I even missed his endless teasing, and the mischievous smile on his face whenever he'd done something to embarrass me beyond redemption.

But at least I had the box. It had been delivered to me by one of Jamie's favorite nurses about a month after he'd died. Inside were exactly one hundred letters, each sealed with a specific directive about when or where I should open it.

For the day you receive this box.
For your first day at a new job.
For a day you're feeling sad.
For a Valentine's Day when you're single.
For your first night in a new apartment.
For the first birthday you celebrate without me.
For a rainy afternoon.
For the day you get married.
For the day my first niece or nephew enters this world.

The letters' contents were always a surprise. Most were light-hearted, meant to bolster my spirits or make me laugh. Some were full of hope, encouraging me to try new adventures or broaden my horizons. But a select few, the ones I treasured most, were both poignant and heartrending — interwoven with memories and the poetic injustice of a resilient young man forced to leave this earth too soon.

I'd opened about a third of them in the three years since I'd lost him, and read them so many times I'd nearly memorized their words. The others remained unopened, as crisply sealed as they'd been the day they were composed, waiting for their prescribed time. Occasionally, when I was really sad, I'd get the urge to tear them open all at once and devour Jamie's words on a binge, as if doing so might somehow repair the cracks in my soul and mend the missing pieces he'd taken with him.

I never did, though. Jamie would've been pissed at me for ruining his carefully thought-out plans.

Today, I reached for a familiar blue envelope that sat near the front of the stack. I ignored the tear-stained, finger-smudged paper as I read the words scribed across the front.

For a day you wish my handsome mug were there to make you smile.

I pulled the thin sheet from the envelope and felt my lips twist up as Jamie's sloping hand came into view.

HEY SIS,

Obviously, since you've selected this particular envelope, I'm going to assume you've either had a rough day or Doritos has finally decided to stop producing the Cool Ranch variety. In either case, try not to panic.

If it's the former — rough days pass. The sun will set, the earth will rotate, and a month from now you probably won't even care that your best friend was a bitch or you had a bad day at work.

If it's the latter — I'm sorry, because I know how much you love your Doritos, but honestly sis, at some point that metabolism of yours is going to slow down and you'll be the size of a house. Don't shoot the messenger! (You can't, I'm already dead.)

Sorry. I can't seem to stop weaving death jokes into these letters. I'm really beating a dead horse, aren't I? (See what I did there?) Anyway, not to play the cancer card or anything, but at the very least you can be glad that your rough day probably didn't involve a nurse walking you to the bathroom and watching you poop because you're not quite steady on your prosthetic leg yet. Do you know how hard it is to perform with a captive audience right outside the door? Sheesh.

I love you, sis. I know none of this has been easy on you, and I know you aren't happy right now. But you share my DNA and, since I'm no longer around, you're pretty much obligated to share that Kincaid awesomeness with the world in my place.

Do me proud, sis.

Chin up. Smile through the tears — it helps them pass faster. (Coincidentally, I use that same strategy when trying to pass certain other bodily fluids with Nurse Charlene standing right outside the door.)

Love you.

Jamie

I smiled as I reached the bottom of the page. There was no one in the world who could cheer me up like Jamie — even now, when he was gone. I folded the letter with care and placed it back in the box, taking one last glimpse at the photo of us inside before the lid snapped closed.

In some ways, I was lucky. Not everyone who lost a loved one got to say goodbye; unexpected losses do little in terms of delivering closure. Jamie's letters had allowed him a semblance of immortality. His body might be gone, but he'd left his heart behind with me — small pieces of himself, enmeshed in handwritten letters and imprinted on my spirit.

Every sacrifice I'd ever made for him had been worth it. I just wished they'd been enough to keep him here with me.

Chapter Eighteen

NOW

I WAS UP WELL BEFORE SUNRISE THE FOLLOWING MORNING, unwilling to be late on my first day working for Sebastian, and hoping to avoid any further incurrence of his wrath. Slipping into a sleek navy pencil skirt and a flowing white silk top, I topped off the outfit with peep-toe Louboutins and simple silver jewelry — Vera's bracelet included. I pulled the top layer of my hair up away from my face with a clip but left the majority hanging loose around my shoulders, and applied my makeup with more care than I typically bothered with.

I might not be in Cara's league, but that didn't mean I had to arrive looking like the fashion-illiterate schoolgirl I'd once been. The clothes, the shoes — they were my battle-armor for the gauntlet I was about to run. I stared at myself in the mirror and tried to summon the cultured, city woman who exuded confidence, walking around *Luster* like she'd been raised shopping at Bergdorf Goodman, rather than the local Goodwill. I searched for her in my reflection, assuring myself this would be no different than any other day at *Luster*, but she was nowhere to be found. In her place, I saw the same insecure girl who'd worn a brave face each day of high school. The girl on the outskirts. The subject of every whispered rumor that left the venomous lips of Amber and her minions.

I groaned, dropping my forehead into my palms and wishing I'd taken Simon up on his offer to pick out my outfit and do my makeup before I faced the firing squad. Sure, he had a penchant for turquoise 1980's inspired eye-shadow, but at least he'd have been there to kiss my cheeks, slap me on the ass, and tell me how fabulous I looked.

The sound of my phone ringing made me look up. Speak of the devil...

"Simon?"

"Baby! Just calling to tell you good luck and, even without my expert fashion advice, I'm sure you look divine. That man of yours won't know what hit him."

"He's not my man," I told him, rolling my eyes. "And I'm pretty sure he's dating a model, so..."

"Baby," Simon chided. "You've got boobs and booty. Trust me — those skinny little skanks have nothin' on you, honey."

"Thanks, Simon."

"Thank me by telling me all about it over drinks tonight before your date with Desmond," he said. "Now go, or you'll be late and sexy Sebastian will have to spank you."

"Simon!" I protested.

"Kisses!" He clicked off.

I laughed at his antics, feeling monumentally better than I had before his call. I squared my shoulders, grabbed my travel coffee mug, and was out the door before I had time to psych myself out again.

Maybe today wouldn't be so bad after all.

I WAS WRONG.

Who'd have predicted that a ring of hell could be contained within the walls of the fourteenth floor of a perfectly innocuous looking skyscraper in Midtown Manhattan? Not me. Yet here I was, damned to an eternity of servitude in a place of nightmares. All that was missing were the fiery pits and ghoulish architecture. Satan was here, though — in the form of a buxom brunette, no less.

Cara: the devil incarnate.

I'd arrived with fifteen minutes to spare, but there were already several people milling about the office. A flurry of activity was in progress — assistants rapidly scribbling notes as their superiors tossed out concepts for photo shoots and set designs. Three men, each carrying several large photo canvases of famous *Luster* spreads from past decades, exited the elevator behind me and immediately began setting them up on easels around the room perimeter.

I stood near the wall, taking it all in as my stomach clenched with nerves. The floor was one large open space, with several work stations set up around the room and a conference table long enough to seat thirty by the far windows. There was a space cordoned off with racks of clothing and a small, mirror-enclosed platform, which I assumed was used for model fittings.

Recognizing no one, I had absolutely no idea where to start and, like a stream around a rock in the riverbed, people filtered by as though I were invisible. Which, at first, was fine, but after a few minutes began to piss me off. I was Lux Kincaid. No longer the high school wallflower, unsure of my place in this world. If Sebastian wanted me here to work, I was going to work. I didn't wait around for orders like a meek intern. I was a professional, successful, career-driven woman. And if he didn't like that, well, he could send me back to *Luster* and this whole ordeal would be over before it began.

Pulling my shoulders back, I threw procedure out the window, strode toward the center of the room, and jumped into the fray. I'd never been particularly good at following the proper decorum rule-book, anyway. After introducing myself as the *Luster* writing correspondent for the Centennial issue series, I'd immediately become engrossed in a conversation with two friendly designers — both of whom, coincidentally, were named Jenny. We were so enmeshed in our discussion of a possible 1960's revolution-themed photo shoot, we didn't notice our audience until it was too late.

"I think just focusing on the hippie, flower-girl angle is going to limit us. It's tired, it's been done before," I told them, impassioned as the idea bloomed in my mind. "We need a fresh angle — something that focuses on the huge changes that happened in society during that decade."

The two Jennys nodded in unison, their eyes thoughtful as they absorbed my words.

"Clothing evolved with the culture — we could explore the fashion revolution theme. From the refined elegance of Jackie Kennedy and Audrey Hepburn — arguably two of the classiest 1960's icons — to the sexually liberated culture of the late 60's, where everyday women were finally free to wear what they wanted — from mini-dresses to go-go boots," I prattled on, foolishly unaware of the reason my two conversation partners had grown wide-eyed and silent. "I just think that would be more interesting than a photo spread of the same frizzy-haired, headband-wearing model, running through a field of tall grass in a flowing floral print dress."

"Well, *thankfully*," an icy voice snapped from behind me. "No one cares what you think."

Shit. That tone of unparalleled bitchery was unmistakable.

I turned slowly, dreading the encounter, and came face-to-face with Cara, who dwarfed me ridiculously in her five-inch stilettos. I tried to shutter my annoyed expression but was likely unsuccessful, given the fact that Sebastian was standing immediately to her left, gazing at me stone-faced and giving me heart palpitations.

"You're a nobody," Cara sneered. "No one here wants your opinions. Why don't you stop breathing my air. Oh, and go get me a latte while you're at it. Double shot espresso, skim milk, extra foam, no whip."

Bitch.

I felt my cheeks heat with embarrassment, and I could practically feel the sympathy radiating off the two Jennys, who had front-row seats to my humiliation. My gaze moved from Cara to Sebastian, who was staring at me with an unreadable look in his eyes. Obviously, I'd be getting no help from *that* front. I turned to leave, but stopped when I heard Sebastian's voice.

"Wait, Ms. Kincaid."

Ms. Kincaid? There was that forced formality again. I pivoted in place, meeting his eyes, which were as inscrutable as ever. Sebastian sighed and raised one hand to pinch the bridge of his nose.

"Cara, Ms. Kincaid is not here to fetch your coffee. She is not an intern. She's a consultant and will be treated with the respect normally afforded one. She also reports to me, not you." He didn't bother to look at her, but his tone was cold, nearly scolding, as he spoke.

My eyebrows lifted in surprise and I heard Cara's displeased huff, but didn't tear my gaze away from Sebastian's face. It was still fixed in what seemed to be a permanent frown.

"Cara, don't you have a fitting to get to?" He may've phrased it as a question, but it was clearly an order. She cast one last scathing look at me before stomping away to yell at whatever poor soul had been assigned to do her fittings.

"Everyone!" Sebastian yelled, causing the thirty or so people in the room to fall instantly silent. "Huddle in for a minute. Morning meeting."

I watched, fascinated, as designers, artists, assistants, and consultants all dropped what they were doing and rushed to the center of the room where we'd gathered. Sebastian commanded a lot of respect around here, that much was apparent. And though this wasn't what Jeanine would consider an official meeting, considering we weren't jammed into a small conference room listening to her drone on needlessly for a half hour, Sebastian's short and sweet, informal approach seemed equally, if not more, effective.

"We'll be working chronologically through the decades: the 1910's through the 2010's," Sebastian said, once everyone was close enough to hear him. "Each decade gets a unique set, costumes, everything. Brainstorm new ideas, seek out fresh angles," he said, locking eyes with me for a brief moment.

I felt my breath catch in my throat, but his eyes were fleeting, moving away to scan the rest of the crowd.

"Use the old shoots for inspiration." He gestured toward the room perimeter, where a series of easels displayed a multitude of shots from *Luster* history. "We'll get this done as quickly as we can, shooting two or three sets each week, if possible. Angela, my production manager, has split you into teams for this week — see her for your assignments. Use today and tomorrow to develop ideas. Wednesday, we'll meet as a large group to finalize the plans for the first few shoots. Thursday and Friday we'll do sets and trial runs. Next week we'll begin shooting for real," he explained, his tone brisk and to-the-point.

"Any questions?"

The pervasive silence in the room gave him his answer.

"This is a unique project. Try to have fun with it, guys," he said, nearly — but not quite — smiling with tight-pressed lips. "Thanks."

At his dismissal, everyone except the two Jennys and me hurried over to a beautiful petite Asian woman in her mid-forties — Angela, I presumed — who was handing out color-coded badges and assignments. I was about to follow suit when Sebastian spoke again.

"Jenny S. — you'll be working with Philippe on the 20's set design concept. Jenny P. — you'll be with Sam over in costumes. Ms. Kincaid — you'll be with me."

With that, he stormed away toward the large conference room table on the opposite side of the room. People scurried out of his way and trailed in his wake — he was the epicenter of activity and attention for every worker in the room. I stood in a daze, my eyes trained on his back, until I realized that everyone else had scattered as soon as he'd doled out their duties and I was now alone in the middle of the room. Hoping no one had seen my momentary Sebastian-stupor, I hurried after him.

I came to an abrupt halt when I reached him on the far side of the room by the windows. He stood with his hands planted against the conference room table, looking over a wide array of photographs from previous *Luster* shoots. It felt foolish to interrupt him by announcing my presence, so I simply hovered by his elbow unsurely, staring out the glass panes at the skyline below. I wasn't even sure he knew I was there, until he spoke.

"It's funny," he muttered in a serious tone that undermined his words. "I thought I knew exactly what I'd say to you if I ever saw you again, after all these years."

He pushed up from the table, turning to face me. His hazel gaze immediately captured my own, and in a fraction of a second the air between us became tense, growing thick with seven years of unspoken words and unkept promises. I fought the urge to move a step back from him, wary of whatever he was about to say.

"But now, with you standing here in front of me, all my words seem to have fled." He laughed, but it was mirthless, bitter. "I don't know what I was thinking."

He might've been looking at me, but I'd swear he was talking to himself. When his words trailed off, we simply stared at each other until the silence became unbearable. I had to say something — anything — to smooth things over between us, even if it was only on a superficial level. Otherwise, we were both in for several weeks of torture while the Decades project came together.

"Maybe we can just start fresh?" I asked naively, holding out my hand for him to shake. "Clean slate?"

It was the wrong thing to say.

He flinched back from me, staring at my hand where it hung in the space between us with a mixture of disbelief and disgust. I'd been wrong — very, very wrong — to assume things with us could ever be wiped away with a few pleasantries and some misguided wishful thinking.

"Why don't you go get that latte for Cara after all," he bit out in a cold tone. "After that, report to Angela. I'm sure she'll find some use for you."

He turned on his heel and walked away, leaving me staring after him in near tears. I'd been dismissed. Snatching my hand back from where it was still suspended in midair, I headed for the elevators. In the future, I'd have to tread more carefully. With Sebastian, each conversation would be like walking through a field of live land mines without a guide — make one wrong move, and things would explode.

Cara grinned and waggled her fingers at me as I passed by the costume fitting area, no doubt having witnessed my arctic encounter with Sebastian. If I were a lesser woman, I'd have contemplated spitting in her latte. As it was, I'd just order one with whole milk instead of nonfat — that would be enough to set her off in a caloric panic of epic proportions.

I smiled as I headed for the Starbucks in the lobby.

⚜

THE VICTORY FROM MY LATTE-TRICKERY WAS SHORT LIVED AND, unfortunately, the day spiraled even further downward from then on. Not only did Cara insist that I bring her another latte with the correct milk, she told two of her model friends that I'd be their designated coffee and errand girl for the entirety of the Decades project. The three of them expressed unmasked delight in rejecting the lattes and macchiatos I'd procured each time I returned with a new cardboard tray of drinks, sending me back down to the lobby four separate times before noon.

I became fast friends with Greg, the barista; every time I reappeared in the lobby he'd grin sympathetically and tell me a coffee-themed joke to lighten my spirits. Who knew caffeine humor could be so sexual?

When I was finally released from Starbucks duty, I found Angela and quickly discovered that despite her short stature, she was a force to be reckoned with. In fact, she was kind of a self-important bitch — one of those people who thought the world would cease to turn if they failed to show up for work one day. She didn't even look up from her clipboard when I asked her for an assignment.

"See those issues?" she asked, gesturing at the mountain of magazines sitting on the conference room table across the room.

I nodded.

"Some of the designers flipped through them for historical inspiration earlier this week and scanned the images they liked onto their computers. Now the magazines are a jumbled mess. They need to be reorganized and carted back to the stockroom. Go through each issue and catalogue it by month and year. You'll find boxes, string, and a label-maker over by the wall," she said, her brow furrowed as she scribbled a note on her clipboard. "Tie the 12 issues from each year together, ordered by month, with a piece of string. Then stack the years together by decade. Each decade gets stored away in a box." She spoke rapidly, flipping through her notes as she fired off instructions. "And don't forget to label the boxes by decade."

"Alright, thanks."

"Oh, and — what was your name again?"

"Lux."

"Well, Lux," she said, finally looking up from her notes to examine me. Whatever she saw, she evidently found lacking, if the slightly distasteful crinkling of her nose was any indication. "Make sure you finish them before you leave tonight. Men will be coming to take the boxes back to storage first thing tomorrow morning."

I nodded and walked away, figuring any assignment was better than an eternity of coffee runs for Cara and her snooty posse.

My mistake. I might not be a math genius, but even I should've realized that organizing 100 years worth of magazines — in which each year has approximately 12 issues — is equivalent to a hell of a lot of work.

Unfortunately, I had this realization a little too late — pretty much the exact moment I reached the conference room table and saw the extent of back-stocked magazines littering the tabletop and stacked in messy piles inside the ten large cardboard boxes beneath the table. The stack sitting on the tabletop was in a similar state of disarray, seemingly having been piled without order or organization. It looked like a pack of rabid toddlers had been looking through the stacks, rather than a group of professional designers.

Joy.

Four hours later, my stomach was rumbling in protest after skipping lunch, my eyes were tired from ceaselessly reading issue dates, my back was aching, and my fingertips were coated in a slightly dusty residue from flipping through century-old pages. With a growing sense of dismay, I glanced from the watch at my wrist to the still largely unorganized pile of magazines. Work would be over in an hour or so, and people would soon start to filter out of the office. Seven boxes sat on the ground to my left — organized, labeled, and ready for pickup. But to my right, nearly four hundred remaining issues were still piled in a haphazard fashion.

I sighed and got back to work, subtly slipping my phone out of my purse to text Desmond.

Stuck at work. Can't make it to dinner. Sorry.

Poor Desmond. This was the third time in a row I'd cancelled on him. He deserved better, but I could honestly say that — this time at least — it wasn't my choice. I also texted Simon, warning him that I'd probably miss happy hour. If I failed to show up without any explanation, he'd be on the phone with the police trying to issue an Amber Alert within the hour, regardless of the fact that I was a legal adult.

The thought of Simon cheered me enough to jump back into my task. I picked up my pace, becoming so absorbed that the rest of the office faded away and the next time I looked up, I was nearly the last one left on the floor. A few costume designers conversed by the fitting area, and Angela was seated at one of the workstations, her cellphone clutched in one hand and her clipboard in the other, but other than that, everyone else had gone home for the day. I hadn't seen Sebastian since our terse encounter this morning, and I thought that was probably for the best. If we were going to attempt to be civil and professional, he'd likely steer clear of me from now on.

I tried to be okay with that, reminding myself that I was here only to serve my sentence and move on. I shouldn't have expected him to treat me with anything but disdain. After all, I was here to be punished — and on his orders, no less.

It was already well past five, and magazines from two whole decades remained on the table before me — at least another hour's worth of work, maybe two. Once Angela — and her watchful glare — left for the night, followed soon after by the two designers, I was alone on the floor and could finally collapse into one of the conference table's leather swivel chairs. The lights, programmed on automatic timers, dimmed considerably after their departure, but I didn't bother to find the switch. I was far too comfortable to move.

I began to pick through the issues spread across the table, thinking as I did so that the 1990s grunge fashion era was better left unresurrected in *Luster* history. I stretched my arms above my head and arched my back, letting out a low groan as my cramped muscles found some relief. Hunching over a table for the last five hours had pulled my muscles tighter than a bowstring.

When I'd worked the kinks out of my spine, I made short work of pulling the clip from my hair, the intensity of my headache ebbing as soon as the heavy locks tumbled free. My fingers combed through the strands, then moved to rub my temples in an attempt to eliminate the ache altogether.

The chime of the arriving elevator froze my hands in place, and my head swung immediately toward the sound.

I gasped soundlessly as the doors slid open and Sebastian stepped through them. He took several strides into the room, the dim lighting no doubt lending the impression that he was alone here. His expression, for once, was unguarded. With his brow furrowed and his eyes trained on the floor, he appeared distressed, as though he were waging an internal war within his mind.

I was captivated by his sudden appearance — so much so, I didn't realize how awkward it would be when he inevitably reached the conference table and found me sitting there, practically drooling at him.

Shit. He was closing in — barely fifteen feet away.

Uncomfortably, I cleared my throat.

"Um, hi," I called loudly, wincing at the sound of my own voice as it echoed through the empty room.

Sebastian's head snapped up, his eyes going wide as he saw me at the table. He started and took a half step backwards — I couldn't help but wonder if he was considering making an abrupt about-face and heading for the elevators to escape me — but eventually stilled and seemed to resolve himself to stay. Straightening his shoulders to full height, he held himself as though he were about to do battle with a formidable enemy.

"I'm sorry," I said, my voice quieter this time but my words flowing out in a torrent. "I didn't know you'd be back here tonight. I'm supposed to finish these before I leave, but I'll just come back early tomorrow morning and do it." I pushed my chair back and stood, shuffling the messy magazines into a singular stack as fast as possible and grabbing an empty box from the floor by my feet. "I'll be out of your hair in just a minute," I babbled on, not meeting his eyes. "I didn't know how long this would take. I'm sorry."

I was repeating myself, filling the silence with everything I could think of, as if that could somehow reduce the awkward strain of the moment. I lifted the stack of magazines and was preparing to drop them into the empty box when he spoke.

"Don't." His voice was soft, and much closer than I'd antici-pated — he'd moved toward the table at some point during my nervous monologue. I didn't dare look up to see just how near he now stood. "It's fine, Ms. Kincaid."

"It's okay," I murmured shakily, eyes still trained on the magazines clutched in my shaking hands. "I'll be gone in just a minute."

"Ms. Kincaid," Sebastian said, so close I could practically feel the heat emanating from his body. "I said *stay*."

A tremble moved through my entire body at his words. I had no idea what expression was playing out across my face — fear, attraction, embarrassment? — I just prayed the dim lighting would be enough to conceal my emotions.

A frozen moment passed between us. I didn't move, I didn't speak, I didn't even *breathe*, for fear of shattering the stillness. I could feel the weight of his gaze on me, but kept my own eyes aimed down at the table.

I'd been right, at least partially, this morning when I'd thought that each interaction with Sebastian would be like walking through a live minefield. I'd just forgotten to consider that for the perilous journey through an expanse of armed bombs, I'd also be blindfolded and spun in several dizzying circles first. And right now, at this moment, I had the feeling that one of my feet was poised millimeters above the earth, a hairsbreadth from triggering a fatal detonation that would claim both our lives.

I'm not sure why, but Sebastian chose to diffuse the bomb. He moved away.

I felt his jacket sleeve brush against my arm as he passed close by my side, heading for the opposite end of the conference room table, and a shaky exhale of relief escaped my lips. I couldn't help myself — I raised my eyes to watch as he walked and took the seat directly across from me at the head of the table. We were now separated by about twenty feet, which should've eased my mind but in actuality set me even more on edge. He, on the other hand, seemed completely unbothered, flipping open a file folder I hadn't seen clutched in his hand and leafing through its contents with composure.

When he suddenly looked up and caught me staring, I dropped

my eyes back to the table and took my seat. I found some small comfort in the fact that he couldn't see me where I sat behind the tall stack of magazines, but remained largely uneasy as the minutes began to tick by in silence.

I tried to focus on my work, but sorting, stacking, and labeling only captured so much of my attention. The rest was honed on the man across the table — and on the fact that with each stack of magazines I organized and boxed, the wall concealing me from his view began to shrink. Within minutes, I could once again see Sebastian over my dwindling pile, but I resolutely tried to keep my eyes — and thoughts — from straying to him.

A half hour passed in silence.

Then another.

I began to fidget in my seat, needing some kind of outlet for the building tension in the room. Tucking my hair behind my ears, crossing and uncrossing my legs on five-minute intervals, and tapping one heeled foot against the tiled floor, I was on my way to a mental breakdown from the sheer strain of not looking at him.

And the more I tried not to think about him, the harder it was.

I shouldn't have been surprised. My freshman year of college I'd taken Psych 101, and my professor had made my class recreate a famous study on thought suppression. In the experiment, half my peers — myself included — were instructed not to think about a white bear for five minutes. In the same time period, my professor told the other half of the class they could think about the bear as many times as they wanted. Every time a thought of the bear popped into one of our minds, we were supposed to ring the small bell we'd each been given.

Would you believe that my group, who were supposed to be suppressing our thoughts about that damn bear, ended up ringing our bells three times more than the other group?

It was basic human nature. The more forbidden something — someone — was, the more we wanted it.

It became almost painful, not looking at him. Like I might die if I didn't simply tilt my head up and meet his eyes to ensure he was still sitting there, across the room, and not some twisted figment of my imagination. My hands began to move faster, stacking magazines in neat piles and tying them together with string. My foot tapped an ever-quickening tempo against the marble, matching the rapid beat of my heart. And finally, *finally*, when the table before me was clear, when each magazine had been categorized and labeled and stacked away neatly in its proper place...

I looked up.

His eyes were already there, locking onto mine with a burning intensity I felt mirrored in my own gaze. I knew it was wrong to want him, wrong to feel the stirring attraction in my body as he looked at me, but I couldn't stop myself. The heat in his stare was too hot, too raw, to bear without combusting.

And we were a box of fireworks. A sixty-gallon drum of gasoline. An unstable container of napalm.

One spark, one look, was all it took.

We went up in flames.

Chapter Nineteen

✦

NOW

SEBASTIAN WAS OUT OF HIS SEAT AND AROUND THE TABLE BEFORE I knew what was happening, the space between us vanishing so quickly I had no time to prepare for impact. When he reached me his fists locked tightly around my wrists, and I was pulled bodily from my seat and lifted up onto the table.

I gasped in shock and pain. This was no gentle placement, no tender lift. He'd slammed me down hard enough that the backs of my thighs smarted on contact and my teeth rattled in my mouth. His grip was biting, his fingers digging into the flesh at my hips with a force that hovered on the razors edge between carnality and brutality.

"Bash," I protested, shocked at the way he was treating me. He'd never touched me like this when we were together.

"My name is Sebastian," he bit out, removing one hand from its hold at my hip. His fingers slid around to the nape of my neck, fisting the hair there tightly enough that I whimpered. "Or Mr. Covington. It's your choice."

I stared into his eyes, not recognizing the look in them. They swam with desire and anger, lust and hatred. He wanted me, and he loathed the fact that he did.

I wish I were strong enough to say I was outraged at his treatment. I wish I could say that the feeling of his hands on me, even though they were rough and lacking the tenderness of the boy he used to be, didn't set my blood boiling in my veins. I'd never been so turned on in my life — not by a long shot. Not even when we were kids, sneaking around on the back roads in his gardener's borrowed pickup truck and discovering one another beneath a blanket of stars.

The memory snapped me back into reason. This couldn't happen. This *shouldn't* happen.

"Bash, you're hurting me," I told him, my eyes wide.

"My name," he leaned forward, eyes burning into mine. "Is *Sebastian*. You lost the right to call me anything else seven years ago, *Ms. Kincaid*."

He was so close now, I could feel each word as it took shape on his lips. He hadn't ever handled me with anger before. At seventeen he'd been gentle, loving, respectful. The man holding me so roughly now was a different creature entirely — one stripped of any genteel fronts a young lover might construct in hopes of shielding his partner's more delicate sensibilities.

Before me was a man, not a boy. Passion warred with anger in his eyes. Pressed so tightly against him, I could feel how much he wanted me, yet his words were cruel when he spoke again.

"What's my name?"

I whimpered in response, ashamed of the dampness I felt gathering in my underwear, of the telltale tightening of my nipples beneath my bra. This shouldn't turn me on. This was wrong.

"Say it," he growled, clutching me tighter against him. His other hand left my hair and found its way to the base of my skirt, viciously bunching the fabric in a clenched fist as he pushed it higher up my thigh. He ground himself against me, and I let out a whimper as the last of shred of my control slipped away.

"Sebastian," I gasped out finally, arching my body against his chest.

"Say it again."

"Sebastian," I breathed, my head falling back.

"I should fuck you right here, like the little whore you are."

My eyes snapped open and my spine went rigid at his cold words. There was no lust in his eyes anymore — only anger and distrust. Vengeance. Maybe some hatred.

He raised a hand to grip my chin firmly between his fingers, with just enough pressure to keep me in place without causing pain.

"You," he whispered, leaning so close our lips brushed. "Are the most selfish, manipulative woman I have ever had the displeasure of knowing, and I have regretted our every moment together for the past seven years. Frankly, the very sight of you makes me sick. But I suppose it's nice to know if I still wanted you, I could have you on your knees begging in under a minute."

I glared at him and raised my hand to slap him across the face, but he caught my flying fist midair within one of his own.

"Lucky for you," he murmured, his eyes trapping mine. "I don't do sloppy seconds."

With that, his right hand disappeared from my chin and his left released my fist, which I let fall to my lap like deadweight. He turned without a backward glance and headed for the elevators, leaving me sitting on the conference room table like a naive little girl — legs spread, skirt rucked, hair tousled.

Like I was a cheap, five-dollar fuck you didn't bother to ask for a phone number or even a first name.

Only when the elevator doors had closed at his back, did I hop down from the table, smooth my skirt, and allow the tears to fill my eyes. I was a fool. He hated me for what I'd done to him all those years ago. And, clearly, he wasn't the same man I'd loved back then. I needed to let go, to harden my heart against him.

If only he'd give it back, first.

Tears of humiliation and grief — for both myself and for the man Sebastian had become — streamed down my face as I collected my things and headed for the elevator. It was time to go home.

⚜

I SET THE CARTON OF BEN & JERRY'S DOWN ON THE countertop, staring forlornly off into space.

Mrs. Patel had already bagged my Doritos, but had yet to reach for the ice cream. When I looked up, she was staring at me from her chair with her hands planted on her hips. Her beautiful bright orange sari was concealed from waist down by the lumpy brown crocheted blanket she always kept over her lap for warmth, her shock of silver hair was groomed impeccably, and her dark brown eyes were narrowed at me with suspicion. I wasn't sure how she managed to look intimidating from down there, but the stern expression on her face was enough to make me un-hunch my shoulders and stand up straight.

"Wine." She made a disapproving *tsk* sound, her eyes focused on the bottle I'd had cradled like a precious babe in the crook of my right arm since I left the liquor store. "Is *not* a food group, Miss Lux."

I thought about it for a minute.

"But wine is made of grapes, Mrs. Patel," I countered. "And grapes are fruit. So technically, I'm pretty sure wine is a food group."

She stared at me, her hands still firmly planted, apparently unmoved by my words. I sighed.

"Okay, fine. It's not a food group," I admitted. "That's what the Doritos and ice cream are for."

Mrs. Patel made a face — I'm not sure I could classify it as pure disapproval, because there were strains of disgust and revulsion woven in as well — and called out to her son, who was stocking the shelves. She rattled off several orders in rapid Hindi, and I watched avidly as he nodded in acknowledgment before scurrying away and disappearing into the back room. When I turned back to face her, her lips were pressed together in a mysterious smile and she made no attempt to explain herself.

"$8.99 please," she said, extending one hand for payment. I shook my head back and forth, dumbfounded. I swore, every time I was in here, the little old lady behind the counter got more bizarre. Laughing lightly, I handed over a ten-dollar bill.

She was passing me my change when her son, Ravi, returned from the back room with a basket in his arms. I was stunned when he appeared next to his mother behind the counter and handed it to me. I looked from his outstretched offering to Mrs. Patel, who was nodding emphatically.

"Take it," she insisted.

Mutely, I reached across the counter with my free hand and took hold of the basket handle. Whatever was inside smelled amazing, and my stomach rumbled immediately in response. Then again, since I'd skipped my lunch break earlier, I was so ravenous I could've gnawed off my own arm to appease my appetite.

Ravi grinned and hurried back to his stocking tasks.

"Naan, chole curry, and chicken tikka masala." Mrs. Patel nodded at me, pleased with herself. "*That* is a dinner — not wine and snack food."

My eyes watered at the gesture. I guess, after a year of watching me purchase nothing but junk, Mrs. Patel was familiar enough with my eating habits to know that home cooked meals were few and far between. And after the day I'd just had, her timing couldn't have been more perfect.

I set the basket down on the counter along with my bottle of wine and the bag of unhealthy contraband I'd just purchased. When I walked around and approached Mrs. Patel, her eyebrows drifted so far up her forehead they nearly disappeared into her hairline.

"What are you doing?" she asked, her face once again set in a frown and her arms crossed over her chest in an unapproachable manner.

"I'm hugging you," I told her, smiling as I leaned forward and wrapped my arms around her petite frame. She was stiff as a board in my embrace and didn't even feign an attempt to reciprocate my hug, but I didn't really care. That wasn't the point.

"Thank you," I whispered, squeezing her lightly. When I moved back a step, she was staring at me with wide eyes, but I could tell by the twitching of her lips that she was fighting off a smile. I winked, moving back around the counter and grabbing my items, just as another customer walked through the doors.

"Bye, Mrs. Patel," I said, beaming at her.

"Don't get any ideas," she told me, trying to maintain her stern face. "It's just one dinner."

"We're totally friends now, Mrs. Patel." I laughed. "You like me, don't deny it."

She harrumphed. "You talk too much and only eat things that come prepackaged. Your insides are probably rotten. It was a civic duty, nothing more."

"Uh huh, whatever you say, Mrs. Patel," I said, still grinning at her. "See you soon."

She sighed, but the beginnings of a smile graced her lips. "See you soon, Miss Lux."

"Bye, Ravi!" I yelled in the direction the storeroom as I pulled open the door and headed outside.

So, overall my day had sucked. Big time. The thing with Sebastian was messed up beyond belief, I was pretty sure Cara was trying to singlehandedly ruin my life, and work tomorrow would probably be even worse than today had been. But for some reason, as I looked down at the basket clutched tightly in my right fist, I couldn't keep the smile off my face.

I LEANED BACK AGAINST MY SOFA, BOTH HANDS RESTING ON MY now-bloated stomach, and surveyed what remained of the feast Mrs. Patel had provided me. The dinner she'd prepared had been incredible — more authentic and flavorful than any of the gourmet meals I'd eaten at Indian restaurants across the city — and I hadn't let any of it go to waste. All that remained were naan crumbs and whatever curry remnants I'd been unable to scrape off the sides of the plastic containers with my fork. I may have gone a little — okay, a lot — overboard, and I'd have to go for a run tomorrow morning if I ever wanted to fit into my jeans again, but it had been worth it.

Once I'd digested enough to move, I hopped in the shower and tried to wash off the day's negativity. I forced myself to accept that there was nothing I could do to fix things with Sebastian. I couldn't tell him the truth about the past, and even if I did, there was a still a good chance he wouldn't forgive me for what I'd done. All I could do now was resolve to handle it better in the future, and hope that our little scene on the conference room table would never be repeated.

I remembered the look in his eyes — so conflicted, so intense — and prayed that somewhere deep down, beneath the caustic mask he now showed the world, a gentleman still existed. With any luck, that would be enough to rein in his anger and save us from any more explosive encounters.

I'd just slipped on my bathrobe when my door buzzed. Puzzled, I walked over to the intercom and pressed a button to activate the small speaker.

"Who is it?"

"It's Desmond!"

I sighed and buzzed him in. There was never a *good* time to break up with someone, I supposed. But Desmond deserved better than me — better than a girl who could only commit a fraction of her time and an even smaller fraction of her heart to the relationship. Whether I liked it or not, Sebastian's reappearance in my life complicated everything. He consumed my thoughts, ruled my actions, even though we weren't together.

I was just thankful that I'd never gotten serious with Desmond. We were casual. Heck, we'd never even talked about exclusivity — I could be one short name on a long list of girls. I tried to console myself with that thought.

I'd barely had enough time to tighten my robe a little more securely when his knock sounded at my door. A cursory glance in my peephole had me sliding the chain and granting him entrance.

"Hey," he said, leaning in to kiss my cheek. He'd bounded up five flights of stairs and he wasn't even winded — the boy had some serious stamina working in his favor. Unfortunately, I wouldn't be the girl benefitting from it.

"Hi, Des."

We walked over to my sofa and sat a few paces apart. A week ago, I might've snuggled into his side, or he might've hauled me onto his lap and taken advantage of my skimpy silk bathrobe. Now, the careful distance between us only compounded the awkwardness of the situation.

"I'm sorry to just show up like this," he said, dual red spots appearing on his cheeks. "It's just, well, you seem distant. I wanted to see if you were okay."

Shit. Of course he had to be the most considerate guy on the planet. Why couldn't he be a selfish jerk? That would make things so much easier for me.

"I'm really sorry, Desmond." I took a deep breath and tucked my legs up beneath me on the sofa cushion. "You're completely right. I've been distracted and upset and... well, just a mess, lately."

"What's wrong?" He reached across the space between us and settled a large hand on my knee. His comforting squeeze made my eyes fill with tears. "You can tell me, babe."

"I've been completely unfair to you," I confessed, my voice shaky. "You deserve someone much, much better than me."

"What?" He stared at me, taken aback by my words. "Lux, that's crazy."

"You don't know about my past." I took a shuddering breath, trying to regain control. "I had a relationship when I was young that didn't end well. For either of us. And I thought I'd never see him again, but last week I bumped into him at *Luster*, of all places. Now he's pretty much my boss for the next few weeks. I just don't think I can handle all the history that seeing him dredges up while trying to start a new relationship with someone else."

I looked at him apologetically, dreading his response. Hurting such a good guy felt supremely shitty, but it was necessary. It wouldn't be fair to string him along while my thoughts were wrapped up in Sebastian.

Desmond squeezed my knee reassuringly. "And this guy, he's—"

"He hates me," I blurted out. "And I don't blame him. But it doesn't make it any easier to see him, or be around him."

"And there's no possibility of a future toge—"

"No." I cut him off. "I'm sorry, I shouldn't be burdening you with this."

"Hey," he said, reaching out and entwining his hand with mine. "Don't worry about it, Lux. I know all about first loves — they're complicated and messy, and they rarely end well. I understand if you need some time and space to sort out your thoughts." He took a deep breath. "And maybe I'm an idiot for telling you this while you're in the process of breaking up with me, but I'd be an even bigger idiot for walking away without telling you that I think you're amazing. I've never met someone like you before. And I'm not saying we'll be able to just put things on hold and pick them up exactly where we left off. But maybe in a few weeks or a few months, when you've figured things out... give me a call."

I felt my chest swell with feeling. He was seriously the perfect guy. Something was definitely, fundamentally, inexplicably wrong with me for walking away from him right now and sabotaging the only shot I had at happiness. Any girl in the world would be lucky to give her heart to a man like Desmond, because he was one of the rare men out there who'd be sure to treasure it forever.

But I'd given my heart away a long time ago, and I'd never gotten it back.

He cupped my face between his hands and dropped a kiss onto my forehead. I squeezed my eyes shut, unsurprised when tears escaped beneath the lashes and tracked down my cheeks.

"I'm sorry," I whispered.

"Don't be," he whispered back. "I'm not. And... maybe someday."

"Maybe someday," I echoed quietly as he walked out the door, my mind a messy snare of conflicting thoughts. If I moved on, if I loved someone else — even if it wasn't the epic, once-in-a-lifetime kind of love I'd shared with Sebastian — was I betraying the memory of that love? Would loving a man like Desmond detract from the memory of my love with Sebastian?

And, the real question: did I want it to?

Because those memories, though they gave me pain, were a part of us. A part of *me*.

Maybe I wasn't the kind of girl who wanted a simple love, with the joys of shared conversations and mutual interests. Maybe I didn't want Valentine's Day cards, a chore wheel to split up domestic tasks, or nothing-fights in the supermarket about whether or not there was any laundry detergent left at home.

No.

Maybe instead, I wanted the kind of love that devastates you. The kind that rips your insides open and leaves you gutted, out in the cold. Maybe I wanted that great, epic, once-in-a-lifetime love, that consumes with the brightest of flames. And maybe, even though I knew the hottest fires often burn out the fastest, even though it couldn't last... it was worth it.

People say love isn't supposed to be painful. But maybe the best things in life are the ones that hurt the most after they're gone.

୧୭୧

THE NEXT DAY AT WORK WAS BETTER AND WORSE, ALL AT ONCE.

It was better because Sebastian wasn't there. Whether his absence had anything to do with our scene on the table after hours last night, I had no idea — and, frankly, I didn't want to. Seeing him would only add to the tangled bird's nest of thoughts and emotions I'd yet to begin to unravel.

It was worse because, without Sebastian there to rein her in, Cara was more demanding than ever. After another morning spent doing coffee runs for her and her friends — seriously, pumping that much artificial vanilla sweetener into a latte could *not* be good for you — Cara decided that I could run the rest of her errands while I was at it.

"Here's my grocery list," she said, staring down at me from her perch on a director's chair in the fitting area. "Go to Whole Foods, then bring everything to my apartment. My address is on the list. I've already called the concierge — he's expecting you." She smiled at me, extending the list with one manicured hand.

"I'm not doing your grocery shopping, Cara."

"What's that?" she asked. "Did I hear someone protesting? Because I'm pretty sure I have your boss' number right here in my phone. Want me to call her? Give her a little progress report on your work ethic?"

I glared at her, watching as her finger scrolled through her contact list and hovered over Jeanine's name.

"I'm sure she'll be upset to hear about your performance as a *Luster* representative." Cara shook her head in faux sadness. "Such a shame for you to lose your job over a little laundry."

"Laundry?" I bit out between clenched teeth.

"Oh, yes. I'll need you to pick up my dry cleaning as well. Didn't I mention that before?" She smiled at me maliciously.

"No," I snapped, snatching the sheet of paper from her grasp. "You didn't."

"My mistake." Her tinkling laugher filled the air, mocking me.

"I'd hurry up, if I were you. It's already past noon, and you've got a full day of errands to keep you busy!" She clapped her hands together excitedly, like a giddy child.

I turned to go, defeated. Cara might look like a total bimbo, but apparently she possessed enough brains to blackmail me. If she called Jeanine, I had no doubt I'd be out of a job. And no job meant no paycheck, so I'd be out of my apartment and living on the streets in a matter of weeks.

She had me cornered, and she knew it.

I'd gotten about five feet from her when her voice rang through the air, loud enough to draw attention from nearly everyone on the floor.

"Lux!"

I turned and faced her, filled with foreboding. Her expression was gleeful, but her eyes showed a deep malice. I wasn't sure what I'd done to this girl, besides accidentally drop a salad she likely had no intention of ever consuming, but she seemed to hate me a great deal.

"I forgot to put condoms on the grocery list. Would you be a dear and swing by Duane Reade to grab some? Oh, and Seb—" She broke off, grinning at her *accidental* slip up. "My *boyfriend* has been practically insatiable for the last few days, so make sure it's the jumbo pack."

Her words were a kick to the gut. I nodded robotically and turned on my heel, so I didn't have to look at her anymore. An icy weight dropped like a stone into my stomach and my limbs felt leaden and uncoordinated, as though my neurons had frazzled and the entirety of my system was shutting down.

I made it to the elevator on autopilot, trying my best to tune out Cara's triumphant laughter. When the doors closed behind me, I leaned back against the mirrored wall and forced deep breaths into my lungs. I hated how much her words had affected me, but the thought of him going home to Cara after what had happened between us last night made me feel physically ill.

The worst part, though, was that Cara had only been toying

with me — piling on one more degrading task to my list of chores. She wasn't even aware how deeply her words would cut or how very personal her attack had been. If she ever found out about my past with Sebastian, I could only imagine the extent to which she'd go to torture me.

I prayed that day would never come as I hailed a cab and headed off for an afternoon of errands.

Chapter Twenty

NOW

MY GAZE SCANNED THE COFFEE SHOP TWICE AS I WALKED through the doors, but I didn't spot Miri anywhere. I was running twenty minutes late, so I hoped she was still waiting for me. As it turned out, Cara actually did ingest more than Starbucks lattes and salad; her grocery list had been quite extensive. I'd spent most of the afternoon trying to discern the difference between sushi and sashimi, attempting to track down the exceedingly rare — and apparently highly in-demand — imported white sapote fruit so Cara could make her morning smoothies, and asking three different Whole Foods employees to help me find a very specific brand of raw milk artisanal cheese. Though my own eating habits had evolved in recent years to include Merlot and the occasional box of macaroons, for a girl who grew up on spray-cheese and Spam, I was a bit out of my comfort zone.

In a shocking turn of events, I'd "forgotten" to swing by Duane

Reade to restock Cara's condom supply. *Oops.* Thankfully, picking up her dry-cleaning had only taken a few minutes and, as promised, her concierge was expecting me when I arrived at her building. He'd helped me lug the grocery bags up to Cara's apartment and even stayed to unload them with me.

Still, getting across town during the evening rush was always a nightmare, and by the time I reached the Village I was late for my meeting with Miri. Hopefully, she was still around here somewhere and we'd get a chance to talk. I approached the counter and ordered a chai tea latte. After the day I'd had, I was in desperate need of something soothing to sip on while I waited.

"Name?" the girl taking my order asked, her sharpie poised over my paper cup.

"Lux."

She stared at me for a beat, her dark blue, heavily-lined eyes evaluative. When I blinked and averted my gaze, unsettled by her intense stare, she scribbled my name onto the cup and passed it down the line to the barista.

"Were you meeting someone here?" she asked, rather strangely.

My eyes flew back to her face and I nodded.

"Young girl, around fourteen? Brown hair? Foreign accent?"

"Miri," I breathed, instantly uneasy. "I was supposed to meet her here at six, I'm running late."

"She left this for you," the girl said, reaching one tattooed arm beneath the counter and revealing a sealed white envelope. I grabbed it from her hand, staring at the three swirling cursive letters that had been scribed across the front: **LUX**.

"What did she say?" I asked, my eyes fixed on the envelope as I handed over a five-dollar bill.

"Not much." The cashier shrugged and passed back my change. "Seemed kinda scared though. Flighty. Looking around in every direction, like someone was watching her or something."

My heart picked up speed and my fingers itched to tear open the letter.

"Thanks," I murmured.

As soon as the barista called my name, I headed for a small table in a quiet corner of the cafe with my latte in hand. My drink sat before me untouched, growing cold as I read Miri's letter over and over. My eyes scanned the handful of short lines so many times they began to blur together into one smeary brick of black text.

Lux,

I'm sorry I couldn't wait for you. Santos was standing outside my apartment when I got home yesterday. He was watching me. I'm scared, Lux. They can't know I talked to you, or I'll disappear like Vera. Please don't come back to see me. It's too dangerous. I'm sorry again.

Your friend,

Miri

PS: Be careful. He's a bad man.

I sat for so long the sun set and gave way to full darkness outside the cafe windows. Miri's words played on a never-ending loop in my mind, stirring within me a tidal wave of guilt, despair, and fear so strong I worried I'd be pulled under, never to resurface.

They can't know I talked to you.

I'll disappear like Vera.

Be careful. He's a bad man.

Had I put an innocent child's life in danger with my foolish insistence to get involved? My intentions had been pure, of course, but did that matter when Miri, a fourteen-year-old girl, was afraid for her life?

Her request was a double-edged sword. If I went back to see her, I might endanger her further; if I followed her wishes and stayed away, I'd live in a constant state of worry that something awful had happened. Either choice would slice me open.

No matter how much I wanted to make sure she was okay, I couldn't risk another trip to Two Bridges. If she was right, rather than just paranoid, my presence in her neighborhood might make her situation worse. But I couldn't just walk away from this — not now that I knew girls were disappearing by the handful.

Santos.

The police officer who watched the young girls. He was the only clue I had to go on. I hoped it would be enough, as I rushed from the cafe to the closest subway platform. It was time to do some research.

⚜

I QUICKLY DISCOVERED THAT FINDING SANTOS MIGHT BE A bigger feat than I'd originally estimated. He was one, small navy-uniformed needle in the mountainous haystack that was the NYPD.

Hunched over my laptop with one hand clutching my phone to my ear and the other holding a very full glass of wine, I tried to convince my best friend that I wasn't crazy.

"You're nuts," Fae said, snorting into her receiver.

I was off to a good start. "I'm not nuts!"

"You honestly think Vera's disappearance has something to do with the NYPD?"

"Miri said Vera isn't the only girl who's disappeared. And, Fae, the stuff I've been reading..." I trailed off, eyes peeled on the screen in front of me. "It's messed up."

"What do you mean?"

"Did you know the NYPD employs over 50,000 people? That's more than the entire FBI! And there are thousands of stories posted online about police brutality and internal corruption on the squads."

I heard Fae exhale a long huff of air.

"I'm not making this up, Fae. I've been reading this stuff for the past few hours, and there are more on-duty murders and cover-ups than you can imagine. Just go online, it's all there at your fingertips." My voice was intent. "Plus, did you know $4.6 billion dollars from last year's city budget went solely to fund the police force? Our freaking mayor referred to the NYPD as the 'seventh largest army in the world.' Don't you think that's a bit excessive?"

"Excessive, maybe," she agreed. "But it doesn't change the fact that you sound like a crazy conspiracy theorist."

"Power tends to corrupt, and absolute power corrupts absolutely," I muttered into the phone.

"Don't quote Lord Acton to me," Fae protested. "I was a freaking History major in college."

I sighed. "Well, I found a picture of Santos and it's beyond creepy. Maybe you'll change your mind when you see it."

"Maybe," Fae said, humoring me. "I have to go, the delivery guy is here with my Chinese. Promise me you won't obsess over this all night."

"Yep. I promise," I agreed, rolling my eyes as I hung up.

Clearly, I wasn't going to get much support from Fae. But I couldn't shake the feeling that I was on to something.

My first hour of searching had been spent mainly sloughing through internet archives filled with useless factoids and anecdotes about the police force. I hit my first stroke of luck when I typed the name *Santos* in combination with my NYPD search and found a story from last August on the *New York Daily News* website. The article itself contained useless information on new city transit laws, but it was accompanied by a photo of a man in a navy blue uniform surrounded by a group of small children. One of the little girls, who was no more than five or six, was wearing his peaked officer's cap and giggling at the camera as the brim fell down over her eyes.

The caption read: *Officer Martin Santos, fifteen year NYPD officer and investigator for the narcotics unit, shares a laugh with neighborhood kids on their way to school in Little Italy early Friday morning.*

Officer Santos wasn't "sharing a laugh," or even looking at the camera; his gaze was focused intently on the laughing girl wearing his cap. Despite the matte photo, his eyes appeared to gleam with excitement and one corner of his mouth was lifted in a knowing smirk.

My stomach turned at the sight of him.

If I had to describe Santos with one word it would be *nondescript*. He was utterly unremarkable, average in every way — medium height and build, with slicked-back dark hair and brown eyes so light they were nearly colorless. He was maybe in his late thirties or early forties; stocky without being overweight, his hair thinning out but not balding, and his features plain but not unattractive.

He was someone you wouldn't look twice at if you passed him on the street.

Well, I planned to do more than look at him, I thought, as I scribbled down the address of the downtown precinct that served as home base for the NYPD Vice Crimes unit. I was going to track him down and shadow him for the day. And if I got so much as an inkling that Officer Santos was somehow involved in the disappearance of underage immigrant girls...

I was going to take him down.

With a deep sigh, I swallowed a large gulp of wine and set the empty glass on my bedside table. My fingers hovered over the keys for a minute and I contemplated what I was about to put into my search engine. A string of simple words I'd never have guessed I'd one day find myself typing.

Immigrant girls disappearing.

In a fraction of a second, Google had retrieved over 10,000,000 results for my perusal.

I read, with a growing sense of horror, about young girls all over the world who were being lured away from their families and forced into pimp-driven prostitution rings or escort services. I was haunted as I saw, over and over, the same words flashing across my screen.

Sex trade.

Human trafficking.

Child slaves.

The thoughts were so revolting, my first instinct was to shy away, to deny that it could be possible. Things like this didn't happen in this day and age. And certainly not in America.

Right?

I refined my Google search to sex trafficking in the United States and forced myself to look on. My eyes blurred with tears as I read firsthand accounts from girls who'd escaped. Adolescents, barely on the cusp of adulthood, who were promised money or fame or fine clothing, and who instead received nothing but a short life on a dirty mattress in the back room of a modern day brothel. Most of them never saw a dime of the spoils earned from the exploitation of their bodies.

I read stories of preteens who were snatched off the streets. Often, they were drugged, raped, and beaten into submission by a sadistic pimp. Their spirits broken, their childhoods stolen, their lives eventually lost.

And what of the victims who hadn't escaped? For every one who broke free of this life and somehow gathered the courage to discuss it afterward, there were countless whose stories went unvoiced.

This seemed like some alternate reality — some other, darker version of the nation and the city I'd come to love. This was America. The best country in the world. Yet, for all our prosperity and progress, it seemed that the gross majority of us — myself included — walked around with bags over our heads, so blissfully ignorant and caught up in our own lives that we didn't even blink when children disappeared from our streets without a trace.

I felt a chill race down my spine as I stumbled onto a website with statistics. Though data was scarce, there were a few persistent trends. For one, the girls were almost always poor immigrants, between the ages of twelve and sixteen. They were usually undocumented, so no one took notice when they vanished. Plus, even if someone were to notice, the girls had no real legal status in our country — no protections against predators. As a port city with a large unregistered population, New York was one of the biggest trafficking hotspots in the country.

Could Vera somehow be caught up in all of this?

I wasn't sure. But it seemed far too coincidental that several young girls were now missing from the same neighborhood. And now that I'd dragged Miri into the fray, I was even more obligated to find out what was going on.

My fingers traced over the shiny silver cuff on my right wrist. I thought of Vera, her beautiful warm brown eyes dulled and lifeless as heroin thrummed though her system, while a man grunted and sweated and stole her innocence for a flat rate in a cheap motel room, or on a seedy street corner somewhere. Her inner light snubbed out into eternal darkness, on a semen-stained mattress in a room full of strangers.

My eyes pressed tightly closed at the images I'd conjured, unable to bear the thought of my sweet friend meeting such an end.

Jamie'd always said that the people who most deserve our help are the ones who'd never ask for it.

Vera hadn't asked, but she needed someone to stand for her. To fight for her. And maybe there were more qualified people out there, who'd do more good than I could. Maybe I was the wrong girl for the job. But I'd never be able to meet my own eyes in the mirror again if I didn't at least try to figure out what was going on.

It was time to pull the bag off my head. Time to stop shielding my eyes from the world around me. Time to see past the illusion, and expose the truth.

No matter how dark that truth may be.

❧

"WHY ARE YOU DRESSED LIKE CATWOMAN?"

"We're on a stakeout. This is total stakeout attire." Fae gestured down at her all-black ensemble.

"Actually, I'm pretty sure the point is to blend in," I noted dryly. "You look like a burglar."

"But a sexy burglar," Simon added consolingly, leaning over the center console to wink at Fae as she settled into the backseat of his car. "The Jimmy Choo biker boots are a nice touch. I approve."

"Aren't they cute?" Fae said, brightening immediately.

I rolled my eyes heavenward, praying for some kind of divine intervention as Simon peeled away from the curb and out into the flow of traffic. I was riding shotgun in the rust-bucket sedan he charmingly referred to as "Lola" and was seriously regretting the fact that I didn't know anyone else in the city who had a car. Not only had Simon made me explain, in detail, why I needed to borrow it, I also was forced to accept the fact that once I explained, there was no possible way he'd let me do this on my own.

Not that I couldn't use his help. After all, he'd spent his college years as a semi-professional celebrity stalker. A simple stakeout would come practically second nature to him, at this point. But where Simon went, Fae soon followed. And, though I loved my best friend, when the name of the game was stealth, she wasn't the first person who came to mind. With her knockout good looks and designer fashion addiction, she made a lasting impression every-where she went — which just so happened to be the exact oppo-site of my intentions for this mission.

Alas, beggars can't be choosers, so here we were, crammed into what I think at one point in ancient history had been a Volvo, but now more closely resembled a dumpster with wheels. There were so many mismatched replacement parts in various colors, it was impossible to tell what the original hue had been. None of the four doors were the same shade, nor did the trunk match the hood. What resulted was a patchwork of lemon yellow, dark red, shiny green, and matte blue, that came together in the approximate shape of a car.

Totally incognito. A trained police officer would never spot us tailing him.

I groaned and began to bang my head against the dash, wishing I'd never dragged the two of them into this. It had all the makings of an impending disaster and, frankly, I'd have been better off alone, on foot, holding a large sign that said "HEY SANTOS, I'M FOLLOWING YOU!" Because, let's face it, even *that* spectacle would probably draw less attention than Fae and Simon's secret-mission shenanigans.

"Baby, you're gonna mess up my dash if you keep that up," Simon chided.

I glanced at the dusty, peeling, faux-leather dash incredulously, wondering what Simon's version of "messed up" looked like. Fae giggled from the backseat.

"This is going to be a disaster," I muttered.

"Chin up, sweets." Simon grinned at me. "I've got mad stalker skills. Just you wait."

⚜

As much as I hated to admit it, Simon was kind of right. He did indeed possess mad stalker skills.

Finding out which station Santos worked at had been easy enough with the help of the internet. Once I'd finished my own search last night, Simon and Fae had come over. I'd quickly brought them up to speed on the Miri situation and they'd helped me hatch a plan to track down Santos. They were excited enough about the adventure we'd schemed up; whether they actually believed any part of my crazy theory or were just going along with it out of friendship, was a different matter entirely.

Simon had the wheels and the surveillance experience. But it was Fae, the Yoda of flirtatious Jedi mind-trickery, who really came through for us in the end. She called the station during her Wednesday lunch hour, while the more seasoned officers were likely to be out grabbing food, and caught a young recruit in her web. A few minutes of giggling at his lame jokes were enough to charm the love-struck rookie into slipping up about Santos' shift schedule — especially after she mentioned how much she wanted to come by in person to "thank that nice older officer named Santos who'd helped her when her heel got stuck in a grate last week." The young officer, all too eager for a chance encounter with the girl on the phone, promptly revealed that Santos came in each evening to work the night shift, from 6:00 p.m. to 2:00 a.m.

Fast-forward six hours, and the three of us were on our way to the 6th Precinct Station, in the heart of the Village. I supposed the only plus side to our mission was the fact that Simon and Fae were too distracted channeling Bonnie and Clyde to press me for details about my first three days of work with Sebastian. If I told them what had happened Monday night, they were liable to obsess for hours on end, dissecting each remark and gesture Sebastian had made until I was forced to throw myself from the moving vehicle. And, honestly, I'd been doing quite enough of my own obsessing, especially in light of Sebastian's unexplained absence both yesterday and today.

We pulled up across the street from the police station and found a parking space about half a block down. According to Simon, that way we were close enough to watch who came and went, without being obvious about the fact that we were watching. I decided to take his word for it. The photograph of Santos I'd printed out last night was sitting on the dashboard, so we could be sure we'd spotted the right guy. I studied it as Simon hopped out of the car and crammed a handful of quarters into the meter. Fae was busy in the backseat, rooting around her seemingly bottomless black hobo bag.

"Aha!" Fae exclaimed, pulling a small item from her purse.

"What?" Simon asked, sliding back into the driver's seat.

"Tell me those aren't what I think they are." I groaned.

"Binoculars!" She laughed excitedly, pulling the lens caps off and lifting them to her eyes. She fiddled with the focus knobs for a minute, turning fully around in her seat to check her view of the station through the rear windshield. "Oh yeah. These babies are ready to rock."

"I'm not even going to ask why you have those," I told her.

"She has a hot neighbor," Simon explained. "Sometimes he hangs from his chin-up bar and does crunches..."

"Enough said."

"Guys!" Fae interjected.

"Usually he does core workouts on Thursday nights," Simon added. "You should come next week. It's quite a show. We make popcorn and everything."

I giggled.

"Guys!" Fae repeated.

"But anyway, I keep telling Fae she needs to ask him out. Those ab muscles alone would be rea—"

"GUYS!" Fae yelled, finally managing to get our attention. "Isn't that him?"

Simon and I whipped around in our seats, trying to catch sight of whoever Fae had spotted leaving the precinct. The man was walking this way, toward one of the unmarked police cars parked across the street. Dressed in street clothes with a black duffle bag slung over one shoulder, he didn't look like the uniformed officer I'd been expecting. I had to glance back at the photo on the dash to confirm it was him.

"That's our guy," I murmured quietly, watching as Santos climbed into his vehicle and pulled out onto the street. We were silent and still as his car rolled past ours and joined the flow of traffic.

"Let's get him," Simon added in a hushed tone, turning over the ignition until the car rumbled to an unwilling start.

"Why are we whispering?" Fae whispered.

"I don't know, it just seemed appropriate," I said, laughing as we pulled away from the curb and started to tail Santos' car. Traffic in the city was rarely navigable at any time of day, but thankfully we were an hour or so beyond the nightly post-work jam that tied up each avenue in gridlock. There were enough cars to conceal our presence, but not so many that we lost track of Santos up ahead.

"The trick is to stay a half block behind them," Simon advised us. "Use directionals and follow traffic laws. Go the speed limit. Otherwise, you draw attention to yourself."

"Okay, Mr. Bond." I snorted.

We followed Santos' car for an hour as he looped around the Village, cut down through Alphabet City, and zigzagged his way across Chinatown. He stopped a few times — once to grab a coffee at 7-11 and again to grab a burger and fries at a greasy spoon near Columbus Park — but other than that, he was pretty much the most boring target of all time. As the minutes ticked by and gradually turned into hours, Fae passed out cold in the backseat and even Simon began to yawn.

It was past eleven. We were about ready to admit defeat and head back to Simon's loft for the night, when Santos took an abrupt turn and headed for the bridge that crossed over the East River to Brooklyn.

I looked over at Simon, my brows raised in question.

"We've come this far," he muttered, taking the exit that would lead us across the bridge. Twenty minutes later, we followed Santos into a rundown neighborhood on the west coast of Brooklyn. Red Hook or "The Point" as it was best known by its residents, was a gritty, working class district that jutted out into the bay, bounded on three sides by water. The former industrial port had at one time been viewed as a great location for gentrification, with transplanted businesses breathing new life into its downtrodden streets. Over time, though, the isolation and inaccessibility of The Point, coupled with a crumbling economy and a lack of funding, had stalled the efforts to revitalize, leaving Red Hook in a limbo state — half gentrified, half in ruins.

It seemed Santos was headed for the still-impoverished section, where overgrown weeds and garbage filled the vacant lots interspersed between Civil War-era brick row houses and Brooklyn's largest public housing projects. Along with the empty warehouses that lined its waterfront, the neighborhood was marked by strips of deserted businesses and a series of ramshackle boat docks that no longer saw any traffic. During daylight hours, it wasn't the most genteel of places; at night, it seemed even more desolate. It was empty of life — the forgotten, destitute, dark southern twin to Manhattan's effervescent, ever-vital boroughs.

The traffic was thin here, with fewer cars to hide amongst as we trailed Santos deeper into the neighborhood. Simon put on the brakes and let a little distance grow between our cars. We slowed to a crawl when Santos turned onto a small side street by the water and parked in front of an abandoned brick warehouse. Its windows were boarded up, its foundation was chipping away, and if I had to wager a guess, I'd say it had probably been constructed at the start of the 20th century, when the Industrial Revolution swept the nation with a wave of new technologies and Brooklyn bloomed with factories and manufacturing plants. The building sat on the very outskirts of The Point, abutting a private dock which likely once served as a lively distribution port for shipped goods.

Now, the pier was dilapidated — the perfect counterpart to the factory it formerly serviced. Many of its wooden support beams hung down into the bay, waterlogged and termite-eaten with age. The planks were so brittle, one miscalculated stride might find you stepping down on sawdust and open air.

Santos' brake lights glowed like twin red halos on the dark street around the corner. Simon cut his headlights and shifted into park on the cross-street just before the intersection — far enough away that we could watch inconspicuously through the vacant lot across from the warehouse. Fae stirred awake when the car jolted to a stop.

"Where are we?" she mumbled, her voice slurred with sleep.

"We're not in Manhattan anymore, Toto, that's for damn sure," Simon whispered, his eyes following Santos as the officer climbed from his car and looked around.

"Otherwise known as Brooklyn," I murmured, following

Simon's lead as he hunched down in his seat to avoid being spotted.

Fae wrinkled her nose in distaste as she peered out her window at the garbage and graffiti littering the abandoned streets. This was a far cry from the sleekly sophisticated bars of her usual late-night stomping grounds.

Though many of the overhead streetlights had burned out and been left in disrepair, there was enough light from the few remaining illuminated posts to make out Santos, his black duffel still in hand, as he crossed the street and walked out onto the pier abutting the warehouse. He walked confidently, as though he'd been here many times before, and casually shifted the bag's strap over his shoulder as he lit a cigarette. I held my breath and watched as he took a few slow drags, his eyes cast out over the still, gray waters of the Hudson. When he'd finished his cigarette, he turned back for the warehouse and approached a rusted metal emergency exit door on the side of the brick building. The jarring sound of his fist pounding against the metal reverberated in the night. Santos waited calmly before the door, wholly unaware of the watchful eyes trained on him.

After a few seconds, what looked like a slotted metal peephole slid open, allowing whoever was inside a glimpse at Santos. He was obviously recognized, as the door immediately swung open to admit him. It closed behind him as soon as he stepped through the entryway.

It didn't open again for two hours.

Fae was snoring lightly in the backseat and Simon was nodding off sporadically, slumped over the steering wheel with drool pooling in one cheek, when the warehouse door finally creaked open and Santos walked out. I elbowed Simon in the stomach and he jerked awake with little grace.

"Whaaasgoinon?"

"Look," I hissed, pointing toward the windshield.

Simon wiped the drool from his face and turned his eyes to Santos.

"Duffel."

"What?" I asked, thinking he might still be half asleep and babbling nonsensical dream words.

"The duffel bag," he clarified. "Look how full it is."

I looked. He was right; Santos had definitely picked something up in the warehouse. The question was, *what?*

"When he went in, it was limp. Now, it's practically exploding," Simon noted.

"That's what she said," Fae chimed in from the back seat with a faint giggle.

I rolled my eyes. "Really, Fae?"

"It's two in the morning." She shrugged. "My humor isn't exactly on-point at the moment."

"So what's in the bag?" I muttered.

"Could be anything. Money, drugs, you name it." Simon's brow furrowed as he watched Santos start up his car and pull away from the curb. "But he was in there for more than two hours. His shift is pretty much over now, and he barely patrolled. I don't think that's standard operating procedure for an NYPD officer."

We all fell silent as we contemplated what that might mean.

Simon waited until Santos was a few blocks out of sight before starting the car and steering us back to Manhattan. I didn't know how I'd do it, but I needed to find out what was in that duffel bag. And then, I had to come back here to see what was going on behind the tightly sealed doors of that warehouse.

As we wound through the streets and back across the bridge to the bustling island we called home, I thought about the missing girls, and how I was essentially no closer to finding out what had happened to them. But mostly, I thought about Simon and Fae, both of whom had work in less than six hours, and how they'd insisted on coming along with me on this charade just so I wouldn't be alone. As it turned out, stakeouts weren't like the movies. I'd been bored to tears, my butt had gone numb after sitting for hours in the same position, and I'd learned virtually nothing about Santos other than the fact that he liked to frequent strange, abandoned places in the dead of night. Which may have been suspicious, but was certainly not illegal.

I wanted a smoking gun, something we could easily pin on him. I wanted to feel like I was doing something other than spinning my wheels while more girls became targets and vanished off city streets. I wanted Vera back home, and Miri safe again.

But, as I knew better than most, life rarely works out the way we want it to.

Chapter Twenty-One

NOW

REMEMBER WHEN YOU WERE EIGHT YEARS OLD AND THE MOST entertaining thing on the planet was challenging someone on the playground to a staring contest? And the most important thing on the planet was winning said staring contest and becoming the dry-eyed, unblinking champion of the recess yard?

I was engaged in a new kind of staring contest right now, and it was imperative that I win. Because, you see, I wasn't eight anymore, and Sebastian and I weren't gazing into one another's eyes willing the other to blink and cry uncle. Oh, no. We were in a uniquely adult version of the staring game, with new rules. In this round, the goal was to see who could go the absolute longest without so much as a glance in the other's direction.

So maybe it wasn't so much a staring contest as an *avoid-at-all-costs* contest.

An *absolutely-do-not-stare-at-me* contest.

An *I'm-afraid-what-might-happen-if-I-look-at-you* contest.

Anyway, I think he was winning.

See, after his absence for the last two days, I'd kind of gotten used to not seeing him. Yesterday, Cara and her posse had been at a fashion event across the city, modeling for a new fall line, and I'd had a gloriously normal day of discussing set designs and hashing out costume ideas with the designers for the 1920s shoot. The roaring twenties was an exciting era, so our team had a lot of options to play with. And despite a terse email from Jeanine, reminding me that I was still on the hook for my normal *Luster* column at the end of the month, I'd had a great time.

So when I walked in on Thursday morning, yawning widely after my late night of stalking and stakeouts, I'd been content with my new position. I'd even been looking forward to the coming day, knowing that I'd be surrounded by creative thinkers and working on a project unlike any in the magazine's history.

Those warm fuzzy feelings deteriorated as soon as I arrived.

I'd slept fitfully, my mind racing with thoughts of Vera, before finally giving up on sleep altogether and rising before dawn. I was too tired for a run, so I'd headed into work early, hoping I could become an asset to the 1920s team and avoid another errand-girl assignment. When I arrived at the ArtLust building, the lobby was quiet and empty but for a security guard, who nodded at me from his desk before turning his attention back to his crossword puzzle.

I'd hit the button for the fourteenth floor and was watching the elevator doors slide closed when a deep, masculine voice called out.

"Hold the elevator!"

I froze, horror dawning as the voice registered in my ears, but it was too late. His hand slipped between the closing doors and they sprang apart to allow him entrance. *Damn.*

Sebastian stopped in his tracks. His eyes widened but otherwise his expression was stony as ever. There was no remorse in his gaze, nor was there any recognition that Monday night had happened. With a deep inhale, he stepped across the threshold and into the elevator with me. I shuffled a few steps left and looked away as the doors closed behind him.

It grew painfully quiet.

No other riders were there to break the silence with their chatter and no tinny elevator music detracted from the building tension between us as we ascended slowly up fourteen stories. It was just the two of us, trying not to breathe too loud or make any sudden movements, looking anywhere but at each other.

I wanted to laugh. Or cry. I wasn't sure which.

We were about halfway through our ascent when I felt Sebastian take a step toward me, so his front hovered mere inches from my back. I could practically feel the molecules in the air between our bodies compressing, compacting, as he leaned closer into my space.

If you pressed two strong negative magnets together, they'd repel with every bit of force they could muster. And maybe if you were strong enough, you could hold them against each other for a short period of time, though doing so might eventually sap all your strength. Once you let go, though — once you stopped using all your energy to force them together against their will — chances were, those damn magnets that had repelled with such intensity would flip, changing course and snapping together so fast you couldn't believe your eyes. And, once they'd realigned, no amount of pulling was liable to separate them again.

What once repelled quickly morphed into an unbreakable pull.

Oh, and how quick that flip was, from abhorrence to attraction, from disdain to desire. Love and lust, hostility and hatred—they were two sides of the same coin. So though Sebastian had made it clear how he felt for me, the charge between us grew anyway, despite all sense and reason. I could hear the pounding of blood in my ears as I mentally calculated the exact amount of space separating his body from mine. I could feel the sharp pain radiating in my mouth as I bit the inside of my cheek to keep myself in check.

Attraction was a life-force. A physical presence, swirling in the air around us and tethering us together. With my hair twisted up in an elegant knot, my neck was exposed to him and I felt his breath there, at my nape, closer than any stranger had a right to be. I fought against the pull, replaying his words in my mind and trying to snap myself back into reality.

I should fuck you right here like the little whore you are.

I loved him.

I hated him.

I wanted him.

I wanted to kill him.

He's isn't your Sebastian anymore, the reasonable side of my brain whispered.

Maybe you could bring him back, a small, insane portion of my cerebrum — probably my hypothalamus, that sex-driven little slut — countered.

Thankfully, before I could address the fact that my brain wires were severely crossed, the elevator chimed, the doors slid open, and the moment was shattered. I felt Sebastian step away and the breath I'd been holding slipped from my lips in a relieved whoosh. Stepping from the elevator, I hurried for the bathroom across the room, not once looking back at him. To my relief, when I emerged ten minutes later Angela was there with a group of assistants, firing off orders at hyper-speed, and Sebastian was on the opposite side of the room by the conference table, staring out the windows in deep thought. His right hand rubbed at the back of his neck in a familiar gesture.

Some things never change, I suppose.

I tore my eyes from him, headed for Angela and, from that moment on, I'd fully committed to our non-staring contest. Or tried to, anyway. I couldn't speak for Sebastian, but I was having an extraordinarily hard time keeping my eyes off him. Especially when Cara arrived just before noon.

"Baby!" she squealed, sauntering from the elevator with long-legged strides and crossing the room to where he stood with a group of designers. Disregarding the fact that he was in a conversation with his colleagues, Cara sashayed her way to his side and wrapped her abnormally long arms around him from behind. I cursed myself as I broke my own rules and turned to watch their encounter.

"Take me to lunch," Cara whined loudly, leaning in to kiss his neck.

I felt my eyebrows go up.

"Cara." Sebastian reached up and took light hold of her wrists, removing them from where they'd locked around his middle. "I'm working." His tone wasn't playful in the least and, though his back was to me, I could only imagine what his face looked like.

"But I want to go to lunch!" Cara began to pout, jutting out one hip and crossing her arms across her chest. I saw Sebastian's shoulders heave upward in a deep sigh, before he turned to face her. "You have to take me," she carried on in a childish tone. Reaching out one manicured finger, she poked Sebastian in the chest to further emphasize her words.

"Right." Poke. "Now." Poke.

Oh my god. I winced as Sebastian's expression clouded over with annoyance.

The entire office held its breath in silence, waiting to see the fallout from Cara's actions, and I could feel the beginnings of a laugh building in my chest. This girl was ridiculous. If I'd liked her at all, maybe I'd have warned her to quit while she was ahead, before she completely embarrassed herself. As it was, though, I'd happily watch her dig her own grave with Sebastian.

"Cara, I'm not going to lunch with you. Look around. What do you see?" Sebastian's tone was cool, dismissive. "People are work-ing. I am working. And *you* are causing a disturbance."

"But—" Cara protested.

"And, for the last time," Sebastian cut her off. "Don't come here again until we need you for test shots next week." With that, he turned his back on her and resumed his conversation, as though she didn't exist. Cara huffed in outrage, whirled around on her heels, and stormed out in a Prada-patterned blur, leaving nothing in her wake but the faint, lingering scent of Chanel No. 5. I had to hand it to the girl, though — on her way to the elevators, she somehow managed to simultaneously throw a severe glare in my direction and mouth "bitch" at me as she trounced her way to the exit.

A solitary giggle escaped my lips as the elevator doors closed at Cara's back.

My boring, bland life had somehow become a telenovela in the space of a week.

I'd reached my drama limit for the day — for the year, actually — and I could feel the hysteria coming on. My lips twitched until I could no longer contain myself. My giggles turned to full out laughter, then erupted into gasps. As tears gathered in my eyes, the two Jennys made identical concerned faces — no doubt worried I'd had some kind of psychotic break — which really only made me laugh harder.

I reached up to wipe my tears away and in the process locked gazes with a set of hazel eyes that were staring hard across the room in my direction. The laugh caught in my throat and I nearly choked, but not before noticing that Sebastian's lips were upturned just the slightest bit around the corners.

He was almost smiling at me.

Of course, as soon as we made eye contact, his expression shuttered and his lips pressed into an uncompromising frown of disapproval. If not for the idiotic flare of hope that had erupted within me at the sight of his smile — which was still burning an uncomfortably optimistic hole in my chest cavity — I'd have thought maybe I'd imagined that expression on his face, or that it was some kind of deluded product of wishful thinking.

Delusions notwithstanding, I had to turn my face away to hide the private smile twisting my lips. Maybe my Sebastian was still in there after all, buried somewhere so deep down he'd been forgotten entirely. Perhaps I hadn't destroyed him all those years ago and, somehow, he could be redeemed.

And that gave me hope.

Not for myself, not for my own future — but for his.

⚶

AFTER WORK, I HOPPED ON THE SUBWAY AND TOOK THE F TRAIN down through Manhattan and over into Brooklyn. I didn't text Simon or Fae, knowing they'd either want to come with me or try to talk me out of going altogether. I would've been better off in a car, of course, but this was something I needed to do alone, without drawing unwanted attention.

I'd changed into my well-worn black UGA sweatshirt, flats, and a pair of dark skinny jeans in the lobby bathroom before leaving work. I had a feeling that I'd stick out like a sore thumb in my freshly pressed skirt, blouse, and heels on the streets of Red Hook, so I'd stuffed my work attire deep down in the small canvas backpack I'd slung over my shoulder. Plus, I'd be walking and, if I'd learned anything at all since moving to the city, it was to never risk ruining designer footwear if it could be avoided.

The Point was a dead zone — meaning that the subways didn't run there and cellphone reception was spotty, at best. I rode the F as close as possible, hopping off at the Carroll Street station and hailing a cab to bring me the rest of the way.

"Red Hook, please," I directed the driver, settling into the backseat and rattling off the cross street we'd tracked Santos to last night. "By the old waterfront."

The gray-haired cabbie glanced over his shoulder at me, his thick Brooklyn accent booming through the plastic and metal partition dividing our seats. "You sure, lady?"

"Yeah," I agreed, swallowing my nerves and pulling my hair up into a ponytail. "I'm sure."

He drove for about ten minutes, the streets outside my window growing emptier the closer we got to the waterfront. When I judged that we were about a block away from the pier, I asked the cabbie to pull over.

"Thanks," I said, handing him a few bills to cover the fare.

"You sure this is where you want me to drop you?" He accepted my money, shoving it into his pocket as he looked out his window and scratched at his graying beard. "Not the best neighborhood."

I nodded in agreement. The view outside my window was bleak.

It had begun to drizzle. The sky had darkened as a thick cloud cover rolled in overhead, casting the streets further into shadow and sending whatever pedestrians had been outside scurrying back indoors as fast as possible. The streetlights had yet to illuminate, as it was still relatively early, and the rain-slicked streets looked both desolate and uninviting. I had no desire to venture out in them alone. Still, I made myself smile at the concerned cabbie, forcing my tone to reflect a cheery disposition I didn't feel.

"I'll be alright. Thanks for the ride." I reached for the door handle.

"Wait, lady." The cabbie flipped open a compartment on his dashboard and grabbed a business card from inside. "Here, take my card. You need a ride back, you call me."

I accepted the card with a smile — genuine, this time — and stepped out of the cab. Once his taillights had disappeared around the nearest corner, I turned and walked a half block until I reached the waterfront. The old pier abutting the warehouses to my left stretched for at least a hundred yards; if I could find a safe enough path across the rotten wooden planks, maybe I could approach the warehouse Santos had disappeared into from the back side. With any luck, the metal door I'd seen last night was the primary entrance, and I wouldn't be spotted from this alternate vantage point.

And if I was... well, I was just a girl out for a walk in the rain. I'd play the dumb-blonde card and hope they bought it. The fact that I didn't exactly look like a super-sleuth would likely work in my favor.

My hair grew damp in the constant drizzle as I picked my way along the pier, the wood groaning beneath my sneakers with each tentative step I took. I stopped to pull up my hood, and looked out over the dull gray waters of the bay to the Statue of Liberty. This could've been a beautiful spot — a home to waterfront condos, or a historically preserved neighborhood filled with boutique shops and vendors. Instead, everything out here seemed leached of color — as though the cloud of factory smoke which had once poured from the chimneys and smokestacks of these warehouses had permanently stained the atmosphere, coloring it faintly gray even after a hundred years of inactivity.

I held my breath each time I decided to trust that the neglected pier would hold my weight, hoping I wouldn't plunge into the dirty, trash-strewn harbor waters below. Skirting my way along two boarded up warehouses, I came to a stop when the third came into view. That was it — the one Santos had vanished into last night. In the dim light, I squinted to make out the faded, peeling paint which had once proudly proclaimed the business name in bold hues and a scrawling font on the side of the building.

Rochester Brewery

The old beer factory's smokestack had caved in long ago, and I wondered about its structural integrity as I crept slowly closer. The three story building had stone-framed windows placed at regular intervals, their shattered panes boarded over on the street level — presumably to keep people out or, quite possibly, to shield whatever was inside from prying eyes like mine. There was a skinny alleyway running alongside the warehouse, piled high with wooden crates and pylons, overflowing garbage cans and years of amassed refuse. I held my nose as I edged around the corner into the mouth of the alley, blocking out the unmistakable stench of rotting trash and decomposing waste.

Closing my eyes, I focused my senses on the brewery yet heard nothing except the patter of light rain as it fell onto the asphalt and rippled into the bay. The sturdy brick walls were too thick to emit any sound from inside. I walked further into the narrow passage, my concentration honed so intently that I almost missed the abrupt scrape of metal against stone as a recessed door swung open behind me.

My heart in my throat, I darted even deeper into the alleyway and crouched behind a large stack of wooden pallets. Curling in on myself, I held both hands over the bright red BULLDOGS lettering on my black sweatshirt, praying I hadn't been spotted. I felt the cold water puddled beneath me seep into my sneakers and soak through my socks, and tried to ignore the torrent of dirty rainwater dripping off the roof onto my head.

Two men stepped through the doorway into the mouth of the alley, mere feet from where I'd just stood. Both were relatively young and stocky, with dark hair and thick, vaguely European accents. I watched as they took shelter beneath the small doorway overhang, lighting their cigarettes and puffing smoke into the damp air. Their voices were faint — I strained my ears to make out their words.

"Don't know why boss makes us smoke outside." The grumbled complaint came from the one whose nose looked like it had been broken four times too many and never properly reset, resulting in a crooked mess that divided what had at one point been a rather handsome face.

"Boss makes the rules. We don't question them." The second man, whose voice was so gravelly it rumbled like a freight train, looked like he'd never evolved past the Paleolithic Era, with his low-hanging brow and small, wide-spaced eyes. His hulking muscles only added to his Neanderthalish appearance; he made every club bouncer I'd ever seen look scrawny.

"Well, are we at least getting a new shipment in soon? We haven't had a new one for days," Smash-Nose whined.

The Neanderthal grunted in response, taking a drag on his cigarette.

"We're almost out of GHB, so Santos better come through soon." Smash-Nose chuckled under his breath. "Otherwise we'll have to find more... *creative*... methods of controlling the next arrivals."

My stomach turned and a wave of nausea washed over me. I clenched my shaking hands into fists and tried to slow my racing heartbeat, watching as the Neanderthal turned, grabbed the smaller man by his shirtfront, and abruptly shoved him backwards, pinning him against the brick wall with brute force.

"Man! What was that for?" Smash-Nose yelped in pain. "I didn't say nothin' to—"

"Don't talk about the shipments outside," the Neanderthal growled. "You know what Boss says."

"Who's gonna hear me?" Smash-Nose goaded. I was beginning to think he had a death wish, given the fact that he was still pinned against building. "We're practically inside."

The Neanderthal tossed his cigarette into a nearby puddle with one hand and used the other to shake Smash-Nose roughly. "Keep your mouth shut, or I'll shut it for you. Permanently." With those friendly parting words, he released his companion, yanked open the metal door, and disappeared back inside the warehouse.

"Fuck you," Smash-Nose sneered quietly, after the door had closed and the Neanderthal could no longer hear him. Grumbling under his breath, he took final puff of his cigarette, stubbed it out beneath the heel of his boot, and vanished inside. When I heard the soft boom of the metal door as it rejoined its frame, I let out the breath I'd been holding since the men came outside.

GHB.

Shipments.

Santos.

I remembered enough from the date-rape pamphlets I'd received on my college campus to know that GHB was a drug — specifically, one of the most popular "roofies" on the market for sexual predators. Colorless, odorless, and practically tasteless, it was perfect for slipping into an unwitting girl's drink at a party. I'd learned even more about it when I wrote a column last year about Manhattan's most desirable drugs, as I'd spent two full weeks researching different substances and their effects — I had little doubt I was on a DEA watch-list somewhere, thanks to my browsing history.

In small doses, GHB was practically harmless. Some called it

"Liquid X" because of its ecstasy-like qualities in lowering inhibitions and revving up one's libido. It relaxed you, slowing your heart and breathing rates, and supposedly making you more sociable. In large doses, however, GHB could be fatal, sending its users into such a deep state of unconscious they could simply slip into a coma and never wake. Its other side effects — dizziness, disorientation, and amnesia — only added to its allure as a date-rape drug.

It wasn't a huge mental leap to forge the connection between Santos' presence at the warehouse and the delivery of the drugs. After all, he worked Vice. As a part of the narcotics unit, he'd have plenty of access to confiscated drugs leftover from raids across the city or, at the very least, know how to track down dealers who could provide him with the supplies he needed. Whatever his motive — money, power, or pure malice — Santos was involved.

This was it — my smoking gun.

If they were moving large quantities of GHB in and out of that warehouse, there was really only one purpose — and Smash-Nose had practically spelled it out for me.

We'll have to find more... creative... methods of controlling the next arrivals.

They were drugging girls, I was certain of it now. Subduing them to be sold or traded or forced into sexual servitude.

Young, defenseless, kidnapped girls.

Girls like Vera.

I clutched my stomach with one hand and held my ponytail away from my face with the other as I succumbed to the nausea, vomiting up my lunch onto the pavement by my feet.

Chapter Twenty-Two

THEN

I brushed the tears from my eyes when Jamie began to stir awake.

"Hey," he croaked, cracking one eye open. I scooted my chair a little closer to his bedside and grabbed hold of his hand.

"Hi." I tried out a smile. "Good nap?"

Jamie stared at me carefully as he struggled to sit up in bed. I was instantly on my feet, my hands supporting his underarms and helping to lift him upright. Once he was settled against his pillows, I sat back in my chair and forced a cheery smile. He was looking back at me with sadness in his eyes, even as a small grin touched his lips.

"You know, don't you?" he whispered.

He could read me so well. My eyes filled with tears. "Why didn't you tell me?"

Jamie scoffed. "Maybe because I didn't want you to look at me with the exact expression you've got on your face right now?"

"Jamie—"

"And maybe because things are finally *good* for you. You've got someone who loves you — which, let's face it, is a miracle in itself. You're applying to college. You're happy. I won't apologize for not wanting to ruin that."

"James Arthur—"

"And also maybe a little bit because if I told you, it would be real." Jamie's voice broke on the last word, but his smile didn't waver. "I really didn't want it to be real, this time."

My tears spilled over and I clutched his hand tighter. "How long have you known?"

"A few weeks."

I pressed my eyes closed. With a cancer as aggressive as Jamie's, weeks could make a world of difference. I always tried my best to watch for changes, to be on guard for signs that it had returned, but Jamie was rarely honest about his pain levels — ever one to put on a brave face or to "handle things like a man," as he was fond of saying. But for the last week or so, he'd been sleeping more and more. Avoiding my eyes when I asked if he was experiencing any symptoms. Snapping at me to mind my own business which, frankly, was just not like the brother I knew and loved.

Did he torment me? Sure, frequently.

But *yell* at me? That was something he never did.

After spending almost six months at the hospital and then in the rehabilitation center, he'd finally recovered enough to come home in late June. And for nearly five, blissful months, I'd had my Jamie back. In the summer, Bash would pick us up and we'd strap Jamie's wheelchair to the bed of his truck, as had become our custom. Hot days were spent by the lakefront, rainy ones at the local movie theater. We laughed often, joking with the ease of old friends — often at my expense, of course, but I couldn't complain when I saw Jamie grinning — and enjoying the freedom that only youth affords.

It was a picture-perfect summer. I was young and carefree, utterly wrapped up in a boy who'd flipped my world on its head.

And for a while I let myself believe that Jamie had been cured for good this time, and that things might stay this way forever.

But inevitably, the days grew shorter and the temperatures began to drop off with the arrival of fall. Our summer days slipped away, Sebastian and I returned to school for our senior year, and, once again, Jamie found himself alone all day, which he complained wasn't much better than being in the hospital. He'd opted not to return to Jackson High. Having missed so much school, he'd essentially have to retake all his junior year classes to catch up. Rather than be left behind as his friends entered our final year, he instead chose to work from home and complete his GED.

Each day, I'd spend time with Jamie before my shift at Minnie's. Sometimes, if he didn't have football practice, Sebastian would come with me and the three of us would do homework together, cramped over the tiny, wobbly kitchen table. And if Bash minded the less than elegant quarters, he never said as much to me. I think he was just happy to be out of his mansion, away from his parents for a while.

But now, the cancer was back. I'd called Jamie's doctor earlier this morning to confirm it. Over a week had passed since his monthly check-up scans and it was unusual for results to take more than a few days, at most. Knowing Jamie, he'd intercepted the phone call in hopes that I wouldn't find out.

"We'll be fine, Jamie." I stood and climbed onto the bed next to him, forcing him to scoot over to accommodate me. "We'll beat it back again, just like last time."

"I know, sis." He sighed. "I'm just getting tired of fighting."

We fell silent for a moment, lying shoulder-to-shoulder on his thin mattress — staring up at the ceiling, each lost in our own thoughts.

"They're going to take my leg this time," Jamie whispered. His tone wasn't mournful or bitter. It wasn't a complaint or a grievance. It was a simple acceptance of fact: he'd be an amputee at seventeen.

"You don't know that." My whispered assurance was more

wishful thinking than actual truth. We both knew it was almost certain that he'd lose his leg with the next operation — it was the doctors' only remaining recourse, after the bone grafts and salvage surgeries had failed.

"Did you tell him yet?"

I knew he was asking about Bash. "I wanted to talk to you first."

Jamie nodded. "Do you think he'll still want to throw a football around with the crippled kid?"

I tried my best to hold in the tears, forcing a laugh and jabbing Jamie in the side with my elbow. "Well, he dates *me*, so I think his standards are pretty low."

Jamie snorted in laughter. "That's true," he noted, wrapping an arm around my shoulders.

I felt a small smile break out across my face. No matter how bad things got, making fun of myself was always a surefire way to cheer Jamie up.

⚜

"I HAVE TO GO"

"No you don't."

"I really, really do."

"Nah," Sebastian breathed against my collarbone. "I think you can stay a little while longer."

His mouth trailed wet kisses up my neck as his hand worked its way beneath the skirt of my work uniform. I pressed back against the smooth leather of the passenger seat, cursing the confined space that was his Mercedes. I had no easy escape from his persistent, wandering hands and, while that was normally not a problem for me, right now I had to get home and finish a mountain of homework before school tomorrow.

Plus, I wasn't in the best mood. He'd picked me up from the diner after my shift and driven us out to one of our favorite spots by the lake. In the summer, it was a hive of activity for daytime swimmers and late-night barbecuers alike, but the arrival of autumn left it still and quiet. With the moon casting a perfect reflection on the mirror-still water, it was perfect place to be alone to talk — or *not* talk — depending on the mood.

Tonight had been a lot of conversation and very little physical interaction. As was the norm lately, our discussion had drifted to the coming end of senior year and college applications. Bash had applied to every Ivy League school, of course, and his father had his sights set on Princeton, where his son could carry on the family legacy. My parents didn't even know I was applying to state school and, if they had, they'd likely have discouraged it.

Suffice to say, it wasn't my favorite topic.

"I applied to another school today," Bash told me, tracing one of his fingers across my upturned palm.

"Mmm," I murmured noncommittally, not really caring which pretentious school was undoubtedly preening over his application at this very moment. I didn't want to talk about the fact that in a year's time he'd be thousands of miles across the country, in California or the northeast, while I'd still be in Jackson. Or, if by some slim chance I managed to snag a full academic scholarship to UGA, in Athens. The most likely scenario would find him returning home for his first winter break with a new collegiate, senator-approved girlfriend in tow, while I worked sixty hour weeks at *Minnie's* in order to make ends meet.

"No interest in which school, huh?" he asked, calling out my indifference.

"I'm sorry, I'm being terrible." I sighed, turning to face him with an apologetic look. "I'm probably the most unsupportive girlfriend of all time. Tell me, please."

"I don't know, maybe I shouldn't tell you now," he teased, one side of his mouth lifting in a half grin.

I looked at him with pleading, puppy-dog eyes until he caved.

"Fine, fine, I'll tell you." Bash grinned fully at me. "Go Bulldogs!"

I froze, stunned. "You applied to UGA?"

He nodded, a self-satisfied smirk crossing his face. "Well, it wouldn't be showing much state pride if I didn't at least apply."

"Does your dad know?"

Sebastian's grin faded slightly and he shook his head. "No. But I'm the one who has to spend four years getting a degree I don't want in political science — I figure I should at least get to pick which school I receive the damn thing from."

"You did this for me," I whispered, grinning at him. I couldn't believe it.

"I don't know what you're talking about." He shrugged casually. "I happen to have a vested interest in the UGA football team. I have absolutely no opinion whatsoever about whether the girl I love happens to be attending that same school next fall."

My world stopped as his words registered. *The girl I love.*

He'd said it, right? Out loud and intentionally? I hadn't hallucinated or experienced severe brain trauma or fallen across some kind of dimensional shift into a world where our deepest desires were fulfilled?

My mouth was gaping like a fish and my thoughts were a tangle of elated disbelief as I tried desperately to formulate a reply — *the* reply. Because there was really only one thing to say.

But Sebastian didn't give me a chance to say it.

Abruptly, his hands circled my waist and he hoisted me over the center console so I was sprawled across his lap. I squealed in protest but it did nothing to deter his movements, and I quickly ended up with my back resting against the steering wheel, my knees straddling Bash's thighs, and my arms draped loosely around his neck.

"That's better." He grinned, leaning forward to kiss the freckles on my nose. When his hands began to drift down from their hold at the small of my back to pull me against him, a soft groan slipped from between my lips.

"You're evil," I muttered, as his hands pushed my uniform skirt higher up my thighs so it bunched around my waist. His fingers toyed with the thin straps of my underwear as his mouth captured mine in a brief kiss.

"Are you sure you want me to drop you off? I have serious doubts that your Latin homework will be as..." His teeth scraped lightly against my earlobe as he shifted closer to whisper. "...interesting... as what we can come up with in the next thirty minutes."

"I suppose Ms. Ingraham can wait a while," I whispered into his collarbone, grinning. My hands locked around his neck tighter and I pressed myself flush against him, feeling a wave of desire crash through my system as his hands skimmed my back through the cotton *Minnie's* t-shirt. All thoughts of verb conjugations and worksheets fled as I pressed our lips together hungrily, my body moving against his in a slow, rhythmic grind. His tongue brushed against mine, my fingers traced his arousal through his jeans, and the point of turning back was quickly lost.

"I need you," I whispered, not caring that I sounded like some cheesy romance-novel stereotype. Because, in that moment, it was the truest thing I'd ever felt — my life was falling to pieces around me, and only Bash could make it whole again. I needed to be full, complete, reassured that this life wasn't all misery and misfortune. That love and joy still existed, and were strong enough to outweigh the sorrow or, at the very least, balance it out.

My hands tore at the buttons of his shirt and I was suddenly, achingly, desperate to feel his skin against mine. His fingers fiddled with his zipper then came up to roughly rip my panties aside, their thin straps no match for his urgency. With one swift motion, they were torn away. Sebastian's hands wrapped around my waist, lifting my entire body slightly into the air. His gaze burned into mine as he brought me back down, ramming himself inside me with one fierce, fantastic stroke.

I cried out as he filled me, my hands bracing against his shoulders as I began to ride him. His jaw was clenched, his gaze saturated with heat as he fought to remain in control. Palming my breasts in his hands, he watched me move against him through slivered eyes. My head fell back as I began to unravel, the dizzying passion sinking my eyelids down to half-mast. The car ceiling over my head grew slightly unfocused, blurred as though I'd been slinging back shots of vodka all night.

I felt drunk — on love, on lust. Utterly inebriated by this ludicrous feeling of distorted perfection that was setting off fireworks within my body. Was this insatiable need to be joined as one — not only physically, but emotionally — a mere symptom of infatuation, of teenage lust? Or was it love, this fire burning in my veins, spinning me out of control until I felt so off balance I knew I'd never again be able to stand on my own?

"Look at me," Sebastian gritted out between clenched teeth. I pulled my eyes from the ceiling and tilted my head back down to meet his gaze. "Do you feel that? Do you feel us, Lux?"

And I did — it was there in the air around us. A chemical reaction, an altered state of being, that occurs when two separate elements collide and change on a fundamental level — fusing together into a new, wholly unique compound. Their joining triggering the creation of entirely new matter: love in its most essential form.

"I feel it." I gasped.

"This is real. We're real." His thrusts intensified to match the strength of his words.

I nodded, feeling my limbs begin to go languorous as pleasure overtook me completely. I rocked myself up and down against his length, his long strokes growing faster as we spiraled together toward delirium.

"You're my girl. I'm not going to let anything happen to us. That's a promise."

I leaned forward and brushed my lips against his, feeling my heart flip over in my chest. I knew this feeling wasn't the product of two new lovers exploring the wonders of a good fuck. This was stronger, more passionate — this was what all the songs and sonnets ever written had been about.

This was making love — literally constructing it from the union of our hearts and bodies.

"I love you," I whispered against his lips, unable to contain the words a moment longer. His eyes widened fractionally and he clutched me tighter against him, as though he were afraid I'd somehow vanish from his arms, taking those three little words with me as I went.

"I love you more." His fervent words were a binding promise.

Afterward, I lay draped across his chest, utterly spent. My forehead rested in the crook of his neck, my breaths labored and uneven as I thought about this wonderful boy, who'd seen past my rough exterior to the girl beneath. He'd taken a chance on me. It was time to take a chance on him, to trust him, as well.

"I have to tell you something." My words were a shaky whisper, as I tilted my head back to meet his gaze. I watched as his eyes cleared of the cloudy, thoroughly-sated look, turning serious between one blink and the next.

"Anything." His fingertip traced my cheekbone in a light caress. I listened to the light rain falling against the metal roof, remembering our first moments together in this very car, and steeled myself with a deep breath.

"It's Jamie."

I felt Sebastian's body tense beneath mine, going completely still in preparation for the words he sensed were coming but could never have prepared for.

"He's sick," I whispered flatly. "The cancer's back."

There was a moment of total silence as he absorbed the news.

"He—" Sebastian's voice cracked. Clearing his throat, he tried again. "He'll be fine, though. He'll get through it again."

I nodded, my eyes filling with tears. "I keep telling myself that. It's just..."

"Hard." Bash finished for me, swallowing roughly. "I know. But we'll get through it. Together."

"Together," I echoed softly.

"You don't have to do this alone anymore, Freckles." He leaned forward to press a soft kiss to my forehead. "I'm here. And everything will be alright."

"*Aut viam inveniam aut faciam*," I breathed, so quietly barely a whisper left my lips.

"We'll find a way, Lux. We'll always find our way."

⚜

THE EMPTY VODKA BOTTLE RATTLED ACROSS THE FLOOR, crashing to a noisy stop against the refrigerator. Flipping on the light with one hand, I clutched my stubbed toe in the other and attempted to massage some feeling back. I took in the state of the kitchen, cursing under my breath. My parents' most recent party favors littered the floor like confetti. Vodka, gin, scotch — they weren't particularly particular when it came to their alcohol. As long as it burned going down and deadened their pain for the night, that seemed to be enough of a selling point. Usually, though, they took their festivities to the local bar. That they were here meant tonight must've called for a special level of inebriation — the kind that even the shadiest of local watering holes frowned upon, because it too often led to drunken misconduct and bar fights.

It was late by the time Sebastian dropped me off, almost midnight. I closed my eyes and prayed they'd already passed out.

"Lux!" The slurred voice came from the small den off the kitchen. The room was dark except for the flickering, intermittent light cast on the walls by the muted television, as scenes from late-night infomercials flashed across the screen. My shoulders slumped defeatedly as I exhaled, picking my way through the discarded bottles toward the doorway.

"Mom."

Her stringy blonde hair hung over her face, unwashed and unkempt. She'd been beautiful once, my mother. A fading pageant queen, with crowns and tiaras from every county fair and homecoming festival around. With Marilyn Monroe curves and a Grace Kelly smile, she could've gone to Hollywood and made it as an actress, as she'd dreamed of doing as a teenager.

Those dreams had died the day she went into the girl's locker room after gym class one day toward the end of her senior year, peed on a little white stick, and watched as it turned blue. And that woman she'd been back then had died too — not at first, but over time. A gradual withering away, like a penknife scraping against the bark of a mighty tree. Her curves had disappeared, unsustainable on a diet of liquid alone, and the lines appearing on her face each day were not from laughter, but stress and sorrow. As a little girl, I'd sometimes catch her staring at herself in the mirror, tracing the weathered skin as though it belonged to a stranger, as slow tears dripped down her face and fell onto her tattered blouse.

Her drinking had increased with age, spurred in part, perhaps, by my father's addictions. She couldn't care for Jamie and me — she could barely care for herself — but I couldn't bring myself to hate her. How could you hate someone who'd had her heart broken by life? Who'd been beaten down by her fate and never found the strength within herself to rise again?

No, I didn't hate her. I simply didn't understand her.

"Where you been? 'S late." She was slumped over in her chair on the far side of the room. My father was nowhere to be seen — assumedly, he'd already fallen into a liquor-induced stupor in bed. I thanked my stars for that.

"Out," I told her, still hovering near the doorway. I tried to stay as far from her as possible when she got this way. Not because she was a mean or abusive drunk — quite the opposite, actually — but because I couldn't bear to see the wasted potential that her life had boiled down to. Talent, ambition, beauty, charisma — all of it squandered in the bottom of a bottle of gin. A ghost of the woman, the mother, she might've been.

"Don' get sassy with me, girlie," she slurred, gesturing at me with a near-empty tumbler. She nearly toppled over with the effort, the glass falling from her hand and rolling under the coffee table. I sighed. I'd be spending my pre-dawn hours cleaning the house before school tomorrow.

"Let's get you to bed, Mom." Judging that she'd never make it by herself in this condition, I walked over to her and placed one hand on her arm. "Come on."

She turned to me, her eyes clearing of the haze for a moment as she examined my face. "You're a good girl, Luxie."

"Okay, Mom, come on," I said, rapidly blinking away the film of tears that had appeared in my eyes. "Time for bed."

"Dunno what we'd do without you 'round here," she continued, refusing to budge from her chair despite my tugging.

I rolled my eyes. "Quite the party you had here tonight."

"It's a goin' away party." She giggled.

"What?" I dropped my hands, staring at her intently. "Mom! What did you just say?"

"I *said*," she whisper-yelled between fits of laughter. "It's a goin' away party."

"For who?" I asked, my heart beginning to race.

As quickly as her levity had arrived, it vanished, replaced by a forlorn look and hunched shoulders. "For us, for the house. Bank called. Can't pay the bills. Gotta move."

The blood began to pound in my ears. "When?"

She shook her head back and forth in slow denial.

"Mom!" I snapped my fingers in front of her eyes, trying to focus her attention. "*When* do we have to move?"

"End of next month," she mumbled, her eyes drifting closed again. "Where's my drink?"

I stood stock-still, contemplating her words and feeling my heart sink down to my stomach. If it were true, if the house was in foreclosure, there was no way we'd be able to pay for the best care for Jamie. And without the best care, he might not make it at all.

I stood for a long time in the flickering darkness, looking down at my mother passed out cold in her chair. I could see nothing but an unscalable mountain before me, with no visible footholds or convenient paths up the massive peak. It was the most treacherous of cliffs, ascending in a straight sheet of rock and ice, up into the clouds and far out of sight.

Even attempting a climb would be futile — a hopeless endeavor.

But then, from a tiny corner in the back of my mind, a single image forced its way to the forefront of my thoughts.

Hannibal.

I saw him looking up at that selfsame crag and telling the wisest, most trusted of his generals to fuck off, before making his way resolutely over the Alps. Despite everyone's doubts, regardless of their predictions of certain death... he'd found a way. He'd *forged* a way.

And, for Jamie, so would I.

Chapter Twenty-Three

NOW

It was hard to get out of bed the next morning. In all honesty, I contemplated calling out sick, but ruled against it when I realized it was Friday — not to mention the fact that my boss was also my ex-boyfriend who, coincidentally, hated me and would most certainly notice if I didn't show up.

I'd been up all night, ensconced in a bundle of indecision about the things I'd learned in Red Hook. Half of me was impulsive, craving action and immediate results. That half wanted to call the police, the FBI, the mayor, and the freaking President, just so I could tell someone what I suspected was happening on a forgotten dock in a dark corner of my city. But my other half, the half that had studied journalism for four years, urged caution, warning me that I might not know the full story just yet. Not only did I lack any physical proof, if I went forward with this information too soon I could end up warning Santos and his friends of an impending raid before it happened. The people operating out of the old brewery obviously had police connections — just how high those connections went was yet unclear. Until I knew for sure, I'd have to proceed with the assumption that Santos might not be the only officer involved.

The way I saw it, I had one shot. One chance to involve the authorities and bring this organization down for good. Because if I misfired — if I cried wolf and called in the cavalry at the wrong moment — I could miss my chance forever and end up jeopardizing everything I was trying to accomplish, as well as the lives of Vera and the other missing girls.

Without law enforcement at my back, there was really only one recourse — an exposé. A story in every newspaper, at every breakfast table across the country that would stop people in their tracks as they sipped their morning coffee or prepared for their commute to work. A tale so awful, so unforgettable, that people couldn't stand by impassively anymore, swaddled in their safety blankets of denial, convinced that bad things only happen in third world countries.

I had to write something to make sure that Vera was the last girl that disappeared. It was my obligation as a journalist, but also as a basic human being. So as much as I wanted to storm that warehouse, guns blazing, with a hundred armed SWAT team members by my side, I had to do this the right way, with irrefutable evidence that would not only bring the ringleaders down, but ensure they stayed down for good.

I took a deep breath and tried to assure myself that I could do this.

I'd keep my personal feelings at bay. I'd be methodical, calculated, and smart. After all, I was a reporter — this was what I'd been trained for, even if I had been out of practice for the past few years, writing about booty-blasting workouts and natural facial exfoliant alternatives.

So, after tossing and turning for several hours, around midnight I'd given up on sleep and struck an internal compromise to reconcile my own indecision. Research, writing, surveillance — those would be my outlets for action, while I bided my time for concrete evidence. With my computer propped in my lap I typed for hours like a woman possessed, the words pouring from my fingertips in a flood, filling the blank word document on my screen. I typed everything I could remember from my conversations with Miri and my trips to Brooklyn, creating a timeline of events and detailing what little I knew about the brewery operation.

There was Santos, who supplied drugs and perhaps played a part in scoping out vulnerable girls using his NYPD connections. Then there were Smash-Nose and the Neanderthal, lackeys who apparently provided pure muscle and handled new "shipment" arrivals. And, lastly, there was the mysterious "Boss" they'd mentioned more than once during their discussion. Other than those few small details, though, my picture remained vastly incomplete. I needed to figure out exactly how many players were involved, and I knew there was only one way to do that.

I had to go back.

I had to somehow find a way inside that warehouse without detection and get a good look around, taking photographs and gathering proof as I went. The plan sounded simple enough on paper. Somehow, though, I had a sinking feeling that no matter how many episodes of *Veronica Mars* I watched, I'd never possess the P.I. skills necessary to succeed at such a stunt.

But I'd cross that bridge when I came to it.

I used up an entire ink cartridge, printing out pages of documents related to sex trafficking in America. Statistics, figures, common trends — anything I thought might be useful. Then I printed out my notes, along with photos of The Point and any images I could find online of the pier and the old Rochester Brewery. I even found some photographs of the brewery interior that a local historical society had scanned and uploaded to their website.

Finally, using nearly ten pieces of paper, I printed out a massive street map of the city and used clear tape to adhere the puzzle back together into one cohesive chart. I laid the map alongside everything else I'd printed on the floor next to my bed, my head pounding with stress as I stared down at the collection. The sheer amount of information before me was overwhelming, and as I looked at the images, the small nervous pit in my stomach expanded to become a cavernous crater of anxiety.

There were too many sheets jumbled together to make any kind of sense or begin to think things through logically; I needed a way to see everything at once and to track my progress through the city. Grabbing the large chart by an edge, I walked over to the small kitchen table that doubled as my desk area and grabbed an unopened container of thumbtacks.

I paused in the middle of my studio and deliberated for a full minute, contemplating whether I was standing on the threshold of whatever normal boundaries exist between a reporter and her story. Turning my apartment wall into a pin-board of notes and theories didn't feel exceptionally detached. Was I about to cross the line of demarcation between overly-obsessive, verge-of-insanity involvement and normal, professional interest?

Staring at the blank wall adjacent to my kitchen, I shrugged my shoulders, thought of Vera, and told that line to go straight to hell. I wasn't just any journalist, and this wasn't just any story. It wouldn't do me — or Vera — any good to pretend I didn't have an emotional stake in this.

I crossed the room, positioned my map with one hand, and jabbed a pin into its corner with the other. Within minutes, I'd used most of my thumb tacks and my studio wall had been trans-formed into a virtual storyboard, much like those used at *Luster* when planning out an issue but, instead, full of macabre images and figures. Thankfully, when I'd moved in last year I'd run out of money before spending a big budget on wall decorations — but who needed Crate and Barrel when you had a creepy, DIY serial-killer-esque shrine of photos and clippings to color your walls?

I studied my work with a mixed sense of accomplishment and concern. It felt good to do something with my hands, to make a small amount of progress, even if it was only the illusion of produc-tivity. The map spanned a good chunk of the wall, framed on either side by charts, images, and notes. A portrait of Vera and me that Fae had snapped on my camera phone one day last summer hung on the left, the picture of Santos I'd found online was pinned on the right. Miri's handwritten letter was tacked up at eye level, and I'd marked distinct locations — the tenement in Two Bridges, the coffee shop in East Village where I'd met Miri, the precinct where Santos worked, the brewery on The Point — with red pins, so I could keep track of all the different locations I'd visited since this misadventure began.

A resigned sigh slipped from my lips. Creating a conspiracy-theory mosaic — à la Carrie in *Homeland* — was typically an indicator that someone was about to plunge straight off the deep end into Crazytown. If Simon and Fae saw this, they'd have me committed to a mental facility immediately, no questions asked.

Fae had been right that day in Two Bridges, when she'd said I'd stumbled down the rabbit hole.

Naive blonde girl wandering a strange, unfamiliar landscape? Check.

Enemies lurking around every corner, waiting gleefully for a chance to chop off my head?

Double check.

৩✻৩

I SHOULD'VE KNOWN THE DAY WAS GOING TO BE A TRAIN WRECK when I spilled coffee down the front of my favorite little black dress and got whacked in the head by four separate umbrella-wielding madmen on the way to work.

Rain in New York is always an experience. Never in your life can you be nearly bludgeoned to death by the overwhelming volume of commuters' umbrellas competing for airspace overhead, except on a rainy day during rush hour in the city. As if the overflowing sewer drains and traffic jams didn't cause problems enough, whenever the slightest drizzle fell from the sky, New Yorkers would have their umbrellas out in spades, poking each other in the eyes and pushing one another off the sidewalks rather than risk a single raindrop wetting their hair.

I'd have to check the city records to verify it, but I wouldn't be surprised if there were far more casualties on rainy days than sun-drenched ones. I'd nearly died just this morning, when an overzealous power-walker elbowed me off the street into the path on an oncoming taxi. I'd escaped with my life, but my black and white Miu Miu pumps hadn't been so lucky — the puddle I'd landed in was deep and spilling over with grime, leaving stains no amount of suede-cleaner would ever lift.

Work itself hadn't been so bad, I guess. Sebastian wasn't there to torment me from afar and Angela had finally assigned me a project in my wheelhouse, writing a period piece that would be sandwiched between the 1920s and 1930s photo spreads in the Centennial issue. I spent my day settled at one of the work stations in a quiet corner, researching the years leading up to the Great Depression and immersing myself in a world that was, surprisingly, not all flapper dresses and finger curls. It was hard to tear myself away to break for lunch — I'd become enthralled by all the fashion and flagrancies that made the Jazz Age so deliciously immoral — but when the two Jennys invited me to grab salads with them, I couldn't say no. We ended up at a small cafe just around the block, where the lines weren't too long and the food was inexpensive but remarkably good.

"This project is so much fun," Jenny S. squealed, pouring some vinaigrette over the bed of lettuce on her plate. "Way better than some of the other spreads we've been working on lately. Remember the sex position shoot we had to do last month, Jen? With the chocolate sauce we had to smear all over that model's ti—"

"Please!" Jenny P. interjected forcefully. "*Don't* remind me." She grimaced before stuffing a forkful of salad into her mouth.

I laughed, easily envisioning the horror. Practically every month *Luster* featured a photo spread of scandalous poses inspired by the Kama Sutra, typically accompanied by a user guide of helpful tips and tricks to spice up our readers' sex lives. Despite all my complaining, at least I could say my column rarely strayed in that direction.

"Seriously, though, we are so totally lucky to be working on this," Jenny S. gushed. "And with Sebastian Covington of all people. I mean, the man is like the hottest thing in photography right now."

"Not to mention the hottest thing in a five hundred mile radius," Jenny P. chimed in.

When I remained silent, they both turned to stare at me expectantly. I felt my cheeks heat.

"Yeah, he's hot I guess," I mumbled, dropping my eyes to my plate. "Why is it so delicious when they put strawberries on top of salad? I mean, you'd think fruit and lettuce would be a totally gross combo, right? And yet—" I stuffed a large bite into my mouth. "—delicious."

My oh-so-subtle attempts to drive the conversation elsewhere were ignored. *Sigh*.

"Ohmigod!" Jenny P. had a terrifyingly astute gleam in her eye. "You totally like him!"

I shook my head in denial. "That's ridiculous," I snorted.

"Oh, girl, you've got it bad." Jenny S. nodded her head in sympathy.

"He's dating a model!" I deflected. "I'd never be attracted to someone who was into girls like Cara." I crossed my fingers under the table as the white lie slipped out.

Both Jennys gaped at me.

"What?" I asked, wondering if there was a lettuce leaf stuck between my front teeth.

"Sebastian isn't dating Cara," Jenny P. said.

"He's not?"

"Of course not." Jenny S. laughed. "Maybe they're together in Cara's deluded dreams. But definitely not in reality."

"Cara follows him around like a puppy after her master, and he lets her because it's the only way to get her to pose for photos."

Jenny P. explained. "She's not the most cooperative model in the industry, or so I've heard."

"No kidding." I laughed, thinking of my trips to Starbucks and Whole Foods.

"Apparently Sebastian took this job as a personal favor to Mr. Harding. He wouldn't do anything to jeopardize it. Plus, he's a total professional. I really doubt he'd ever get involved with someone he works with." Jenny P. smiled at me reassuringly. "But, girl, you've totally got a shot. You're hot."

"Plus, I've seen him watching you a few times," Jenny S. murmured, her gaze distant with thoughts. "With this sad, almost-longing look."

"That's crazy." I dismissed her words in a flat tone, though my heart was racing inside my chest. "Have you been huffing too much glue over there in set design?"

Jenny S. responded as any mature adult would — she stuck out her tongue in my direction.

Jenny P. clapped her hands three times, a sunny smile crossing her face. "This totally calls for some matchmaking, don't you think, Jen?"

"Please, don't do anything," I begged them, watching in horror as they locked eyes and grinned at one other.

"Ooookay," Jenny S. drawled. "We promise."

Jenny P. winked at me. "Yep, pinky swear."

"Shit," I muttered. They laughed in unison.

I was so screwed.

❦

AFTER LUNCH, I BECAME SO WRAPPED UP IN WRITING AND researching my 1920s story that I stopped worrying about the Jennys and their undoubtedly devious plans to force Sebastian and me into some kind of staged interaction. So at a quarter to five, when Jenny S. approached my work station with a stack of files in her arms and said that Angela wanted me to bring them down to the billing offices on the fourth floor before I went home for the night, I thought nothing of it.

"Thanks, Lux!" Jenny S. called, bouncing away with a pleased look on her face. I chalked it up to the fact that it was nearly happy hour and went back to my story.

That was my first mistake.

My second mistake was waiting until after five to complete her task. I figured I'd simply stop at billing on my way down to the lobby, rather than make two trips but, as usual, I lost track of time, so it was closer to five thirty when I actually made it into the elevator with the stack of files in hand. The building had already begun to empty out, as most people had a tendency to race for the exits as soon as possible, especially on a Friday. So, when I stepped out of the elevator onto the fourth floor, I found the billing offices completely deserted.

"Hello?" I called, looking for signs of life. The only sound I heard was the dull clicking of my heels against the smooth marble floors as I crossed to an empty secretary's desk. From the looks of it, everyone had already gone home for the weekend.

"Anyone here?" I walked further into the office, thinking perhaps someone in the back was still lingering to finish up paper-work or a final report. When no one answered, I reached into my purse with my free hand and began rooting around for my cell-phone. I'd have to call Jenny S. and ask where to leave the files. Hopefully they weren't time sensitive.

"Ms. Kincaid."

The unexpected sound of a man's voice breaking the quiet of the office startled me and my phone slipped from my grasp, landing hard against the shiny floor and rattling to a stop beneath a nearby desk. My hand flew up to clutch my chest while my head whipped around to get a look at the man who'd just appeared from the back office.

I was going to murder the Jennys. Preferably with some kind of slow, painfully archaic torture device that gave them an eternity to reflect on their poor matchmaking decisions before they finally succumbed to the darkness.

"Hi," I blurted, staring at him. He looked wonderful, even dressed casually in dark jeans and a fitted henley. A little more informal than usual, perhaps, but it suited him. He'd never been one for suits or ties. I had to curl my hands into fists to keep them from smoothing out the wrinkles on my dress or fidgeting with the tendrils of hair that had escaped my clip.

Sebastian cleared his throat and my eyes flew back to his face. I was sure my cheeks were on fire — inappropriately checking out your boss' chest muscles was a definite no-no, especially when he was the ex-boyfriend you were supposed to hate.

"Files," I said dumbly, gesturing toward the stack still clutched in my right hand.

Sebastian's brows rose but otherwise he didn't move, standing with his hands stuffed into his jean pockets in a relaxed fashion.

"These are, um..." I swallowed, trying to clear the nervous lump that was lodged in my throat. "They're, um... files... Obviously."

I knew I was rambling and not making any sense whatsoever. But he was looking at me and still not saying anything and, well, I couldn't concentrate worth a damn. He left me totally unbalanced, reeling like a wind vane in a storm. I gulped again, worried my airway might seal permanently if I didn't take a breath soon.

"I was supposed to drop these, um..." I trailed off like the babbling, incoherent idiot I'd evidently become, at an utter loss for words. "Um..."

"Files," Sebastian supplied, a ghost of a smile crossing his lips.

"Right, of course, they're files," I agreed, cringing internally. I wanted nothing more than to curl up in a ball of embarrassment and die rather than continue this conversation. "I was supposed to drop them off here tonight. So, um..."

Grimacing at my total lack of social grace, I edged backwards slightly so I was next to the secretary's desk, and piled the files in her wire inbox basket. With a fleeting glance back at Sebastian, I bobbed my head and turned to go. "Okay... have a good weekend, then, Bas—Seb—" I cleared my throat, blushing furiously. "I mean, Mr. Covington."

Fuck, shit, damn. Could I *be* anymore awkward if I tried?

I made it about three steps toward the elevator before Sebastian finally spoke again.

"Ms. Kincaid," he called softly.

So close, I thought, staring longingly at the elevator doors. I sighed and turned to face him. He was standing a bit closer now, and in one hand he held my battered phone.

"Oh!" I exclaimed, slapping my forehead with one palm. "Completely forgot about that."

I approached him, trying to walk with confidence even though I was shaking like a leaf. His silence was terrifying, but the possibility of what he might say when he finally broke it was infinitely more so. My fingers trembled visibly as I reached out into the air between us, and he watched their progress with the intense gaze of a predator stalking his prey.

Our hands brushed as I removed the phone from his palm and, in what was quite possibly a figment of my overactive imagination, I swear I felt a jolt of electricity shoot up my arm straight to my heart. Yanking my hand backwards, I lifted my gaze to meet his.

"Thanks," I whispered.

"You're welcome," he whispered back.

I spun to go, but found my progress halted by a firm grip on my arm. A glance down confirmed it — Sebastian's hand was wrapped around my bicep in a gentle but insistent hold. I lifted confused eyes to meet his, which had softened to show a hint of remorse. There was no time to dwell on the fact that he was less than a foot away, that he was *touching* me, because he opened his mouth and said two little words that short circuited my entire thought process.

"I'm sorry."

I blinked at him, stunned. "What?"

"For the other night, for the way I've treated you all week... I'm sorry."

I barely kept my jaw from falling open. He released his hold on my arm and sighed deeply, running a hand through his hair and mussing it in an instant.

"I thought — well, it doesn't really matter what I thought. The bottom line is, I brought you here for the wrong reasons. And I've been punishing you for something I should've gotten over a long time ago. We were kids, we didn't know anything back then. It's not fair to blame you. I mean, after all, what we had?" He laughed lightly, though his eyes were deadly serious. "That wasn't even real."

He stared at me, watching as his words hit home. I tried my best to mask my expression, to conceal the pain his statement caused me, but I could only withstand so much before my facade splintered.

Because it had been real. It was *still* real — the realest thing I'd ever felt.

"Right?" he asked, his voice low and his eyes searching mine.

"Right," I agreed in a small voice, forcing myself to nod.

Something flickered briefly in the depths of his eyes, but disappeared too quickly for me to identify it.

"I'm tired of tiptoeing around one another at work. I'm sure you are too. And from everything I've seen, you're an asset to this project. So from now on, I'll play nice. I promise." He held out a hand for me to shake. "Sound good?"

I subtly pinched the fleshy part of my hand to ensure that I was, in fact, awake and not lost in some strange dream-fugue state. Was he really giving me a clean slate? Letting me off the hook after everything I'd done to him? It seemed too good to be true. But if he had an ulterior motive of some kind, for the life of me, I couldn't figure out what it might be.

With my eyes fixed on his face, I slipped my hand into his and tried not to show how much the simple act of our palms meeting affected me. Outside, I was professional, shaking his hand with the perfunctory composure of any colleague. But inside, I felt that small touch radiate up my arm and out through every corner of my body. His touch filled me, made me feel truly alive, as though my most vital atoms and particles had lain dormant and were only now rousing after a seven year hibernation, stirred awake by the siren song of Sebastian's touch.

It took all the strength within me not to let my eyes drift closed at the sensation, not to lean into his touch like it was the only source of oxygen in an airless room. Instead, I forced my fingers to unclasp and my palm to drop, falling like dead weight to my side. His eyes still trapped mine, searing into me with their intensity, but I managed to simply nod. I took a step backward, so there was a bit more space between us.

"Thank you," I said, accepting his apology as though he were any other coworker who'd eaten my yogurt out of the communal fridge in the break room, or "borrowed" my favorite pen from my desk drawer and never returned it. I shifted my weight from one heel to the other, wholly uncertain about what to do next.

"We might never be friends again," Sebastian acknowledged. "But there's no reason to be at war. Plus, I can't imagine Jamie was pleased to hear that we're acting like enemies."

I stilled. The air caught in my lungs as Sebastian talked on.

"Actually, knowing him, he's placed bets on who'll come out victorious. God, if you've told him about any of this, he probably thinks I'm a real asshole now, doesn't he?" Sebastian shook his head, a small smile on his lips — one of the first I'd seen from him since our unexpected reunion. "Oh, well. Tell him I said hello and if he's up for it, I'd love to grab a beer sometime."

Sebastian looked up at me, that little grin still playing out on his lips, and finally seemed to notice my silence. His smile faltered a bit and something changed in his eyes.

"He's here in the city, right?" he asked. "I can't imagine you two would ever live very far apart."

I took a deep breath, my chest aching with the effort, and felt my eyes well up with tears.

"Lux?" Sebastian asked, finally using my name. Hearing it from his lips only pushed me closer to the edge. "How's he doing?"

A single tear fell down my cheek as I struggled to find the words. My lips parted but, looking at Sebastian as the hope slipped from his expression, I found I couldn't speak at all. It didn't matter, though — my strangled silence said everything he needed to hear.

The realization came swiftly for him, an arrow straight to the heart, and with it a total change in his demeanor. His forehead furrowed in shock and his mouth pressed firmly into the frown I'd come to know so well, but it was his eyes that changed the most. The soft look faded away, replaced by two chips of greenish brown ice that glared at me with every ounce of dislike he could muster.

"When?" He bit out the word like a curse. Another tear tracked down my face.

"Three years ago." My voice cracked.

He stared at me, a dark look clouding his expression. "Three years." His laugh rang out in the empty office and I flinched at the bitter, mirthless sound. "How could you not tell me? He was my friend, too. I should've been there. I had a fucking *right* to be there, Lux."

He advanced on me and I felt my shoulders hunch involuntarily. Curling in on myself was my only defense — there were no words I could offer him to ease the pain of this loss, of this betrayal. Keeping him from Jamie, though I'd certainly had my reasons, was both the worst and the hardest thing I'd ever done. The regret of it still kept me up at night, an unwanted bedfellow that haunted my thoughts and stalked my memories.

"I'm sorry," I told him. There was nothing else I could say.

"You're sorry." Sebastian leaned into my space, fury radiating from him like a physical forcefield. "That's just perfect. That makes it all okay."

My tears dripped faster, spurred by his stinging words and the sharp pain I felt inside. I'd struck a deal, and this was the price, I reminded myself. Choices had consequences. I thought I'd mastered that lesson seven years ago, but it seemed I still had some learning to do.

"You nearly had me fooled a second time." Sebastian's voice dripped with disbelief and his eyes flashed with outrage and pain. "I can't believe you almost drew me in again. Your talents are wasted here — your true calling is clearly as an actress, since you've mastered the art of deception."

I averted my eyes as his words landed against me like lashes, each one slicing deeper into vulnerable flesh.

"Tell me, is there anything but ice beneath that pretty exterior?" he whispered, his face inches from mine.

My gaze lifted to stare at his face, my spine straightened, my shoulders un-hunched and, for the first time, I felt it flutter to life, deep down at the depths of my soul — my own anger at this situation, finally coming alive. I was being treated as the villain here when, in actuality, I was as much a victim as he was. We'd been screwed, the both of us, by the same situation seven years ago. And yes, I'd played a role in the terrible end we'd come to that fateful June. But I couldn't undo what had been done to our love, anymore than I could bring my brother back to life or travel through time to make my parents quit drinking so my teenage home wouldn't be seized by the banks and debt collectors.

When I'd worked at *Minnie's* as a teen, many nights found me in the back kitchens with Minnie herself, stirring soups or helping her wash and cut vegetables for big recipes. I remember one night, when the diner had been particularly slow, we'd set ourselves up at the stainless steel prep table and peeled about fifty potatoes for a huge shepherd's pie someone had ordered for some kind of family event — a wedding reception or maybe a reunion. Minnie, wielding a razor sharp knife, had stopped peeling in the middle of a potato and held it up for me to examine.

"See that?" she'd asked, gesturing to the dark brown rotten spot on the side of the potato. "Some people'd throw this one out, thinkin' it'd spoil the whole pie. But potatoes are hearty — you cut out the rot, the rest is just fine." With a practiced swirl of her knife-tip, Minnie expertly removed the brown portion. I watched as it dropped to the tabletop, landing in a pile of discarded skins.

"Some people, baby girl, they're your brown spots. And some of us got more spots than others, a'course. But, point is, they don't spoil you forever. You cut 'em out of your life, you gonna be just fine."

She'd winked at me and gone right back to peeling.

I liked to think that Minnie had been right that night — that if someone or something awful entered your life, you could cut it out cleanly and move on, as though that spot had never been there at all.

But what if you didn't have just one — what if you were full of brown spots?

How many people could you walk away from? And how much of yourself could you cut away before there was nothing left behind?

No matter how much you wish it, you can't rewrite the past. It's set in stone — unshakeable and uncompromising. So it made no difference whether Sebastian blamed me or badgered me about our history — I couldn't make things better for him. The only thing I could do was vanish, cut myself out of his life completely once more, and hope that someday he might forget me all over again.

"Say the word and I'll go," I whispered in a broken voice, my watering eyes locked on his furious ones. "Say the word and I'll fade away, and this, right here, will be the last time you see me."

His eyes lost a little of their fury, but his jaw remained tightly clenched. I tried to gauge his emotions, but his expression was guarded. My throat constricted, and I thought I might choke on all the words I wanted to say but couldn't ever voice.

"You brought me here; you can send me away." I forced myself to go on. "Let me go back to *Luster*. Back into your past. You and I both know it's where I belong — and where I'm supposed to stay."

He stared at me for a minute in silence and for just a moment, I caught a glimpse of the boy I'd loved beneath the surface — he was there in the flash of sadness in Sebastian's eyes, in the tense fists his fingers curled into when those words left my lips.

I hiccupped for air, the choked sobs rattling my chest and finally breaking free. Tears blurred my vision, appearing faster than I could wipe them away.

"I'm sorry, Bash. You have no idea how sorry I am." I looked up at him with wet eyes, wishing I could tell him all of it — every secret, every false truth — but knowing I couldn't.

He opened his mouth to speak, but I took an abrupt step backward and cut off his words with my own.

"Let me go," I pleaded, feeling an unpleasant sensation of déjà vu as I told the man I loved, the man I'd *always* loved, to watch me walk away.

I turned and darted for the elevator which, for once, opened almost immediately. I boarded and pushed the button that would carry me down to the lobby, my shoulders heaving with sobs as I wept. I didn't — couldn't — look back at Sebastian before the doors closed.

"Goodbye," I whispered into the empty elevator, pressing my eyes tightly closed against the tears.

Regret was an emotional cancer, destroying you from the inside out. Eating at your most vital parts until there was nothing left but scar tissue and sorrow. It chipped away at you in small increments, shattering your defenses and tiring you out. But, unlike a physical cancer, which might eventually go into remission or be cut out with a few careful strokes of a surgeon's scalpel, regret would stay with you forever. It was chronic, but not terminal — a constant companion that would haunt you until your deathbed. And there were no cures to diminish its influence. No salves to counteract its effects.

Regret didn't break your body. It crushed your spirit.

Mine had just been broken beyond repair.

Chapter Twenty-Four

NOW

I DON'T REMEMBER MUCH OF MY WALK HOME, BUT I KNOW IT wasn't pretty. More than a few people stopped to stare at the girl with mascara running down her face, mussed up hair, and a trembling lower lip, but no one spoke to her. New Yorkers were rarely phased by something so minor as a girl having a total breakdown while wandering the streets of Midtown. Times like this made me miss Georgia, where I'd have been stopped immediately and tucked under the wing of a concerned neighbor, who'd have insisted on bringing me home with her for a glass of sweet tea and a slice of homemade pie.

I supposed a bottle of Merlot would have to do as a substitute.

When I got home, I didn't even take my dress off before collapsing onto my bed in a heap of misery. Though the tears had finally stopped, I was exhausted from my crying jag and had no desire to look in my mirror at the puffy-eyed mess I'd become. I slipped my sleep-mask over my eyes to block out the light, burrowed my head beneath a mound of pillows to muffle the sounds of rush hour traffic, and fell into a fitful sleep, in which I dreamed of cemeteries and flashing hazel eyes.

⚛

"Do you think she's dead?"

"I don't know, poke her foot."

"*You* poke her foot. I hate dead people."

"Does anyone *like* dead people?"

"Necrophiliacs?"

The sound of two people giggling like hyenas pulled me back into consciousness.

"Ungh," I muttered. I really needed to change my locks.

"Oh good, she's alive." A voice I now recognized as Simon's drifted closer, and the weight of someone's body landed next to me on the bed. Seconds later, another body settled in on my opposite side. To my dismay, my cocoon of pillows and blankets was ripped from my body and shoved to the floor. With a resigned sigh, I pushed the sleep mask up onto my forehead and cracked my eyes open. Simon and Fae were staring at me with horrified expressions.

"What?" I asked, my voice scratchy with sleep.

Simon looked at Fae. "Do you want to tell her, or should I?"

"Sweetie, you look like death warmed over. You've got raccoon eyes." Fae's lips twitched as she pointed at my face. "What happened?"

"And what's with the psycho serial-killer wall over there?" Simon asked, gesturing toward the mosaic of notes and photos I'd pinned up on the other side of the room. "Does someone need a Prozac?"

I groaned, pulling my sleep mask back over my eyes to block them out.

"I think this calls for serious measures," Fae noted.

"Yep." Simon agreed. "You thinking what I'm thinking?"

"Wine," they chimed in unison.

A hand grazed my temple, peeling the sleep mask off my face and up over my head, and bringing my best friends back into view. Fae, sleep mask in hand, was staring at me with concern while Simon headed across the room toward the kitchen area, no doubt in search of the jumbo bottle of Merlot I'd stashed on the counter. I sat up in bed when he returned with a full glass of wine and a warm, wet washcloth. I accepted both gratefully, gently wiping at the mascara on my face and taking a large sip from my glass.

When I'd gotten myself together, I took a deep breath and faced Simon and Fae, who were watching me from their perches at the end of my bed.

"It's time to spill, baby," Simon said, squeezing my thigh. Fae nodded in agreement.

With a sigh, I set my wine glass on the bedside table, climbed from the bed, and crossed to my desk, where I'd dropped my keys earlier. Fingering the smallest brass key on the ring, I headed for the small excuse for a closet embedded in the wall by my bed. On the top shelf, tucked behind the Jamie Box, I had a small lockbox where I kept a few things safe — the tiny diamond stud earrings my grandmother had left me when she passed, some of Jamie's old medical records, my college diploma, and, of course, the document that had sealed my fate all those years ago.

The NDA.

I pulled the lockbox down from its place on the shelf and used the small key to open it. My fingers flipped through several documents before reaching the file that lay on the very bottom. I grasped the papers lightly, as though they were laced with toxins and holding them might allow fatal poison to seep through my fingertips and into my bloodstream. The pad of my index finger traced the lettering typed in boldface across the top of the first sheet:

Non-Disclosure Agreement

The tempo of my heart picked up speed as I walked back

toward Simon and Fae, who hadn't moved from their spots on my bed. I stopped about five feet away.

"If I tell you everything, I'm violating this contract," I told them, gesturing to the papers in my hand. "And, technically, I'm breaking the law."

"What is it?" Simon breathed, the light in his eyes equal parts excitement and trepidation.

"It's a non-disclosure agreement." I swallowed roughly.

Fae's expression was unreadable. "It has to do with Sebastian?" she asked.

I nodded. "I've never told anyone about this. Not even Jamie. I didn't ever want to look at it again," I whispered, my grip tightening on the slim stack of paper. I wanted to rip it to shreds, but instead I forced my grip to loosen and looked up at my friends. "But I needed you to know that this isn't a secret I keep lightly. It's not something I ever wanted in my life, and I probably shouldn't even be talking about it, but I trust you guys. I love you. And if you need to know, I'll show you — I'll tell you everything."

They were quiet for a long time, the silence stretching out as I waited for them to make a decision. They locked eyes, staring at one another for a few seconds before nodding in sync and turning back to face me.

"We don't need to see it." Fae smiled softly at me. Simon nodded in agreement.

"Are you sure?" I asked, wavering. There was a large part of me that didn't want to keep all of this to myself anymore, even though sharing wouldn't have been the soundest decision I'd ever made.

"Put it away, baby," Simon ordered in a gentle voice.

"I don't want this secret to come between us or cause a problem in our friendship," I said quietly, voicing one of my biggest fears. Since Jamie died, Simon and Fae were the closest thing I had to family.

Simon snorted outright. Fae's laugh was a little more subdued, but not much.

"Now you're just being a dumb blonde," Simon chided, rolling his eyes. "I thought you'd finally dispelled that stereotype but I see my work with you is not yet done."

"Lux, don't you understand?" Fae asked with a grin. "We love you too. Being friends with someone doesn't mean that everything is perfect all the time."

"Clearly," Simon chimed in, rolling his eyes.

"As I was *saying*," Fae continued, smacking Simon lightly on the arm. "A perfect friendship doesn't mean everything is perfect — it means you love each other enough to forgive the imperfections."

I'd thought I was cried-out for the day, but I suddenly found my eyes watering.

"Jesus, all this sweet bonding is giving me cavities," Simon complained. "Put that damn thing away and come drink your wine."

With a laugh, I walked to the lockbox and slipped the NDA inside before placing it back on its shelf in my closet. When I returned to the bed, I sat in the space between Fae and Simon, who immediately enveloped me with their arms.

"What would I do without you guys?" I asked, leaning my head on Simon's shoulder.

"You'd probably be dead in a ditch somewhere." Fae giggled.

"Or, at the very least, you'd have an abominable fashion sense and never get into the good nightclubs," Simon added.

I smiled and sipped my wine.

※

BY THE TIME SIMON AND FAE LEFT ME FOR THE NIGHT, I WAS thoroughly buzzed and swaddled in the pale blue silk pajama set I never wore because it was too pretty to wrinkle and, anyway, didn't only women in classic movies wear fabulous designer nightwear? Most nights I slept in the first oversized t-shirt my hands landed on when they reached into my dresser drawer, but tonight I had little choice in the matter — Simon was being insistent.

The pajamas had been a Christmas gift from him last year,

purchased because they'd apparently "bring out the blue in my eyes" and, as an added bonus, help to trick men into thinking I was the kind of classy lady who wore silk to bed. While rummaging through my wardrobe — as was his habit, whenever he was cooped up in my tiny studio for too long — Simon had been dismayed to find them folded in a neat pile with the tags still attached, in a small nook at the back of my closet. He'd retrieved them, made a fuss about my neglect of a perfectly good pajama set, and, of course, forced me to put them on immediately.

I had to admit that his taste was impeccable. As soon as I pulled the sleek tank top over my head and slid my legs into the flowing kimono pants, I fell in love with the feeling of silk as it brushed against my skin like a caress. And he'd been right — my gray-blue eyes did look brighter in the mirror in contrast to the fabric.

During the pajama drama, Fae located a bag of microwave popcorn somewhere in the depths of my cabinets — quite possibly leftover by the previous tenant, but I had a good buzz on and I wasn't feeling picky tonight — and popped a comedy into my DVD player. The two of them clucked over me like mother hens for nearly an hour before I finally forced them out of my apartment. They would've stayed with me all night if I'd asked, but I was craving some alone time after the day I'd had.

The credits were rolling and my eyes were drooping when the buzzer rang sharply three times in quick succession. I rose and stretched the kinks out of my back, walking to the door with my wineglass in hand. I figured it might be Simon and Fae, back to ensure that I hadn't pulled a Sylvia Plath and put my head in the oven or started bottling my own urine like Howard Hughes.

I pressed the intercom and was surprised by the voice I heard on the opposite end.

"Babe! It's Desmond!"

What was he doing here?

"Um, hey, Des. Did you need something?" I buzzed back, my brow furrowed in confusion.

"I have your jacket! You left it at my place after the movie a few weeks back. I was in the neighborhood so I figured I'd swing by and return it to you."

I glanced at my watch — it was 9:00 p.m. on a Friday night. Maybe he really had been in the area, but it seemed unlikely. Guys who looked like Des didn't spend their free evenings playing errand boy for former girlfriends. Then again, I could be totally overthinking things. I'd had too much wine to judge properly.

I sighed and buzzed him in.

"Hey, babe." Desmond leaned down and kissed my cheek as soon as I pulled open the door. "Nice jammies."

I smiled. "Thanks."

"You okay?" he asked, his eyes scanning my face. My makeup was long gone and I knew that my eyes were still puffy and red from earlier.

I nodded, but didn't explain the residual traces of tears.

"Here," he said handing over my jacket.

"Uh, thanks," I repeated, feeling awkward. Southern hospitality practically demanded I let him in, rather than leave him standing on the stoop like a stranger, but I didn't want to give him the wrong impression. I was half-inebriated, braless, and feeling vulnerable after the day I'd had, so a visit from an ex was probably not the greatest idea. As I deliberated, I watched a delivery man walk through my hall toward Mrs. Johansson's apartment next door, the brown bag in his arms wafting the deliciously greasy aroma of lo mien noodles and egg rolls.

My stomach growled loudly.

"Hungry?" Desmond asked, arching one eyebrow in the direction of my stomach.

"No," I lied, trying to conceal the Pavlovian response I was having to Mrs. Johansson's takeout. It was a miracle I managed to hold in the long tendrils of drool threatening to leak from my mouth.

"What'd you eat for dinner?"

"Um." I winced. "Stale microwave popcorn?"

"Babe." Des shook his head. "My idea of gourmet may be macaroni and cheese, but even I know that popcorn is not a meal."

I opened my mouth to protest, but Desmond kept talking.

"And no, Doritos and wine don't count either."

My mouth snapped closed. The delivery guy, now empty handed, smiled at me as he headed for the stairwell at the end of the hall.

"Come on," Des said, edging inside my doorway. "I'll make you something."

"My cupboards are empty."

"Well, then I'll order you something." He grinned at me, stepping further through the entry so I had no choice but to move back a step — it was either that or initiate a sumo-wrestler-esque chest bump standoff, which I was in no way prepared for seeing as I wasn't wearing a bra.

"Listen, Des..." I trailed off. I didn't want to hurt his feelings, but I also didn't want to lead him on. His smile slipped a little. "I just don't think it's a good idea for us to—"

"Hey, it's cool," he said, holding both hands up in a gesture of surrender. "No worries."

"Thanks for the jacket," I told him, meaning it. "And I'm sorry."

"Come 'ere, Kincaid." He smiled sadly as he stepped forward and pulled me into an embrace. It wasn't one of seduction, but of sheer comfort. Of friendship.

What a freaking good guy, I thought, bringing my arms up to return his light hug. I cursed my own inabilities to date him, but hoped that one day we could, at the very least, be friends. A warm, happy bubble of contentment rose within me at the thought.

Unfortunately, that bubble burst when a familiar icy voice shattered the silence and stopped my heart — for the second time today.

"I hope I'm not interrupting."

My arms stilled around Des, and I felt every hair on my body stand on end.

Shit, shit, shit.

Sebastian *fucking* Covington was at my door.

༺༻

M Y EYES FLEW OPEN AND SPOTTED HIM OVER DESMOND'S shoulder. He was standing in the partially open doorway, the hand he'd raised to knock drifting slowly back toward his side. His glaring eyes were, for once, not directed at me, but were locked on the back of Des' head. With my eyes on Sebastian, I pulled out of the embrace. Desmond's arms dropped away from me, and he turned to face the man who'd just appeared in my doorway.

"This was a mistake." Sebastian's eyes were wide, his tone incredulous. "I just can't seem to stop making those with you. I shouldn't have come here."

Desmond looked from me to Sebastian, then back to me. "This the guy?" he asked.

I glanced at Sebastian, who'd turned to go but halted when he heard Desmond's question. When Bash's eyes met mine, I nodded reluctantly.

"Seems like a dick," Desmond muttered. One corner of my mouth twitched and my gaze returned to Des.

"Actually, I'm pretty sure I'm the dick in this situation," I admitted. I could sense Sebastian's presence by the door, where he stood paralyzed with momentary indecision — to stay or to go. As much as I was worried about another confrontation like the one we'd shared earlier, the curiosity of why he was at my door — hell, of how he'd even tracked down my apartment and gotten inside without buzzing — was tearing me up inside.

"You gonna be okay with him if I leave?" Des asked. I smiled softly at him before my eyes drifted over to Sebastian. He was watching me closely and I saw something flare in his eyes when I nodded my head.

"Yeah," I said, my gaze steady. "Yeah, I'll be fine with him."

"You need me, you call." Des took hold of my chin and turned my face back toward him, so I was looking into his light blue eyes rather than the hazel ones that had a tendency to ensnare me.

"Thanks, Des," I whispered. "You're the best."

"I know that, babe." His grin was cocky. "I'm just waiting for you to catch up."

I laughed as he dropped a light kiss on my forehead, turned for the door, and came face to face with Sebastian — at which point all levity was sucked from the room and my giggles died in my throat. Des drew himself up to full height and made sure his not-insignificant muscles were on display as he leaned toward Bash.

"Do not upset her." His tone was surprisingly cordial, even if his stark order left something to be desired.

To my surprise, when Sebastian responded it was with equal civility. "I won't," he promised.

"Good." Des nodded, then turned back to look at me. "Bye, babe!"

With a final wink, he was gone — leaving me not only in the company of my ex, but also wearing a ridiculous silk freaking pajama set and three sheets to the wind after downing two brimming glasses of wine.

Perfect.

I stared at Sebastian. Sebastian stared back at me.

When neither of us spoke, the tension grew into a living, breathing entity — coiling around us like a dark, malevolent snake. With each passing second, the cobra constricted more tightly, its deadly embrace squeezing until the strain of simply staring at one another became too much to withstand. I cleared my throat, sick of this silent stalemate, and gave in.

"Well." I stepped back into my apartment so the doorway was clear. "I guess you should come in."

He took a step inside and shut the door behind him with a soft click that, for some reason, sounded more like a jail cell locking into place than a thin piece of particle-board closing on crappy hinges.

I walked over to my kitchen area and immediately topped off

my wine glass, taking a healthy gulp for strength. When I turned back to Sebastian, his eyes were sweeping my small space in an intense but not altogether critical evaluation. They lingered for a moment on my wall of notes, photos, and mapped locations, his brow crinkling in confusion and curiosity as he took in the sight.

"Wine?" I offered. He shook his head.

I walked over to my couch, skirting him with several feet of safe distance between us. Settling into the cushions, I turned to look at him. He hadn't moved much past the doorway and his gaze now seemed to be locked on my bed, examining the rumpled comforter and widely strewn throw pillows with more than cursory interest.

"You didn't tell me you had a boyfriend." He spoke the words with indifference, still refusing to look at me.

I rolled my eyes. What was this — jealousy?

"You didn't ask," I snapped back, my inhibitions far lower than usual due to the wine sloshing around in my system. Sebastian turned to me, surprise clear in his expression. I'm not sure what answer he'd expected, but it hadn't been that one.

"He's not my boyfriend," I admitted, this time using a quieter tone. With a sigh, I turned away from him and burrowed deeper into my couch cushions. "So are you going to tell me why you're here, or should I start guessing?" I didn't look at him as I asked my question — two could play that game — nor was there any real insistence in my voice. I was too worn out to fight with him any more today.

There was a moment of silence before I heard the sound of footsteps on hardwood. Seconds later, Sebastian settled onto the other side of my couch, leaving an empty cushion in the space between us.

"I'd apologize, but the last time I tried it didn't go very well," he said quietly.

My lips turned up in a small smile. "True," I acknowledged.

"I meant what I said earlier, before...everything exploded." He looked over at me, his expression earnest. "I'd like to try civility.

Hearing about Jamie, it just — it floored me. But I shouldn't have said those things to you."

"Well, I shouldn't have kept his death from you," I countered.

We fell silent, neither of us knowing how to move past this stage of anger and animosity to a reality in which we were kind to each other. We'd ignored, tormented, and nearly broken one another in the past. We'd approached every interaction like two hostile combatants, locked and loaded with enough ammunition to blow each other to pieces. And sure, maybe those barbed, explosive interactions were dangerous and practically guaranteed to destroy us both — but somehow, the thought of laying down our arms and negotiating peace seemed a far more daunting task right now. The accusations and antagonistic words that had colored our previous conversations were, for all their brutality, simpler to face. Holding a gun on someone as you stood in your suit of body armor was much easier than trusting that as soon as you lowered your weapon, they wouldn't blow you away with their own.

That was really what it all came down to: trust.

I'd broken Sebastian's a long time ago. And trust was a funny thing; once it was gone, I wasn't entirely convinced it could ever be reconstructed or made whole again. There would always be small chinks in the foundation, compromising the structural integrity of everything you managed to rebuild on top of it.

But what was the alternative?

If you didn't try to reconstruct — if you chose to live in the ruins and attempted to convince yourself that you were happy there — you'd never even have a chance at seeing the beautiful view from the sky. You'd spend your life looking up at what you could've had, lying in the rubble of a broken relationship.

It was time to lay my weapons aside. To strip away my armor. To try to rebuild. And to hope, above all things, that Sebastian might do the same.

"I can't," he said abruptly, shattering the silence and drawing my gaze to his face.

"What?" I whispered, wondering if he could somehow read my thoughts.

"You asked me to let you go — like it's this simple, easy thing. But I can't let you go." Hunched forward with his wrists resting on his knees, Sebastian shook his head and a deep frown troubled his expression. "I've had seven years of unanswered questions. Seven years of doubts. Seven years of calling myself an idiot, and cursing your name, and hating you for what happened. And I've tried to drink you out of my head with booze, and screw you out of my memories with other women."

I cringed, but forced myself to listen to the rest of his words.

"I've traveled across the world, trying to outrun my memories of you. But damned if I didn't get to every fucking continent and still see your face on the other side of my camera lens — in a crowded Tibetan market, on the cliffside of a snowy Himalayan peak, in the reflection of a muddy river in Thailand. You were always there, haunting me, around every corner."

I curled my hands into fists in my lap. He looked over at me and our eyes caught immediately. I knew my every emotion was playing out on my face for him to read — a running script of remorse for the things I'd done, regret for what we'd both endured in our time apart, and longing for the love we might've had.

I'd honestly thought that he'd been fine without me all these years. That he'd moved on and forgotten the carefree months we'd spent beneath the sun when we were young and innocent, wrapped up in love. Because, though he'd been the brightest star of my life, I'd always assumed I had just been a minor, forgotten constellation somewhere in his massive stratosphere. A tiny asteroid, shooting across his distant horizon.

"I don't know what to say to you," I admitted, my words hesitant. "I don't know how to do this. All I can tell you is that I'm sorry for hurting you all those years ago, and again this afternoon. I'm sorry, Bash."

He nodded. "I know. Me too. And honestly?" he added, the

specter of a smile crossing his face. "Hating you is absolutely exhausting."

I laughed lightly. "You too."

Once again, silence descended.

"You moved here when he died?" he asked eventually.

I took a deep breath, prayed for composure, and nodded. "After, I needed a clean break. It was too hard to be there without him...too many memories."

Our gazes caught once more, and I knew he sensed I wasn't just talking about Jamie.

"You never came back." He looked at me with a question in his eyes. "That summer, after that day, you were just gone. Both of you. You vanished from Jackson, from my life like ghosts and I never saw you again."

"I'm surprised you noticed," I teased, hoping to steer the conversation out of dangerous waters. "With all your adventures at Princeton I can't believe you even had time to think about Georgia, let alone visit."

He looked at me as though he were staring at a mountain of puzzle pieces, trying to align them in his mind and figure out which ones were missing altogether. When he spoke again, his voice was even quieter than before.

"I didn't go to Princeton."

My eyes flew to his face. "*What?*"

"I didn't go." His expression was blank but there were thoughts working in his eyes.

I took a steadying breath and tried to keep my voice free of malice. "But what about your father and all his grand plans?"

"I told him to go fuck himself."

Sebastian smiled — a real, genuine grin that made the corners of my own mouth lift. I thought about his words for a moment, and small bubbles of hysteria began to dance within me like popcorn kernels just before they burst open. They filled me, vibrating and expanding in my chest until I could no longer keep them contained, and I burst into laughter. Spurts of giggles popped from my mouth into the air like a flurry of exploding kernels.

"I'm sure that went *really* well," I gasped out between fits of laughter, my mind conjuring up images of the senator's face as his golden boy broke the news. My reaction probably didn't make much sense to Sebastian, but I couldn't help myself — there was a tremendous amount of karmatic justice in the fact that, after everything the senator had done to ensure it, Bash still hadn't ended up on the path to the presidency or even followed in his father's footsteps.

I glanced over at Sebastian and was pleasantly surprised to find him still grinning, rather than looking at me like I was a crazy person. "Sorry," I whispered. "Just the thought..."

"Of his face?" Bash shook his head, grimacing. "Yeah, not pretty at the time but, in retrospect, pretty damn hilarious."

"So no Princeton..." I trailed off, an unspoken question hanging in the air between us.

"He cut me off, of course," Sebastian said, his happy smile still in tact. Evidently, he hadn't been too upset about this turn of events. "I went to art school out in California. To pay my tuition, I worked my ass off every night doing freelance for local magazines and spent my mornings as a waiter, serving breakfast at this tiny diner. Then I g—"

"Wait, wait, wait," I interrupted, holding out a hand to stop his words. "You, Sebastian Michael Covington, were a *waiter?*" I contorted my expression into a mask of horror. "The same boy who didn't know the difference between an omelet and a frittata? Who'd never even been inside a kitchen unless it was to sneak cookies from the pantry? Who'd never eaten a waffle until he was eighteen?" I stared at him in disbelief. "How on earth did you manage to deliver orders?"

Bash dropped his forehead into his palm. "Thanks for the vote of confidence," he muttered, groaning at the memory. "Though you're right — the first few weeks were pretty brutal. It's actually amazing they didn't fire me after my first shift. I spilled an entire pot of coffee, accidentally gave an order of huevos rancheros to a vegan, and mistakenly charged someone's credit card for another table's order."

"Oh my god." I snorted. "And they chose *not* to fire you because...?"

"I begged the owner for another shot. She was a great lady. Plus, it's hard to say no to this face," he joked, winking at me.

I laughed and rolled my eyes.

"After graduation, I got lucky. National Geographic had an opening doing some foreign correspondence stuff overseas. They needed someone young without any attachments back at home — someone who'd be willing to drop into dangerous places to shoot photos, with the knowledge that they might never come back. Frankly, at the time, it sounded perfect," he told me, some of the light fading from his eyes as he thought back. "And for a while it was. I saw pretty much all of the Middle East, and a lot of Asia. Some of Africa, a few cities in Europe. I didn't come back to the States for almost three years."

"Sounds amazing," I murmured. *Sounds lonely*, I added in my thoughts.

"It was." He looked over at me. "Though if I never eat rice or see sand again, I'll die a happy man."

I laughed again and this time, though he seemed almost uncertain how, he joined in with me. His deep chuckle resonated through the room in perfect harmony with my own giggles, and filled me with an unrelenting joy. I watched his face alight. Unbeknownst to him, his expression revealed his own surprise at the sound of years of shored up laughter spilling out into the air around us. It was clear he'd not laughed like this for a long time — perhaps so long he'd become convinced it was no longer possible.

I'd forgotten how wonderful it was to laugh with Sebastian. I savored the moment, memorizing the sound of his rumbling laughter, the warm look in his eyes, the faint smell of his aftershave. I bottled up the memory and tucked it away in a far corner of my mind so that one day, when he was once again just a thread in the fabric of my past, I could replay it, relive it, as many times as I wanted.

When our breaths grew short, we finally fell silent, staring at one another across the sofa. We'd ended up in identical poses, with our bodies turned inward toward the unoccupied cushion between us, our sides pressed against the couch back, and our heads leaning against the fabric.

He reached over slowly, his hand moving to my shoulder blade where the thin strap of my silk tank had fallen down over my left shoulder. His entire body moved toward mine, and I held my breath as he entered my space. I pressed my eyes closed when I felt his light touch on the skin of my upper arm, and shivered lightly when he dragged the strap back into place. The graze of his finger was featherlight as it traveled down the length of the strap to the space below my left collarbone, where it stilled abruptly and pressed into the skin with more pressure than before.

"A tattoo?" His voice was husky.

My eyes flew open. *Shit.* He could not see my tattoo.

With my inhibitions dulled by the wine and — fine, I admit it — the pull of his presence, I hadn't realized that the small line of script was visible near the edge of my tank top. Only a portion of the last word, but still — enough to make him curious about the phrase I'd inscribed in ink over my heart.

My hand came up to cover his, shielding the tattoo from his eyes.

"It's, uh, it's nothing really." My mind searched desperately for an excuse to keep him from seeing the mark, and when my eyes landed on the small door to my bathroom, I blurted the first words that popped into my head. "I have to pee!"

I jumped to my feet as Sebastian laughed, my abrupt admission clearly a case of over-sharing. God, I was such a dork. I averted my eyes from him and hurried for the door. "Be right back!" I called.

He was still laughing when the door closed behind me. I leaned against it and sank slowly down to the floor, the cool tiles chilling me through the thin fabric of my pants. I curled my knees to my chest and proceeded to smack my forehead repeatedly with the open face of my right palm, hoping it might knock some sense back into me.

Seriously, what the hell was wrong with me?

Where was my self-control? My common sense? My ability to ignore the fact that the most beautiful man in the world was sitting in my living room?

Ah yes, that's right. They'd fled somewhere around the time I'd poured that third glass of wine.

Crap.

I had to go back out there and regain control of the situation. I could totally do this — be his friend, without letting him see how much I still loved him. Pretend I felt nothing more than mutual respect. Restrain myself from staring at him like I'd given up ice cream for Lent and he was a large, delicious cone of mint chocolate chip, begging to be consumed.

Damn, Des had been right. I really was hungry. Even my mental metaphors had devolved to become food-oriented.

I scrambled to my feet and stared at my reflection in the mirror over the sink, trying to collect my thoughts. I reached up and pressed my fingertips against the still-swollen bags beneath each of my eyes. Staring into their cloudy grayish depths, I prayed for composure, straightened my shoulders, and shook my fingers through my hair from root to tip, as though I could somehow shake out my nerves.

When I stepped back into the studio, I saw immediately that Sebastian was no longer sitting on the couch. He was standing by the far wall with his back to me, examining my mosaic of research. I was silent as I approached him, coming to a stop by his side with a few feet left between us.

"What is this?" he asked, all laughter gone from his voice.

"It's for a story," I explained, my serious tone matching his. "It's nothing."

"This isn't for *Luster*."

"No," I agreed. "It's not."

His eyes caught on the photo of Vera and me — our matching smiles stretching our cheeks so wide they'd ached with happiness, our arms looped around each other's waists in an embrace, my silver bangle gleaming in the summer sunshine. Sebastian's slow gaze migrated from the pinned photograph on the wall, down to where my wrist hung at my side. Its only adornment was the same beautiful thin bracelet I wore in the picture and, when his eyes came up to meet mine, I knew he'd figured out that my involvement in this story was more than that of a simple reporter.

"Why haven't you gone to the police with this?" he asked.

My eyes moved up to examine the photo of Santos. "It's complicated."

"So un-complicate it."

"I don't want you to get involved," I deflected, crossing my arms over my chest. "It's none of your business."

"Jesus, I forgot how goddamn stubborn you are." His tone was exasperated, and I'm sure if I'd looked, I'd find his expression matched it. "If this is dangerous, you shouldn't be doing it alone."

"Who says I'm doing it alone?" I countered maturely, using avoidance tactics a seven-year-old wouldn't deign to. I stopped short of sticking out my tongue at him or taunting *nah-nah-nah-nah-poo-poo*. How totally adult of me.

I suppose it was better than the alternative — better than admitting how terrified I'd become of this whole thing. The doubts were there, circling like wolves, ready to take me down. I was in over my head, and I knew it. I was scared for Vera's safety and my own. I didn't know what to do, or where to turn next. But if I let those fears in — if I let them take hold — I'd never be able to finish this investigation or do anything to change those missing girls' fates.

"Lux, this isn't a game. If this is what I think it is..." He looked over at me, concern furrowing his brow. "It's dangerous. These aren't good people."

"You think I don't know that?" I fired back, my eyes flashing as I thought of Vera. "Believe me, I know. But it's none of your business. We aren't dating. We aren't even friends. Until twenty minutes ago, I'm pretty sure we hated one another. So please just leave it alone, Bash."

He stared at me for a long moment, then held his hands up in surrender. "Fine, if you don't want my help, I'll drop it. And you're right — we aren't dating and we aren't friends. But you couldn't be more wrong about that last part, Lux."

I felt my eyes widen slightly and my breath caught as I waited for him to explain. He leaned in closer and when he whispered in my ear, his warm breath sent a small tremor through my entire body.

"See, I'm pretty sure you never hated me. In fact, I'm nearly positive of it." His lips brushed my earlobe and I tried to keep my body completely still, my face clear of the emotions that were raging behind my mask of impassivity. My heart raced faster as he spoke on. "I wasn't sure at first — I thought I might be imagining it, seeing things that weren't there because I wished they were true. But now, after watching you for the last week, after sitting here with you, after laughing with you, after seeing the way you react when I do this..."

He pressed his lips against the sensitive hollow beneath my ear, his tongue flicking out to brush the skin in the briefest of caresses, and I couldn't stop my reaction. It was involuntary — the instinctual arching of my spine, the slight tilting of my head to give his lips better access, the breathy gasp that escaped my mouth.

"Or this..." he breathed, his lips trailing down my neck to the ridge of my collarbone, where he pressed another openmouthed kiss. I whimpered slightly, cursing my wanton reaction internally but powerless to stop it.

"See, Lux, if you hated me, you wouldn't tremble at the thought of touching my hand to take back your cellphone. You wouldn't cast your eyes away, as though looking at me caused you acute pain. You wouldn't smile at my jokes, or breathe in my laughter like you need it to keep on living."

Damn. Apparently, he'd been paying pretty close attention —

which meant I was royally screwed. I took a step away from him and ran my fingers through my hair, before opening my mouth to formulate a protest. I needed to be a minimum of three feet from him if I wanted to be at all convincing or coherent — any closer and it seemed my mouth was more likely to produce a torrent of uncontrollable babble. Unfortunately, as I stepped back, he advanced on me, matching each of my strides and maintaining our close distance.

"You're crazy," I muttered.

"Yeah?" He arched an eyebrow at me skeptically.

"Delusional," I confirmed, retreating another step.

"Mhm."

"Seriously, this is pathetic," I lashed out, falling back on hostility to dissuade him. It had worked before. "Look, I get it. You're rewriting the past to make it less painful for yourself. But that doesn't mean you're right."

"Oh, burn," Bash mocked, grinning as he advanced on me. "You got me."

Shit.

Abruptly, I felt my back hit the wall. He'd boxed me into a corner. Before I could squirm away, his arms came up on either side to form a cage around me, and he leaned down so we were face to face.

"I didn't see it seven years ago. I was too hurt, too mad. But I see it now."

"What?" I bit out, glaring up at him.

"You lied then. Just like you're lying now." He leaned closer so our lips aligned perfectly, separated by the smallest sliver of space. "I still don't know why. But you know what, Freckles?"

My breathing stopped entirely as the endearment left his lips and he moved fractionally closer, closing the gap between us until our mouths brushed in the hint of a kiss. When he spoke again, I felt his words before I heard them.

"I intend to find out."

His eyes were solemn, his voice more serious than I'd ever

heard it. They weren't just words — it wasn't just a statement of curiosity or an expressed desire to solve a seven-year-old mystery.

It was a vow. It was a promise.

He breathed his declaration into my mouth and deep down into my soul, where it fanned the flames of panic and passion raging simultaneously within me. And before I could move, speak, breathe, think — he was gone. Striding to my apartment door and out into the hallway without another word.

I lifted a hand to trace my still-tingling lips with my fingertips, staring at my closed door with disbelief. I simply couldn't believe it — my mind refused to process that whatever had just happened was real. Because if it was...

Bash knew. Maybe not everything, but certainly enough to send him digging into our past.

Shit.

Chapter Twenty-Five

❦

THEN

"Where's the bathroom?" I asked in a soft voice, praying Greta spoke English.

The quiet Swedish maid kept mostly to herself, speaking infrequently and making eye contact only when she received a direct order from Mrs. Covington — or "Judith" as she'd told me to call her when I'd arrived, donning her arctic smile and studiously ignoring my presence from that moment on.

Thankfully, Greta smiled and pointed down the hall off the kitchen. "On the left," she whispered, turning back to the island countertop where she was artfully arranging a spread of hors d'oeuvres on several large silver platters. It was enough food to feed four times the number of guests milling about the mansion — most of it would likely be thrown out with tomorrow's trash. For a moment I hesitated, looking down at the mini vegetable quiches and bacon-wrapped scallops until I felt my stomach rumble beneath the pale white lace of my dress. But when images of my own empty refrigerator and Jamie's painfully thin face flashed in my mind, a bitter taste filled my mouth and I forced myself to look away.

"Thanks, Greta." I nodded at her, then wandered down the hallway to find the bathroom. I'd purposely sought this one out, knowing most guests would use the main bathroom off the front hall and that I'd be less likely to bump into anyone in this part of the house. I needed a moment alone to collect myself before heading back into the lion's den of well-moneyed socialites, acquaintances, and associates that "Judith" and the senator had deemed appropriate company at Sebastian's eighteenth birthday party. Personally, I didn't care how wealthy or well-bred they were — all I knew was, they were no fun at all.

One of the senator's friends had just engaged me in a condescending conversation about the difference between our Congress and the British Parliament. When he'd expounded for nearly five minutes without coming up for air, I decided to excuse myself rather than risk falling into an irreversible coma in the middle of the Covington's foyer. Beelining for the bathroom, I spotted Bash across the room by the door. He was flanked on either side by his parents, greeting guests as they arrived with a glazed look in his typically animated eyes.

Considering the invitees, I couldn't blame him.

These people were cold. Dead inside.

For all their fashionable clothing and sophisticated mannerisms, they were lacking that vital spark of life possessed by the truly vivacious. They seemed to walk around half alive, bored to death by the utterly predictable prosperity that defined their ostentatious existence. I watched them gliding through the mansion like elegant zombies, their empty eyes dulled by a lackluster life of overindulgence — perhaps weary of their own wealth, but too afraid to ever let it go.

There's a kind of freedom in poverty, I suppose — in the total lack of posturing or pretension. It's easy to think of the rich as the only ones who are truly free in this life, but it seemed to me that most of the genuinely affluent were held down by more shackles and obligations than I'd ever been, for all my lack of fortune. Money may've lent the illusion of freedom, but ultimately it seemed to bind its possessor in enough chains of expectation and apprehension to render spontaneity and self-fulfillment impossible.

It was hard to bear witness to such extreme indulgence, when my family didn't even have enough to pay for Jamie's treatments or keep up with the mortgage. We'd gotten a medical hardship extension from the bank, which would keep us out of foreclosure for another few months, but it was just a temporary fix. I knew it was only a matter of time until they took the house — yet that remained the least of my worries.

Weakened by his most recent round of treatments, Jamie was back in the hospital with a severe bout of pneumonia. And, with Christmas a few short weeks away, he'd be there for the remainder of the holidays. Over the past few months, he'd been through more chemotherapy and radiation, with minimal results, and the doctors had ruled against another bone-graft. They were scheduled to amputate his leg as soon as he'd recovered enough strength to endure the operation.

Merry Freaking Christmas.

When I reached the bathroom, I headed for the sink and splashed cool water on my face, careful not to do irreversible damage to my makeup. I contemplated hiding in here for the rest of the night, but knew my disappearance would eventually be noted — if not by the pompous party guests, then certainly by my boyfriend. Bash knew how nervous I'd been to come tonight. He was fully aware that I'd feel out of my element — the impoverished, ugly duckling in the company of swans.

Plus, I was faced with the uncomfortable reality of meeting his father for the first time. I'd managed to avoid him for this long because he spent most of his time in the nation's capital, flying home only a few days a month to visit his family. But, around the holidays, he made a point to return to Georgia for several weeks, in celebration of his only son's birth as well as Christmas and New

Year's. If the senator was anything like his wife, I feared I'd have a hard time keeping my polite smile in place when I finally did merit an introduction.

A soft knock sounded at the door.

"One second!" I called, grabbing one of the white disposable towels from the basket on the marble vanity and dabbing at my face. When I'd wiped away most of the moisture, I smoothed a hand over my errant waves and took a final glance in the mirror.

Three more hours. I could do this.

I steeled my shoulders, took a deep breath, and turned to pull open the door.

"Hi." He was leaning against the wall directly across from the bathroom, grinning at me with a warm look in his eyes.

"Hi," I returned, grinning back at him as I moved a step forward into his space.

"You hiding out in here?" he asked. Both of his arms came up to circle my waist and tug me against him.

Pressed close, I propped my chin against his chest and tilted my head up to look at his face. "Only for a minute," I admitted, my lips twisting in a sheepish expression. He leaned down and kissed the tip of my freckled nose.

"I know this isn't your ideal night. It's not mine, either," he said, hugging me tighter. "Thanks for helping me endure it. You have no idea how much better it is, having you here with me."

The warmth in his eyes melted away all of the discomfort I'd felt since stepping through the massive oak front doors in a hand-me-down dress Minnie had scrounged from one of her daughters' closets.

"It's your birthday," I said, rolling my eyes at him. "I wouldn't miss it for the world. Plus, have you tried those mini quiche things? They're pretty fantas—"

"Lux." Bash leaned down and brushed his smiling lips against mine. "Shut up."

"Shutting up," I promised, grinning as I lifted onto my tiptoes and kissed him back.

The downside of being the guest of honor at an event?

You can't just disappear to make out with your girlfriend for an hour, or make an early escape if things get boring. So, after a few, too-brief stolen moments, we were eventually forced to tear ourselves apart and head back to the party.

"Come on." Bash sighed resignedly, linking our hands together as he led me down the hallway to the main room. "My dad wants to meet you."

His words made my stomach churn with nerves, but I said nothing as we entered the main room and approached his parents. Judith's clear blue eyes narrowed as soon as she spotted my hand entwined with her son's, but her Botoxed smile didn't waver. My eyes skittered away from her to take in the man on her left.

I'd seen him in pictures, of course, but they hadn't done Senator Covington justice. He was classically handsome in the way that benefitted the most memorable politicians. He could've passed for a Kennedy with his broad white smile, boyish charm, and sandy blond hair. His eyes were a startling shade of green, but they were wide and full of welcome — a total contradiction to his wife's icy stare.

"Lux!" He stepped forward and grabbed my free hand, cupping it within both of his. With a gentle tug, I was pulled away from Bash and into his father's space. "So nice to meet you. I've heard so much about you and your interesting little family from Sebastian."

"Dad." The warning in Sebastian's tone unmistakable.

"Oh relax, son. I'm not going to embarrass you." The senator pulled me against his side and wrapped an arm around my shoulder, squeezing lightly. His enthusiastic greeting made me feel infinitely more welcome than Judith ever had, but a creeping sense of unease was stirring to life in the recesses of my mind. That unsettled feeling only magnified when I looked at Bash and saw how tense he was — his pulse throbbed in the protruding vein on his neck, his jaw was tightly clenched, and his eyes were locked on his father.

"So tell me, Lux," the senator said, loosening his hold on my shoulders so he could peer down at my face. "What are your plans for next year?"

I swallowed roughly. "Well, Senator, I—"

"Andrew," he corrected, beaming at me.

"Okay, Andrew," I repeated, feeling an uncomfortable blush spread across my cheeks. "Hopefully, I'll be at UGA."

"She received a full academic scholarship," Sebastian offered, still staring at his father. His expression was entirely closed off — nothing I'd ever seen from him before — and though his words were supportive, his voice was defensive.

"How wonderful," Andrew said in a happy tone, staring back at his son with smiling eyes. When he turned his gaze on me, I barely stopped myself from taking an involuntary a step away from him. It was like looking into two empty glass orbs — up close, I could see that no genuine emotion or affection filled his stare, no warmth or welcome suffused their depths. He was hollow.

"Lux, tell me," he continued, squeezing my arm tightly. "Has Sebastian given you the good news yet?"

My eyes darted to Sebastian, unsure of what to say and afraid to get in the middle of whatever was happening here.

"Dad." Bash glared at his father, his reprimand even chillier than before.

"But I'm so proud!" Andrew gushed, his spirited laughter filling the room. "See, Lux, he's been accepted to Princeton in the fall!"

I stilled, forcing a happy smile onto my face and avoiding Bash's stare, which I could feel scanning my expression. "That's fantastic," I said, my fake enthusiasm discernible even to my own ears. I'd never been a very good actress.

"I don't know what we'll do without him around here — Princeton's in New Jersey. That's nearly two thousand miles away!" Andrew added, as though I didn't possess basic, elementary-level geographic knowledge about the location of our states. The moment was beginning to feel less like a conversation and more like a chess game between Sebastian and his father — each careful syllable a rook, each nuanced word a knight, sliding across a board of unspoken meanings and moving in for the kill.

"With you here in Georgia and my boy up north, well, it'd be a miracle if you managed to make something like that work." The senator smiled happily, his white teeth so perfect I wondered if he'd had them capped with porcelain veneers.

"That's enough," Bash growled, reaching a hand across the space and grabbing my hand. With one sharp tug, he pulled me out from his father's grip and settled me into his side. "We're leaving."

"But we've barely gotten to know one another!" the Senator protested, grinning at Bash and me with an uncomfortably excited glint in his eyes. "Don't steal Lux away yet. We've so much more to explore."

I felt the blood drain from my face as I watched Andrew's eyes travel slowly down the length of my body, perusing my every curve with a blatantly sexual stare. Hoping for some kind of intervention, I turned my horrified gaze toward Judith only to find her staring impassively at the wall, a crystal tumbler of amber liquid clutched in her hand. She appeared completely uninterested in her husband's actions — either she was well-practiced at looking the other way during his indiscretions, or she was so caught up in her own thoughts of glamorous gatherings and guest lists she failed to even notice his inappropriate leering.

"Come on," Bash whispered, pulling me away. "Let's go."

"So nice to meet you, Lux!" Andrew called after us. I made the mistake of glancing back over my shoulder at him, and felt my stomach flip when he winked lecherously. "See you soon, dear!"

Sebastian led me to the kitchen and outside, walking at a brisk pace. His anger was apparent in each stride he took, his steps pounding against the grass at an unmatchable pace as we made our way down the sloping lawn to the tree line. The sun had set hours ago and there was a chill in the air — I shivered, pulling my thin cardigan tighter around my short dress and trying not to stumble on my flimsy, borrowed pumps. I wasn't used to walking in heels and, as I stumbled over a stray rock on the path through the woods, I knew I'd never become the sort of woman who wore them every day. They were so impractical.

Guided by the faint glow of Sebastian's cellphone, we eventually made it to the clearing. Bash pulled our wool blanket from the tree hollow in the giant oak. He spread the blanket across the grassy bracken and settled in, immediately pulling me down beside him. I lay across the blanket, my long hair spread out in the grass around me and my white dress glowing luminous in the moonlight. Bash rolled onto his side to face me, his head propped against his hand and his eyes on mine.

"Lux, I'm so sorry," he whispered. "My father, he's—"

"Shh," I breathed, reaching a finger up to press against his lips. "Don't."

"The Princeton thing, it's not definite. It's just what he wants. And the way he looked at you..." Bash pressed his eyes closed at the thought and his upper lip curled in disgust. "I don't know how to make this up to you, but I swear I will."

"Bash," I said, rolling onto my side so we were face to face. "Stop. There's nothing to apologize for."

"But my family—"

"So they aren't perfect. Think about who you're talking to." I smiled at him. "The only reason you haven't met my parents is because they're always at the bar, or passed out drunk on the couch. 'Dysfunctional' is inscribed somewhere on our family crest."

A small smile crept across Bash's face.

"You aren't your family. You aren't your father," I told him, leaning in to press a kiss against his lips. "I love you because of who you are — not because of them. You could've been raised by a troupe of con artists or circus performers and I'd still love you."

"Yeah?" he asked, quirking an eyebrow at me.

"Yeah." I kissed him deeply, twining my arms around his back and looping one of my legs around his waist. He pulled me flush against him, rolling onto his back so I was sprawled across his chest.

"You know what I think, Freckles?" he asked, his hands skimming down my back in a possessive gesture.

I shook my head.

"Babies have no say about which crib they end up in. I didn't pick my parents anymore than you chose yours. I think real family is the family you get a say in — it's the family you build with someone you love. And I know one day, when we're married and you're the size of a house, pregnant with my baby inside you..." His hands stilled on my sides as he stared into my eyes. "I'll have made my real family. *Our* family."

My heart fluttered in my chest and my eyes began to tear, but I forced a stern expression onto my face. "Maybe I don't want babies with someone who thinks I'll be the size of a house."

Bash grinned. "Yeah, you do."

"I don't like you," I informed him, trying my best to maintain a glare.

"I know," he whispered, cupping the back of my neck and guiding my lips against his. "But you love me."

"Yeah, yeah, yeah," I grumbled, smiling as our kiss deepened and we forgot all about the party still going on inside, and the parents we'd had no choice in.

❦

"I'LL GRAB YOUR COAT. MEET ME BY THE CAR IN FIVE MINUTES," Bash said, leading me back toward the house.

"Okay," I agreed, squeezing his hand tightly as we approached the dark mansion. The party guests had all gone home, but I didn't want to chance an encounter with either of Sebastian's parents. "I just want to say goodbye to Greta."

Bash smiled. "She likes you."

"I like her," I countered, bumping my hip against his.

He kissed my forehead quickly, then headed for the side door into the house. "See you in a minute."

"Not if I see you first!" I whispered, grinning as I made my way across the patio toward the back entrance to the kitchen. The glass paneled door swung open on soundless hinges, and I stepped into the dim room. Only the faint light above the stove was left illuminated — all of the other kitchen lights had been switched off for the night. I scanned the space for Greta, hoping she was still awake, and my eyes caught on the light creeping out beneath the crack of the ajar pantry door across the room.

She must've gone in there to put away the party leftovers, I thought, skirting around the kitchen island and heading for the small entrance. The sound — a terrified, mewling protest — reached my ears just as I reached the door. What I saw through the open crack made my blood run cold.

Greta wasn't alone in the pantry.

Andrew's hands roamed the maid's body freely, despite her cowering. She didn't attempt to fight him off, but her distress was clear on her face. He groped at her breasts and though his back was to me, I imagined the lascivious look on his face.

"Shh," he muttered, moving one of his hands down to the bottom of her uniform. "Be a good girl, Greta. It's only me. I thought we resolved all this, the last time."

When his hand moved beneath her skirt, Greta cried out in despair and her wide blue eyes flashed with horror. My mind reeled, searching for an explanation, seeking some kind of justification for this, but there was none. This was no tawdry dalliance between master and maid — no secret affair between two willing partners. This was rape.

I watched my hand like it belonged to a stranger, as it lifted and pushed the door open with enough force that its impact against the pantry wall set the cans rattling on their shelves. The loud bang was enough to stop the progression of Andrew's hands. When he turned to me, his eyes still swirling with lust, I saw surprise flash in his expression.

He hadn't expected it to be me at the door.

Greta's face showed both terror and relief, and as her hands worked to smooth her uniform back into place, she cast a grateful look in my direction.

"I'm sorry to interrupt," I said, my cold tone saying otherwise. "I was just looking for Greta. I promised her a ride home."

"How odd — Greta usually drives herself home," Andrew said, still panting slightly as he stared at me with a challenge in his eyes.

"Her car battery died," I added, lying through my teeth with my furious eyes locked on the senator.

"Well, that's very generous of you to offer, Lux, but I'm happy to drive Greta home. After all, she is mine." He smiled at me and I thought I might be sick. "My employee, that is."

"I insist," I bit out between clenched teeth. I kept my eyes on the senator, but extended my hand into the open space and spoke to the frightened woman. "Come on, Greta. Let's go."

I waited until I heard her hesitant shuffle and felt her hand slip into mine.

"Goodnight, Senator." I took a step backwards through the doorway, unwilling to turn my back on this man even for a moment. He was evil.

His grin never faltered, but his eyes had gone cold the moment he was forced to release his victim. "Goodnight, Lux. I'm sure I'll be seeing you again. Very soon." His gaze moved to the woman at my side, and I felt fury boil in my veins as his eyes drooped down to half-mast and scanned her trembling body. "Greta. Always a *pleasure*."

I squeezed the maid's hand and pulled her behind me, practically running for the patio door that would take us out of this house and away from these people. When we reached the side garage, I looked around for Sebastian, but he hadn't arrived yet.

"Thank you," Greta whispered, her eyes filling with tears as she stared at me. "Thank you so much."

I took her by the shoulders and stared into her face. She was only a few years older than me — maybe in her mid-twenties — and I suddenly saw how fragile she was. "Listen to me," I whispered fiercely. "You get in your car and you go. Don't come back here."

"But my job...the money..." Greta bit her lip and her anxious expression tugged on my heartstrings.

"There are other jobs, Greta," I said, staring into her eyes. "There's only one of you. This is your life. You can't live it here — not under the same roof as that man."

Her tears spilled over and she nodded weakly in agreement.

"Here," I said, reaching into my small clutch bag and pulling out my tattered wallet. There wasn't much — just what little grocery money I'd managed to save for next week — but I pulled the bills out anyway. Pressing them into her hand, I knew in this moment, she needed them more than I did. "Take this."

"I can't—" She began to protest, but I stopped her.

"It's not much, trust me. I wish I could do more for you." I used my hand to curl her fingers closed around the wad of money. "Just promise me you'll get away from him."

Greta clung to the money like a lifeline, then wrapped thin arms around me in an unexpected embrace. Her wet, tear-stained cheek brushed mine as she hugged me. "Thank you."

"Go," I ordered, fighting off my own tears as I stepped away and pushed her lightly toward the small, beat-up Honda she'd parked next to the garage. She nodded and hurried for her car.

When her taillights disappeared down the long driveway, I brushed the dampness from my cheeks and turned away.

"Good luck," I whispered into the night.

Sebastian emerged from the house a few minutes later. He draped my jacket over my shoulders and led me to the car, staring at me with worry in his eyes. Three times during our ride home, he asked why I'd gone so silent. I shrugged off his concern and stared out the passenger window, lost in my thoughts, until he dropped me off at home.

I couldn't tell him.

Not tonight, anyway. This was his father, after all. Plus, it hadn't escaped my notice that his father was an important political figure. If this got out, it wouldn't only ruin the senator's career and reputation, it would set off a media storm that would shatter Sebastian's family — and, in all likelihood, his future.

But, at the same time, I couldn't *not* tell him.

His father was the worst kind of man — one who abused his power to exploit the innocent, who used his strength to force others into submission. Bash had a right to know.

I'd tell him in a few days, I reasoned. I needed time to process and figure out the right way to break it to him. For now, as I remembered the crazed look in Andrew's eyes when I'd led Greta away from him, all I could think about was the fact that I'd just made a very powerful enemy — one who'd stop at nothing to protect himself.

And destroy me.

Chapter Twenty-Six

NOW

THE BOARDS GROANED BENEATH MY SNEAKERS, EACH STEP sending up a plume of dust into the stale air of the warehouse. This was, by far, the stupidest thing I'd ever done in my entire life. Did that stop me from attempting this insane quest?

Of course not.

After work on Monday, I'd hurried to the lobby bathroom and performed another quick change into sneakers, jeans, and a sweatshirt before boarding the subway to Brooklyn. As I rode to Red Hook, I distracted myself from thoughts of what I was about to attempt by replaying the day I'd had over in my mind.

I'd arrived at work purposefully late, figuring a tardiness reprimand was better than another early morning elevator ride with Sebastian. Walking in while the daily briefing was already in progress, I avoided any possibility of being cornered alone. I weaved through the group and headed immediately for the Jennys, shamelessly using them as a human shield to protect me from the hazel eyes that roamed the gathered team. Sebastian had stood at the center of the circled workers, discussing the 1950s and 1960s sets he'd be shooting today and doling out responsibilities to the design crew.

"I'll be up on the fourteenth floor most of the day, shooting," he'd informed us.

Thank god. I smiled as I listened to him hand out assignments, cowardly relieved I wouldn't have to see him all day.

"Tech support, you're with me. Models should already be in hair and makeup upstairs. Costume design, you can head up there immediately to ensure everything's set up." Sebastian glanced at his watch. "I want this to go as smoothly as possible. Set design, be on standby to set up the '60s set as soon as '50s is done. Last week it took too long to roll out the '40s set after we finished with '30s and we were here late." Sebastian's eyes abruptly cut through the crowd straight to me, where I'd ducked partially behind Jenny S.'s petite frame. Apparently, he hadn't missed my stealth entrance or been fooled by my makeshift hiding spot. He smiled when our eyes met.

"I don't want to be here late tonight," he continued, his eyes locked on mine. "I've got plans."

Shit.

His grin widened as he turned his head away, scanning the crowd a final time before he broke up the meeting. "The rest of you, continue working on whatever research or writing projects Angela has assigned for the upcoming shoots. Any questions, ask her — she's in charge while I'm gone. Let's have a good day, people."

When everyone began to disperse, I made a point to engage the two Jennys in a conversation about their troubled love lives — they always had plenty of weekend horror stories to share — and studiously avoided looking in Sebastian's direction again until I was sure he'd disappeared upstairs for the photo shoots. My own weekend had been blessedly quiet after his visit Friday night — I'd locked myself away from the world, researching and drafting the beginnings of my story on sex-trafficking, watching old movies, and eating so many Cool Ranch Doritos I was sure the chip company was going to write me a thank you letter for single-handedly helping them meet their third quarter sales quota.

Work on Monday flew by and as soon as the clock struck five, I was on the elevator, heading down to the lobby with my black backpack in hand. I didn't know what "plans" Bash had in mind, and I had no intention of sticking around to find out.

When I finally reached the waterfront, plucking my way across the dilapidated pier as I approached the warehouse, I was having serious doubts about my plans for espionage. Armed only with my total lack of experience, Fae's borrowed binoculars, and the disposable camera I'd picked up at *Swagat* yesterday as a backup in case my cellphone ran out of battery, I grew increasingly nervous as the brewery came into sight. I snapped a few pictures from a safe distance, leaning around the corner of an adjacent warehouse to keep my body out of sight from any lookouts — as I'd seen any number of Hollywood-manufactured spies do. Instead of approaching the brewery directly, like I had last week, I slipped down an alleyway on the far side of the abandoned building next door. The adjacent warehouse was a cannery, long fallen into disrepair, and not somewhere I'd normally want to explore. But, unlike the neighboring brewery, this cannery was special.

Its windows weren't boarded up.

It had come to me last night as I tossed and turned in bed, mulling over possibilities for breaking into the brewery. I wasn't a complete idiot — I knew a petite blonde woman with no covert training would never be able to sneak into such a place, especially with thugs like Smash-Nose and the Neanderthal patrolling the grounds. In a face-to-face altercation, I wouldn't be able to overpower or evade them and — even on the off chance that I did — there was nothing to stop them from calling their friend Santos, who could issue a warrant for my arrest faster than I could say "in over my head."

But then, as I conjured an image of the brewery in my mind, I had a realization.

I didn't need to get inside. I just needed to *see* inside.

While the ground level windows were thoroughly boarded up to keep out prying eyes and looters, the upper floors' panes had been left unbarred. If I could get into one of the adjacent buildings, climb to the third floor, and see through the windows, I'd have an all access pass to whatever was happening inside the brewery.

So here I was, spending my happy hour climbing a termite-eaten stairwell to reach the third floor of a dusty, decaying cannery. Simon and Fae had each called me twice already. Either they were pissed I'd been avoiding them all weekend, or they'd finally caught on to the fact that I'd shut them out of my investigation after our Santos surveillance run last week. They may've let the presence of the sex-trafficking storyboard in my apartment slide the other night, because I was in the midst of a Sebastian meltdown, but now that they'd had time to reflect, their worries about my sanity had probably reached DEFCON 1 levels.

After everything I'd learned, I didn't want them involved. If something went wrong, I was going to land in a world of trouble. Plus, if I were trapped in a car with those two for any amount of time, the saga of Sebastian would inevitably come up — and for that conversation I'd need to fortify myself with at least a pint of Ben and Jerry's. Possibly two.

I froze as a loose floorboard creaked loudly underfoot — I'd reached the top of the stairs. Stepping onto the third floor of the cannery, I tried to be light-footed as I crossed to the bank of windows that faced the brewery. There were faint signs of life here on the upper floors — a candle burnt down to a stub, a dusty blanket riddled with holes, a discarded book. Remnants of squatters long gone from here, if the thick coating of dust was any indication. My sneakers left a trail of footprints in the grime, like walking through a fall of snow on an early December morning.

When I came to the windows, I spent several minutes using

the cuff of my sweatshirt to wipe the dusty residue off one of the panes at eye level. Peering out, I could just discern the building across the street through the smudged glass. From what I could see at this distance, the room directly across from me inside the brewery appeared to be an office. There was a wooden desk stacked high with papers, a laptop computer, and a small lamp that helped to light up the gloomy room.

About twenty minutes passed without any activity inside the brewery. I was about to head down to the second floor, to test my view from there, when the office door swung inward and two people entered, the dim lighting illuminating their figures in shadowy profiles. As they walked closer to the window, I strained my eyes to make out their faces.

I lifted my phone to eye-level, made sure the camera flash function was switched off, and snapped a few pictures through the dirty glass. Pulling back, I used my fingers to zoom in on the photos I'd just taken. As I zoomed, the resolution blurred and the images became grainy and useless. I couldn't make out much of the figures inside the room, though I thought one of them might be a woman — the smaller stature was apparent despite the fuzzy quality.

Reaching into my backpack, I rummaged around until my fingers grazed Fae's mini-binoculars. I popped off the lens caps, raised them to my face, and leaned closer to the pane. They were poorly crafted out of cheap plastic — I think Fae had purchased them at Duane Reade as a spontaneous two-dollar add-on item— but they magnified the room enough to see the larger of the two figures, who was standing closest to the window. It was definitely a man — a hulking one at that. It could easily be the Neanderthal I'd seen the other day or another like him.

I cupped my hands around my eyes to block the light and pressed the binoculars to the glass, squinting to bring him into better focus. His shirt was black, but there was something written in bold green script across the back of the garment.

Labyrinth

What was *Labyrinth*? My mind spun with possibilities.

A restaurant? A club? A business?

Before I could delve further into speculation, I felt it — that slow awareness that overtakes your system when you sense that someone is watching you. The tingling instant of time in which all the fine, feathery hairs on the back of your neck rise because you know, with instinctual perception, that you have ceased to be the hunter and are, instead, the hunted.

The hand clamped down over my mouth before I could take a single step away from the window, or even turn to face my attacker. My phone and binoculars clattered to the floor, and I began to struggle — my hands came up to tear at the fingers blocking my airway, my torso thrashed violently, my feet fought for purchase against the dust-coated wooden floor.

None of it mattered. As soon as his mouth brushed my ear and his whisper registered in my mind, the struggle was over.

"It's me," he said, his voice hushed. "There are two men in the alley directly below us. If you scream, they'll hear you."

All the fight left my body and I hung limp in his arms, relief coursing through my bloodstream and chasing the terror from my system. Though the relief was short-lived — anger took its place in matter of heartbeats.

"I'm going to take my hand away now," he added. "You good?"

I nodded and his hand slipped away from my face. Whirling around on the balls of my feet, I planted my hands on my hips and glared at him.

"You followed me!" The outraged whisper flew from my mouth with enough heat to sear the flesh from his bones.

Bash nodded. His face was set in stone and there was no humor in his eyes — they were flat as two greenish ponds on a windless day.

"What the hell, Bash?" I glared at him.

Without saying a word, he bent over and grabbed my phone and binoculars from the ground by my feet.

"What are you— Hey!" I yelped as his free hand shot out and grabbed hold of my arm just above the elbow with a fair amount of pressure. His vice grip didn't loosen as he began to stride across the room toward the stairs.

"I'm not finished here!" I struggled against him, but made no progress. "Bash, let me go! This is crazy!"

He stilled so abruptly, I had no time to slow my forward momentum and crashed face first into the broad planes of his back. I winced and rubbed my forehead with my free hand. Turning his head slightly over his shoulder, so his face was visible in profile, Bash's icy words were enough to stop my protests.

"Those men in the alley? They're armed. So you can either walk out the back entrance with me, or I'll carry you out. Your choice. But either way, we're leaving. Now."

It took me about two seconds to evaluate my options and realize that he wasn't kidding around. Admitting defeat, I nodded to signal my cooperation and allowed him to pull me to the stairwell.

Sebastian walked quickly, leading us down to the exit and out onto the pier in less than a minute. Before I knew it, we'd left the row of warehouses behind and were back on the streets of Red Hook, heading for a small alleyway around the corner where a parked black Land Rover sat waiting. He yanked open the passenger door, shoved me inside, rounded the hood, and settled into the driver's seat in a series of aggressive movements that betrayed just how angry he was.

"I don't know why *you're* mad," I said, crossing my arms over my chest in a defensive maneuver.

Sebastian turned over the ignition and pulled out of the alley with such speed my body pressed back against the cushioned seat and my stomach turned over.

"So dramatic," I muttered under my breath.

He didn't bother to acknowledge that I'd spoken, but his fists clenched tighter around the steering wheel as we sped along Brooklyn's waterfront toward the bridge. Realizing he likely wasn't going to speak to me until we reached our destination — wherever that might be — I sighed and flipped on the stereo system. Strains of familiar classical music filled the car and I immediately regretted my decision.

Vitali. Of course.

My hands itched to turn it off, but that seemed a far too obvious show of discomfort. I tried to appear unaffected as the violins crescendoed, though the desire to fidget in my seat was nearly irrepressible. Sensing my distress or perhaps feeling some of his own, Sebastian reached forward and flipped off the music, sending us back into a weighty silence. I turned my eyes out the window and allowed my attention to drift for a while. My thoughts were so wrapped up in the brewery and whatever "Labyrinth" might be, I didn't notice that we weren't heading for my apartment in Midtown until we'd slowed to a crawl on the streets of SoHo. Several blocks from Simon's loft — and several hundred thousand price-points higher, in terms of real estate value — the converted brick factories here were upscale lofts, complete with climate controlled underground parking and security systems.

Sebastian pushed a button on a sleek box affixed to his windshield, and we pulled into a gated, ground level garage. The gate lowered behind us and he nodded to a security guard as we rolled past the enclosed glass office.

"Where are we?" I asked nervously, seeking unnecessary confirmation.

Tight-lipped, Bash pulled into a parking spot and shifted the car into park.

"Can you please just take me home?" The hopeful naivety in my tone bordered on desperation.

He didn't answer or even look at me as he climbed from the driver's seat and walked around to open my door.

Shit.

I SPUN IN A CIRCLE, TAKING IT ALL IN. THE LOFT WAS GORGEOUS in an understated, luxurious kind of way. The entire space was white, with gleaming hardwood floors and lots of exposed wooden rafter beams crisscrossing the vaulted ceiling overhead. The kitchen was all stainless steel and chrome, a stark contrast to the warm earthy tones of the wood, and the walls were covered in a series of framed, black and white photographs from Bash's many travels across the globe. I recognized famous landmarks and cities in many of the photos.

Dubrovnik, Sydney, Venice, Paris, Beijing, London, Amsterdam.

There were so many photos, the loft could've easily passed for an art gallery — except for the bed, of course.

King size, low to the ground, draped in a white down comforter, and scattered with huge black throw pillows that looked like they'd be heavenly to sink down into, the bed took up a big portion of the loft space. It was bathed in light from the setting sun, as it sat by a bank of windows. There was no head-board; instead, the space on the wall above the bed was taken up entirely by a huge canvas, at least ten feet across, which showcased the only color photograph in the entire apartment.

I stepped closer, bringing the vivid photo into better focus, and felt my breath catch.

It was a tree — *our* tree.

His lens had captured the huge oak at its most beautiful — in the heart of fall when the leaves had begun to redden and wither, drifting down to lay like fallen soldiers beneath the huge sentinel. The massive tree towered over the clearing, its graceful boughs backlit by a warm autumn sun and its leaves a kaleidoscope of orange hues.

It was beautiful — there was no question about that.

But as to why it was here, in Sebastian's apartment, after all these years — I had no explanation.

I turned to him, the question on my lips, but froze when I saw his face. He was staring hard in my direction, a thunderous expression clouding his features. I felt my hackles rise immediately and whatever warmth I'd felt at the sight of the photograph began to dissipate.

"What?" I asked, crossing my arms over my chest and glaring right back at him.

He stepped closer to me. "What the hell did you think you were doing?"

"Excuse me?"

"You heard me." He stared at me with narrowed eyes. "You have no good reason to be going down there alone."

"You have no idea what my reasons are or what I was even doing there," I countered.

"Sneaking around in warehouses that are practically falling down? Spying on dangerous fucking people with a fucking iPhone camera?" Bash snorted. "Yeah, I've got you pegged, Nancy Drew. You're looking for that girl — your friend. And you're going to get hurt in the process."

He was probably right, so I couldn't really argue with that statement. But I could still glare at him.

Bash took a few steps closer. "I'm not going to stand by and watch you stumble into a situation you have no idea how to handle. And, Freckles, from what I've seen — there's not much you *can* handle."

"You're a condescending ass!" I yelled, taking a step toward him. My entire frame trembled with barely-contained rage. I knew I wasn't an expert investigator, but I was doing the best I could with the few resources I had at my disposal — and rather than acknowledge that, he'd chosen to belittle my every effort.

"Well, you're a naive little girl!" he shouted back at me, the vein throbbing in his jugular.

"I hate you!" I spat the words, getting right up in his face.

His hands shot out, grabbed hold of my upper arms, and yanked me closer, crushing our bodies together so tightly the breath was stolen from my lungs. "Yeah, I hate you too," Bash muttered, just before he closed the remaining gap between our faces and his lips crashed down on mine.

Once our lips met, there was no stopping us. It had been far too long since our hands had explored the secret places of each other's bodies. An eternity since my fingertips had skimmed over his rippled abdominal muscles. Eons since his palms had slipped down my sides and beneath the bottom hem of my top. Forever since my shaking fingers had worked at the buttons on his shirt, or tugged his belt from its loops with impatience.

His lips were relentless in their pursuit, his kiss demanding as he stole my breath and pushed my control to its absolute limits. There was a small part of my brain that was screaming out that I should stop this, *now*. That this couldn't go on, or I'd be triggering a scenario that would end badly for everyone involved — a conclusion doomed from its very inception.

But that part of my brain was quickly overridden by the wave of passion that swept through my system as I savored the feeling of finally, *finally*, having my lips pressed against Sebastian's. I'd hungered for this moment — longed for it, wept for it, even prayed for it — for seven years, like an addict who needed her fix. Now, I was a junkie confronted with her greatest vice on a veritable silver platter; there was no way I could summon the strength to walk away.

And so, reason was lost. Inhibitions, shredded. Clothing, discarded.

Sebastian's lips moved down to kiss my neck and his fingers dug into my flesh as they roamed the bare skin of my back, beneath my shirt. With one swift tug, he pulled the sweatshirt over my head and tossed it to the ground, his mouth only lifting from my skin for the fraction of time it took the material to slide past my shoulder blades. I wound my hands into his thick hair, luxuriating in the feeling of the smooth strands against my fingertips, and he raised his head to look at me.

His eyes burned into mine, their normal frozen hazel tundra

now a molten pool of desire. He pulled me closer roughly, as though any amount of space between us was far too much, and cupped the sides of my face in his palms. My hands slipped from his hair and twined around his neck, our faces hovering so close we shared the same breath.

"You are so fucking beautiful," he whispered, his voice laced with awe.

His right hand moved from my cheek and up to the clip in my hair. One deft motion of his fingers had it spilling free, my long blonde locks tumbling down around my body in a cascade of curls that fell to mid-back. Bash's eyes turned scorching at the sight, and his lips crashed down again on mine. His hands moved to trace the straps of my bra and tank top, pulling them down off my shoulders with twin tugs. His lips followed his fingers' path — down my neck, across my collarbone, and between the valley of my breasts. I felt my breath catch when he moved up over the swell on my left side, his lips trailing kisses as they went.

And just when I'd reached the point of combustion... When I was ready to tumble to the ground and lose myself completely... When his lips and fingers were about to bring me to my knees...

Everything stopped. Or, more specifically, *he* stopped.

My eyes opened, my spine straightened from the arch it had unknowingly bent into, my head lifted, and I saw that Bash was immobile — frozen with his burning eyes locked on the ink over my heart. I watched as he mouthed the words, each soundless syllable forming on his lips and contorting them into varying shapes of astonishment.

aut viam inveniam aut faciam

Shit.

I tried to step back, to turn from his sight, but it was no use — not now that he'd seen it. His hands clutched my shoulder blades and he lifted confused eyes to meet mine. There was really only one question for him to ask and though I braced for it, I still didn't have an answer prepared for him.

"Why?"

I stared at him, frustrated with myself but unable to tell him what he wanted to know. I wanted to scream at the top of my lungs, *Because you were right. Because I love you, you idiot! I've always loved you. Can't you see that?*

But I couldn't.

"Lux, *why* do you have this?" His thumb skimmed over the tattoo, his eyes never wavering from the inked skin.

I didn't answer, but my eyes were tingling with the formation of useless tears.

"This isn't fresh. When did you get this?" His disbelieving stare moved across the script as he read the words over and over. When I remained silent, he finally managed to tear his eyes away and raise them to meet mine. His grip on my shoulders tightened and he bent in close to my face.

"Tell me." His tone was ardent, his eyes desperate. "Tell me what happened back then. Why did you run? What made you go? I have to know, Lux."

Walk away, my brain shouted at me. *For your own good, and his, walk away. Now.*

"I know there are things you think you want to know but, in all honestly you *don't*," I whispered in a small voice, taking a step backward and watching as his hands fell limp to his sides. "You think I'm the victim here, but I'm not. As much as you might wish it, I'm not the damsel in distress in your story, Bash — I'm the villain. The sooner you accept that, the easier this will be."

"Goddammit!" Bash cursed, running one hand through his hair and rubbing the back of his neck with the other. "You are fucking impossible."

"I have to go." I turned and headed for the door, picking up my fallen sweatshirt on the way.

"Walk away again, Lux. You've had plenty of practice at it," Bash called after me.

I flinched, but kept walking.

"All that tattoo does is prove that I was right," he called to my back. "You didn't leave me back then, not by choice anyway. Something drove you away. And even if you won't tell me, I'm going to figure it out. I'll either find a way or make one — thanks for reminding me."

Freaking fantastic. I was such a monumental fuck-up.

"So I wouldn't run too far, Freckles," Bash added, his voice a blend of frustration and determination. "Because we're not finished. Not by a fucking long shot."

Chapter Twenty-Seven

❧

NOW

"Baby, what are you doing here? Not that I'm not glad to see you — I am, always." Standing in the doorway, Simon tilted his head sideways and looked me up and down. "But first you pull a vanishing act for the past three days and then you show up on my doorstep unannounced and, it *must* be said, disheveled in an I-just-had-sex kind of way?"

Damn, he was good.

"Do you have tequila?" I asked in a voice that was pathetically close to begging.

Simon's brows went up. I was a wine girl — he knew this better than most — so if I was asking for liquor, the shit had really hit the fan. I shoved my way past him through the doorway and headed for the kitchen, passing by a shirtless Nate who was sitting on the sectional drinking a beer. He lifted his glass to me as I barreled by, but I didn't stop to chat. I was a woman on a mission.

Simon trailed me to the kitchen and made short work of grabbing two shot glasses from the cabinet over the sink. I pulled the bottle of Patrón from its spot on top of the fridge.

"You're drinking too?" I asked him, raising one eyebrow at the sight of the second glass.

"Friends don't let friends do tequila shots alone."

I smiled as I poured out two helpings. I lifted one, clinked it against Simon's mid-air, and prepared to toss it back.

"What are we toasting?" Simon asked.

"Bad decisions," I said, tilting the shot glass and pouring the burning liquid down my throat.

"Which, of course, are only ever improved when tequila is involved," he noted in a wry voice, before throwing back his own serving. He coughed delicately, set both of our glasses in the kitchen sink, and put the cork back in the bottle. "Come on, baby. I have a surprise that'll make you feel better, and then its story time."

"You're going to read me a story?" I felt my brow furrow as I laced my fingers with Simon's outstretched hand and allowed myself to be led across the open loft toward his bedroom.

He snorted. "No, don't be an idiot. You're going to tell *me* the story of why you're at my apartment at—" He glanced at his watch. "—8:15 p.m. on a Monday night. Call it payment for the tequila shot."

I rolled my eyes and followed along in his wake. "What's my 'surprise'? It better not involve anything with glitter — and no, before you ask, I will not let you wax my eyebrows again. Last time, I ended up looking like Lindsay Lohan pre-rehab."

"That waxing pot was defective!" Simon protested. "It wasn't my fault!"

"Mhmm."

"You'll be sorry you ever doubted me when you see what I have for you." He dropped my hand when we reached the door to his bedroom, and I hopped up on his bed.

"The suspense is killing me," I drawled.

"No need for sarcasm." Simon crossed his room and grabbed a

large garment bag from his closet. I looked from the bag to his face, which bore an alarmingly happy expression as he approached.

"Oh, no," I muttered, realization dawning.

"Oh, yes," Simon squealed, unzipping the bag with a flourish to reveal a floor-length, Grecian style gown in ice blue. Elegantly draped fabric covered each shoulder and an ornate, silver-gilded belt gathered the material below the breast line to create an empire waist and a plunging v-neck. The daring neckline was far riskier than I'd ever choose for myself and would be sure to turn heads if I tried to squeeze my C-cups into it — but the dress' real eye-catching feature was the back.

Or lack-thereof.

On the other side of the dress, material from each shoulder fell straight down on either side and draped in a low cowl at the small of the back, leaving the entire spine exposed. From there, the sheath of blue fabric cascaded to the floor in a short yet elaborate sweeping train that was designed to drag several inches on the ground with each step.

"Ta-da!" Simon yelled. "Surprise!"

I stared at him, more confused now than I'd been the time he told me I was no longer allowed to wear wedge-heeled sandals because they were 'cheating' — apparently, in his world, heels don't count as heels unless they're a chore to walk in.

"Um, Si, are you sure this isn't for Fae?"

His face contorted into a look of disgust. "Of course I'm sure. Fae's an olive-toned brunette — a summer color girl, not a winter. Ice blue would be a disaster on her. You, on the other hand, will look fabulous in this. That creamy skin and blonde hair — my little ice princess." His eyes gleamed with anticipation.

"But where would I ever wear this?"

Now it was his turn to don a look of disbelief. "Um, I don't know, maybe to the huge, once-in-a-lifetime celebratory ball we're required to attend next week at our place of employment?"

Shit. In all the madness of my investigation and Sebastian, I'd completely forgotten about the upcoming *Luster* party — and the fact that I had yet to purchase a dress.

"Centennial," I muttered.

"There's the lightbulb!" Simon grinned and pulled me from my perch on the end of his bed. Leading me over to stand before his full-length mirror, he circled around behind me and held the dress to my front.

"It's perfect," he whispered.

I stared at the dress in the mirror, picturing the frost-blue against my porcelain skin and my hair twisted up in an elegant knot. I'd look like Cinderella – – a sluttier version, perhaps, but a princess nonetheless. If not for Simon, I'd have been attending in whatever I could find last minute at Macy's.

"I'll never be able to pay you back. This must've cost a fortune," I murmured, thinking it was worth every penny even as I mentally reconfigured funds in my bank accounts to cover the expense.

Simon simply chuckled.

"Where'd you get this?" I asked, breathless as I examined the gown more closely. "It's amazing."

"I made it," he said, shrugging as though it was no big deal. "Figured I should put all those skills I learned at Parsons to good use. It's not like I use them at *Luster*."

"Simon!" I exclaimed. "Are you serious? This is an incredible dress! It should be on a model, walking down a runway somewhere."

"I know," he huffed. "Took me freaking forever to get the draping right. But every incredible girl needs an incredible dress to match."

"Thanks, Si." Our eyes caught in the mirror and I reached up to squeeze his hand.

"Anytime, baby girl." He grinned at me. "Plus, a model totally wouldn't have the boobs to fill out this top, let alone the booty needed to hold up that train."

I rolled my eyes. "I'm going to take that as a compliment."

"As you should."

Careful not to wrinkle the dress, I turned to face him and wrapped my arms around his frame. "Love you."

"As you should," he repeated.

I laughed into the crook of his neck until he complained that I was messing up his new bow-tie and pushed me away.

WHEN I GOT BACK TO MY APARTMENT, STILL GLOWING HAPPILY from my visit to Simon's, it was past ten but I knew I'd be up for quite a while. I changed into comfortable clothes, grabbed my laptop from my desk, and climbed into bed. First, I updated my blog. It had been over a week since my last *Georgia on My Mind* posting, and my followers were likely wondering if I'd fallen into a manhole or been hit by a train. After posting an apology for my absence, responding to a week's worth of backlogged comments, and composing a brief anecdotal story about my first time in a city-wide blackout, I logged off and pulled up a blank word document.

It was time to catch up on my typical *Luster* column for Jeanine. I had deadlines rapidly approaching and I'd been procrastinating, as was often the case when I was confronted with writing about a topic I had little interest in. This month, it was juice cleanses. I laughed to myself as I wrote about the latest, greatest cleanse that promised to keep you full for days, drinking only a unique blend of lemon juice, honey, and cayenne pepper. I wasn't sure what women out there could possibly be satisfied by a diet of pure liquid, but I didn't ever want to meet them. Personally, I got pretty damn grouchy if I didn't eat every four hours — after a week, I'd be ready to commit double homicide for a doughnut.

Thankfully, I'd done all the research for the piece already, so it was written and ready for edits within two hours. I emailed it off to Jeanine for her inevitable critical feedback, pulled up a Google page, and typed "NYC Labyrinth" into the search bar.

Nothing. Not one credible result popped up.

There was a company out of Jersey called Labyrinth Fences, but their website boasted a poppy-red logo and pictures of a family-run, small-time business. There was a story about a prostitute who'd legally changed her name to "Labyrinth" after ten years working the streets. There were countless movie credits and photos from the set of *Pan's Labyrinth*. But there was absolutely nothing that would help my investigation.

My eyes grew tired as I scrolled through page after page of Google results. I'd been searching for hours, growing more frustrated with each dead-end I clicked on, and was ready to call it quits for the night when something caught my eye. A single link to a forum of questions about New York City's best-kept secrets. A conspiracy theorist's paradise.

I clicked it and scanned the screen with raised brows.

There, at the bottom of the page, was a thread of comments from anonymous posters. My eyes devoured their words, and I felt my heartbeat begin to race.

STARGAZER86: ANYONE ON HERE EVER HEARD OF *LABYRINTH*? On weekends, I bartend at this bar on the Upper East Side. Over the past few years, I've heard some patrons whispering the name, but I've never been able to figure out what it is.

PINKYSWEAR91: Supposedly, it's a club. Caters to the elite, members-only. Lots of rumors about backdoor deals and political alliances being made there, but no one knows for sure. It's all speculation.

STARGAZER86: So... secret society or urban legend?

GOODGUY33: Urban legend. It doesn't exist.

PINKYSWEAR91: Agreed. Probably a myth made up by someone with an overactive imagination. Tourists love the idea of secret clubs and shit. Makes them excited about the city — excited tourists spend more money. Simple.

STARGAZER86: Damn, too bad. I was hoping it would be something cool.

MADHATTER666: It's not a legend or a myth — *Labyrinth* is real enough. It's on E. 65th between Madison and Park. Though I wouldn't recommend walking through the front doors. Not unless you've got a death wish.

GOODGUY33: A name like MadHatter really makes you sound legit, bro. Go back to playing World of Warcraft and stop cluttering our threads with bullshit.

THERE WERE NO MORE COMMENTS, AND THE THREAD HAD BEEN inactive for more than four years.

I felt a chill race up my spine. So, it wasn't the most credible lead. GoodGuy33 was probably right — MadHatter666 was likely insane.

But what if he wasn't?

There was only one person I could think of who made knowing about the city's most exclusive venues a priority. If there really were a secret society called *Labyrinth*, she'd have heard of it. I scrolled through my phone to her name and dialed, wincing when I saw it was past midnight. Fae was a big proponent of beauty sleep and, as such, had a strict *no-calls-after-ten-unless-you-are-dying-or-pregnant* policy on weeknights.

Oh well. The phone rang in my ear three times before it connected.

"I know you're not preggers, so you better be dying," she muttered into the receiver.

"Well, I mean, technically we're *all* dying. Just at different paces," I noted. "But am I bleeding out at this exact moment? No."

"Hanging up, now."

"Wait! I'm sorry to call so late, but it's important." She couldn't have missed the strain in my words. "Please."

"Fine, five minutes," she agreed, sighing. "What is it?"

"Have you ever heard of *Labyrinth*?" I asked. "It could be a club or a restaurant, I'm not sure."

There was a pause over the line. I pictured her lying in bed, her tired mind reeling through thousands of restaurants, nightclubs, and organizations as she tried to conjure up a memory of the place I'd mentioned.

"Is it in Upper East? Near Madison and Park?"

At her words, I felt my throat constrict. I stared at MadHatter's comment with wide eyes. "Yeah, that's the one," I whispered.

"I don't know much." She yawned audibly. "I think it's members-only. Elite — *very* exclusive. We're talking old money. Some of the city's oldest, wealthiest families are supposedly affiliated. Politicians, professional athletes, mega-wealthy power players. But I don't know for sure; no one does. They don't exactly publish members' names in the *Post* on Sundays."

A sinking feeling turned my stomach when I realized that, if Fae and MadHatter were correct about *Labyrinth*, it would throw a major wrench in my plans to search the building. I couldn't simply follow this lead and walk through the front doors. Places like this, with their closely guarded velvet ropes and multitude of bouncers, were harder to get into than the White House.

"Hypothetically, if someone who wasn't a member wanted to get in... how would someone do it?"

Fae was silent for a moment, then sighed deeply. "Please tell me you're joking."

"Humor me," I appealed.

"It's impossible," she said. "You can't get in unless you're either a member yourself or the guest of one."

Damn. I thought for a moment before further querying my annoyed friend.

"Hypothetically, if someone wanted to find out the members' names... how would someone go about it?"

"Hypothetically?" Fae's tone was skeptical but amused. "That *someone* would have to call her best friend at well past a decent hour, in the middle of the night, and ask said friend to make a call."

"Seriously?"

"Seriously." She sighed. "I know a guy. He makes it his business to find out this city's secrets. I'll call him in the morning, see what he can do. No guarantees, but it's worth a shot."

"I owe you a bottle of wine," I said, feeling my spirits lift. With any luck, Fae's mystery man — who I totally had to ask about at a later date because, um, how cool was it that she 'knew a guy' who dealt in secrets — would come through for us and I'd have another lead to chase down.

"More than one," she observed. "And don't think I don't know what you're up to. This is about Vera and that crazy-town collage of theories you've plastered all over your apartment wall. We're overdue for a chat about your conspiracy obsession. No more secrets."

"Oh, like you don't have secrets of your own." I snorted. The girl was practically a Pandora's Box of mystery.

Fae sighed, but didn't contradict my words. "I'll call you tomorrow after I hear back about *Labyrinth*. We can meet after work."

"Thanks, Fae."

"Yeah, yeah. Call before ten next time," she grumbled, clicking off.

Despite her grouchiness I knew no matter what time I called, Fae would always answer. I smiled as I stashed my phone on my bedside table, closed down my laptop, and snuggled deeper beneath my comforter. It had been a pretty awesome day, if you didn't count my interaction with Sebastian — which I wasn't. The last thing I saw before my eyes drifted closed was my Cinderella gown hanging on the door of my closet.

◈

THE BARTENDER SLID A GLASS OF MERLOT ACROSS THE mahogany bar top, grabbed the bills I'd placed on its sticky surface, and moved on to take another order. I stared into the deep crimson swirling in my glass, mired in a bad mood I hadn't been able to shake all day.

Not since Cara had shown up at the office this afternoon, anyway.

She'd sauntered in, two lesser-known models following at her heels as any proper minions should, and immediately headed for Sebastian. Sure, I'd been studiously ignoring him all day as I worked on a new piece about how the 1960s fashion evolution echoed female empowerment, but once Cara made a move in his direction, all of my senses shifted into high-alert. I watched her progress with narrowed eyes, listened intently to her girlish greeting, and flinched when I saw her wrap skeleton-thin arms around his torso.

My head told me in a calm, rational tone that I should be glad he had someone else to distract him from his mission to discover what had happened between us seven years ago.

My heart let out a battle cry and decked itself out in war-paint, beating a drum and sharpening a spear as it prepared to engage Cara in a savage altercation that would leave no doubt about who Sebastian belonged to.

I fought against my more primal instincts and managed to talk myself off the edge. Not very far off — just a step or two back from the brink — but enough that I could turn my eyes back to my laptop and at least pretend to focus on my story. My gaze may have been averted, but my ears were finely attuned to every word that escaped Cara's Maybelline-endorsed Very Berry lips.

"Baby, wait until you see my dress for Centennial! It's Vera Wang. Totally gorgeous."

"Cara, you're late." I was relieved to hear the frustrated undercurrents in Sebastian's voice — a common occurrence whenever he spoke to the model. "We had the '50s shoot this morning. You missed it."

"Well, I'm here now," Cara whined, her voice that of a petulant child. "Let's go shoot it."

"I don't need you here, Cara. Go home."

"What do you mean, 'you don't need me?' I'm the lead model for this spread."

I could sense her pouting from across the room.

"We shot it without you," Bash said, his voice weary. "So come back tomorrow. On time."

"What did you say?" Cara screeched.

"You heard me, Cara. And don't act so surprised — you know my rules. You didn't show up; I replaced you. End of story."

"This is ridiculous!" Cara's shrill tone made everyone in the office flinch. "I'm calling Jeanine about this."

"Go ahead."

Cara stormed to the elevators — or so I thought. When the unmistakable sound of her clomping heels came to a halt directly next to my work station, I looked up to find the model's glaring eyes narrowed on my face.

"While I'm on the phone with Jeanine, I'll be sure to tell her what an absolute fuck up you've been here," she sneered at me. "After the stunt you pulled with my salad, I wanted you fired right away. Sebastian convinced me that your working here would make up for it, though, so I didn't say anything." She looked at me with the malicious excitement of a small boy who'd pinned an ant beneath his magnifying glass on a hot summer day. "But you haven't suffered here at all. In fact, the way I see it, he treats you better than he treats me. So I'll be speaking to Jeanine about you after all, skank, and I'll make sure you walk away from here without your job."

With a final glare, she turned and exited the building. My wide eyes flew from her retreating form to Sebastian, who was already striding in my direction. Beneath the watchful eyes of the score of people in the office, he grabbed my arm and led me to the emergency exit stairwell. When the heavy metal door swung shut at my back, isolating us in the abandoned stairway, he turned to me and let out an exasperated breath.

"What did she say to you?" he asked, running one hand through his hair.

I leaned back against the cool cinderblock wall, as far as I could get from him on the small landing. "Just that she's going to call my boss and get me fired."

"Shit." With a sigh, he leaned against the opposite wall, directly across from me.

"Yeah." I swallowed roughly, trying to quell my worry.

"Well, it's not like you enjoy your job, anyway," Bash's tone was amused and a quiet chuckle escaped his lips. "Writing about bubble bath and Beyoncé isn't really your style. No huge loss."

I lifted incredulous eyes to him. "You think this is *funny?* Losing my job and only source of income is *laughable* to you?"

"Lux, I was kidding." He cracked a smile. "You don't have to worry about your job. Cara has no power. She might huff and puff and blow a whole lot of smoke up your boss' ass, but at the end of the day nothing will come of it. She's a pretty face, nothing more."

"Oh."

"Yeah." He grinned, taking a step in my direction and closing some of the gap between us. "But if you want, I can call Jeanine and smooth whatever feathers Cara manages to ruffle."

"Really?" I asked, swallowing nervously as I watched him move closer.

"Of course." His smile was warm as he took one final step and entered my space fully. I felt my mouth go dry when he leaned down so our faces were at eye level. "For a price," he whispered against my lips.

I let out an embarrassing nervous squeak and tried to shrink back against the wall, but there was nowhere to go.

"Nervous, Freckles?" he asked, his voice amused. "Whatever for? You haven't even heard the price yet. And from what I remember of last night — I think you might enjoy my price quite a bit."

Breathe. Just breathe. Ignore everything he just said. Don't think about how much you would definitely *enjoy any price he set for you. Don't drool on him — that would be bad. And do not, under any circumstances, let him kiss you.*

"I'm not nervous," I lied, placing both palms against his chest and pushing him slightly out of my space. "You should be, though. I'm pretty sure this is sexual harassment." My small grin of triumph dissipated as soon as he leaned against my hands, his breath once again ghosting across my lips and sending shivers down my spine.

"Freckles, you can sexually harass me any time you want."

"I hate you, remember?" I smiled at him caustically, not realizing my poor word choice until I saw his eyes go liquid with heat — there was no doubt he recalled yesterday evening, the last time I'd said those words to him.

Shit. Seeing those memories in his gaze, I felt my own control slipping away.

"Oh, I remember," he whispered. His eyes watched my mouth as he leaned forward, his pupils dilating when my tongue darted out to wet my parched lips. He came ever closer, and I waged an internal war. I wanted his kiss, *needed* it, more than my next breath — but that didn't mean I could have it.

I should've moved away, skirted around him, darted for the door.

Instead, I froze and simply watched as his lips came toward mine. Our mouths were mere millimeters apart when a knock sounded on the metal stairwell door, snapping me out of my lustful haze. We sprang apart just as the entry swung open.

Angela popped her head inside. "Sebastian, we need your opinion on the final proofs. We're about to send off the first five decades to the publication team for review."

"Okay, be right there," Bash called. Angela disappeared back into the office, the door swinging shut behind her with a resounding boom. He turned his head back to meet my eyes, an amused smirk on his face.

"Saved by the bell," he murmured, his eyes still burning. "Any chance you want to pick this up at my place after work?"

I crossed my arms over my chest and tried to get my breathing under control. "Absolutely not."

He smirked. "Right. 'Cause you hate me."

"Right." I nodded sharply.

"That's fine, Freckles. You're just making this more fun." He grinned. "See, I've got a new strategy."

I didn't dare ask what he was talking about, but steeled myself when he stepped close once more and backed me up against the wall with his frame. He pressed a soft kiss against my lips, then whispered a string of words that made me curse myself for my own inability to walk away.

"You might think you're the villain in my story, Lux, but what you don't seem to realize is that *I don't care*. Princess or Evil Queen, I want you standing by my side when the tale comes to an end. So I'm not walking away — I'm going to wear you down, until you're ready — no, until you're *dying* — to tell me what happened back then." Another kiss landed on my lips, and I fought off a tremble of desire. "And Freckles?"

My eyes flickered up to meet his searing gaze.

"It's going to be a hell of a lot of fun."

෪

I WAS STIRRED FROM MY REVERIE BY A FAMILIAR VOICE.

"What's with the horse impersonation?"

Turning on my stool, I quirked an eyebrow at Fae, who'd just arrived at the bar with Simon in tow.

"Excuse me?"

"The long face," Simon explained.

I rolled my eyes. "Hardy har har."

They settled in on the stools to my either side and quickly put in orders for their own drinks with a passing bartender. I was still nursing my first glass of Merlot.

"Bad day?" Fae asked.

"The worst."

"Well, cheer up, chicky. I've got good news," she said, fishing around in her purse for a moment and pulling out a legal-sized envelope. She slapped it down on the bar in front of me, a self-satisfied smile on her face. "Am I good, or am I good?"

"If this is what I think it is, you aren't just good — you're freaking *great*." I picked up the envelope lightly, hope flaring to life in my chest at the feeling of the thick paper beneath my fingertips.

"Yeah, yeah, yeah, we're all wonderful," Simon intoned in a bored voice. "Open the damn thing."

I worked my right index finger beneath the seal, ripping the thin package open with care not to tear anything inside. I held my breath as I reached into the envelope and pulled out a stapled stack of sheets. There were probably at least twenty printed pages, but with just a cursory glance I could tell Fae's "guy" had come through for us. Big time.

The first few sheets contained a brief history of *Labyrinth*, which I mostly skimmed through. The final section of papers held the most vital information — a master list of members' names, dating back fifty odd years. I heard Fae's audible intake of air and could feel Simon vibrating with excitement as their eyes scanned through some of the figures on the list. My own heart began to race as I saw this was no mere collection of socialites and society members.

No, the monikers that caught my eye were household names — business moguls, multibillionaire technology mavens, United States congressmen, movie stars, political party leaders, and even, if I wasn't mistaken, the Vice President himself. They were the people you saw on your television every morning when you turned on the news, and every night when you sat down for some mindless after-dinner entertainment.

The leaders of our country were on this list. Powerful, far-reaching people with a vested interest in keeping any affiliation with a place like *Labyrinth* a secret. The information in this dossier was prized. And it had somehow landed in the hands of three over-worked, underpaid, fashion magazine employees at a trendy bar in Midtown.

Suddenly, it didn't seem like a good idea to be reading it out in public. In fact, it didn't seem like a good idea to be reading it at all.

"Maybe we should..." Simon trailed off, casting his eyes around the bar at the fellow happy-hour indulgers.

Fae was already reaching for her wallet. "Pay the bill and get the fuck out of here before anyone sees that?" she finished.

"My thoughts exactly," I muttered, shoving the papers back inside the envelope and tucking them deep down in the recesses of my purse where they couldn't be seen.

As soon as the tab was paid, we headed for the door. The three of us waited for a cab, shrouded in an uneasy silence so unlike our typical nonstop chatter, until Fae leaned forward to whisper in my ear.

"Did you see it?"

"See what?" I whispered back.

She held my eyes for a beat, a flicker of unease flashing across her face. "One of the names on the list..."

"Yeah?" I prompted.

"It was Senator Covington."

Chapter Twenty-Eight

❧❧❧

THEN

"YAHTZEE!"

"How are we even related?" Jamie snorted. "This is poker. You don't yell 'Yahtzee' in poker."

"I have a royal flush and just whooped your ass — I'll yell whatever I damn well please!" I grinned.

"She must be cheating." Bash shook his head. "Maybe she's counting cards?"

Jamie snorted. "Oh, please. She's not that smart."

"Hey!" I objected.

"I think it's more likely that you're going easy on her," Jamie said. "To keep her from whining about her losses all night."

"Or maybe Bash is just a shitty dealer," I chimed in, sticking out my tongue in my boyfriend's direction.

Bash raised his brows at me. "Oh, really? Well maybe you should walk home tonight."

I turned to Jamie with a shameful look on my face. "He forgets that his keys are in my purse," I said, nodding in Bash's direction. "It's all looks, no brains with this one."

At that, Bash leapt from his seat and pulled me into a playful headlock. "Someone's asking for it, today," he muttered, tickling my side with his free hand. I giggled, squirming in his arms so I could look up at his face.

"I might be asking for it," I whispered slowly, a telltale blush rising to my cheeks. Bash leaned in to bump his nose against mine.

"Later," he promised in a whisper.

Jamie began to wretch loudly, his fake-vomiting antics a clear protest of our mini PDA session. "Seriously, you guys are gross. Watching that two second interaction was more painful than a two hour round of chemo, I swear to you."

Laughing, I detached from Sebastian and hopped up on the bed next to Jamie. I snuggled lightly into his side, laid my head on his shoulder, and wrapped an arm around his midsection.

"You nervous?" I asked in a quiet voice.

I felt Jamie's body tense slightly. "A little," he admitted, his voice unsteady.

I hated that he was afraid.

"You're gonna do great, man," Bash said, settling into the chair on the other side of Jamie's hospital bed.

"Dr. Huntington has a spotless record, and I asked all the nurses about him," I revealed. "He's one of the best surgeons on staff. You'll be in great hands, Jamie."

"It's not that," he said flatly, staring down at his left leg which, after tomorrow, wouldn't be there anymore.

"I know," I whispered. "I'm sorry. I wish there was another way."

We fell into sad moment of reflection, each wrapped up in our individual musings, until Sebastian cleared his throat and shattered the heavy silence.

"I know this is a few weeks late, and I feel like a real dick for hanging onto it for so long," Bash said, reaching into the pocket of his jeans and pulling out an envelope. A red adhesive Christmas bow, flattened from its time in his pocket, was affixed to the top. "Merry Christmas, man."

He handed the thin package to Jamie, who accepted it with a stunned expression.

"You didn't have to get me anything," Jamie said, eyeing the envelope curiously. "And now *I* feel like a dick. Your gift may be late, but I didn't even bother to get you anything."

Bash laughed. "Well, before you convince yourself that I'm entirely selfless, just open it."

Jamie happily tore into the paper and pulled out two vouchers. The familiar hammer sigil alongside trademark blue and red script made them instantly identifiable.

"Dude! This is sweet!" Jamie grinned, holding the Braves tickets aloft. "I've never been to a major league game!"

"That second one's for me," Bash noted, grinning. "See? Not so selfless after all."

Jamie laughed, reading the tickets more carefully. "Wait, are these..." he trailed off. "No way! No freaking way!"

He sat straight up in bed, his excitement tangible and his sudden movements launching me onto the floor.

"Care to enlighten me?" I asked Sebastian, arching an eyebrow as I regained my balance. I'd never seen my brother so excited.

Bash laughed, watching with a happy smile as Jamie practically bounced up and down in anticipation. "They're VIP Meet & Greet passes. You get to tour Turner Field before the game, meet all the players, take photos, get autographs... It's supposed to be awesome."

"Wow," I murmured, more than a little in awe of my boyfriend. He'd managed to turn this day of mourning and grief into one of light and joy for my brother — a price I'd never be able to repay. Slipping one hand into his, I squeezed lightly and dropped my head against his shoulder. "I love you."

Bash kissed the top of my head. "The tickets are flexible, so we can choose a game once the season kicks off and Jamie's feeling up for it."

"Dude, if this isn't motivation for me to master my prosthetic in record time, I don't know what is," Jamie muttered, still unable to unglue his eyes from the tickets in his hands. "I'm gonna run a lap around the bases."

I turned to face the wall, not wanting Jamie to see the moisture filming my eyes. But, in a happy twist of fate, they weren't sad tears.

They were joyous.

⚬❦⚬

"Lux?" Minnie called from the kitchen. "That boyfriend of yours called. Said his plans changed and he can pick you up tonight after all."

"Okay thanks, Min!" I called back. I was in the front, wiping down tabletops and refilling condiment bottles after a busy Saturday night at the diner. Her announcement was a pleasant surprise. Bash made it a habit to pick me up after my shifts each night — tonight was one of the rare nights he'd said he couldn't make it. His mother had dragged him away for the weekend to visit one of his great aunts who apparently controlled a vast amount of financial assets and required some annual ass-kissing to guarantee the Covingtons weren't forgotten in her will. I wondered how he'd managed to escape early enough to pick me up.

Most nights he waited inside for me to finish cleaning after closing time — he'd charmed Minnie during their first meeting and from then on she'd been more than thrilled to let him keep us company. At the beginning I'd protested, saying he had much better things to do with his nights than help fill empty salt and pepper shakers, but he'd worn me down, insisting that no time spent with me was wasted. Tonight, as the minutes ticked by and Bash failed to appear at the front door, I felt a flutter of unease in my stomach. Maybe he wasn't coming after all.

Sure enough, though, when I stepped out of the diner into the brisk January night, his Mercedes was there idling in the parking lot. Dismissing my rattled intuition, I waved goodbye to Minnie as she locked up and hurried for the car, eager to see Sebastian. The dark tinted windows were impossible to see through from the outside, but I knew he saw me — I heard the locks click open as I approached. Reaching for the handle with a smile on my face, I slid into the passenger seat and turned to kiss him hello.

Before I could so much as strap on my seatbelt, the car lurched forward with a jolt that slammed my still-open door shut and sent my stomach reeling into my throat. Yet the shock induced by our abrupt departure was quickly overshadowed when I realized the man in the driver's seat was not my boyfriend.

It was his father.

"Lux!" Andrew grinned over at me, then looked back at the road. "So glad you could make it."

I reached for my seatbelt and strapped it on, my heart pounding as I eyed the speedometer. We were hurling away from the diner at breakneck speeds, inching past fifty miles per hour within seconds of leaving the parking lot.

"Senator." I tried to keep my voice steady. "What a surprise."

"Ah, well, I knew my boy was out of town tonight. Figured you could use a ride home."

"Minnie would've taken me."

"Nonsense! I'm happy to drive you." His perfect smile was too unwavering to be genuine. "Plus, this way we can chat."

I didn't want to "chat" with him. I didn't want to be in this car, traveling at this speed, without anyone knowing where I was or who I was with. I wished more than anything that I had a cellphone to call Bash, Minnie, or Jamie. Hell, I'd even call my parents at this point, I was so eager to escape this man's presence.

"Want to hear something funny?" Andrew asked.

I didn't respond. I had nothing nice to say – any words I spoke would only anger him.

"No?" He laughed with forced good humor, his tone disingenuously cheery. "I'll tell you anyway. My maid, Greta — you remember Greta, don't you?"

I clenched my hands tightly together in my lap and I looked out the window at the trees speeding by in a greenish blur. In the movies, people always jumped out of cars going a hundred miles per hour and walked away without a scratch; at what speed could I hurl my body from the passenger seat in real life and still survive?

Not this fast, that much was certain.

"Well, Greta didn't come back to work after you were sweet enough to drop her off the night of Sebastian's birthday party a few weeks back. Quite unlike her — she'd never been late a day in her life. And then suddenly she simply doesn't return?" He made a disapproving *tsk* sound. "Very unlike her. Strange enough to make you think someone else might've convinced her to stay away."

My palms began to sweat — I wiped clammy hands against my jean skirt, focusing on the feeling of denim scraping against my skin to regain a sense of calm. "Where are you taking me, senator?" I bit out in as polite a tone as I could muster.

"Home, of course, darling girl." He laughed boyishly. "After we've finished our chat."

Great.

"Anyway, like I said, it's been a terrible time at the house without Greta." He paused for a beat. "We all miss her, but Greta and I had a... special bond... you might say."

I flinched.

"But anyway, I didn't pick you up to talk about Greta."

"Then why *did* you pick me up?" I muttered.

"Don't get testy, darling." He laughed again. "We've still got a lot of ground to cover."

"Why don't you just skip to the point?" I asked, tired of all the false pretense littering this conversation.

"Fine, have it your way." He pulled the car to the side of the road and shifted into park. My heart leapt into my throat when he leaned across the center console into my space and my hand groped blindly for the door handle, but it wouldn't open — the child locks must've been enabled. I stilled when the glove compartment fell open and Andrew removed a thick white envelope. Still hovering over me, he turned his head over his shoulder and grinned, no doubt emboldened by our proximity and my clear discomfort. For a small infinity of time, with his arm pressed against my torso, I ceased even to breathe. One hand worked its way into my purse, as I searched desperately for my ring of house keys. When I grazed them, I clutched them between my fingers like tiny knives — prepared, if need be, to defend myself.

I felt a surge of relief when Andrew shifted back into his own space.

"Here," he said, tossing the envelope onto my lap. "Open it."

"What is it?"

He stared at me with that unflinching grin. "You'll see."

I felt a chill whisper up my spine as I ripped the package open. Inside, a single sheet of paper — embossed, in a curling archaic font was a phrase that stopped my heart.

DEED IN LIEU OF FORECLOSURE

Beneath the scrawling script were two signatures I recognized easily — they belonged to my parents. I knew, instantly, that this was the document they'd agreed to sign several weeks ago, which granted complete ownership of our property to the bank. We were now existing as renters on what had once been our own property, and still so far indebted to the bank it was hard to imagine ever being free and clear again.

"Why do you have this?" I whispered, not looking at him.

"It's a matter of public record, my dear! Any housing liens or foreclosures can be accessed with a simple trip to the Registry of Deeds." He chuckled. "I must say, I had no idea your family was in such dire straights when I met you on Sebastian's birthday. I suppose it does explain why he was so touchy when I brought them up. But after that night, I was inspired! I looked into your situation, my dear, and I must say, everything I discovered was a pleasant surprise."

I stared at the words on the paper until they began to swim

before my eyes, wishing I could erase them with sheer force of will. When I began to feel nauseous, I closed my eyes against his words, trying desperately to shut him out.

"Shame about your brother, though." His voice was full of false remorse. "James, is it?"

My eyes flew open and my head snapped in his direction. "Do *not* speak to me about my brother."

"I do believe I've touched a nerve." He grinned again. "But James is such an important piece in all of this."

"What are you talking about?" I ground out the words through a tightly-locked jaw.

"Your house is in foreclosure. Your brother is ill — perhaps dying. His osteosarcoma has a precarious prognosis. And you have no resources to pay for his care."

I stared at him, horrified realization beginning to dawn.

"It's simple, really. You need money." He stared at me, a gleam in his eyes. "I have plenty of it."

My mouth went dry and I tried to convince myself that this was some kind of terrible nightmare, from which I would awake at any moment. This couldn't be happening — could it?

"No." I shook my head in denial. "I don't want anything from you."

"Don't be so quick to turn me down, my dear. You haven't even heard my offer yet." He straightened his tie and seemed to gather himself, as I'd seen him do countless times before political rallies and public appearances on television. This was it — he was gearing up before the big pitch. I tried the door handle again, but it was useless.

"You and I both know you aren't meant to be with my son. He's destined for greatness. You are destined for..." His gaze scanned up and down my body, lingering on my chest. "A different life. One with a nice farm boy, perhaps, in a double wide somewhere out in the country. You'll pop out a few babies, eat Hamburger Helper for dinner, maybe even make your way to the polls to vote for a politician like me who promises to really *change* things for you." His eyes were empty of feeling. I didn't bother to answer, afraid to show how much his scathing words mirrored my deepest fears.

"But my son — he could be great. A congressman, a senator. Even the President someday. And you, my dear, are poised to ruin all of that." A flicker of annoyance flashed on his face, but was quickly smoothed away into a clear expression meant, no doubt, to persuade me. "You love him, that much is obvious. Don't you want what's best for him? Don't you want him to have that future? Because, if you do, we both know you have to let him go. To Princeton, to Washington, to the successful life he's meant to live — without you."

I took a steadying breath. "Sebastian is an adult. I think he's old enough to decide what he wants in his future. If that doesn't include you, or your plans, well — I'd say I'm sorry, but I'm really not. You're just going to have to let him make his own choices. It's not my place, or yours, to decide a damn thing for him."

His grin widened in response to the challenge my words had presented. "Even if it meant you could pay off your family's debt? Even if it meant James would have the best care?" He paused to guarantee that his words would have the ultimate impact. "How much is your brother's life worth, Lux? Is one, short-lived, high school romance that, in all likelihood, won't even last, worth your brother dying before he turns twenty? Face it — men like my son might fuck girls like you, but they certainly don't marry them."

I pressed my eyes closed. As much as I hated to admit it, as much as I wished it weren't true, his words had their intended effect. They rattled around my mind like loose marbles in a jar, jumbling everything I thought I knew — turning immovable morals and ethical codes into adjustable, ever-shifting margins. I had to consider his offer. The stakes were too high to disregard it without a thought.

Money could change things for my family — for Jamie, especially. He could have the best treatment, at a state-of-the-art facility in the city rather than a small, regional hospital in Jackson County. He could afford to apply for a place in clinical trials and have a private nurse to help him with rehab for his leg. He'd have the best doctors, surgeons, and medical staff at his disposal. A custom-fitted prosthetic. A unique treatment plan specifically tailored for his condition. A house with more than four rooms — somewhere that he could walk and exercise his atrophied muscles until his strength was fully recovered.

But could I give up the love of my life? My heart began to tear at just the thought.

"I can't," I whispered, seeing the beautiful future I'd painted for Jamie in my mind dissipate and fade to black. "I won't."

I'd find another way to give Jamie that life — this bribe wasn't the right path for us. No one made a deal with a devil and walked away wholly unscathed.

"Tough girl." Andrew chuckled, his Cheshire Cat smile only widening. "I thought you might say that. Thankfully, the first rule of political negotiation..." He reached into his jacket pocket and pulled out another thin envelope. "Never put all your cards on the table in the first round, dear."

He slid a thick, off-white document from the package, his fingers tracing the county clerk's green stamp by the signature line with reverence.

"This, my dear, is a very special piece of paper. Do you see what it says here?" His index finger pointed to a line at the top of the sheet.

DEED OF SALE

When I saw the property address and the name Andrew Covington listed as the new lot owner, I knew, with absolute clarity, that he'd backed me neatly into a corner. I'd been outmanned, outplayed — he held all the cards in this game, and I'd never even had a shot at beating him. There was the date of sale, in clear black and white — signed and stamped last week, by officials at the bank. My home, in the hands of a monster. My life, my family's life, at his mercy.

"This is the deed to your house, dear." Andrew turned fully in his seat to face me. "So, you see, I'm not just holding a document — I'm holding your fate in my hands. I thought you might need a little extra *incentive* to see things my way."

I swallowed roughly.

"What, no brave words? Where did all that honor and courage go?"

I bit my lip to contain my scream.

Andrew chuckled. "I'm really doing you a favor by teaching you this lesson early on in life. See, honor only gets you so far." He leaned in closer and I shied as far away from him as possible in the confined space, my side pressed firmly against the cool glass of the window. "I'll let you in on a little secret: people who fight with honor are the ones who *lose* their battles. The winners write the history books — and winners rarely let things like integrity get in their way, dear."

I took a deep breath. "What do you want?" I forced the quiet words from my lips, feeling like the worst kind of traitor.

"There's my good girl! I knew you'd come around," he crowed, tasting victory. "Tell me, Lux... Do you know what a non-disclosure agreement is?"

Chapter Twenty-Nine

❧❧❧

NOW

"ARE YOU SURE I HAVE TO DO THIS?"

"Yes," Fae said.

"It's the only way," Simon agreed.

I sighed. We'd been going back and forth about this for hours, discussing options and strategies for getting inside *Labyrinth*. Despite the absolutely feasible alternative plans I'd suggested — bribing a bouncer, finding a back-alley entrance or window, locating and utilizing Harry Potter's invisibility cloak — they were resolute: I had to ask Sebastian to get me inside.

"But he'll think this means he's won," I appealed, hoping they'd see reason. "He'll think I'm conceding to tell him about our past. He'll think I want to sleep with him!"

"You do want to sleep with him," Simon pointed out.

"And you should tell him about your past," Fae added.

"You know I can't do that," I muttered. "Plus, I called out sick from work today! If I call him, he'll know I was lying. I could get in trouble."

"Love, chances are he already knows you weren't sick. You're a terrible liar, so it's doubtful Andrea or Angela or whatever her name is even bought your story." Fae laughed lightly. "He probably thinks you're just avoiding him — which is partly true. He just doesn't know the rest of your reasoning."

"True," Simon chimed in.

"Also, I need a copy of that NDA," Fae said in a casual voice, her eyes averted.

"What?!"

"I won't even read it, I swear," she promised in a bored tone, staring at her cuticles.

"Let me guess..." Simon quirked an eyebrow. "You *know a guy?*"

Fae shrugged. "I just want to show it to a friend of mine, see what he has to say. He's a lawyer, he really knows his stuff. Maybe there's a loophole in that contract. If there is — he'll find it."

"If I give you the NDA, do I still have to call Sebastian?"

"Yes," Fae said.

I sighed.

"It's the only option that makes any sense," Simon said, handing me my cellphone. "He's the only one who can get you inside."

I grimaced as I accepted the phone, but resigned myself to their plan. After everything we'd learned about *Labyrinth* since opening that package yesterday, it was more imperative than ever that I get inside that club.

The document had been a manifesto of sorts, containing a detailed history of the exclusive organization as well as a list of members' names. After we'd scanned through a few pages at the bar last night, we'd headed back to my apartment where we could pour through it with a fine-toothed comb, safe from watchful eyes out in public.

From what we could tell, *Labyrinth* was more "secret society" than it was "club" — its history was full of tawdry love affairs between famous members, high profile business mergers that had shaped our country's economy for hundreds of years, and backdoor political deals that had far-reaching effects on our government to this day. The society had been around for so long, no records could pinpoint its exact year of origin. One source claimed that the decision to invade Vietnam had been made in a tea parlor on the second floor of *Labyrinth* in the early 1960s. Another, that the Constitution itself had been drafted by our country's forefathers in the front atrium at the original club site, long before the document ever made its way to the Philadelphia Convention in 1787.

Despite those high profile anecdotes, there was one piece of information that captured my attention more than any of the rest. In 1981, a reckless, still-wet-behind-the-ears rookie of the NYPD had stumbled onto something far above his pay grade.

Thomas Monroe, a twenty-six year-old New Jersey native, was on patrol when a transmission went out over the police scanner about a white moving truck parked illegally in an alley outside a new restaurant in the Upper East Side. When the call came in, Monroe responded that he would follow up. His supervisor also heard the call and quickly radioed back that Monroe should stand down, as another officer was already en route to the scene. But Monroe, eager to prove his worth on the force, disregarded that order and arrived at a chic address on E. 65th Street within minutes.

What he saw that night became the source of immense friction within the NYPD. Monroe attested that he'd witnessed three large men dragging what appeared to be a half-dozen bound, listless women from the white truck into the back door of the club next door to the restaurant — a club, according to city records, by the name of *Labyrinth*. His supervisor contradicted Monroe's statement, reporting that another officer arrived at the same time as the young recruit and had seen no such thing in that alleyway.

Monroe became the laughingstock of his precinct, the butt of every joke from his fellow officers. He was branded a too-keen rookie, an attention-seeker, and accused of imagining grand scenarios in which he'd be the hero of the force.

But the young man refused to recant his statement, despite immense pressure from his supervisor — and his supervisor's supervisor. When they switched his patrol route to the heart of the South Bronx in a crime-riddled neighborhood with a murder rate twice that of the rest of the city, it came as no great surprise that Monroe was murdered one night — knifed and left to bleed out in an alleyway, his assailant never brought to justice. With little fanfare, Monroe's name faded into the annals of NYPD history. And with his death, his far-fetched story about a suspicious club in the Upper East Side also died.

The week following Monroe's murder, the fledgling restaurant owner who'd placed that call to the police abruptly sold his property and left the city. The building was purchased and demolished within days. As soon as the dust had settled, the new owner broke ground on a fully enclosed parking garage, complete with tunnels connecting to the club next door. No truck would ever be carelessly parked in that alleyway again, and the newly-expanded *Labyrinth* now sat on a double-plot of land.

I gripped the phone tightly in my right hand as it rang. Once, twice, three times.

"Hello?"

Deep breath.

"Hello, is someone there?" Bash repeated.

Fae whacked me on the arm violently. "Say something," she hissed.

"Hi," I mumbled into the receiver, rubbing my smarting arm with my free hand. "It's Lux."

There was a beat of silence over the line. "Can't say I was expecting your call, Freckles." I could hear a teasing smile in his voice. "Does this mean you're giving in already? I have to admit, I was expecting a bit more of a challenge..."

"Don't be an ass," I muttered. "This isn't about us."

He laughed. "Oh, so you agree there's an 'us' now?"

"You're impossible," I complained, rolling my eyes. "Can you meet me tonight? I have something to ask you. And, before you get yourself all worked up, you should know — it's for the story I'm working on. The one about the missing girls."

"Where?" he asked, his tone suddenly serious.

"A coffee shop in the East Village. I'll text you the address."

"I'll be there. What time?"

I glanced at my watch. "Seven?"

"See you then."

I clicked off.

⚵⚵

"I MUST SAY, YOU'RE LOOKING REMARKABLY HEALTHY FOR someone with the flu." Bash stared at me with raised brows as I approached him. He was standing on the sidewalk, just below the café awning.

"The wonders of modern medicine," I drawled, coming to a stop by his side. "Thanks for coming."

He grinned at me. "Your wish, my command." I rolled my eyes as he pulled open the glass door and ushered me inside. "After you."

I made my way to the counter and ordered a chai tea. I looked around for the tattooed, eyeliner-wearing barista who'd given me Miri's note, but she didn't appear to be working today. Before I could pay, Bash placed his own order for a cappuccino and a croissant, handed a sleek black AMEX credit card to the cashier, and grinned down at me infuriatingly.

"What are you doing?" I asked, crossing my arms over my chest. "This isn't a date. You're not supposed to pay."

He laughed at me and shook his head, the bastard.

I turned to the cashier. "Can you refund that chai? I have cash."

Bash looked from me to the cashier, who was watching us with wide eyes. "Don't listen to her," he whispered conspiratorially, nodding his head in my direction as he retrieved his credit card from her outstretched palm. "Her money's counterfeit."

"Wha— Are you serious right now—Bash!" I spluttered as he led me away with one hand at the small of my back.

"Just sit, Freckles." He steered me toward a table and pulled out my chair. "I'll get our drinks."

"I can get my own—"

He cast a dismissive frown in my direction, before heading back to the counter to accept our drinks from the barista. I sat, tongue-tied, watching him and feeling spectacularly off balance as I took in the sight of his broad shoulders and well-toned arm muscles from behind. He was too gorgeous for his own good — mine weren't the only set of female eyes on him at the moment – but he didn't seem to notice the attention his looks drew. He tossed a quick smile over his shoulder at me when he reached the counter, and I heard two appreciative girls at a nearby table sigh in unison. Somehow, it was a comfort to know I wasn't the only one left dumbstruck in his presence.

Balancing two mugs and the small plate holding his croissant, Bash made his way back to our table and sat down across from me.

"Thanks," I murmured, accepting my tea mug.

"Anytime," he returned, smiling as he tore off a chunk of his croissant and popped it in his mouth. He chased the bite with a sip of cappuccino, swallowed, and adopted a solemn expression. "So, spell it out for me."

I took a deep inhale. "You know I've been investigating that old brewery down in Red Hook."

He nodded.

"Well, there's a bit more to the story," I admitted.

"I figured as much." A wry smile twisted his lips.

"It started with Vera." My voice cracked when I said her name, but I forced myself to go on. For the next hour, I spoke without interruption, laying out the whole sordid tale as my heart pounded in my chest. The flea market, Roza, the tenements in Two Bridges, Miri, the significance of this very cafe, the note, Santos, Red

Hook, the brewery, and, finally, *Labyrinth*. By the time I reached that portion of my tale, my tea was long gone and all that remained of Bash's croissant was a small smattering of crumbs on the white ceramic plate. As I spoke, his eyebrows lifted higher and higher, the frown lines around his mouth becoming more prominent with each passing moment. He was quiet for a long time when I finally finished speaking.

"Let me see if I have this right," Bash muttered, his wide eyes intent on my face. "You want me to help you get inside a highly-secure, tightly-guarded, entirely dangerous secret society, and then gather incriminating intel on some of the most powerful people in this country."

I gave a hesitant nod.

"Are you out of your fucking mind?" he bellowed, causing several people at surrounding tables to look in our direction warily.

"Bash!" I protested quietly. "Calm down."

"Calm down? *Calm down?*" He snorted. "Yeah, I'm feeling extremely calm after learning you're on some halfcocked mission to get yourself killed. These people are dangerous, Lux. You know that better than anyone. I can't fucking believe you've been going after them alone."

"Well, if you come with me, I won't be alone anymore," I pointed out. "I need your help, Bash. I need to see what's going on inside that club."

"And you don't think, if these people are as powerful as you say, that they'll notice a blonde sleuthing wannabe traipsing through their back rooms and looking through their computer files?" He laughed. "That's optimistic."

"There won't be cameras." I pulled out a page from the dossier that I'd stashed away in my purse before leaving my apartment. I held it out so he could look it over, pointing to a highlighted section. "See? It's apparently part of the club charter. Too many important people are members — they'd never feel safe if potentially illegal actions were being recorded. The only cameras are on the perimeter."

"You're putting blind trust in the research of a guy you don't even know." Bash shook his head. "How can you be sure it's accurate?"

"I know Fae — I *trust* Fae," I said, crossing my arms over my chest. "If she says we can trust him, we can trust him."

Bash stared at me for a moment, an unreadable expression on his face. "You're the same," he muttered eventually, his eyes incredulous.

"What?"

"You haven't changed a bit in all these years. You're still stubborn as a mule — set in your ways and utterly impossible to negotiate with once you've made up your mind about something. Pigheaded, really." He cracked a smile.

I glared at him.

"Relax, it's refreshing." His grin widened. "Take it as a compliment."

"I'll take it as a compliment if you agree to help me," I suggested.

"I'll agree to help you if you go out on a date with me," he countered.

"I'm not going out with you."

"Come on, it can just be a friends thing. If we choose to get naked afterward, so be it."

"You're terrible." I tried to contain my smile, instead forcing a stern glare in his direction. "I think I preferred it when we were ignoring each other's existence."

"Don't you need my help?" Bash steepled his hands on the tabletop and leaned forward. "You should be nice to me if you want me to get you into *Labyrinth*."

"You really think you can get us in just because your family is on the list?" I felt the rush of banked excitement stirring to life within me.

"It's worth a shot." Bash leaned back in his chair and let out a deep breath. "A photographer and a journalist whose last column detailed the many attributes of Channing Tatum's physique, up against the most powerful people in the world. What could possibly go wrong?"

"Have a little faith." I laughed. "And it was Ryan Gosling, not Channing Tatum."

Bash snorted. "My mistake."

"So when are we doing it?"

"Baby, we can do it anytime you like," Bash said, a familiar heat filling his eyes.

"Please, be serious," I implored.

"Fine, fine," he said, laughing. "I guess we can go Friday."

"Friday's no good," I immediately countered.

"Hot date?" he asked, his brows raised and his eyes suddenly serious.

I laughed. "Oh yeah. Me and about three hundred *Luster* coworkers, affiliates, and sponsors, sipping champagne and toasting 100 years of success."

Comprehension flared in his eyes. "Centennial."

"You're going?" I asked.

"Pick you up at six," he said, winking.

"What?" I stared at him. "I don't need a ride, I'm going with Simon and Fae."

"They'll get over it." Bash pushed back his chair and stood, reaching out to grasp my hand. "Those were my terms. I get you in, you go on a date with me. This is the date I'm choosing. Come on, I'll drive you home."

I allowed him to tug me from my seat. "I never agreed to a date, and I most definitely did not agree to a public appearance. There'll be cameramen at the curb, photographing important people as they arrive. You, sir, are considered important — though for the life of me, I can't fathom why." I stuck my tongue out in his direction.

"I see your insults haven't improved with age," he noted dryly. "And as for Centennial — take it or leave it, Freckles. You need me, not the other way around."

I deliberated for a moment. "Can we at least avoid the curbside cameras?"

He grinned, sensing that I was about to give in to his terms. "I'll consider it."

"We still haven't picked a date for *Labyrinth*."

"Eager to see me again so soon, huh?"

"You're hysterical." I rolled my eyes. "What about Wednesday?"

"Tomorrow? No can do," he said, shaking his head.

"Hot date?"

His grin turned wolfish. "Wouldn't you like to know."

I would, actually, but I wasn't telling him that. "Nope, couldn't care less," I said breezily.

He laughed.

"Thursday," I suggested, following him out the door onto the street.

"Works for me." He shoved his hands into his pockets and brought his face closer to mine. "Where are you going now?"

"Home."

"Are you sure?" He leaned in, hovering close enough that if I raised myself the slightest bit up onto my toes, our noses would brush. "We could continue our business meeting at my loft." His lips skimmed my cheekbone.

I pushed him away with a light shove of my palms against his chest. "Why do you keep suggesting that?"

"Because one of these times, you're going to say *yes*."

"In your dreams." I let out an amused huff of air. "I have to go, I have things to do."

"Sure you don't want a ride?"

"I'm sure." I began to walk away, but stopped myself. Turning back, I stared at him for a beat. "Hey Bash?"

His eyes softened to that warm, glowing look I loved so much. "Yeah, Lux?"

"This was kind of fun." I admitted, surprise clear in my tone. "I mean, not the Vera stuff or the part where you called me pigheaded and told me I was 'out of my fucking mind'..." My smile was irrepressible. "But the rest of it."

"You're right — it was fun. You know what would be even more fun?" he asked, the warmth in his eyes beginning to build into a fiery heat.

"Nope," I grinned full out, taking a step backward as he began to advance on me.

"There's that pigheadedness," he said, shaking his head at me. "Can I at least have a hug goodbye?"

"Nope. See you tomorrow!" I called, giggling as I dodged his embrace and rushed down the sidewalk toward the nearest subway entrance.

"Flying away again, Freckles?" Bash called after me.

Without turning around to face him, I held my arms aloft at my sides and pumped them up and down, mimicking flight as I walked further away from him. His laughter chased me all the way to the platform and back to Midtown, where I let it envelop me like a warm blanket I never wanted to remove and lull me into a sort of temporary bliss. I knew this holding pattern of friendly bantering and benign flirtation couldn't last forever between Bash and me — sooner or later, real life would overtake the fantasy we'd shared in the café this evening.

It was as though, through some unspoken pact, we'd both agreed to set aside the past completely and live the life we might've had — two twenty-five year-olds on a coffee date, laughing and arguing good-naturedly as time ticked by and the world spun on without their noticing. We'd been isolated in that bubble of content self-deception for hours, our mirage so convincing we'd deceived even ourselves, for a time, into believing it might last forever.

It wouldn't last — it couldn't.

But for tonight, I'd hold the blanket Bash's words had woven close to ward off the shadows of the past.

I WAS LATE.

My morning run had been painful — I'd been sincerely neglecting my workout regimen lately, and my sore leg muscles were paying the price. The three-mile loop I typically flew through with ease was a struggle for breath, each cramping stride a punishment for my lack of discipline. By the time I made it home and hopped into the shower, I was thirty minutes behind schedule.

Hair still damp, I practically ran to the subway, stopping only briefly to grab a coffee from the food cart parked just outside the platform. I was in the process of dumping two sugars into the steaming brew when someone smashed into me from behind, spilling the entire scalding cup down the front of my blouse and eternally staining my outfit.

There was no way I could go to work like this — I'd have to go home and change, which would put me even further behind schedule.

"Goddammit!" I cursed in the loud, unabashed style I'd adopted since moving to the city, turning to face my assailant and unleash a can of whoop-ass on him. "Watch where you're going buddy, it's—"

"So sorry, miss." The smooth voice immediately drew my attention. My eyes traveled from the shiny black shoes, up two navy, uniformed legs, and came to land on the gleaming chest badge and emblem. Shit — I'd just cussed out a police officer.

"No, officer, it's my fault," I apologized, raising my eyes to meet his. Another sentence was there, on the tip of my tongue, but it dried up when I realized that the face I was staring at was one I recognized. I'd seen it before — infinitely pixilated on the screen of my computer, furrowed into a frown outside the 6[Th] Precinct station in the Village, illuminated by the faint glow of a cigarette on the docks of an old brewery in Red Hook. I'd seen it every day for the last week, affixed to my wall — that permanent gloating smile, seeming to mock me from across the room whenever I glanced in the direction of the mosaic.

Officer Santos.

"Are you alright?" His pressed lips turned up in a small smile. "Looks like you really doused yourself."

I stared into his pale brown eyes, searching for something appropriate to say but coming up short. My mind was otherwise engaged, reeling as I tried to calm myself. All of my mental resources were occupied by one thought — this was no coincidence. Santos was here, following me to work, watching me buy coffee, and staging an interaction, all because I'd been careless. I'd been spotted somewhere along the way, whether at the brewery or on one of my surveillance trips to his precinct. And that meant...

I was no longer flying safely below the radar. I was being watched.

I comforted myself with the knowledge that, if I were seen as a true threat to these people, they'd have already eliminated me from the playing field. There were only two possible purposes served by this confrontation with Santos: either they wanted to warn me away from the story and let me know that they were surveilling me, or they were testing me — trying to see whether I was simply a dumb blonde, who'd stumbled onto their organization accidentally.

For my sake, I prayed it was the latter.

I forced myself to smile at him, emulating the pageant queens I'd seen every year at the Jackson Fall Festival growing up. I played up my Southern twang, pouring it on thicker than syrup on French toast and praying it was enough to convince him that I didn't possess enough brain cells to spell *sex trafficking*, let alone investigate it.

"Aw, jeeze, I'm such a klutz! Always spilling my coffee and tripping over my feet." I let out a sunny peal of laughter. "My boss pretty much expects it by now. She won't even notice this." I gestured down at my coffee-splattered blouse. "I don't think she's ever seen me without a coffee stain somewhere on my outfit."

Santos laughed lightly, and some of the tension lines disappeared from around his eyes.

"I'm awful sorry I bumped into you, officer," I said, injecting my voice with honeyed remorse. "You have a good day, now!"

"You too, miss," he nodded at me.

I beamed and turned away. When I'd made it three blocks from him, I allowed the forced smile to drop off my face and headed down onto the nearest subway platform. I couldn't go home, not if Santos was still watching me. I'd have to hide out somewhere else for a few hours, which meant I'd likely be missing work for the second day in a row. I switched trains at three different platforms to ensure that if someone were, in fact, following me, they'd have a hell of a hard time keeping track of my final destination. When I was convinced I'd muddled my trail beyond recognition, I rode to SoHo.

I pulled out my phone and texted Sebastian.

Lux: Don't kill me — I'll be there as soon as possible. Something came up.

My phone chimed instantly with an incoming text message.

Bash: You okay?

Lux: I'm fine, just a little rattled and covered in coffee. Bumped (literally) into Santos on my way to work.

My phone rang.

"I'm fine!" I whispered into the receiver.

"Where the hell are you?" His voice was demanding and I could hear the sound of his quick footsteps pounding through the speaker at my ear. "Tell me you weren't stupid enough to go straight home."

"Excuse me!" I huffed. "I resent that statement."

"Lux, don't fucking mess around with me. I just left a meeting with six executives. Tell me where the hell you are."

"I didn't go home. I got on the subway, hopped trains a few times, and headed to SoHo. I'm going to Simon's loft."

"I'm coming to get you."

"That's ridiculous. You have work to do, and it'll take you over an hour to get here in your car. Traffic is completely gridlocked."

He sighed and I listened to the sound of his thundering strides

JULIE JOHNSON

grow quiet as he slowed to a stop. As much as he hated to admit it, he knew I was right. "I don't like this. I don't want you alone."

"I won't be alone. Simon's roommates Nate and Shane are usually hanging at the loft. I'll be fine."

"Don't they have jobs?"

"Nate's an artist and Shane's a model — they pretty much make their own hours and spend a large majority of their time in their boxers, eating cereal from the box and sitting on the sofa watching sports reruns or playing video games. They'll be happy to have me there — I'm freaking great at Mario Kart."

A frosty silence passed over the line as he considered that scenario. "Well, I'll be there at eight to pick you up."

"Don't I need to come into work?" I asked, confused. "Angela will wonder where I am."

"Let me worry about Angela. Don't move from that loft until I get there. Understand?"

"Jeeze, Mr. Dramatic." I blew out a puff of air. "Can she at least email me my assignments, then? What else am I supposed to do all day?"

"Get ready for tonight. Make sure you have something to wear — I'm guessing the dress code is formal."

"Tonight?" I asked, crossing at an intersection and heading for Simon's loft.

"I want this damn charade over with. I want you safe, done with this damn investigation. So we're moving up our timetable," Bash said. "Tonight, we're going to *Labyrinth*."

Chapter Thirty

NOW

"I LOOK LIKE A PROSTITUTE."

"You look gorgeous," Simon said dismissively.

"Fae!" I cast a pleading look in her direction.

"What?" she muttered, not looking up from her magazine.

"Help!"

She raised her head to examine me. "I'd veto the blue eyeliner," she suggested with a shrug.

"It makes a statement!" Simon protested.

"Sure, if the statement is, 'I'm a hooker for hire,'" I complained, staring at my reflection in the mirror.

It was wrong, all of it. The dress was too short, the neckline too low, the heels too high to make me look like anything but a streetwalker — a high-priced one, perhaps — working her wares on the corner.

"They're not even going to let me in looking like this." I shook my head as I scanned myself from top to toe.

"Of course they will." Fae sighed dismissively. "That's a three thousand dollar dress."

"What!"

"Relax," Fae said, setting aside her magazine and rising from her perch on Simon's bed. "We borrowed it from wardrobe closets at *Luster*. One of the stylists owed me a favor because I set her up with this great guy from—"

"Fae!" I interrupted what was sure to be a long tangent about her matchmaking skills. "Can we skip back to the part where you said this dress costs more than my *rent*..."

Simon and Fae grinned in unison.

I began to hyperventilate. "What if I tear it? What if I spill something and stain it?"

"Wow, good thing we didn't tell her how much those Manolos cost," Simon muttered to Fae.

"What?!" I exclaimed, looking down at my feet in horror.

"Baby, breathe," Simon ordered, taking me by the shoulders and staring deeply into my eyes. "You won't tear the dress or muss the heels. You'll be *fine*. I'll even take off the blue eyeliner if it makes you feel better."

"Thank you."

"Even though it totally brings out the navy hues in your eyes and—"

"Simon!"

"Fine, fine," he muttered, steering me back to his vanity and grabbing a cotton swab. "Sit down, my little lady of the night."

I narrowed my eyes at him as he began to dab the heavy makeup away.

"So what's the plan, again?" Fae asked.

"Sebastian's picking me up here in—" I glanced at my watch. "Shit! That can't be the time! He'll be here in ten minutes!"

"Deep breaths," Simon ordered, swatting the tip of my nose with a makeup brush. "So you're going to walk into this super secret society, assuming Sebastian's last name even gets you inside, and... then what? Accuse the Vice President of sex trafficking?

Tackle and handcuff a state senator in a civilian's arrest? Kidnap and waterboard the beloved *Good Day America* newscaster until he reveals his sexual deviancies?"

I wrinkled my nose at him. "Of course not. We're going to get inside, make a little small talk, and slip away into the back room when the coast is clear. There must be some kind of an office or a computer where they store files. If I can find a bank receipt or any kind of money exchange proving that they've been doing anything remotely incriminating, I'll have enough to get the authorities involved."

"But who?" Simon asked. "I thought we couldn't trust the NYPD because Santos might not be the only dirty cop working for these people."

I grimaced. "I haven't quite figured it all out yet."

Simon snorted. "Great."

"The FBI," Fae interjected quietly. She'd been listening in silence for several moments, a conflicted expression on her face. "You can go to them. I know someone who will help you."

Simon and I turned simultaneously to face our friend, twin expressions of surprise on our faces.

"You *know a guy* in the FBI?" I asked, my tone full of disbelief.

"Someone has been keeping some serious secrets," Simon chided, planting both hands on his hips and leveling a glare in Fae's direction. "What is this about? First you *know a guy* who can magically produce a dossier of information about *Labyrinth*. Then you *know a guy* who can look over Lux's NDA. And now you *know a guy* who happens to work as a federal agent?" Simon snorted. "What are you, an international spy? A mobster's daughter? A computer hacker leading a double life as a relationship expert?"

Fae shook her head. "You guys, it's not a big deal."

A knock sounded on Simon's bedroom door and Nate popped his head inside. "Sebastian's here."

"Thanks, Nate." I smiled at him and he winked in return before disappearing back out into the common room.

I rose from the vanity stool, straightened my shoulders, and took a final look at myself.

"I can do this." I took a deep breath. "At least, I think can do this. I'm pretty sure I can. Probably."

"Your self-confidence is awe-inspiring." Simon rolled his eyes.

"Oh, shut up." I turned to face Fae. "When I get back, we need to have a long talk about your mysterious connections."

She grinned at me. "Good luck tonight."

"She doesn't need luck, she's wearing Dior," Simon said. "Now go forth and conquer, baby."

⚜

BASH WASN'T SPEAKING TO ME. NOT WITH WORDS, ANYWAY. He'd taken one look at my outfit, and his vocabulary had devolved into some kind of strange, caveman-esque language of grunts and grumbles. Apparently, he wasn't a fan of the hyper-short black dress or its revealing strapless sweetheart neckline.

He'd arrived at Simon's loft looking like a god — if gods were well-built, 6'2" blond men in immaculately tailored dinner jackets. We locked gazes as soon as I emerged from Simon's bedroom, my two crazy friends in tow, and I saw his eyes widen fractionally as he took in my Simon-approved ensemble.

Simon leaned in close to my side to whisper in my ear. "That's a custom Dolce & Gabbana suit." He blew out an amused huff of air. "Ha! And *you* wanted to recycle that old blue dress you wore to Trisha and Stu's wedding last summer. I bet you're glad to be in Dior now! You would've looked like one of the Ugly Stepsisters next to Prince Charming, instead of Cinderella."

"Thanks, Si. Real nice."

"Oh, you know what I mean, baby." He laughed. "Don't get your panties in a twist."

"She's not wearing any," Fae chimed in, linking her arm through mine as we made our way to the door. "This dress is so tight, a panty-line would be glaringly obvious."

"Please, if you care about me at all, both of you *shut the hell up*," I begged as we reached the door and came to a halt in front of Sebastian.

"Hi," I said, blushing.

"Hi," he replied, looking me slowly up and down in a way that gave me heart palpitations. As his eyes returned to study my face, a slow smile worked at the corners of his mouth and the banked heat in his eyes stirred to life. I prayed for the strength to make it through this night without combusting under his gaze.

"Hi, handsome." Simon hip-bumped me to the side and moved close to Bash, his hand extended in greeting. "I'm Simon. I'm sure you've heard about me — all flattering things, I hope." He cast a look over his shoulder at me. "Otherwise, Lux will be getting no more free wardrobe updates or makeup tutorials."

I opened my mouth to protest that I had never *once* asked for either of those things, but Sebastian beat me to the punch by letting out a surprisingly happy laugh.

"Well, to be honest, I haven't heard much — but the things Lux has shared have all been wildly flattering, so you have nothing to worry about." Bash unleashed his most devastating grin — the one that practically oozed charm and sex appeal, delighting women worldwide — and both Simon and Fae seemed to melt a little at the sight. Apparently, even they weren't immune to the Covington charisma.

"I'd love to stay and get to know you better, but Lux and I have a date." He turned that alluring smile on me and I tried to steel myself against it but, even with nearly a decade of practice, I couldn't quite manage to.

"It's not a date," I grumbled, trying to breathe at a normal rate. I flipped my hair over one shoulder — drawing a glare from Fae, who'd spent nearly an hour curling it to perfection with hot rollers — and grabbed my purse from the small table near the door. Narrowing my eyes in what I hoped was a badass manner, I dropped my voice an octave lower to emphasize how serious I was about this endeavor. "Let's do this."

Fae and Simon burst into simultaneous fits of hysterical laughter behind me. I cringed at the sound and turned slowly to face them, my brows arched.

"Her face!" Simon gasped out between laughs. "Ohmigod, did you see her face? She's like, ready for battle!"

Fae had tears running down her cheeks, streaking her mascara into watery trails of black, and was clutching her stomach as she fought to regain breath. "Her face? What about that voice!" Her laughter turned into a snort. "Jack Bauer has nothing on you, Lux!"

"I hate you both." I glared at them each in turn. "And if I die, well, I hope you feel really terrible that the last thing you ever did was make fun of me." At that, I turned and faced Sebastian, whose lips were twitching dangerously.

"You laugh, you die," I threatened, brushing past him and yanking open the door.

"Not laughing," Bash promised in a strangled voice.

"Wait, wait," Simon called breathlessly, rushing forward and leaning against the doorframe as we made our way down the hall. "Lux, you better not die, because... well..."

I stopped and turned to face him, awaiting his apology.

"We really need to return that dress to *Luster*." He grinned. "If you die, we'll be in deep shit."

I flipped him off and turned on my heel, listening to the fresh round of cackles erupting from Fae and Simon. When I heard a much closer laugh bubble up from the man standing next to me, I turned my glare in his direction.

"Not a *word*, mister." Despite my best intentions, their laughter was getting to me. Holding my stern face was a struggle.

Bash tried to nod solemnly but soon lost the battle against hilarity. Within seconds, a chorus of laughter exploded out of him, echoing through the hallway and harmonizing with Fae and Simon's giggles in a melody of mirth even I couldn't deny.

"Such children, all of you," I complained, even as a grin stole across my face and a solitary giggle escaped my lips.

Unfortunately, Bash's amusement quickly fled as the severity of the situation once again descended on us. He grew quiet as soon as we climbed into his Land Rover, his eyes lingering on the hemline of my skirt and the treacherous amount of cleavage threatening to burst from the confines of my neckline.

"Might as well be naked," he muttered under his breath.

"Excuse me?" I snapped, clicking in my seatbelt. "What was that?"

Bash started the car and stared ahead in silence, his jaw clenching and unclenching every few seconds as he tried to reel in his spiraling frustration. He shifted into reverse and backed out of the parking spot. Within minutes, we were rolling smoothly into the flow of evening traffic, headed for the Upper East Side.

I stared out at the passing city, thinking about the night to come, and my stomach churned with fresh nerves. Before I knew it, we'd nearly reached *Labyrinth*. When we turned onto E. 65th St., Bash glanced over at me.

"I don't know who we'll see in there or what will happen. We're going in blind, so we need to stick together. No going off by yourself, no heroics. As far as the members inside are concerned, you're nothing but arm candy — don't speak unless spoken to, don't call any unnecessary attention to yourself. The less they notice you, the better you can observe them without detection. And, trust me, you don't want to be on their radar if you can avoid it." Bash grumbled something indecipherable under his breath. "I don't care if we haven't found anything — if either of us senses any kind of trouble, we leave. End of story."

I nodded in agreement.

When we pulled up at the valet, Bash leaned over into my space, slipped one hand around the back of my neck, and pulled me toward him with little tenderness. His lips landed hard on mine, crushing them in a rough kiss that I knew would leave my mouth swollen and bruised. His tongue invaded my mouth in an abrupt onslaught that left me no time to prepare and utterly unable to even begin to return his kiss. And as quickly as he'd begun, it was over, leaving me dizzied and breathless. His hands released my neck and I fell back against the smooth leather seat, attempting to catch my breath and staring at him with wide eyes.

He cupped my jaw lightly, his thumb skimming over my well-bitten bottom lip. "I had to do that, at least once. Just in case... things don't go well in there."

A warm feeling spread through my chest and my throat went dry. Nipping at his thumb with my teeth, I tried to bring a smile back to his grim face. "Don't say things like that. It's going to be fine. And, if it's not, well... I'll make it up to you."

His wolfish smile appeared.

"Not like *that*, you pervert." I huffed. "I meant I'd buy you a beer or cook you dinner."

"You cook now?" he asked, surprise evident in his eyes.

I laughed. "I can reheat take-out leftovers. Does that count?"

His laughter joined mine, filling the small space with joy and chasing away our apprehension for a brief moment. Eyes warm on my face, he leaned forward once more and touched his forehead to mine. "Let's go," he whispered against my lips.

For once, it was me who initiated. I threw caution to the wind and leaned in, brushing my lips against his. On the surface, it was a small kiss — a single ripple on the ocean of lust we'd been wading in for the past few weeks. But beneath the surface, in the deepest reaches of the sea, a monumental tidal shift had occurred.

When we broke contact, Bash stared at me, his expression totally unguarded and a question burning in his eyes. I opened my mouth to speak but before either of us could say anything, a valet appeared at my window and pulled open my door, extending his hand down to guide me from the car.

I'd always seen movie stars being helped from their vehicles by chauffeurs and laughed, thinking *Jeeze, she can't even get out of a car by herself?* But tonight, I finally understood. There was no way heels this tall and a skirt this short would make it out of the Land Rover unassisted — at least, not without flashing the world a view of the lady bits I'd rather keep private.

The valet, a huge man clothed in a familiar black t-shirt with scrawling green print, led me around the front of the hood and handed me off to Sebastian, who was standing at the curb waiting for me. I slid my hand into the crook of his extended arm and smoothed my face into a mask of serenity. Summoning an air of confidence I certainly didn't feel, I matched Bash stride for stride as we made our way up the elaborate marble stairway outside the towering four-story building. It looked imperial — like some odd mix between a traditional English estate and a gothic French cathedral leftover from ancient times. Not wanting to seem like a naive, wide-eyed tourist, I only allowed myself a quick glance upward, but it was enough to note that there were several turrets and multi-tiered gables ornamenting the stone-shingled roof. I even thought I spotted a baleful gargoyle or two, but was forced to look away before I could make out a clear image. The only flaws in the building's elegant, old-fashioned veneer were the security cameras — sleek, black electronic eyes trained on the stairwell and valet entrance, no doubt there to alert anyone inside about approaching visitors.

The ornate gilded doors loomed before us, at least fifteen feet tall. We reached the top step and waited for several seconds. When nothing happened, Bash shrugged and extended his hand to take hold of the right door handle. Freezing in simultaneous alarm, we shared a quick glance as the sound of lock-bars unbolting and the loud creak of grating hinges rang out in the night. The doors swung inward, revealing a well-adorned atrium of priceless antique furniture pieces and elaborate wall sconces. At the far side of the hall, a huge grand staircase — at least twenty feet across, and solid marble from the looks of it — dominated the wall space and presumably led up to the second floor, though at the moment it was cordoned off with red velvet ropes. A resplendent chandelier in tiers of gold, glass, and light hung from the ceiling, its statement unmissable: this place we'd come to was a haven for the truly wealthy.

We stepped inside hesitantly, unsure how to proceed. My grip tightened on Sebastian's arm as my eyes swept the hall, searching for any living beings and finding none. The click of my heels against the gold-veined marble was the only noise to be heard in the hushed hall, until the delicate clearing of a throat sounded several feet to our left.

Standing in the shadows, so still I'd missed him in my initial scan of the hall, was a well-dressed, diminutive man in a tuxedo. He stepped fully forward into the light, and bowed — yes, *bowed* — slightly at the waist.

"Mr. Covington," he greeted, turning his head from Sebastian to me. "Mademoiselle."

"Hello," I stammered nervously. Bash pressed his hip firmly against mine in a warning gesture that told me I'd already broken one of his rules by speaking and that he was in no way pleased by it. I cringed internally — I knew I'd messed up. But I challenge anyone to remain calm and collected when a 5'2" butler wearing an ultra-sleek, near-invisible electronic earpiece like he's in the CIA or something *bows* to you as if you're the freaking Duchess of Cambridge.

"It's our pleasure to receive you, sir. My name is Charles, one of the concierge's at your service here."

I looked at Bash, wondering if he'd called ahead to inform them of our visit, but his face showed nothing but surprise. I'm not sure which alternative was more disturbing — the idea that they'd known we were coming or the thought that they'd recognized Sebastian on sight as soon as we'd exited his car.

"It's your first time here, correct?" Charles asked.

Bash nodded.

"Wonderful, sir." Charles raised an open-palmed hand and gestured toward a set of doors on the left side of the atrium. "If you'll follow me, I will gladly show you and your guest to the East Parlor. You are, of course, free to explore the first floor at your leisure, but I've found the parlor to be a preferred starting point for many of our newer members."

I felt my brows shoot up on my forehead involuntarily and had to make a conscious effort to lower them back down to their normal heights. It seemed we hadn't just crossed a threshold — we'd been transported into an entirely new world of impeccable manners, spotless clothing, and seamless servitude. A place where servants bowed and used titles, avoided eye contact and catered to your every wish.

I wanted instantly to leave.

Bash caught my eye as we crossed the room, following Charles to the parlor. He nodded slightly in reassurance, reaching up to squeeze my hand where it lay on his arm. *Relax*, he mouthed at me. *Breathe.*

I smiled weakly at him and turned my face forward.

When we reached the doors, Charles ushered us into a sedate room decorated entirely in green hues. The carpets were the deepest shade of emerald, the silk curtains and brocade couches stitched with fabrics of jade and cream. Even the wall tapestries and various gold-framed art pieces — one of which looked suspiciously like a Picasso — had been carefully selected to complement the room's viridescent theme. Each detail — from the small reading lamps illuminating the space by each plush chair to the vast, ornamental bookcase that took up the entire far wall, filled with more tomes than one could read in a lifetime — had been carefully planned and meticulously looked after to create an environment fit for kings.

"The door to your right leads to the Billiard Room and connects through to the rest of the first floor chambers. On your left, you'll find a small sitting room with light refreshments and desserts. Many of our members congregate there in the earlier evening hours, as we have a full dining service until eight o'clock." Charles glanced at his watch. "You've just missed that, I'm afraid. Though there are fresh hors d'oeuvres served hourly until midnight."

"And the upper floors?" Bash asked.

Charles' composure didn't falter, though the skin around his eyes tightened in the tiniest show of tension when he heard Bash's question. "Ah, I'm afraid they're undergoing some renovation. At present, they must remain out of bounds while you are exploring. I do hope you understand, sir."

"Of course," Bash agreed readily. I felt my heart rate begin to quicken.

"Should you need anything at all, please simply press the blue button on the panel by the door. Each room is equipped with a similar one," Charles said, executing yet another perfect bow before backing out of the room and closing the doors behind him as he went.

"Think he'll bring us a map if we ask real nice?" I whispered as the doors clicked closed. This place was huge — we'd never find what we were looking for in one night's visit.

"Doubt it." Bash grabbed me by the hand and pulled me toward the door on our right. "Let's check this place out."

We wound our way through room after room, each with its own color palette and distinct furnishing theme. We soon found that *Labyrinth* was not nearly as big as it appeared from the outside — there were perhaps ten rooms, forming a U-shaped ring around the atrium. The entry hall, with its vaulted ceiling, grand staircase, and grandiose atmosphere, took up a vast amount of space. Most of the sitting rooms we encountered were either entirely empty or nearly so. A few white-haired, male members were scattered amongst the plush chairs of a garish red-toned sitting room with mahogany-paneled walls — they were clustered by a stone fireplace, enveloped by a noxious cloud of cigar smoke as they puffed away, discussing some kind of business deal involving Iranian fossil fuels. When we entered, they nodded in greeting but their murmured conversation came to a swift halt and did not resume until we'd moved on to the adjacent room.

A similar group of female patrons was gathered on the lounges of a pale blue room, sipping tea and discussing the latest society scandals while bestowing disingenuous compliments on each other's dresses and jewelry. They eyed my attire with hyper-critical stares as we passed through.

Within an hour's time, we'd traversed the entire bottom floor and encountered absolutely nothing of note. Mostly, *Labyrinth* seemed like a terribly obnoxious though perfectly innocuous millionaires' club — a watering hole for the über elite.

"We need to get onto the second floor," I hissed. "There's nothing down here and you know Charles' line about 'renovations' was utter bullshit."

"How do you suggest we do that, genius?" Bash muttered back at me. "Do you have powers of invisibility I don't know about?"

I thought for a moment. "We haven't checked the sitting room Charles told us about. It's the only room left."

"What, are you suddenly craving some 'light refreshments'?" Bash snorted.

"Something like that," I mumbled, leading him through a set of doors back out into the atrium. Heading for the entry Charles had led us through on the opposite side of the hall, my mind raced. If there were hors d'oeuvres served hourly in the sitting room, maybe there was a kitchen or back room attached to it.

We nodded to an elderly couple in matching mink-cuffed coats in the atrium, before stepping into the small sitting room. It was dimly lit, with several intimate, two-person tables scattered across the gleaming hardwood floors. Along one wall, a banquet table was laid out with multiple shining silver platters, an array of still-warm appetizers and fine desserts on display. My eyes scanned the walls and I felt a flare of hope when I spotted it — a recessed door set into the wall on the right, so finely crafted it was barely discernible from the cream-papered walls around it.

"Come on," I whispered to Bash, thanking my stars that the room was abandoned and hoping whatever lay beyond that door would be as well. I made my way over to the entryway, tracing my fingertips along the seam as I searched for a way to open it. There was no visible knob, no switch or electronic panel that might open the door from this side. I felt the hope begin to deflate in my chest.

Before I could wilt entirely, Bash reached over my shoulder, placed his palm flat against the door, and pushed inward. To my surprise, the door was spring-loaded — it popped open easily at his touch, two narrow inches of space appearing between the wood panel and its frame. I turned to him with wide eyes.

"Nice work, Mr. Bond."

"The basement door in my parents' house opened like that," Bash said, his eyes distant with memories. "My mother always hated the look of knobs on closets. She said it created 'unnecessary eye clutter' and ruined a room's aesthetic."

I rolled my eyes and pulled the door slightly more ajar, peering through the crack to see the connecting room. It was dark but as my eyes adjusted, I saw something that made me want to high five myself for this stroke of intuition: a stainless steel refrigerator, a small range, a long prep table, a china cabinet, a fully-stocked liquor bar, and, tucked into a far corner, the most thrilling object of all — a small, spiral staircase leading to the upper and lower floors.

"Bingo," I whispered.

"Servants staircase," Bash noted, his voice full of admiration. "Good thinking."

I edged into the room and Bash followed, shutting the door behind him. Once inside, he grabbed my hand and shifted my body behind his as we made our way over to the staircase.

"I go first," he ordered, his tone booking no room for argument.

I nodded.

"Follow me, stay silent, and if we're caught try to play it off. We're new, we're lost — you wanted to see the chandelier up close." He stared at me intently. "Got it?"

"Got it," I echoed.

The journey up the dark stairs was painstakingly slow — each step Bash took on the creaking steps made me flinch in horror, sure we'd be detected if we so much as breathed too loudly in the confined space. My heart pounded so fast I was sure its beat was audible from at least two floors away. I was thankful I'd never suffered from claustrophobia, as the walls seemed to press in closer the higher we rose. We passed the second floor, then the third, but Bash continued to ascend, evidently convinced that anything illegal would be as far from detection as possible — on the highest floor, in the most closely guarded room.

I didn't disagree.

Eventually, we reached the top of the flight, stepping out into a space nearly identical to the kitchen prep room on the first floor, but with no signs of habitation. No lights were left illuminated to aid still-working kitchen staff. There were no utensils lying about, no food remnants of recently-prepared appetizers scattered about the counters — the stainless steel tables were immaculate and not a single tool was out of place.

I held my breath as we crossed to the door, wondering what we might find on the other side. Had this all been for nothing — a misadventure, born of misguided hopes and ill-founded wishes to find Vera? Had I been connecting invisible dots? Seeing illusory correlations between completely unrelated people and places?

Was *Labyrinth* even connected to my investigation? Because, so far, nothing here suggested anything remotely associated with human trafficking.

Short on the heels of that thought came another — one so paralyzing I felt my throat begin to constrict at just the possibility it might be true. I began to wonder if I really was crazy, after all. Maybe my conspiracy-theory wall mosaic was just that — a conspiracy, feigned and fabricated by a sad, foolish girl who couldn't cope with the truth. Maybe, without ever noticing, I'd slipped off the ledge of sanity and fallen so far into lunacy I couldn't even see it anymore.

Or, maybe not.

Because, when Sebastian opened that door, when we saw what lay in the empty space beyond, when I felt the air disappear from my lungs and the saliva evaporate from my tongue as my mouth went dry with dread... there was little room left for doubt.

I wasn't crazy — but that was little validation when the truth was so repugnant.

Horrifyingly, cruelly, abominably... I'd been right all along.

Chapter Thirty-One

NOW

CHAINS HOLD BETTER THAN ROPE, I SUPPOSE. THEY WERE A good choice — sturdy, of course, but also perfectly suited to the archaic nature of *Labyrinth* on the whole.

Why they needed to restrain the girls when they had plenty of sedation drugs at their disposal, I had no idea. Perhaps drugged girls were less attractive than those who could stand on their own two feet. Perhaps there was something thrilling to the men watching from their dark little booths about a small, defenseless girl, bound in heavy, inescapable chains.

I didn't know. I didn't want to ever know.

But as I stood on the threshold of the empty room, I was certain that the small round platform at the center of the space, with its set of carefully coiled ankle chains, served only one purpose: to display property on sale.

This wasn't a brothel as, in the dark corners of my mind, I'd allowed myself to prepare for during the past few weeks. It wasn't a safe haven for sexual predators, or den of depravity, where the wealthy could come to indulge in erotic favors from underage immigrant girls at no personal risk to their careers or reputations.

No. This was something far more odious.

It was an auction block.

The private, dark booths lining the walls were the biggest indication. There were ten booths, arranged in a circle around the platform. To offer a semblance of privacy, each booth was cordoned off on either side with curtains and enclosed behind a wall of tinted glass, facing the small platform at the center of the room. A closer look inside the booth nearest to us revealed an electronic panel with buttons used for placing anonymous bets.

Those partaking in the auction could participate without ever revealing their identities.

I heard Bash swear under his breath as he slipped one hand into his jacket pocket and removed a tiny point-and-shoot camera. As he snapped photo after photo, I realized in a detached way that I was in shock, but couldn't quite muster the energy to do anything about it.

I saw it play out in my mind in startling clarity — the whole organization, clicking into place like pieces of a jigsaw puzzle snapping together.

They scouted girls — young, pretty, poor, and preferably undocumented — on the streets of the city. Watched for opportunities to snatch them away from their families and took them somewhere they could be contained for a while: the brewery in Red Hook, most likely. There, the girls were given GHB, sedated past the point of ever putting up a fight or escaping, and held, like livestock in a pen awaiting their slaughter. Thugs like Smash Nose and the Neanderthal watched them for a time — days, weeks, maybe even months — until the rich men arrived at *Labyrinth* to examine the newly stocked wares and compete for their pretty new possessions. Just as Officer Monroe had witnessed in the back alley all those years ago, the girls were transported here, to this very room, and put on display.

And for a price — likely an extremely steep one — they could be purchased.

I pictured Vera on that stage, ten pairs of lewd eyes glued to her chained body as money changed hands, and had to turn away.

The room began to shake, as though an earthquake was rumbling the entire city and disturbing the building's foundations. I pressed a hand to my stomach, hoping I wouldn't wretch on the lushly carpeted floor. Belatedly, I realized the trembling wasn't the room — it was me. I'd begun to shudder violently, and no amount of deep breathing would soothe me this time.

It was too much. All of it.

"Come on, I have enough." Bash grabbed me by the shoulders and shook me lightly. "Lux, we have to go. Pull it together."

I knew I was spiraling quickly into panic, and would soon be of no use to anyone. Looking up into Sebastian's eyes, I tried to ground myself. The steadiness in their depths lent me strength enough to snap myself out of it.

"I'm fine." I swallowed roughly. "Let's go."

He laced his fingers through mine and pulled me back toward the kitchen door. We flew down the pitch-black stairwell as fast my heeled feet would allow, emerging into the downstairs prep room breathless and fraught with tension. When Bash opened the door to the sitting room, we rushed inside so quickly we nearly plowed straight into the small man standing a few feet away, seemingly waiting for us.

"Charles," Bash said, coming to an abrupt halt and squeezing my hand a little tighter.

"Sir." Charles did not look happy. In fact, he looked downright peeved that we'd been caught outside his carefully laid boundaries. "Were you looking for something particular in the kitchen area?" he asked in a smoothly cultured voice that totally contradicted the vexed glare his eyes were shooting at us.

"No, the door was left open and we wandered inside by mistake." Bash forced a grin. "Sweet knife set — are those custom-made Shun blades?"

Charles glare intensified. "I believe so, sir."

"Excellent." Sebastian sidestepped and pulled me along with him, angling us closer to the exit. "Well, we've had about as much exploring as we can take for one night. You've been a great help, Charles."

"We hope to see you again in the future, Mr. Covington." Charles seemed all too eager to be rid of us, practically escorting us toward the door and back into the atrium. "I'll call for your car to be brought around."

"Thank you, Charles."

"Goodnight, sir." The mysterious butler vanished in seconds, slipping into an alcove somewhere or perhaps simply fading into the wallpaper like a chameleon taught to camouflage itself in the presence of predators. Though I could no longer see him, I felt his watchful eyes still lingering on the back of my neck as we headed for the mammoth front doors and out into the night, leaving behind a well-moneyed, well-secluded auction room where business of the most deplorable kind was conducted — as well as a small piece of my soul.

⚜

BASH WAS PACING.

He'd been pacing for an hour, and I was worried he'd soon begin to wear a tread mark into the lovely hardwood floors of his loft. I was curled up in a ball on the window seat, my borrowed heels discarded on the floor next to me. I didn't know what to say to him — there was nothing I *could* say to make this right. When another twenty minutes ticked by in the dark, silent room and he showed no signs of stopping, I sighed and hopped down from my perch.

I walked over and planted myself in his path, slipping my hands around the back of his neck and forcing him to still. His head was bowed, his breathing labored — it seemed the shock that had hit me in the auction room was only now catching up to him.

"Bash," I whispered. "Look at me."

He raised bleak eyes to meet mine. A moment of silence passed between us, and when he spoke his voice was haunted. "You were right."

I arched my brows in question.

"I'd half convinced myself that you were delusional. I didn't want to believe..." He trailed off.

"I know."

"My father..." Bash's lips twisted in revulsion and his eyes pressed closed. "If he's involved in this..."

I was quiet, my mind fully occupied by memories of a cold December night on the eve of Sebastian's eighteenth birthday. Andrew Covington — his hands roaming the body of a defenseless young maid in his pantry. I knew, with unshakeable clarity, that the senator was capable — more than capable — of rape. Why shouldn't he be capable of this as well?

"You aren't your father," I said, cupping Bash's face between my palms and drawing his gaze back to mine. "You cut him out of your life a long time ago."

"He's my family." Bash's voice held both contempt and disgust. "His blood runs in my veins."

"You once told me that you believe family isn't determined by the crib you're born into — it's the family you *make* with someone you love." I held his gaze intently. "Blood isn't always thicker than water, Bash. I believe things like friendship, things like love — the things you get to *choose* in this life — are the most important things we have. They're what we have to hold on to. Don't you still believe that?"

Some of the ghosts cleared from his eyes as he stared back at me. "I should've fought for you," he whispered, reaching up to tuck a loose strand of hair behind my ear.

"What?" I breathed.

"Back then," he said, swallowing hard. "I should've fought for you. Instead, I spent a long time blocking out every emotion I felt for you. And when I finally stopped being hurt and confused and headstrong, when I started to let feeling back in... six years had passed and I was alone, on the other side of the world, without the only person I'd ever wanted standing by my side."

I felt my breath catch.

"I hated myself for getting lost in that anger, for all that time I'd wasted running away from the one thing that truly scared me."

"What was that?" I asked, afraid to hear the answer.

"Whether or not you'd been honest that day," Bash whispered. "I knew if I found you, if I saw you again, and you were indifferent to me — as cold and calculated as you'd been the day you broke my heart — I'd never survive it. So staying away became an act of self-preservation."

I skimmed my fingers against his close-shaved jawline, hoping to sooth him.

"If there was even a possibility that you still loved me, I should've done everything it took to fight for you." He closed his eyes tightly. "But I didn't. Because it was easier to block you out, to shut out any possibility of finding you again and learning if my fears were right. I was afraid — a coward."

"Bash—" I interjected, but he spoke over me.

"But after six long fucking years, I finally realized something." His eyes opened and began to burn into mine. "I could love you, or I could hate you, or I could miss you from ten thousand miles away, but none of it did me a damn bit of good, because none of it gave me what I wanted." He cleared his throat roughly. "None of it gave me you."

"Bash..." I whispered.

"Just let me get this out." He reached up and covered one of my hands with his. "You blame yourself for what happened to us — I get that. I see it on your face every time you look at me. But you weren't the only one at fault."

I felt my heart skip.

"I always said, when I found the love of my life, I'd fight for her. That I'd do whatever I had to do to earn my soulmate. I walked around, spouting Hannibal's words..." His eyes dropped to my heart, their focus so intense I feared they might singe a hole through the neckline of my dress to where the ink lay beneath. "But when it came time to really live those words — I stumbled. I didn't fight for you. I didn't question it. I let my own pride and heartbreak cloud my judgment. I let you walk away. And then I hid, halfway across the world, unwilling to — What? Get my ego bruised a second time?" He blew out a huff of air in self-deprecation.

"Bash—" I tried again.

"I love you." He said simply, his eyes fierce. "I've loved you since the first moment I clapped eyes on you in Latin class. Since that day in the rain, when you climbed into my car and slipped my sweater over your head to get warm. Since the first time I watched you with Jamie, laughing and joking even though the weight of the world was on your shoulders. Since I saw you running in crazy, breathless circles around the circumference of my favorite tree, a look of absolute joy on your face." He traced a finger down my cheek. "I've loved you since before I even knew what love was."

"Bash—" My voice was thready.

"No, you don't get to talk. No more telling me I'm crazy or running away from this." His hands slipped around my shoulders and wound up into my hair. "I've been playing it your way, waiting patiently for you to come around. And, Freckles?"

He leaned close and our lips brushed.

"My patience has officially expired."

His lips landed on mine — consuming me, devastating me, stripping away my every defense. I didn't try to fight it — I didn't want to fight it. Instead, I kissed him back, just as hungrily. I met his kiss head on, my hands clinging tightly to his shoulders to steady myself. He broke away to curse under his breath as one of his hands worked at the tiny, stubborn zipper on the back of my dress. I worried he was about to tear it off me — which would probably get me, Fae, and Simon fired from *Luster* — but the jammed tread finally gave and slid open. The dress pooled by my feet, and I heard Bash growl at the sight of what lay beneath.

Simon and Fae had insisted on the sheer black corset, instead of the plain strapless bra I'd wanted to wear. They'd argued that the bustier's garter straps were necessary to hold up my stockings, tying me into the tightly-bound contraption before I could so much as mutter the words *Why aren't there any underwear?* At the time, I hadn't been too thrilled with the idea but now, as I watched a carnal, possessive look fill Sebastian's eyes while he took in my ensemble, I was more than happy to have such overbearing friends.

"Holy hell," he muttered, his eyes locked on my body.

His hands reached around to my back and worked at the bindings there as my fingers unbuttoned his shirt and yanked it upward, untucking it from his pants. My palms slid up his bare chest muscles and beneath the jacket on his shoulders. With a swift movement, I pushed the garment to the ground, followed soon after by his crisp white shirt. They landed in a heap next to my abandoned dress.

I laughed as Bash struggled to untie the corset, and he glared at me. "I'm about to cut you out of this thing," he threatened, the serious look in his eyes telling me his words were no idle threat.

"Here," I said, turning in his arms so he had better access to the laces at my back.

His hands worked faster now, finally making some headway and loosening the ties enough to slide the corset off. As it fell to the floor, Bash's hands skimmed from the small of my back, around my bare hips, and finally to my breasts. I pressed into his touch, my head resting against his shoulder blade and my eyes locked on his bed across the loft. Just above it, the photograph of our tree was visible even in the shadows — a perfect beacon of the past, its beauty immortalized forever on canvas.

My breaths grew ragged and my focus went fuzzy as one of Bash's hands worked its way down my body, his expert fingers quickly making my knees go weak. When he felt me beginning to lose control, he spun me around in his arms to face him. Leaning down, he gently pulled the gartered stockings from my feet, pressing a kiss to each kneecap as he did so. On his journey back upward, Bash kissed a path along my body, stopping at a few sensitive areas that made me gasp and weave my fingers into his hair, pressing him as close against me as I could manage.

A moan slipped from my lips — a low, instinctual sound that reverberated in my throat — and at the noise, Bash abruptly stood, hiked his hands beneath my thighs, and lifted me against him. I wrapped my legs around his waist and kissed his neck as he strode toward the bed, carrying me with hurried impatience.

It had been a long seven years, waiting for this moment.

When he lowered me onto the bed, I fell back against plush down pillows and watched through half-closed eyes as one by one, he removed his shoes, undid his belt, and let what was left of his clothing drop to the floor.

"I can't believe you're here, in my bed." His voice was husky with lust, deeper than I'd ever heard it. "I've had this dream, over and over, so many nights I've lost count. I keep thinking any minute I'll wake up and you'll be gone, just another figment of my past I can't get back."

I didn't think about repercussions or consequences. I didn't think about anything but Sebastian, and how desperately I needed to feel his bare skin on mine. I extended my hand up to him. "Touch me, Bash. I'm no dream — I'm real." My voice was breathy. "Touch me. *Please*."

At my words, his restraint shredded completely. He was on me, *in* me, before he'd even settled fully on the bed, his thrust making us both gasp in unison at the feeling of being whole again, rejoined and connected, for the first time in so long I'd nearly forgotten what it could be like. Our eyes locked, the inferno of passion blazing so strongly between us I thought his gaze might burn me to ashes, but I couldn't look away.

My view was perfection — the man I loved hovering over me and, on the wall above us, a gorgeous backdrop of the most beautiful oak tree in the world. And, to me, it was somehow right, somehow *perfect*, that after all this time, our joining should happen once again beneath the shadows of our tree, sheltered under its sweeping boughs as we'd been one spring day a million afternoons ago... Back when we were two dumb kids, fumbling and stumbling upon the joys of one another for the first time. Young and in love and, for a brief time, full of infinite dreams for a bright future together.

Those kids we'd been weren't gone — they were still inside us, calling out in ecstasy at having found each other again after all this time. And as the grown man and woman we'd become reveled in the joy of rediscovering each other, so did the souls of our youth. They sang out, a hymn of passion and reunion, their joyous melody guiding me down the path to sheer oblivion, and I felt my chest swell with pressure.

I felt a short, sharp sensation within the left side of my breast — a pang, as though my chest was overflowing with too much blood — followed by the most intense feeling of completeness, of utter *wholeness* I'd ever experienced. Pleasure built to a tipping point, crashing me down into release, and my last thought as I spun madly into euphoria was that after seven long years, it had finally happened.

I had my heart back.

❦

I USED THE ILLUMINATED SCREEN FROM MY CELLPHONE TO GUIDE me around the loft. A glance back at the bed revealed that Bash was still fast asleep, sprawled across the down comforter with his limbs askew. I wanted nothing more than to climb back in bed with him, but that would have to wait for a while.

I had something to do first.

The familiar ping of my cellphone receiving a text message had woken me from a deep slumber. I'd opened my eyes to find my limbs completely entwined with Bash's. His leg was wrapped around mine, one arm was thrown over my midsection, and his face was nestled into the hollow of my throat. I'd smiled as I slowly untangled myself from the knot of limbs and linens on the bed, moving cautiously so as not to wake him. There were deep shadows under his eyes from one too many sleepless nights of work and worry. It was easy to forget that in addition to everything we now knew about *Labyrinth*, the weight of the entire Centennial issue was on his shoulders as well.

Bash stirred once as I worked myself free, but simply shifted and sighed before falling back into a deep sleep. When I managed to make my way to the edge of the bed, I turned back around to look at him with a small smile on my lips. I wasn't sure how I'd managed to survive so long without seeing his face every day, without hearing his laugh or being the subject of his jokes, but I wasn't going to do it anymore.

Screw the honorable Senator Andrew Covington and his NDA. If he wanted to play hardball with me — threaten to take my parents' house, come after me for repayment of Jamie's medical bills, or demand restitution for breaking the terms of our contract — that was just fine. After what I'd learned tonight at *Labyrinth*, there was only one of us who should be worried about the fallout from their actions — and it wasn't me.

When I reached the center of the loft, I grabbed Bash's discarded white button down and pulled it on. In the darkness, I stubbed my toe on his coffee table, letting out a subdued scream of pain as I hopped silently toward the countertop where I'd left my purse. I pulled my cellphone out just as another low ping sounded, alerting me to an incoming text. Sliding my finger across the screen, I saw I had three unanswered messages from Fae.

Fae: Are you awake?

Fae: Are you awake now?

Fae: How are you possibly still asleep? If you don't text back, I'm coming over.

Lux: I'm here. Relax.

Fae: Well, I was worried. You didn't text me after your super secret mission.

Lux: Long story — will explain in person.

Fae: Perfect! Come downstairs.

Lux: What?

Fae: I'm here. Come to the parking garage — black limo waiting by the elevator.

Lux: What on earth are you doing here?

Fae: Just come down and I'll explain everything. Don't bring your boy toy.

Lux: I'm getting the feeling I'm not going to like whatever you have to say...

Fae: COME DOWN.

Lux: What if this isn't even Fae? What if it's someone who stole Fae's phone and is trying to kidnap me?

Fae: You have watched way too many Lifetime murder mysteries. It's me.

Lux: Prove it.

Fae: Fine. Your deepest regret — last summer you were eating a pint of Ben & Jerry's as you walked down 42nd. You dropped your spoon on the dirty sidewalk. Rather than let your ice cream melt, you wiped off the spoon on your t-shirt, stuck it back in your mouth, and proceeded to eat the entire pint.

Lux: I'll be down in a second.

⊗

I TRIPPED MORE THAN ONCE ON THE TOO-LARGE SWEATPANTS I'D borrowed from Bash's closet, but eventually I made it downstairs to the parking garage. Stepping out of the elevator, I spotted the limo immediately — as well as my best friend, who was leaning against it with an amused smile on her face, totally unbothered by the fact that it was three in the morning. She was dressed in all black again — her designer version of "stealth attire" — and exuding a poised, confident air. Or, at least, she was until she caught sight of me in Bash's clothes.

"Ohmigod!" Her smile was so wide and bright I feared it might blind me. "You totally got some."

"Shut up," I grumbled coming to a stop next to her.

"I need details. Like, very explicit, graphic, step-by-step details of everything that happened since I last saw you." She grinned. "Simon is gonna flip! He owes me twenty bucks."

"You two *bet* on whether or not I'd have sex with Bash tonight?"

She nodded. "Simon thought you'd hold out till after Centennial, but my money was on tonight!"

"That is beyond disturbing. You do realize that, right?"

"Yeah, I know." She shrugged, still grinning. "But I'm pretty sure you should be eternally indebted to me, since I was the one who found that bustier and garter set on sale." She arched an eyebrow at me as a scarlet blush stole across my cheeks. "Oh yeah, you totally owe me, you little slut."

"Was this the reason you dragged me out of bed and away from the best sex of my life at three in the morning?" I asked.

"No, it's not the reason," Fae said, sighing.

"Then what is it?"

The sound of the back window rolling down in the limo had both of us swiveling our heads in the direction of the automated glass pane. A male voice called out from the back seat. "That would be me. I'm the reason."

Fae rolled her eyes. "No need to be so dramatic, Gallagher."

"No need to waste my time, Montgomery," the man fired back.

My brows went up.

"Just get in the car. He'll explain everything better than I can," Fae said, pulling open the back passenger door and climbing inside the dark limo. After a brief moment of deliberation, I sighed and followed her in. As I settled onto the seat on the right side of the car, I was surprised to see an attractive man with stunning blue eyes, a day's worth of stubble, and well-mussed, overgrown black hair falling over his eyes, sitting in the seat directly across from me. He was probably in his late twenties or early thirties, wearing a rumpled black suit that needed some serious attention from an iron.

"Ms. Kincaid?" he asked.

I nodded.

"I'm Agent Gallagher." The man leaned forward and extended his hand, and I shook it hesitantly after a quick glance at Fae. She nodded reassuringly. "I'm with the FBI. I believe Fae told you about me?"

"Oh, wow," I stammered, casting a scathing glance at Fae. "Yes, sir, I'm sorry — Fae didn't warn me you'd be coming. I would've dressed..." I trailed off, mortified by the fact that I wasn't even wearing a bra in front of this super-hot, deadly-serious federal agent. Really, couldn't she have given me even a five-minute head's up?

"Not a problem, Ms. Kincaid. I'm sorry to wake you at this hour, but I needed this meeting to be as private as possible." His eyes were beautiful but held no humor or comfort. "I work with the New York field office, in the Organized Crime unit." He flashed a shiny gold badge at me from across the limo.

"You're the one who got the dossier on *Labyrinth*," I said, putting the pieces together. I turned to Fae. "This is your *guy*."

She nodded, and a small smile twitched her lips up at the corners.

Agent Gallagher cast a brief glance at her from his peripherals, before turning his attention back to me. "Ms. Kincaid, I've been aware of your investigation for a while now."

"You have?" I was dumbfounded.

"Believe me, you're not the only one who's been keeping close watch on that brewery. I've been working this case for nearly two years now, and before my partner died, he worked it for five." Sadness flickered in the depths of his eyes. "I nearly pulled you out of there twice, afraid you were going to jeopardize my entire investigation."

"Oh, jeeze." I gulped. "I'm sorry, Agent Gallagher, I had no idea..."

"I know." He nodded in acknowledgement. "But these are dangerous people, Ms. Kincaid. You can't get too close without disappearing. My partner was a good man, but he stepped on too many toes. Made a lot of enemies."

"So that's why you're here? You want me to back off?" I asked, beginning to deflate at the prospect.

Agent Gallagher leveled me with a serious look. "Not exactly," he said, leaning forward. His eyes were suddenly intense. "I've been trying to get eyes inside *Labyrinth* for months, with no success. I don't have enough cause for a search warrant, and breaking in would be impossible — it's a fortress. Every perimeter is closely monitored by armed guards and more cameras than you can count. You can't get in unless you're a member."

Comprehension came swiftly. "That's why you helped me. You knew I could get in, with Sebastian's help."

"I shouldn't have given you that dossier. If my boss found out — let's just say this city would have one less FBI agent walking its streets come tomorrow morning. But when Fae contacted me and told me about you and your boyfriend... Things just seemed to fall into place. I gave you the information you needed, left you on a long leash, and let you run. I knew anything you saw inside could potentially help my investigation."

"And, I suppose, if things had gone poorly for me and Bash in there, you'd be free to deny any involvement," I said, my lips twisting in a wry smile at the thought. "Convenient."

"It was a calculated risk." Agent Gallagher shrugged without remorse.

Fae snorted and crossed her arms over her chest. "Nice of you."

He ignored her. "What I need to know, Ms. Kincaid..." He rubbed at his stubble, a nervous habit. "Did you see anything in there — anything at all — that might tie *Labyrinth* to the brewery at Red Hook and the trafficking ring I suspect they're running? Think hard — it could be something small, just a tiny detail that didn't seem important at the time but, in retrospect—"

"What's your name?" I interrupted his somewhat patronizing tangent.

"Excuse me?" he asked, taken aback that I'd cut him off.

"Your name. Your first name. The one your momma gave you. What is it?" I asked.

He stared at me for a moment, no doubt judging how serious I was. My resolute expression must've convinced him I wasn't joking, because he finally sighed and relented. "Conor."

"Hi, Conor. I'm Lux." I smiled at him. "I believe you're asking me for a favor. Where I come from, people who ask favors have to, at the very least, display a little bit of common courtesy. Especially at three in the damn morning."

"He's always like this," Fae noted. "It could be three in the afternoon, he'd still be this unpleasant."

"Ms. Montgomery, please be silent." Conor's jaw clenched. "I know it's a constant struggle for you, but I'd appreciate any effort."

Fae rolled her eyes and sighed.

"I'm sorry if I've offended you, Ms. Ki—" He broke off when he saw my chastising look. "Lux," he amended. "It's just very important that you think really hard—"

"Conor, I'm going to stop you right there, before you dig yourself into an even deeper hole." I met his eyes with a serious look. "I can sense that this is important to you. But you don't seem to realize how important it is to me as well."

He opened his mouth to speak but I plowed onward.

"I'm not some dumb blonde who stumbled across this mess and thought *Hey! That sounds like a neat story to investigate!* I'm not doing this for fun, or for fame, or for whatever reason you've thought up." I touched the silver cuff I'd forgotten to remove from my wrist when I fell into bed earlier. "A friend of mine is missing. This isn't a game to me."

"I'm sorry," Conor said, his eyes softening a little.

"Downstairs, *Labyrinth* is everything it promises to be — a sanctuary for blue-bloods. Tea parlors, cigar rooms, and the like, but nothing of interest to you." I took a deep breath and tried to prepare myself. "Most of the people down there probably have no idea what's going on upstairs."

"Upstairs?"

"It's an auction," I told him, feeling the crushing sadness return to lay against my chest like a heavy weight, as though someone had spliced open my ribs and poured a batch of concrete inside.

His brows rose. "Excuse me?"

"They're auctioning off the immigrant girls to the highest bidder. There's a room, on the top floor. Ten private betting booths, facing a small round platform with a track of spotlights overhead to illuminate the space." I swallowed roughly. "There are chains attached to the stage — ankle bindings, so the girls can't run."

I heard Fae gasp. Conor's reaction was more subdued — he released a low expletive under his breath, and the skin around his eyes tightened with tension. "Could you describe it for a sketch artist? We could replicate the space..."

"No need." I stared at him for a weighty moment. "We have pictures."

Chapter Thirty-Two

❧

NOW

As I rode the elevator back upstairs, I thought about the conversation I'd just had with my best friend — a woman I once thought I knew everything about, from her deepest secrets right down to her favorite shade of nail polish. I knew now, I couldn't have been more wrong about that assumption.

I'd climbed from the car clutching Agent Gallagher's business card in one hand, feeling more than a little shell shocked at the fact that I, Lux Kincaid — sunny Georgia girl and all round believer in the good things in life — had just had a conversation with a federal agent about a secret human trafficking ring on the Upper East Side, potentially involving people who had the power to wipe me off the face of the earth with a single phone call.

I'd leaned against the car for some time, lost in my thoughts and half-listening to Agent Gallagher bark orders into his cellphone, until I felt Fae settle in next to me. Her hipbone pressed against mine, our elbows and shoulder blades bumped lightly.

Glancing over at her, I'd seen an unfamiliar look in her eyes — it took me a minute to recognize it as worry.

"Are you mad?" she whispered.

"What?" My brow furrowed in confusion.

"I didn't tell you about any of this."

I looked over at her. "About your double life?" I smiled faintly. "No, I'm not mad. If you didn't tell me, I'm guessing you have a pretty good reason."

She nodded. "Remember that night at the bar a few weeks ago, when Simon said he'd always wanted to know someone in the Witness Protection Program?" Her voice was hesitant and hushed.

I felt my eyes widen.

"Surprise," she muttered weakly.

"Jesus," I whispered, my mind whirling with possibilities. "I know you probably can't tell me much, but I have to know... Are you safe, at least?"

She nodded. "For now, I'm safe enough."

"You're hiding from someone," I guessed.

Fae looked over at me for a moment, her eyes intense and sad. "My husband."

I felt my eyes well with tears as I leaned over and wrapped my arms around her. "Oh, Fae. I'm sorry, love."

"It was a long time ago," she whispered into my neck, her arms coming up to return my embrace. "I'm fine."

The threads of sadness and regret interwoven in her tone said otherwise, but I didn't push her.

"No wonder you never date," I murmured.

Fae laughed lightly and squeezed me tighter until Agent Gallagher ended his phone call and leaned out the open window.

"Alright, ladies, time to break up your little love-fest. It's four in the morning — I'm beat. I want to get home."

Fae sighed as she detached from me and turned to face the undeniably handsome, undeniably rude agent. "You could at least ask nicely, Conor," she muttered.

"It's Agent Gallagher to you, sweetheart."

"Lux gets to call you Conor and I don't?" Fae's face morphed into a scowl. "That doesn't seem fair."

"Lux is about to hand me a promotion on a silver platter by helping me bring down a group of criminals the Bureau has been after for years," he said, smiling for the first time since we'd met. Though handsome even with his typical glower, Conor's entire face lit up when he grinned. If he'd show off that set of pearly whites a little more often, he'd have women lined up around the block for him. "You, on the other hand..." He looked Fae up and down. "Only ever come to me for favors or when things in your life need fixing."

"You're an asshole." Fae's eyes shot daggers at him.

"Well, you're an entitled princess." Conor didn't attempt to conceal his look of dislike.

They glared at each other for so long, I began to think they'd forgotten my existence entirely. Wondering what could've happened between them to brew a relationship of such anger and animosity, I cleared my throat lightly and took a step in the direction of the elevator. "Well, then, I'm gonna go..."

In sync, their heads swiveled toward me.

"You'll email me those photos as soon as you get inside, Lux?" Conor reminded me, his eyes once again serious.

I nodded, pushing the button to call the elevator. "I have to get back before Bash wakes up and flips out because I'm not there."

"Tell him I said hi," Fae said, winking at me. "And plan on drinks with Simon tomorrow night. He'll want the low-down — and so do I."

I waved before boarding the elevator and heading back upstairs to the man waiting in bed for me. I was nearly giddy at the thought, my huge grin unstoppable as it spread across my cheeks. Just as the elevator reached the top floor, I felt an insistent vibration coming from the pocket of Sebastian's sweatpants — my cellphone. I fished it out as I walked down the hall to Bash's front door, glancing at the screen just as I came to a stop outside the entrance to his loft. I sighed and slid my finger across the screen to answer the call.

"Hi."

"Where the hell are you?" His voice was ragged with worry. "I woke up and you were gone."

"Breathe, Bash."

"Don't tell me to breathe. We finally work things out and you fucking vanish in the middle of the night." I heard his harsh intake of air as he tried to regain calm. "I thought we were past this, Lux."

"We are!" I protested.

"Then why did I just wake up in my bed alone?"

"I had to meet someone!"

Silence blasted over the line. "What possible reason could you have for meeting anyone at four in the morning?"

"You don't exactly say 'no' to the FBI, Bash." I rolled my eyes and tried the doorknob — it was locked.

"You're with the FBI? Why?"

"It's a long story. Remember Fae's *guy?*" I reached up and knocked lightly on the door.

"Yeah."

"Turns out his name is Agent Conor Gallagher — he's with the New York field office. Organized Crime."

"He wants to know what we found at *Labyrinth,*" he deduced.

"I have to send him the pictures." I reached up and knocked harder on his front door. "Are you going to answer your door, or not?"

"What?"

"I'm literally standing at your front door freezing my ass off in this damn, uninsulated hallway, waiting for you to open up. I've been knocking for three minutes."

I heard the sound of his footsteps echoing through both the door and the receiver at my ear. He pulled open the door and stared down at me, surprise etched on his features and not a stitch of clothing covering his chiseled, naked body. I whispered into the phone, a huge smile stretching across my face.

"Took you long enough."

"Sorry, I was a little distracted between waking up to find my girlfriend missing from my bed in the middle of the damn night and hearing about her clandestine meetings with federal agents." He grinned down at me so warmly, I decided to ignore his casual use of the g-word, for the moment.

"You about done with your super-spy antics for the night?" he asked.

"Just about," I said, hanging up my phone.

"Good." He placed his phone on the small table by the entry-way, removed mine from my hand, and tossed it alongside his. Before I could retreat, he bent forward, propped his shoulder against my stomach, and threw me over his back in a fireman's carry.

"Bash!" I squealed. "What are you doing?"

He kicked the door closed with one bare foot and carried me across the loft to the bed. As we went, he pulled the over-large sweatpants from my legs and tossed them to the floor. I squeaked in protest when I felt cool air against my suddenly exposed backside.

"Bash! Put me down!"

"Gladly," he muttered, tossing me onto the bed and settling above me. He straddled my thighs, staring down at me with a look I couldn't quite decipher. With one hand, he reached down to move a strand of flyaway hair from my face; with the other, he began to slowly unbutton the white shirt I'd borrowed.

"I like my clothes on you." His voice was deep, his eyes dark with lust.

When his hands moved beneath the fabric, I arched up into his touch and felt my eyes droop to half-mast, my gaze still locked on his face.

"I like you in my bed," he added, slipping the shirt down my arms and casting it quickly aside.

I felt my limbs turn liquid beneath the heat of his gaze, as his eyes roamed my body. A small, distant thought niggled at the back of my mind, nagging that there was something I had to do — something important — before I could lose myself between Bash's sheets for the next several hours.

Agent Gallagher's scowling face flashed in my mind — Ah, yes. The *Labyrinth* photos.

"I have to email those pictures to Conor," I managed to mumble between gasps, as Bash lowered his head to kiss the column of my naked throat.

"He can wait," Bash muttered. "I can't."

I opened my mouth to object, but all that escaped was a breathy moan of pleasure as Bash thrust into me and my mind went blank.

۞

I WALKED INTO *SWAGAT* THE NEXT DAY WITH AN IMMOVABLE grin on my face. My cheeks had begun to ache from my constant smile several blocks ago, but nothing in the world could dampen my spirits today.

"Hey, Mrs. Patel!" I called as the door swung shut behind me.

She waved begrudgingly from her post behind the cash register. Her sari was purple today, covered from the waist down with her usual dull brown crocheted blanket, and her hair was twisted into a high knot at the crown of her head.

"Love that color on you. Purple looks great with your skin tone." I grinned at her as I walked past the counter and headed for the frozen section, chuckling when I heard her responding grunt of acknowledgement. The doorbell chimed overhead, signaling the arrival of another customer, but I was far too busy contemplating ice cream flavors to look up.

"What do you think, Mrs. Patel? Black cherry or chocolate chip cookie dough?" I called, opening the clear refrigerated door and swirling my index finger through the icy condensation on the glass. "I know I usually get the cookie dough, but today feels like a perfect day to switch things up."

I wasn't surprised that she didn't answer as I made my decision and pulled the carton of black cherry from the shelf— she rarely did. But I *was* surprised to hear a man's voice close to my ear, to feel the heat of his body press against my side far too intimately for a stranger.

"I would've gone with cookie dough, personally," he whispered, one hand clamping down on my arm in a rough grip. He whipped me around so fast the carton slipped between my fingers and clattered to the ground, rolling down the aisle and coming to a stop beneath a shelving unit. Pressing me close to the fridge, he brought one meaty hand up to cover my mouth before I could scream for help. I struggled, thrashing so hard my vision went blurry, but managed to make out one distinct feature on my assailant's face.

The nose — more mangled than Rocky Balboa's after a fight, hit one too many times and never set properly. In my peripherals, I saw another man hovering just behind my attacker — big, strong, and silent, waiting to step in if his partner couldn't control the situation. My veins flooded with panic as I realized that I knew these men.

Smash-Nose and the Neanderthal, come to collect me.

Correction — to *try* to collect me. I wasn't going without a fight.

My teeth sank into Smash-Nose's palm with enough force I knew I'd broken the skin. I tasted the coppery tang of blood on my tongue even as his curse pierced the air.

"Fuck! You little bitch!" he howled, clutching his bleeding hand inside his uninjured fist. I paid him no attention as I turned and ran toward the counter, screaming as I went.

"Help! Mrs. Patel, call the police!"

I heard the Neanderthal close on my heels, his pounding footsteps chasing me through the store faster than I could run away. I rounded a wire shelf display filled with chips too fast and felt my toe catch on the bottom corner. Sailing into the air, I was perilous to stop the crash. On my way to the ground, I locked eyes with

Mrs. Patel for a fraction of a second — not long enough to draw in a breath or brace myself for impact, not long enough to scream for help one last time or plead for intervention.

Just long enough to watch as she — my knight in shining purple sari — threw off that brown, crocheted blanket I'd always thought was terribly ugly, stood on trembling legs, and aimed a sleek, state-of-the-art, semi-automatic pistol at the men behind me. As I hit the ground, a dull ache spreading through my body from my battered knees and elbows, I heard the most beautiful sound in the world.

Mrs. Patel's faintly accented voice, ringing with authority, along with the telltale click of her Glock as she cocked back the barrel.

"Leave Miss Lux alone! Get out of my store!"

I scrambled to my feet in time to see Smash-Nose and the Neanderthal freeze, eyeing the elderly woman skeptically. I could see them weighing the odds — how serious was this little old lady? Would she really shoot? Did she even know *how* to shoot?

I recognized the change in the Neanderthal's eyes the moment he decided to risk it — his irises darkened as he edged closer to where I was standing with my body pressed tightly against the counter.

Apparently, Mrs. Patel recognized it too.

The shot rang out so loudly I jumped, a dull ring resounding in my ears as soon as the gun recoiled. I smelled the sharp sulfuric pungency of gunpowder in the air and watched in what felt like slow motion as a bag of Doritos on a shelf halfway between Smash-Nose and the Neanderthal blasted apart in an explosion of orange chips.

"That was a warning shot! Next time, I aim for you!" Mrs. Patel yelled, her arm steady as a sniper's as she held the gun on their retreating backs while they ran for the exit.

"Don't come back!" Mrs. Patel called, as the door swung closed behind them.

Once they were gone, a moment of total silence fell. I stared at Mrs. Patel in shock, unable to process what had just happened but knowing, without a doubt, that I owed this ornery old woman my life.

"You saved me," I breathed, limping around the counter toward her.

Mrs. Patel exhaled deeply, dropped the gun on the countertop, and collapsed back into her armchair. When I reached her side, I placed one hand on her arm. "Are you okay?" I asked.

She tilted her weathered face up to look at me, her brown eyes shining with exhilaration even as her weak legs shook with overexertion. "I could use a scotch."

I laughed lightly, reaching beneath the counter as I'd seen her do once before and pulling out a bottle and two short glass tumblers. Unscrewing the cap, I poured out two dollops of amber liquid, passed one glass to her, and clinked mine against it.

"Cheers," I said. "To you, Mrs. Patel. You saved my life."

"And to you, Miss Lux," she muttered. "You always keep things interesting around here."

We both smiled — well, I beamed and she kind of smirked, but I was still counting it — before sipping our scotch. As we set our empty glasses down on the countertop, the sound of approaching sirens became audible.

Hopefully, it wasn't Officer Santos, reporting for duty. That would just be the cherry on top of a fantastic morning.

Not that it had all been bad.

Before my near-abduction, I'd been incandescent — practically levitating off the ground with sheer lightness of being. Waking up wrapped in the arms of the man you love will do that to you, I suppose. Even after he'd left for the office and I'd headed back to my apartment, in need of fresh clothes for work, my happy mood had lingered. In fact, I'd been in such a good mood, I'd decided only one thing could make it better: ice cream. Who cared that it was only seven in the morning?

Life was good.

I had a feeling my day was about to take a turn for the worse as soon as the door flung open and uniformed officers poured through the entryway, their guns drawn and their expressions solemn. I sighed and looked at Mrs. Patel — who'd just finished stashing the scotch back beneath the counter — as the officer in charge approached and asked if we were okay.

Bash was going to flip his lid when I told him about this.

◌⟐◌

THANKFULLY, THE POLICE INTERROGATION WAS RELATIVELY brief. The officers were all extremely polite and efficient as they took our information, asking several times if I needed medical attention for my scraped knees. They confiscated the VHS tape recording from the store's security camera and promised to be in touch soon with any leads, climbing back into their squad cars and vanishing into the flow of traffic within an hour.

I was just happy I hadn't had to make a trip to the station. Bumping into Santos at the water cooler wouldn't exactly help matters.

It had taken a huge amount of self-containment not to spill the beans about the fact that I knew exactly who my attackers had been. They weren't random street thugs looking for cash, as I'd led the officers to believe — they were pawns in an organization far more deadly than any city gang. But I'd given my trust to Agent Gallagher and, for the time being, I'd have to leave my life in his hands. Getting the NYPD involved in an FBI investigation would only complicate matters. Not to mention the fact that these same officers possibly worked alongside Santos. The last thing I wanted to do was tip him off, if he wasn't already aware of my trip to *Labyrinth*.

As soon as the police left, I called Ravi and made sure someone would come relieve Mrs. Patel of her duties for the day. My next call was to Conor.

"Gallagher," he clipped, answering on the first ring.

"It's me. Lux."

"I got the pictures by email this morning. You didn't need to follow up." His voice was terse.

"It's not about that." I sighed. Fae was right — he really was grumpy all the time. "I had a visit this morning."

"What?"

"Smash-Nose and the Neanderthal came to see me."

"Who?"

"The brewery thugs."

"I told you last night, their names are Peter Miller and Tim Walsh," he said, a note of impatience creeping into his tone. "Ex-cons, both of them."

"Conor, I don't give a flying fuck what their names are. I care that sixty minutes ago, they attacked me in broad daylight at a convenience store."

"Fuck," he cursed quietly. "They know about your trip to *Labyrinth* last night."

I rolled my eyes and infused my voice with sarcasm. "You think?!"

"Don't worry. I'll fix it." He sighed. "I'll put eyes on you at all times and see how far we can push up the timetable. I have to check with my boss — and my boss' boss. Fuck."

"This is making me feel *so* much better," I muttered.

"You'll be fine. If you see a black sedan parked outside whatever building you're in, don't worry — it's either me or one of my men. Don't go to work. Go to your apartment, pack a bag. Move in with someone you trust — I'm sure Ms. Montgomery will let you crash with her." Just the mention of Fae's name added strain to his voice.

"You guys really don't get along, huh?"

There was silence over the line. "Call me if anything else happens."

He clicked off.

"Rude," I mumbled, texting Fae **SOS** — our universal code for extraction from any kind of bad situation, reserved for only the direst of circumstances. The last time I'd used it, I'd been at a five star restaurant and my date had just plucked a hair from my head and used it as floss at the dinner table. One text and *viola!* Fifteen minutes later Fae was at the curb in Simon's borrowed car, speeding me away as fast as the rust bucket could manage.

After texting her the *Swagat* address, I shoved my phone into my pocket and walked back to the counter to hang with Mrs. Patel. I hadn't called Bash — I didn't want his head to explode in the middle of a board meeting. And, anyway, I figured a few hours of keeping him in the dark wouldn't change anything. I'd tell him later. Preferably when he had a large glass of liquor in hand or a convenient wall to punch. I was only keeping it quiet so he could have a normal day — he couldn't possibly be mad at me for that.

Right?

⚬❧⚬

Oops.

I was partially right. He wasn't mad — he was *pissed*.

The first text arrived soon after I didn't show up for work on time. Even after I messaged back that I was totally fine and assured him he had nothing to worry about, Bash was persistent. He called twice and I let it go to voicemail both times, feeling awful but hoping he'd eventually get caught up in work and forget about me for a few hours.

On his third call, I realized he had no plans to give up, so I bit the bullet and answered.

"Are you trying to give me a heart attack?" he yelled into the phone. "One week with you and my hair's going to start turning gray with worry."

"Sorry, Gramps." I smiled. "I'm fine. I didn't want to bug you at work. I know how much stress you're under."

"You not answering your phone does *nothing* to alleviate my stress, Freckles."

"Well, I'm sorry, but I figured it was the lesser of two evils." I chewed on my bottom lip nervously.

He was silent. "What does that mean?" I could hear the tension in his tone.

"Promise you won't freak out."

"Lux."

"Promise!"

"Fine, I promise. Tell me."

I took a deep breath before launching into the story. I spit out the words as quickly as possible in hopes that if I talked at twice my normal rate he might not fully process everything I was saying. "I was at *Swagat*, that little convenience store I told you about, and I kind of got attacked by Smash-Nose and the Neanderthal." I took a quick breath and hurried on. "But I bit Smash-Nose and bolted — *so* gross, but I had no choice — and then Mrs. Patel went totally badass and pulled out her Glock. She fired a warning shot and held it on them 'till they ran away. It was actually pretty awesome."

I paused, waiting for Bash to interject, but he was surprisingly silent for once. I kept talking to fill the quiet, my nervous prattle doing nothing to soothe my nerves.

"Then Mrs. Patel and I did shots of scotch, which really wasn't appropriate at seven in the morning but, I mean, how often are you attacked by thugs in a convenience store? If any occasion called for alcohol, I think it was that one."

I paused. He was still silent.

"So then I talked to the police and gave them a statement, but I obviously didn't mention anything about the fact that I *knew* Smash-Nose and the Neanderthal because, well, that would've just made things worse..."

I trailed off, listening. I heard nothing over the line. No words, no background noise, not even his breathing. I pulled the receiver away from my ear and checked the screen to see if the call was still connected — it was.

"Bash?" I asked. "You still there?"

When he finally spoke, his voice was choked with tension. "I promised you I wouldn't freak out. If I talk right now, I'm going to freak out."

"Oh."

"Where are you?" he forced the words out through clenched teeth.

"My apartment," I whispered.

"Alone?"

"Fae's here. I'm going to crash at her place for a few days, I just need to grab some clothes. Really, Bash, I'm fine."

"I'll be there in twenty."

He clicked off.

Shit.

I turned to Fae, who was sitting on the other side of my sofa listening to our conversation. She shook her head in resignation. "Don't look to me for sympathy," she said, shrugging her shoulders. "I told you that you should've called him right away."

"He was working!" I protested.

"He loves you. He wants to be with you. That means, when shit like this happens, you tell him about it." She sighed. "I know you've been taking care of yourself and everyone around you for your whole life. You supported your family. You held your parents together. You were there, everyday, when Jamie was sick and he needed you. I get that, love." She grabbed my hand and squeezed it tightly, staring into my eyes with an intensity I'd rarely seen in the past. "But Lux, you have to realize that people love you. We want to take care of *you*, occasionally. And you have to let us."

"I'm sorry," I whispered. "I didn't see it that way."

"Don't be sorry. Just stop being so damn self-sufficient. It's okay to lean on other people, sometimes."

"I lean on you and Simon all the time," I pointed out.

"Only when we force it on you," she contested.

I sighed. "I'll try to be better about it."

"Good," she said, grinning. "Now let's pack before Sebastian gets here. I have a feeling things are going to be a little tense when he arrives."

I felt my stomach flutter with nerves as I walked to my closet to retrieve my suitcase.

TWENTY MINUTES LATER, I WAS NEARLY PACKED. I'D SQUEEZED as many clothes as I could manage into my luggage, and I'd filled a large tote bag with other essentials — hair products, makeup, my computer, a journal, a book to read, and the tiny iPod shuffle I used while running. The bags sat by the entryway, ready to be loaded into Simon's car. The garment bag containing my Centennial dress hung on the back of my door, where I'd be sure not to forget it.

When the intercom went off, I let Fae answer and buzz Sebastian in. Within seconds he was at the door, stepping through and crossing the room to me with a stern expression that made my stomach flip. As he came close, I backed away from him, wary that his anger might make an appearance at any moment.

I felt like a fool as soon as he reached me. He didn't scream or tell me I was an idiot for not calling sooner. He didn't freak out. Instead, he wrapped his arms around me in a gentle embrace, propped his chin against the crown of my head, and exhaled a breath he'd seemingly been holding for quite some time.

"You're okay," he whispered into my hair, his arms tightening around me. "You're not hurt."

I brought my arms up around him and pressed myself as close as possible. "I'm fine. Better now that you're here."

Bash kissed the top of my head and pulled out of our embrace, but wrapped one arm around my waist so our connection wasn't entirely severed. He turned to look at Fae. "Thank you for taking care of her. She's too stubborn for her own good."

"Believe me, I know." Fae grinned.

"I'm all packed," I told Bash, nodding at the stack of luggage. "I'm crashing at Fae's until this is over."

"You're crashing with me," Bash countered.

I turned startled eyes up to stare at his face. "What? Why?"

"First of all, because I want you there. Secondly, because you'll be safer with me." He glanced at Fae. "No offense to you, I'm sure you're more than capable of taking care of yourself. But my building has 24-hour security on site, plus an alarm system. Anyone who tries to reach Lux won't even make it past the parking garage. And if they do, well, let's just say I did more than take photos during those years in Iraq. Our men in arms taught me enough to handle myself, with or without my gun."

My eyes went wide. "Does everyone I know carry a gun?"

"Probably," Bash said, shrugging.

"Pretty much," Fae agreed, grinning as she reached into her purse on the coffee table and pulled out the smallest handgun I'd ever seen in my life — it was barely bigger than my fist.

"Jesus Christ," I muttered under my breath.

"Time to go," Bash said. "I'll grab your suitcase and the tote, you grab the dress."

I cast one final look around the apartment, sure I was forgetting something vital. When my eyes landed on the closet, I smacked myself on the forehead with an open palm. I couldn't believe I'd almost left them behind.

"Wait," I called, crossing the room and pulling open my closet door. I pulled down the Jamie Box first, followed by the lock box. Stacking them, I carried both back toward Bash and Fae, who were hovering by the doorway. "Now I'm ready."

Bash stared at the boxes for a moment with a question in his eyes, but managed to contain his curiosity for the time being. We headed out into the hallway and, locking the front door behind me, I walked away from my apartment, unsure how long I'd be away from it. I felt sad as I loaded the car, hugged Fae goodbye, and climbed into Bash's passenger seat but, looking over at the man sitting next to me, I knew everything would be okay in the end.

Chapter Thirty-Three

✿

THEN

JAMIE COUGHED VIOLENTLY. HUGE, HACKING COUGHS THAT wracked his entire body where he lay in the hospital bed. I rubbed his back in a soothing gesture, waiting for his heaving to subside.

"You okay?" I asked when he finally grew still.

"Water," Jamie rasped, his throat dry.

I poured a glass and handed it to him, settling in on the bed beside his body. "Small sips. I don't want you to choke."

Jamie rolled his eyes at me. "Sure thing, *mom.*"

I laughed, but it was a weak, unconvincing sound. I couldn't be happy — not seeing him like this. There were so many tubes in his frail body, I'd lost count. He was fighting off another bout of pneumonia, brought on by his rigorous treatment schedule.

Since moving away from Jackson, we'd had the best doctors and medical care and, at first, things seemed to get better. After the amputation of his left leg, Jamie recovered almost completely. He was practically in remission.

It didn't last, though.

The cancer came back, metastasizing in his lymph nodes and lungs. He was labeled Stage IV, which, I knew, meant the odds of his survival dropped radically. The nodules appearing in his internal organs were, for the most part, totally inoperable. The chemotherapy drugs were no longer effective.

His doctors had predicted he'd live a year, at most.

He'd lived another three.

My brave, resilient twin had fought for his life — fought hard — these last few years. And though I'd stood by his side the whole time, this was one thing I couldn't fix. One battle I couldn't wage in his stead. I could only watch, helplessly, as he got sicker, weaker, thinner. As the life was gradually leached from his body.

"Come on, why don't you try to eat something. Get your strength up," I suggested, gesturing toward the tray of untouched hospital food that was slowly growing cold on his bedside table. "You have to eat if you're going to get better, Jamie. You know that."

"I'm not."

"You're not eating?" I asked, narrowing my eyes at him. "Well, that's just plain stubborn."

"No," Jamie said, shaking his head weakly. "I'm not getting better."

I stilled, my breath catching in my throat.

Jamie smiled wanly. "Don't look so shocked, light of my life. You had to know it would happen at some point."

"James Arthur," I snapped, fighting the tears that were rapidly filling my eyes. "Don't you ever say anything like that to me again."

"Lux," he whispered, his expression grave. "I'm dy—"

"No!" I leapt to my feet beside his bed, tears streaming down my cheeks. "No you aren't. This is just like last time. You've been sick before. You'll get better again. Everything will be fine."

Jamie's eyes were closed and his head moved back and forth, rejecting my words with each shake.

"Don't shake your head at me, Jamie!"

His eyes opened slowly and caught my gaze. "This isn't like last time, sis. You know it; I know it."

I opened my mouth to protest but he cut me off.

"I'm dying," he whispered, his words slicing into me like a knife to the heart. "And you know what? I'm not angry anymore." Jamie sat up straighter in his bed and stared at me with a resigned look in his eyes. "I was angry as hell for a long time. Angry at my diagnosis. Angry at you for being able to walk and run when I couldn't. Angry at Mom and Dad for being so fucking weak. Angry at my goddamn self for ignoring that muscle cramp in my left leg for six months so I might get a shot at playing varsity football."

My tears wouldn't stop — as he spoke, they only dripped faster.

"I'm not angry anymore, Lux. I know that if a total stranger evaluated my life by what he could see my medical chart, he'd think I spent a miserable twenty-one years on this earth. But he'd be wrong. Cancer isn't my life. My diagnosis isn't my destiny." Jamie smiled at me, courage in his eyes. "Sure, it's played a part in who I am. But the significant things aren't written in the doctors' files. I mean, you're the most important person in my life, and there's not a single line about you in the whole James Arthur Kincaid folder."

My lip began to tremble and a sob rattled in my chest. "Don't you dare start being nice to me, Jamie," I ordered in a shaky voice. "Then I'll know you're saying goodbye, and I'll kill you myself. I swear it."

He laughed, but it soon turned into a cough. I raced to his bedside and held his hand until the fit abated.

"I'm not saying goodbye," he said. "Not yet. But I am saying this, while I still have the strength left..."

Jamie's eyes met mine, and his gaze held no trace of his usual jesting.

"You are going to live a long, happy life without me," he began, setting my tears off again. "You're going to get old and fat, pop out a couple of babies — one of which better be named Jamie which, conveniently, is gender-neutral — and marry a guy you love so much it makes you dizzy. You're going to be sad for a while. But, eventually, you're going to find a way through this. Because you, light of my life, will someday find that person who'll do for you what you've done for me all these years — put you first, no matter what."

I was a sniveling, weeping mess.

"Come here, cry baby," Jamie said, extending thin arms to offer an embrace. I readily accepted, leaning against his chest and wrapping careful arms around him. I wept for several minutes and Jamie was silent, the only sounds in the room those of my muffled cries against his hospital gown and the faint whirring of machines as they pumped life into my brother.

"I'm the one with cancer," Jamie eventually huffed, teasing me even in his darkest hour. "I don't know why *you're* crying."

I lifted red-rimmed eyes to meet his. "You're terrible."

"I know." He grinned. "Promise me something?"

"Anything," I whispered.

"Be selfish for a while. Think of yourself, instead of everyone else. Find a way to be happy again. Not for me, or for our parents, or for some guy. Be happy just for you. Do the things that give you joy, that put a smile on your face. And don't let anyone else's needs get in your way. You deserve to know what joy feels like, sis."

"I'll be happy if you promise not to leave me," I murmured, my voice a hollow shell. "I can't do this without you, Jamie."

"You can, and you will." His voice was solemn. "Because, if you don't, I'll make sure to haunt you from the great beyond."

I glared at him.

"I mean it," he scoffed. "If you spend your next few years wallowing in memories of all that you've lost, you'll miss out on all the good things I want for you in this life. I know there's darkness in this world, Lux. Shadows and grief and unimaginable pain. But there's also love and light and laughter." Jamie squeezed my hand as tight as he could, his waning strength making even that small gesture a great task.

"Don't dwell in the darkness, sis. Live in the light."

Chapter Thirty-Four

❧

NOW

"Damn." Simon let out a slow whistle. "This place is seriously awesome."

"Prime real estate," Fae added, pivoting in a slow circle to take in the entire space. I couldn't argue — Sebastian's loft was gorgeous. I'd only been here a few hours and had barely begun to settle in, but I couldn't turn away my best friends when they showed up at Bash's door with wine in hand, determined to make my day better.

When I'd first arrived this afternoon, Bash had insisted on making room for me in his closet and dresser. I'd argued that I would only be here a short time — a few days, at most — but he'd just grinned indulgently in my direction before unzipping my suitcase and tossing a handful of bras and underwear into an empty drawer. The sly look on his face didn't bode well for my plans to move back into my studio as soon as these abduction shenanigans were over, but I had no desire to argue with him after the day I'd had. With a sigh, I'd relented and unpacked my clothing into his space, ignoring the small part of my mind that wanted this move to be permanent.

I was clearly delusional or, at the very least, suffering from brain trauma after my brush with death this morning. That had to be it. Because it was in no way sane to move in with someone you'd started sleeping with yesterday.

Well, technically eight years ago. And then again yesterday.

It was all very confusing. I decided the mature, logical thing to do was put it out of my mind entirely.

So when Simon and Fae showed up at the door, I was more than happy for a distraction. Bash likely sensed that my friends wanted some private time with me to gossip about things he didn't want to hear — such as his performance between the sheets — so he quickly made excuses about a conference call with a client and disappeared into the small office space abutting the main room.

Within minutes, Fae and Simon were totally relaxed on Sebastian's sleek leather sectional, sipping wine and listening to my story about *Labyrinth*. Fae helped me fill Simon in on the meeting with Conor, her face twisting into a sneer as she talked about the FBI agent.

"Why do you two hate each other so much?" I asked. "What happened between you?"

"It's a long story," Fae muttered, sipping her wine.

"Is he good looking?" Simon asked.

Fae shook her head darkly. "Who cares what his face looks like?"

"Is that a yes?" Simon looked at me.

I nodded. "He's gorgeous."

"Ah, I see." Simon's lips twisted into a knowing smile. "Maybe some hate-sex is in order."

"Excuse me?" Fae asked, turning to face him.

"Don't knock it till you've tried it, sweetheart." Simon grinned. "All that bottled up anger and aggression can be... explosive... under the right circumstances."

"He's right." I sipped my wine, smiling privately as my mind filtered back over some of Bash and my first interactions during the past few weeks. "Love and hate — they're two sides of the same coin."

"Can we please talk about something important?" Fae asked. "Like the fact that Centennial is tomorrow night and Lux can no longer leave the apartment for the mani-pedi we booked her?"

I snorted. "Oh yeah. 'Cause *that's* important. I'm so glad you want to talk about truly vital issues, Fae."

"Never fear," Simon said, reaching into the bag he'd brought with him and pulling out a French manicure set. "I always come prepared."

I rolled my eyes but didn't resist as he pulled my bare feet into his lap.

"I can't believe Jeanine won't let me out of going," I complained. "You'd think an attempt on my life would be enough to convince her I can't attend."

Fae shrugged. "She's British. They take attendance and punctuality very seriously."

"You're going with the boy toy?" Simon asked, applying a clear base coat to my toes.

"He helped me get into *Labyrinth*; now I owe him a date," I explained, my voice regretful. "I just wish it were anywhere but at Centennial. All the cameras... I'll probably end up on some trashy gossip site."

"I can see the headlines now." Simon smirked. "'MYSTERY WOMAN SNAGS SEBASTIAN COVINGTON' — you'll be famous!"

I glared in his direction.

"You're worried about the cameras?" Fae snorted. "What about Cara? She's going to flip when she sees you with Sebastian."

"I hadn't even thought of that," I moaned, feeling my apprehension build further. "She'll probably scratch my eyes out in the ladies' room."

Fae laughed, an excited gleam in her eyes. "I'd like to see her try."

"I'm beginning to think you have a fixation with danger," I said, staring at her with concern.

"Adrenaline junkie," Simon agreed, nodding as he applied a light coat of pale pink to my big toe.

"Whatever." Fae shrugged. "I have a feeling that tomorrow is going to be a night to remember."

"Good memories, I hope." I looked at them, trying to ignore the feeling of foreboding that was chewing at the lining of my stomach.

"Don't worry," Simon said dismissively, gesturing toward my Cinderella dress where it hung on the closet door. "When you're wearing a custom Simon Gilbert design, nothing can go wrong."

⚜

BY THE TIME SIMON AND FAE LEFT FOR THE NIGHT, I'D BEEN buffed, plucked, painted, and groomed within an inch of my life — I was more than ready for Centennial tomorrow night. They hugged me goodbye with promises of seeing me at the gala and threats to kill me if I didn't wear my hair up the way they'd instructed. Apparently, if I didn't force my locks into a perfect up-do, it would ruin the lines of Simon's dress and be a grand-scale catastrophe.

I rolled my eyes and promised to replicate the hairdo to the best of my limited abilities.

As I closed the door behind them, I felt Bash press against my back and his arms slide around my waist. His chin came down to rest on my shoulder as I leaned back into him, and for a moment I simply closed my eyes and enjoyed the long-forgotten sensation of a casual embrace with the man I loved.

"Can I show you something?" I whispered, tilting my face back so his lips rested against my forehead.

"Of course," he said, turning me in his arms. He cupped my

face and kissed me lightly. I lost myself in his kiss for several moments, tightening my arms around him and immersing myself fully in the feeling of his lips on mine. When I pulled away, I knew my cheeks were flushed with both happiness and desire.

I twined my fingers through his and pulled him toward the closet, where I'd stored most of my things. Reaching inside, I pulled out the Jamie Box and walked back to the couch with Sebastian close behind me. I set the wooden box lightly on the coffee table, absently tracing the carvings with my fingertips as I turned to look at Bash.

"This is the most important thing I own," I told him, a smile tugging at my lips. "It's from Jamie."

Bash smiled involuntarily at the thought of my brother.

I slid the box in front of him on the table. "Open it."

Bash lifted the lid, his eyes catching immediately on the embedded photograph of me and my twin. When his fingers moved to skim over the letters inside I felt my eyes begin to tingle, the heartache still fresh after three years.

"One hundred letters," I explained. "All for different dates and occasions."

"For the big moments in your life," Bash said, flipping gently through the stack and reading the messages inscribed on the front of each envelope.

"For the small ones, too."

I passed him my one of my favorites:

FOR A DAY WHEN LOVE STINKS (YEAH, YEAH)

As he read, the smile on his face grew to a grin.

Light of My Life,
You're moping. I get it — heartbreak sucks.
Well, I don't really get it, because I've never been in love, per se. Not unless you're counting my obsession with Sophia Vergara who, one of these days — you mark my words — will

realize that the love of her life is a twenty-one year-old amputee in Georgia.

But you, my darling sister, have been in love. And afterward, your little heart was broken and I was forced to listen to John Mayer breakup songs for almost two years. (Our apartment walls are treacherously thin, for future reference.) Maybe even now, a few years down the road, you're reading this letter because you've been reminded of that same heartbreak. Maybe you've experienced a fresh one. I don't know, I'm not there. (Dead, remember?)

I do know one thing, though. You're brave. It takes guts to give your heart to someone else, and trust that they'll take care of it. And some day, you'll find that someone who makes all the other someones in your life seem insignificant.

When that day comes, when you're absolutely sure he's the one you're supposed to be with, give him the red envelope at the back of this box.

I may never have been in love, but I've witnessed more of it than most ever get to.

People think of hospitals as being full of only sickness and sadness — patients dying, relatives mourning. But they're wrong. I've spent a good part of the last five years in and out of hospitals, first in Jackson and now here in Atlanta. Of course I've seen the grief and the illness and the death here. That's all you'll see on surface level. Look a little deeper, though, and those things are insignificant compared to the immense love that fills the walls of these buildings.

The baby wards, where new parents hold their little bundles close and plan out bright futures full of joy. The hopeful families who keep smiles on their faces in spite of the odds. The ones who've traveled around the world to hold the hand of a loved one who's lying in a sickbed with a fate unknown.

That's love.

There are all kinds of love in this world, sis. Great loves and little loves. The fleeting ones, and the ones that last a lifetime. I might be dead, and you might be a crazy person fueled by far too much estrogen, but I love you more than anything.

Well, actually, that's a little dramatic... Maybe not more than anything. But more than most things. More than Cadbury chocolate bars and all of my favorite sports teams. More than ~~Sophia Vergara~~ those really great popsicles they give out during chemo sessions.

Keep your chin up. Things will get better. Maybe not today, or tomorrow, or even this year — but someday.

You'll find that great love again.

Until then, know that I love you.
Jamie

BASH LOOKED OVER AT ME WITH A FILM OF TEARS IN HIS EYES. "I miss him," he said, his voice rough.

I nodded. "Me too. Every day."

He slipped his hand into mine and squeezed lightly.

"He wrote 100 letters." I stared at the box. "But only 99 of them are for me."

Bash's grip tightened on mine, his eyes following my free hand as I reached toward the back of the box and pulled out a bright red, sealed envelope. The script on the front was simple, two short words that held so much significance.

FOR HIM

With trembling fingers, I passed the envelope to Bash and looked up to meet his eyes. "There's no one else I would ever give this letter to," I whispered. "I've never even been tempted. It felt like..." I took a deep breath. "Well, like Jamie would've wanted you to have it, more than anyone else."

Bash inhaled sharply. His fingers gripped the red envelope tightly and his gaze was riveted on my face as I continued to speak.

"Jamie told me to wait until I was absolutely certain that I'd found the one I'm supposed to be with in this life. But I think he knew, all along, that the person I was supposed to be with was you." I leaned in and brushed my lips against Bash's. Pulling back slightly, I stared into his eyes. "I'll be honest — I didn't fall in love with you again during these last few weeks," I told him.

His brows rose and he opened his mouth to say something, but I cut him off.

"Because I never fell out of love in the first place," I whispered, reaching up to cup his jaw with one hand. "You had my heart for all these years — you still have it, Bash."

He pushed a lock of hair behind my ear and pulled me close. "About time you admitted it," he whispered, his smiling lips pressed against my ear.

"I'm sorry it took me so long." I looked into his eyes, my own smile spreading across my face. "I love you. I never stopped."

He kissed me then, and it was as if, for a few moments, my world ceased to turn, my heart stopped its beating, and everything just... *froze*. I knew it was one of those perfect moments I'd remember for the rest of my life.

A flashbulb memory, capturing the exact point in time that the past fell away and my future with Bash began.

When we broke apart, Bash opened Jamie's envelope with reverence, taking extra care not to tear the paper. He pulled out a single sheet from inside, and his eyes scanned it for several minutes. I watched his face as he read the document through once, then a second time, his eyes narrowing as they poured over each line.

As more time passed, I began to grow nervous. What had Jamie put in that letter? Some kind of brotherly threat, intended to protect me? An embarrassing story from my childhood, meant to warn off any potential suitors?

When Bash finally lowered the letter and turned to look at me, his eyes were strange — guarded and intense — and his words were careful. "You should read this," he said, passing me the letter before he rose to his feet and walked to the bank of windows to look out over the cityscape below. I felt my heart turn over in my chest as I watched him walk away, gripping the thin paper between my fingertips so hard I feared it might rip apart.

I forced myself to breathe before looking down at the sheet in my hands.

We haven't met. We probably never will.

But, if you're reading this, it's because you love my sister and, for reasons I'll never get to know about, she loves you too. I'm going to go ahead and presume that you're a nice guy — my sister wouldn't settle for a jerk. I'll even give you the benefit of the doubt by assuming that you've got a slew of redeemable qualities that make you "good husband material" or "good father material" or whatever bullshit standards modern women use to justify their decisions when it comes to choosing a life partner.

You might be wondering why I wrote this letter. Contrary to what I'm sure Lux thinks, it's not to scare you off or to tell you something mortifying about her or to threaten to haunt you from the great beyond if you mistreat her. It's not even to tell you how great my sister is, or that she deserves to be treasured because, again, I'm going to assume that you know that already.

Instead this letter is one I felt compelled to write because, if I know my sister as well as I think I do, she probably won't ever tell you the things I'm about to. Not because she's a big secret keeper — the girl is literally one of the worst liars I've ever met — but because it's too painful for her to talk about. And, trust me, I wouldn't be telling you unless I thought you needed to know, in order to better understand her — to better love her — for the rest of your life together.

It made her who she is today. It shaped the woman you've fallen in love with.

So, I'll rip off the Band-Aid as quickly as possible: you aren't the first man to hold my sister's heart in his hand.

When we were kids, little more than seventeen, she met a boy who changed her life. Their love was the kind that was evident even when they were standing on opposite sides of a room — their bodies would orient like two planets sharing the same orbit, tugged together by forces out of their control. It was there in the light touch of his hand on the small of her back as he guided her into the car. It was there in the beaming grin she unleashed whenever he came to the door. And it was there in the way he loved me, simply because I was the closest extension of her.

I'm not sure I believe in soul mates but, if there were ever two spirits shaped solely for one another, I have to believe it was those two kids from different worlds, who loved so strongly in spite of the many odds stacked against them.

You're wondering what happened — why is she with you when, if I'm even remotely correct, she should be with someone else entirely?

You're also wondering why I'm telling you this — what possible point could my story serve, except to piss you off beyond measure or make your own love for my sister pale in comparison?

Don't worry, I'm getting to that.

As most things eventually do, their love ended. And it shattered her.

I've never seen my sister — my happy, hopeful, full-of-heart sister — so decimated as when their love fell apart. She never told me the reason — I'm sure she thinks I went to my deathbed with no knowledge of her sacrifice — but I'm not a stupid man. I put the pieces together easily enough.

It seems ridiculous even now, so many years later, to be writing these words, but sometimes the truth really is stranger than fiction. And the truth is, my sister was blackmailed into leaving the man she loved. Someone close to him forced them apart. I guess you could say she made a deal with the devil — and she lost.

I don't know the exact terms of their agreement, but I'm guessing it was something like this:

She'd agree to remove herself from the life of the boy she loved and, in exchange, I'd get to live out my days with the best treatment money could buy. Her happiness, her life, traded for mine.

You see, we were poor. We had nothing. The house was in foreclosure and my parents couldn't afford groceries, let alone my bone-grafts and rehabilitation costs. And then, one random Tuesday afternoon, my sister stormed into my bedroom, fresh traces of tears on her face, and said we were leaving — just the two of us. We were getting out of Jackson and never coming back, never to see our friends — or the boy she loved — again.

That same day — miracle of miracles! — the new owner of our house told my parents they didn't have to move out after all. Lux suddenly had funds to put a down-payment on a small apartment in the city. Within a week I was at the best medical facility in the state, receiving treatment from some of the foremost oncologists in the country, whose waiting lists are typically longer than the state of Texas. Whoever bumped me to the top of those lists had serious connections — and, I'm guessing, is the same person who forced us out of Jackson.

At the time, I didn't question it. Selfishly, I was glad for Lux's sacrifice, if it meant I had a shot.

Because of my sister, I lived.

We never saw the boy again.

And I never saw my sister again. At least, not whole and happy.

She puts on a brave face because she thinks that's what the world needs to see. But deep down, she's been hurt, badly, by love. And the true miracle is, despite her own heartbreaks, she's still the most giving person I've ever known. I'm sure you've realized already how much she cares for those closest to her. Once you've found a place in Lux's heart, she keeps you there forever.

So I ask you, please — for the sake of my sister, who gave up her happiness so I might live a few brief years — don't hurt her. Don't manipulate or lie to her. Don't expect her to be something she's not.

And, if that boy should ever come back into her life, don't hate her if she still needs him, if she still loves him.

I won't lie to you or tell you I didn't try my best to get them back together — I wrote him letter after letter, all of which were "Returned to Sender" by the postal service. And you shouldn't lie to yourself by pretending Lux is someone she isn't.

She's human, just like the rest of us. She has flaws, and baggage, and memories that give her sleepless nights, and far, far more than her fair share of grief to deal with.

I hope that if she's found you, it means she can finally put some of that to rest. I hope you'll not take this letter as an attack or a warning against loving her — because that would truly be your loss. I hope, more than anything, that she's found someone who completes her again.

Please — take care of her for me.

Oh, and here's a free piece of advice: if you give her a pint of Ben & Jerry's, a bag of Cool Ranch Doritos, and a bottle of Merlot, she's far easier to deal with. Especially during "that time of the month."

You're welcome.

Jamie

PS: Bash, if it's you reading this, you should know I'm grinning down at you right now, buddy. I knew it all along — you guys were always meant to find your way back. I miss you, my friend. But I'll rest easier knowing our girl is in good hands.

THE TEARS STREAKING DOWN MY FACE BLURRED THE PAGE IN front of me until I could no longer read the words.

He'd known. Jamie had known all along.

Not just about the deal I'd made, but that Sebastian and I would end up back together someday.

Overwhelmed by the tangle of emotions in my head, I turned my wet eyes to Bash. He'd stopped his pacing by the window and was looking at me with a kind of shell-shocked tenderness I'd never seen on his face before. Approaching me slowly, he knelt before me and gently wiped the tears from my cheeks with both of his thumbs.

"Jamie knew it. I know it. You know it." His whispered words were intense as leaned in to touch his forehead against mine, our lips sharing the same breath. "We belong together. We always have."

I nodded.

"I should've known," Bash continued, his voice haunted by regret. "There was nothing you wouldn't do for Jamie. It's one of the things I always loved best about you. If I'd been in your shoes and someone handed me the money to save his life... I don't know if I could've walked away from that deal either."

"It wasn't just the money, Bash." I pulled away so I could meet his eyes. "No amount of money could've made me walk away from you."

His brows lifted in question.

"Wait here for a second," I whispered, pulling out of our embrace and walking over to the closet. I retrieved the lock box, grabbed my keys from my purse, and returned to the couch where Bash was waiting. He watched me open the box with intent eyes, and his surprise was evident when I removed the stapled contract from inside and handed it to him.

"What is this?" he asked, his eyes scanning the document.

"It's a nondisclosure agreement." I swallowed roughly. "I signed it when I was eighteen."

"I don't understand," he said, flipping a page and reading on. "Who gave this to you?"

Fear of his reaction made me hesitate for a few seconds. "Your father," I whispered eventually.

Bash's head lifted and his eyes flew to mine. "What?"

I reached out and flipped past sheets of legal jargon to the last page of the contract, where a copy of the deed to my parents' home in Georgia had been stapled. Andrew Covington's signature was there, plain as day, registering him as the new owner of the house. Bash traced his index finger across his father's signature, followed by the property address.

"He bought your house and threatened to evict your family," Bash guessed, his voice bitter. "Dear old dad was far more cunning than I thought possible, back then."

I grabbed Bash's hand and entwined my fingers with his. "I'm sorry," I whispered, my voice hollow. "My family..."

"Don't apologize, Freckles." Bash turned to me, his eyes dark but his voice soft. "None of this is your fault."

"He made me promise never to contact you again. Never to return to Jackson or tell anyone about our agreement. He paid for Jamie's care, right up until the end. He still controls my parents' property. And..." I trailed off.

"There's more?" Bash's laugh was bitter.

"This was bigger than you and me. It wasn't just about his dreams for Princeton or your career in politics."

He stared at me in silence, waiting for the other shoe to drop.

"I saw something, the night of your eighteenth birthday party. You had a maid—"

"Greta," Bash supplied, nodding. "I remember. But she never came back after that night. My mother said she fired her because she'd messed up one of the appetizer dishes."

I shook my head. "She didn't come back because I made her promise not to. I gave her all the money in my wallet and told her to get as far away from Jackson as she could."

"Why?" Bash's eyes moved restlessly over my face as his mind sorted through memories, trying desperately to piece together the details of that night.

Taking a deep breath, I forged on. "I went to say goodnight to Greta in the kitchen, but she wasn't there. She was in the pantry." I looked into his eyes and forced out the words. "With your father."

Bash pressed his eyes closed — in expectation, in disbelief, in pain. I wasn't sure.

"He was... he tried..." I flinched as the scene played out in my memories. "He was trying to rape her, Bash."

His eyes opened and he looked at me, his expression tormented as his mind filled in the gaps. "And he couldn't let that information get out. Not when it might tarnish his perfect reputation as a southern gentleman." Bash laughed, the sound empty and cold in the air around us. "He had to get rid of you somehow, and make sure you wouldn't talk."

Both of us turned our eyes to the NDA on the table.

"I'm sure he saw it as killing two birds with one stone," I whispered. "I was out of his life, but I was also out of yours. A win-win."

"Ever practical, my father." His voice was more bitter than I'd ever heard it.

Bash stared down at the contract for a long time, the minutes ticking by in silence. It had taken me years to fully process what had happened — god only knew how long it might take Bash to come to terms with this. I didn't speak, knowing that this was something he needed to work through on his own. I simply sat next to him, my hand clutched tightly in his, offering wordless support.

Finally, after a small eternity of waiting, Bash removed his hand from mine, reached out, and lifted the NDA from its spot on the table. His eyes swept the front page one last time before his hands tugged abruptly, tearing the contract straight down the middle and letting it fall to pieces on the glass tabletop. His fingers tore at the paper until all that remained was a small pile of white scraps, littering the floor around us like confetti.

When he was done, he turned his eyes to meet mine. "Now, you're free. *We're* free."

He wrapped his arms around me in a crushing embrace.

"My parents…" I trailed off, my mind racing with worries about their house.

"If my father makes one fucking move to evict them, I'll make a personal trip to *The New York Times* office, offering the exposé of a lifetime. He won't do a damn thing to threaten his reputation." Bash's eyes were intense. "And if he does, I'll buy your parents a new house."

I felt my eyes well with tears and I tucked my face into the crook of his neck. "I should've told you sooner, but I was afraid for my family… and I wasn't sure how you'd react," I admitted. "I thought you might hate me for keeping it from you or for the choice I made back then."

"Hey. Look at me," he ordered, pulling my face out from where I'd hidden it. "There was no choice. Your family was at stake, and you did the only thing you could to protect them. None of this is *your* fault." His eyes went unfocused and anger flickered across his face. "My father's, certainly. And mine, for being an idiot for so many years. But not yours. Never yours."

"All those years apart… All the plans we made… " I drifted off, my tone filled with grief as I pictured the life we should've had. Seven birthdays and seven Christmas mornings. College years spent huddled close over textbooks. A crappy apartment we could call our own. Travel to all the far-flung places we'd always wanted to go together. "So much wasted time."

With a gentle hand beneath my chin, Bash tilted my face up.

"It doesn't matter." He smiled at me for the first time since I'd handed him the red envelope from Jamie. "All that matters is we found each other again. We have a whole lifetime to make up for the years we lost."

"Who says I want a lifetime with you, huh?" I teased, trying my best to contain the happy tears threatening to leak from my eyes.

Bash laughed. "I'm afraid you don't have a choice in the matter, Freckles. Because I'm never letting you walk away again."

"Promise?"

"Promise," he whispered as his lips descended on mine, sealing his vow with a kiss.

Chapter Thirty-Five

✿❀✿

NOW

BASH HELPED ME FROM THE DARK SEDAN, HIS BODY SHIELDING mine from the sudden onslaught of camera flashes and yelling paparazzi at the curb. I forced my face into a smooth expression, tried my damnedest not to trip on the sweeping train of my dress, and focused on the feeling of Sebastian's hand gripping mine as he led me through the gauntlet of media who'd camped out around the blue carpet leading into Harding Tower. Ignoring calls from the photographers — *Mr. Covington! Sebastian! Over here! Who's your date? This way, sweetheart! How 'bout a smile?* — my gaze flickered up to see that the looming skyscraper was illuminated by dozens of blue and pink spotlights — *Luster* colors — in honor of the gala inside.

We traversed the carpet and arrived at the atrium, its glass doors propped wide to receive us. When my eyes had cleared of haze caused by too many camera flashes, they swept the hall to take it all in. One glance around the huge lobby told me the company had spared no expense for Centennial. It was just as grand and girly as Jeanine had promised it would be.

Huge swathes of pink fabric hung from the ceiling, elegantly draped from the overhead steel beams like *Cirque du Soleil* ribbons. I did a double take when I realized there were, in fact, aerial artists performing on each suspended strip of material. Spotlight beams shot up from each corner of the room, illuminating the high vaulted ceiling with colorful lights that pulsed and changed with the beat of the music blasting from the lofted DJ booth across the hall. Waiters dressed in avant-garde pink costumes wound their way through the crowds, trays held aloft as they offered a custom, *Luster* themed cocktail — which was, of course, pink.

I grabbed two from the nearest waiter and took an immediate sip. Despite the girlish coloring, the concoction wasn't terrible — it tasted like strawberries covered in whipped cream, the sharp burn of vodka somehow tamed by the sweetness of the fruit juice. Taking another gulp, I offered the second martini glass to Bash.

His face twisted into a grimace of disgust. "Men don't drink things that are the same color as cotton candy."

I shrugged, taking another healthy swallow from my first glass. "More for me. God knows I'll need it to get through this night."

"Let's find the bar," Bash suggested, wrapping an arm lightly around my body and guiding me across the room.

It took us a while to navigate through the throng of *Luster* employees, all dressed to the nines in glamorous gowns and sophisticated suits, who'd gathered in numbers around the bar — as was the norm for any company party with mandatory attendance and free drinks.

When I heard familiar boisterous laughter coming from the center of the crowd, I glanced over at Bash and grinned. He chuckled as we broke through the crush of people and spotted Simon and Fae, both looking extremely chic as they sat on two barstools holding court for their many admirers. Their inappropriate jokes and sordid stories had the entire crowd in stitches.

"Baby!" Simon squealed when he spotted me, throwing out a

hand and waving me forward. I smiled sheepishly as the cluster of people parted so I could approach, Bash hovering close at my back. "You look fabulous! Whoever made that dress is a marvel!" Simon winked at me playfully, squeezing my hand when I reached his side.

"You two clean up pretty well," I said, grinning as my eyes swept their outfits — Fae's red beaded gown was heart-stopping and Simon looked dapper in a dark gray suit, his red tie exactly matching the shade of Fae's dress.

"And how does Mr. Covington feel about the gown?" Simon asked, his eyes on Bash.

"Right now, I'm wishing there was a little more of it," Bash muttered, glancing around at the men in the crowd, some of whom had their appreciative eyes fixed on my naked back. "But I can't really blame them for looking. She's the most beautiful woman in this room — I'd look too."

"Oh, don't worry, love," Fae said, a small smile on her lips. "Most of the men here are gay."

"True," Simon added. "In the world of fashion, it's probably a five to one ratio, gay to straight. Not that I'm complaining."

Bash laughed as he leaned forward to place his drink order with a passing bartender.

I cast another glance around at the crowd. There were at least four hundred people gathered here, along with more food than I'd ever seen in one place and enough alcohol stocked behind the huge bar to send the whole place up in a fiery inferno if someone were to strike a match.

"This is a pretty elaborate spread," I noted, tilting my head back once more to examine the acrobats entwined in the ribbons overhead. Their costumes were nude spandex, affixed with thousands of clear gemstones that glittered like diamonds each time they caught the light thrown by a pulsing spotlight.

"It had to be — it's Centennial! The most important night of our lives!" Fae gushed in a fake British accent, mimicking Jeanine.

Simon snorted. "Where is that old cow, anyway? I haven't seen her yet."

"Let's hope that trend continues," I muttered, in no rush to see my boss any time soon.

Bash, a fresh scotch in hand, nudged me with his elbow and leaned down until his mouth brushed my ear. "There's Mr. Harding," he said in a low voice, gesturing toward the entryway where an imposing, white-haired man had just stepped into the atrium. "And Cara," he added, nodding subtly toward the opposite side of the room where a group of models had taken up residence in front of the DJ.

"And there's Jeanine!" Simon hissed in a hushed tone, nodding toward the raven-haired woman approaching from our left. "Crap, she's spotted us."

"Great. That woman hates me with a passion," Fae mumbled.

"She hates everyone," I said, sighing as I watched our boss move closer, her eyes narrowed on me.

"She likes me," Bash contradicted with a grimace. "I'll distract her. You three make a break for it. I'll meet you on the other side of the bar as soon as I can get away."

I wrapped my arms around his neck and pulled him down for a lingering kiss. "You're my hero," I whispered in a thick Georgian accent, batting my lashes in a coquettish manner. "How ever will I repay you, sir?"

Bash grinned roguishly. "I can think of several ways."

"Well, think long and hard. I want you to feel like you're getting your side of the bargain." With a tinkling laugh, I pressed another kiss to his lips and winked at him. "See you in a few, handsome."

"Come on, lovebirds, time to break it up." Fae snapped her fingers in the space between our faces. "The shrew is closing in — any more of this sappy banter and we'll never get away."

I blew Bash a kiss as Fae and Simon tugged me from him. We rushed for the bathrooms on the other side of the hall, quickly losing sight of Bash in the crowd. Mercifully, no one we knew was in the ladies room to eavesdrop and no one made a fuss about Simon's presence. A few models and makeup artists chatted by the small mirrored lounge area, but otherwise it was surprisingly quiet. Then again, I suppose it wasn't such a surprise — trays of appetizers had just started floating around the crowd and most people were out gorging themselves, descending on the cater waiters like scores of vultures on a single dead carcass.

"We have a few minutes. Jeanine can talk for at least a half hour without coming up for air," Simon said, chuckling at the thought. "Poor Sebastian. He really must love you, if he's willing to put up with her."

I smiled and a happy flush warmed my cheeks.

"What did you do today?" Fae asked me. "No work again, right?"

My smile faded slightly. "No, Conor said I shouldn't go."

Fae rolled her eyes at the FBI agent's mention.

"I met with Conor, watched four episodes of *Say Yes to the Dress* on TLC, ate an entire bag of Doritos, and forced myself to read last month's issue of *Luster* — which nearly sent me over the edge. I mean, I know we're a 'women's magazine' but, seriously, who the hell approved that story about cup size directly correlating to marital satisfaction?" I huffed.

Simon and Fae glanced at each other. "Jeanine," they chimed simultaneously.

"Of course," I muttered.

"Why'd you meet with Agent Gallagher?" Fae asked, her nose wrinkling in distaste.

"He wanted to discuss the surveillance plans for tonight. Apparently, he 'has a man on me' somewhere inside the gala. He also insisted I wear this," I gestured to the simple bracelet on my right wrist. "Just as a precaution."

"What's that?" Simon asked, leaning closer to examine the silver chain.

I grinned. "Supposedly, it's a tracking device. So they can find my body when it washes up on the beach after I'm abducted and killed."

"Not funny," Fae murmured, leaning close to stare at the bracelet. "It doesn't look like a tracker. Maybe Gallagher just gave it to you so you'd feel better about the prospect of another abduction."

I shrugged. "Maybe."

"Well, it sounds like you had a very fulfilling day," Simon said, laughing.

"Oh, that was all before noon." I studied my cuticles. "This afternoon I got bored, so I spent the rest of my day writing a story."

"For next month's issue?" Fae asked.

I shook my head.

"For the December *100 Years* issue?" Simon's brows raised in curiosity.

I shook my head a second time. "No. It's something I've been working on for a while now, just a bit at a time. It's about my investigation. Details about Red Hook, *Labyrinth*, the auction, the missing girls. Photographs, to substantiate everything."

"But...why?" Simon asked, his brow furrowed.

"I want you to publish it if..." I trailed off and cleared my throat. "Well, if for some reason Conor doesn't come through on his word. Or... if something happens to me."

Fae and Simon stared at me with serious expressions.

"Nothing is going to happen to you," Fae said, her tone firm. "And Conor might be an ass, but he'll follow through."

"I hope so," I said in a quiet voice. "But, if you're wrong... The file is on a memory stick in the lockbox. Just make sure it finds its way into the hands of someone at the *Times*. Please."

Simon nodded. "You know we'd do anything for you, baby. But I don't like you walking around worried you're going to disappear."

"I know. I'm just being paranoid. Let's head back, I bet Bash is in need of an intervention by now." I forced a smile, pushing down the strange feeling I'd been carrying around all night. I couldn't explain it — this wary, foreboding sensation deep in my core — but I couldn't dismiss it, either.

We were halfway back to the bar when I felt my phone buzz in the confines of my small purse. The bag was tiny — a jeweled, ice blue clutch that Simon had designed to perfectly match my dress. Nearly half the inside compartment was occupied by the clear plastic "emergency kit" Simon put together and insisted I bring. The small zip-lock bag was stocked with makeup brushes, the tiniest mascara bottle I'd ever seen, a nail file, a tiny sewing kit for dress malfunctions, breath mints, and even a miniature pair of razor sharp scissors. I'd laughed when I'd first seen it, complaining there was barely enough room for my cellphone. Privately, I'd been amused by his utter preparedness to handle anything that could possibly go wrong tonight.

I paused to fish my phone from the clutch, its insistent vibrations signaling an incoming call from an unknown number. Glancing away from the screen, I looked up to tell Fae and Simon to wait for me, but they'd already disappeared into the vast swarm of people in the atrium. I assured myself I'd find them in a minute, maneuvering my body toward the edge of the crowd where it was quieter and hitting a button on my screen to accept the incoming call.

"Hello?"

"Lux!" The voice was well known to me — young, feminine, filled with fear.

"Miri?" I asked, feeling my stomach flip. My eyes scanned the crowd, looking for Bash and my friends, but I spotted no familiar faces. "Is that you?"

"Please, Lux. You have to come." Her voice was hushed and trembling with terror. "I have to tell you something."

"Don't worry, Miri, it's going to be okay," I told her, trying to conceal the tremors in my own voice. "Tell me where you are, I'll send someone to pick you up."

"No!" Her voice was shrill with panic. "It has to be you! You're the only one I trust!"

I felt my heart turn over as I heard the fright in her voice. "Calm down, Miri. Tell me what's wrong."

"I know where they're keeping Vera," she whispered.

The breath halted in my lungs.

"They saw me. I think they're after me." Her breaths were ragged. "Please, come. I need you to come. Right now."

"Miri, I'll bring help. It'll be okay. Just tell me where you are."

"Please," she pleaded. "Come alone. I need your help. I'm at the coffee shop — you know the one, in the Village where we met before."

"Why do I have to come alone?"

"I don't trust anyone else," Miri whispered into the phone. "If you don't come alone, I'll run. Please, Lux. I don't want to disappear like Vera."

The line went dead.

۞

I DIDN'T THINK.

I should've considered all my options. I should've been logical. Should've planned better, thought harder.

But I didn't.

I don't really have any excuse, other than the fact that, as adrenaline and fear pulse through your veins and your heart races at twice its normal speed, rational thought becomes difficult. I heard the fear in Miri's voice and something inside me snapped, like a twig placed under so much pressure it finally cracks in two. Phone clutched in one hand, the skirt of my dress held aloft in the other, I rushed for the exits.

I didn't think about going to Bash or my friends. I didn't even consider the FBI agent milling about the room with me somewhere. Instead, I moved on instinct, my thoughts consumed by the image of a young girl I had an obligation to protect. Stupidly, I thought I might just slip out for a moment to see her — my absence so brief my friends wouldn't even notice I was missing. I thought I might call Conor on my way, and have him arrange some kind of safe location for Miri to go until this was all over. I thought there'd be more time to plan, to phone for help if I needed it.

I was wrong.

There's a moment in every horror movie when the young, nubile heroine hears a scary noise from the dark, dank basement and decides to go down alone to check it out. And you, watching at home, are screaming at your television as she descends the creaking stairs, straight into the arms of a waiting serial killer.

Go back, you idiot! you yell, shaking a frustrated fist at the screen as the heroine meets her predictable, gruesome end. I'd been that person, rolling my eyes at the girl in the movie and fully convinced I'd never be so foolish. Which made it all the more ironic that, when that moment came along in my own life, I failed to recognize it.

Running for the front doors, I skirted around several arriving guests and held one hand up to shield my eyes from the mob of cameramen eager to snap my picture a second time. I could only imagine tomorrow's headlines:

SEBASTIAN COVINGTON'S DATE FLEES GALA

But, in my mind, that was better than the alternative:

YOUNG IMMIGRANT GIRL FOUND DEAD IN CENTRAL PARK

I wasn't a total idiot, nor did I have a death wish. I simply knew that, with each passing minute, the likelihood something might happen to Miri increased tenfold. As I hailed a taxi, I scrolled through my contacts until I found Conor's name. The yellow cab slowed to a stop before me just as the phone began to ring in my ear.

"Gallagher," he clipped, as I pulled open the door and slid into the backseat.

I opened my mouth to speak but the taxi lurched forward, peeling away from the curb so fast my phone slipped from my hand and landed on the cushion next to me. My eyes flew to the driver's seat, growing wide when I saw who was sitting there.

I'd been neatly trapped — sprinted straight into my enemies' snare. There would be no call for back up made during this ride. No warnings or words of goodbye.

"Hands in the air, whore," Smash-Nose sneered at me from the front passenger seat, one bandaged hand holding a gun against the thin plastic partition between our seats. The Neanderthal grunted as he sped down W 57th past the park, the steering wheel clutched tightly in his fists.

I raised my hands into the air slowly, my mind occupied by thoughts of what a fool I'd been. Miri wasn't at the coffee shop — she was somewhere in the custody of *Labyrinth* thugs, probably forced at gunpoint to call and get me outside... into their waiting taxi.

"We've got you now, bitch." Smash-Nose's grin was full of malicious anticipation. "Boss is gonna have a fucking field day with you."

I felt my stomach clench. A quick glance down at my seat revealed that my cellphone was still connected — I prayed Conor was listening. "Where's Miri?" I asked in a loud voice.

Smash-Nose laughed. "Wouldn't you like to know."

"Where are you taking me?" I tried again.

"Boss wants to see you," Smash-Nose gloated.

"That wasn't my question."

He tapped the partition with the barrel of his handgun. "I don't fucking care what your question was, bitch. Boss wants to see you. Did you really think you could just walk into *Labyrinth* on the arm of Boss' fucking *son* and not be noticed?" He laughed in condescension, enjoying his taunting. "I guess it's true what they say about blondes."

"Shut up!" The Neanderthal growled at his partner, glaring daggers in his direction. "How many times do I have to fucking tell you? Don't talk about Boss in public. Ever."

"We aren't in public," Smash-Nose said, a cruel smirk crossing his face.

My hands were beginning to tingle from being held aloft, the blood struggling to circulate up my arms with each pump of my racing heart. I played Smash-Nose's words over in my mind, struggling to comprehend his meaning.

"Boss' son," I whispered, my thoughts drifting to Sebastian.

Smash-Nose laughed contemptuously. "Oh, you didn't know? You didn't realize you'd nearly staged a little family reunion the other night?" His eyes were wide with amusement. "That's even better!"

The Neanderthal reached out with one beefy fist and cracked Smash-Nose across the cheekbone. The smaller man cried out in pain, reaching up to cup his injured face and emitting a loud howl of pain that made me flinch in my seat.

"Senator Covington is the boss." I hoped my voice was audible through the small phone speaker. I hoped Conor hadn't already hung up. I hoped, somehow, that help was coming.

At my words, Smash-Nose quit his whimpering and turned his eyes to me. A smile crept across his face as he undid a latch and slid the plastic partition open. He leaned forward through the open space, his gun extended menacingly.

"You'll see soon enough, bitch."

That's when everything went dark.

❧

I AWOKE WITH A DULL ACHE IN MY TEMPLE. EITHER SMASH-Nose had hit me with the butt of his gun and knocked me out, or I'd been drugged. Judging by the throbbing goose-egg that had swollen my right eye half shut, I was willing to bet it had been the former.

I cracked my eyes open, surprised to find that I was in a well-appointed parlor of sorts. The room was small but fully furnished with red velvet drapes shielding the window and an ornate, white Victorian-style sofa directly across from me. The priceless Persian rug beneath the legs of my chair was lush, its vibrant red strands thickly woven into a breathtaking pattern. On my right, I saw a small dining table with seating for four. On my left was what appeared to be a closed door, constructed of the thick insulated metal I imagined one might find inside a cold-storage meat locker or a deep-sea submarine. The strange door was totally out of place amidst the refined furniture adorning the room — welded with rounded edges and set deeply into the wall, it was more industrial than Victorian chic. In place of a traditional knob was a broad metal lever that looked like it had to be rotated if one was to open the portal.

The odd door made me wonder where I'd been taken, but I didn't dwell on those thoughts for long. As far as I was concerned, an exit was an exit — and getting out of here was my only concern at the moment.

Disoriented, I tried to stand but soon found that I couldn't move. The fog began to clear from my mind as I looked down and saw that my hands had been bound behind me, the thin cords holding them looped through the wooden rungs at the back of my chair. I pulled with all my strength, but the ropes didn't give in the slightest — the more I tugged, the harsher they dug into my wrists.

I inhaled deeply and tried to get my bearings. I was still in my gown and heels but my purse was on the small table next to the sofa, nearly ten feet away. My phone was nowhere to be seen, either still lying on the back seat of a taxicab somewhere in the city or tucked into my clutch. I twisted in my chair, trying to get a look at my right wrist to see if I was still wearing the tracking bracelet Conor had given me, but I couldn't crane my neck enough to tell.

My heart began to pound as I realized how perilous my situation was. I knew, at any moment, that door might open and the man who walked through would be more than happy to make me suffer.

And Andrew Covington had made me suffer more than enough for one lifetime.

I'd never be able to turn the door lever with my hands bound. But if my cellphone was still inside that clutch, I might be able to call for help before anyone returned to check on me. It was a long shot — but it was also my only shot at escape.

With that thought, I took a deep inhale and tried to rise to my feet with the chair still strapped to my back. My heeled feet wobbled as they attempted to support the awkward, crouched position I'd heaved my body into, and within seconds the chair legs smacked back down against the carpeted floor with a low thud that made me wince. I froze, listening for sounds of anyone approaching. When a minute passed in unbroken silence, I tried again.

Rocking my body forward, I rose once more, bending my torso nearly parallel to the ground. I teetered slightly but managed to steady myself, holding my breath as I focused on remaining upright and not tripping over the long train of my gown. In a series of slow, shuffling steps, I made my way across the rug with my eyes trained on the carpet's sumptuous weaving. After what felt like an eternity I reached my destination, the small sofa table coming into view inches below my nose.

Taking care not to move too fast and jeopardize my precarious balancing act, I leaned forward slightly, opened my mouth, and clamped down on my small clutch, my teeth digging into the bejeweled fabric. Suppressing the small flare of hope in my chest, I retraced my shuffling steps back to my original spot and dropped the chair legs to the ground.

I sighed. Now, for the tricky part.

Once my chair was back in place, I maneuvered my body as far forward as I could manage on the seat, creating a small gap of space between my back and the rungs of the chair, where my hands had been bound. I took a deep breath through my nose to steady myself and took aim, tossing my chin and releasing the bag from its hold between my teeth.

My heart skipped a beat as I watched my small clutch drop like a stone through the air, landing on the edge of the seat and nearly tumbling to the floor, where it would be both useless and unreachable. When the dangling bag steadied on the brink, I exhaled in relief and shifted backwards on the chair once more, using my body to maneuver the bag, inch by inch, away from the edge.

When my fingers brushed the jeweled satin, I nearly wept with relief.

Pulling the clutch between the rungs, I worked at the zipper, my tied hands making it difficult to gain purchase on the fabric. In my clumsy attempts, I almost dropped the purse to the floor and lost my only chance at freedom. When I finally managed to work the zipper open, I was disheartened to feel nothing but satin and plastic inside.

No cellphone.

I fought off a scream of frustration as my only escape method went out the window. I was tied to a chair, totally defenseless, about to face the man who haunted my nightmares. And I was armed only with a clutch purse and Simon's plastic "emergency kit" of makeup supplies.

My breath caught in my throat.

The "emergency kit." Hadn't Simon said there was a sewing set inside? A pair of scissors?

The ropes binding my hands weren't too thick — with enough sawing, even a small pair of scissors might be able to cut through. With newfound energy, my fingers tugged at the clutch. Closing my eyes to better sort the shapes inside, I opened the plastic bag. I felt a small, smooth tube — the mascara — as well as a thicker, indented tube — the roll of breath mints. My fingertips scraped against several stick-like things — makeup brushes — and finally came to rest on something cool and metallic.

Scissors.

I smiled as I worked them from the bag and pushed my clutch back through the rungs onto the seat so I could devote all my concentration to slicing the small blades against my bindings. The smile dropped from my face when I heard the scrape of metal on metal, my head twisting left to watch as the door lever twisted counterclockwise and the thick portal swung inward.

Smash-Nose stood in the doorway, grinning. "Boss is here."

He stepped aside to allow the "Boss" to enter the room and winked at me through the crack as he pulled the door closed with a metallic boom. I sat immobile, blinking like an idiot, as I came face to face with the ringleader of the *Labyrinth* organization. My wide, disbelieving gaze swept from the immaculately styled blonde hair to the icy blue eyes, which hadn't changed in the near decade since I'd last seen them. I struggled to reconcile what I was seeing with what I knew to be true.

The "Boss" was Judith Covington.

Chapter Thirty-Six

※

NOW

JUDITH STARED AT ME WITH THE COOL GAZE I REMEMBERED SO well. She strode several feet into the room, her black sling-back heels clicking quietly against the carpeted floor. Her navy pantsuit was pristine — not a single wrinkle marred the elegant outfit, as though she'd just stepped off the runway at a fashion show.

"Lux." Her tone was cordial and disapproving all at once. "I thought you'd learned your lesson seven years ago about what happens when you stick your nose places it doesn't belong."

I blinked at her, stunned. "You're the Boss." I couldn't quite keep the note of incredulity from creeping into my tone.

She laughed, a brittle sound ringing out in the small room, and walked over to the white settee. She sat and crossed her legs in a polished gesture. "You say that with such surprise. Why is that, I wonder?"

"You're exploiting innocent girls. It was bad enough when I thought it was your husband, doing this. But for a woman to be the

leader of this kind of organization.... To do this to other women..."
I trailed off, staring at her as disgust twisted my features into a
grimace. "It's the worst kind of evil there is."

Judith's eyes went arctic. "My husband doesn't have the brains
to run an organization like *Labyrinth*. He was far too busy with his
whores and his mistresses to do his own job in the capital, let alone
take the helm of a multi-tiered institution."

"How could you do this?" I asked, my eyes narrowing on the
woman seated across from me. "*Why* would you do this?"

"It's so very short sighted of you to ask me that question. *Why?*
Why would I do this?" She leaned forward, her voice intent and
her eyes suddenly gleaming. "I'm the wife of a U.S. Senator. The
arm candy. The Stepford Wife with a great complexion, good
breeding, and no brains in her head. Right?" She laughed again,
and I flinched at the harsh sound, my fingers clenching against
something metallic. Abruptly, I realized I'd been so stupefied by
Judith's appearance, I'd forgotten I still held the scissors in
my hand.

"That was my role. Sit still, stay quiet, look pretty." Judith's
eyes narrowed. "It didn't matter that I had twice the brains of my
senator husband. I'd never have been elected. Do you know
why, Lux?"

I shook my head as my fingers worked silently, angling the scissors to saw at the bonds holding my wrists. Progress was painfully
slow — I knew I had to keep my arm muscles as immobile as
possible to avoid detection.

"Let's play a game," Judith suggested, uncrossing her legs and
folding her hands delicately in her lap. "For every answer you get
correct, I'll let you stay in here a little longer. Too many wrong
answers, and I'll have you taken outside. And, believe me, Lux, you
don't want to go out there until it's absolutely necessary.
Understand?"

Seeing no other options, I nodded. My right hand began to
grow tired and I feared the small blade was growing duller with
each stroke, but I kept sawing anyway.

"How many U.S. Senators are there?"

A third grader could've answered that one. "One hundred."

Judith nodded. "Good. And when was the Senate founded?"

That was a little harder. I thought back to the history classes I'd taken in college, racking my brain for the answer. "1789?" I guessed, holding my breath until I saw Judith smile coolly.

"Someone knows her history. Very good," she praised. "And today, more than two full centuries later, how many women have served in the Senate? Any idea?"

I swallowed roughly. I had no clue — not even the shadow of an inkling.

"I don't know," I admitted, finally feeling one of the bindings on my wrist begin to split.

"Well, that's unfortunate." Judith rose from her seat and walked to the curtained window. Pulling the velvet drapes aside, she stood before the pane. I craned my neck, but could see almost nothing in the black night outside the window. A few industrial lights, some metal fencing — nothing I could properly make out.

"It's getting late. We'll be leaving soon." She turned back to face me. "The answer to my question is forty-four."

I stared at her in silence.

"Forty-four women have served on the Senate." She walked closer. "Not this year. *Ever*. In the history of our country. In two and a quarter centuries."

"I didn't know that," I whispered, feeling one of the cords holding my wrists sever completely.

"There are twenty female senators serving this term. Twenty, out of a hundred. It's considered a banner year for women." She sat on the sofa again, glancing at her watch with a sigh. "And yet, you ask me *why* I would run an organization like this."

I bunched the loosened bindings in my hands so they wouldn't fall to the floor and give me away, sighing lightly as I felt circulation begin to return to my freed fingers. "I'm sorry, Judith, I still don't understand how the underrepresentation of women in our government could possibly justify the things you've done to young, defenseless girls."

"I'll spell it out for you, since you're clearly not intelligent enough to put it together yourself," she said, her eyes coldly excited — as much emotion as I'd ever seen from her. "The answer is simple. *Power*."

As she spoke, I was beginning to realize she wasn't just a shrewd, unfeeling businesswoman — she was totally unhinged. Now that I was free from my bonds, I could make my escape at any time. But I knew the element of surprise was the only thing I had working in my favor. Plus, if I wanted to hear her motives, I needed to bide my time.

"I control *Labyrinth*, which means I control every secret that goes on inside its walls. I know about every major business deal and political decision before it happens. I know which senators prefer the underage brunettes, and which congressmen most enjoy the busty blondes."

Her voice dropped to an impassioned whisper.

"There may never be equality for women in positions of power, and I may never be elected to office — but what does that matter, if I can pull the strings of the most powerful men in this country? I'm the puppeteer — the *female* puppeteer — who holds the end of all their chains." She laughed. "Perhaps, if they'd been able to keep their peckers in their pants for more than twenty minutes, they wouldn't have found themselves in this situation."

"But... you're talking about women's rights. About the need for gender equality...." I shook my head in disbelief. "And, all the while, you're snatching girls from their families and selling them to the highest bidder. How is that remotely sane?"

The smile dropped off her face. "What are the lives of a few immigrant girls in comparison to women finally, *finally*, having some power in this country? I shape national policy. I make sure your right to vote, to choose, to work in a professional field stay in tact. And you have the audacity to question that." She glared at me. "You should be thanking me. Not working against me."

Her voice dropped lower and her eyes turned to blue chips of ice. "Not turning my only son against me."

"I had nothing to do with your son's feelings for you." I glared back at her. "You managed to alienate him all on your own."

"We had an agreement — I held up my side. I footed the bill for that pathetic brother of yours until the day he died. I allowed your alcoholic parents to remain in that hovel they call home," she hissed, her expression enraged. "Did you really think you could insert yourself back into Sebastian's life without me noticing? That I wouldn't do everything in my power to remove you?"

I lifted my chin and refused to give her the satisfaction of a reply.

"I'll remove you again — but this time, I'm afraid it will be much more permanent." She leaned forward. "You were never meant to be a part of my son's life, you little white trash whore. Where you're going, be sure to remember that. And, by the way, your parents?" She smiled again and I felt my heart drop into my stomach. "They'll be out on the streets by tomorrow morning."

Hatred swirled through my veins as I contemplated the woman before me. "No matter what you do to me," I whispered, smiling back at her. "Sebastian will never let you back into his life. You're toxic — you poison everything you lay your hands on. And getting rid of me will only drive him further away."

Her lips pressed into a thin line. She rose, strode quickly across the room, and cocked back her arm in preparation to slap me.

I saw the look of total surprise on her face when my own arm flew up to halt her motion midair. I rose quickly to my feet and used the momentum from her swing against her — one sharp tug in my direction sent her stumbling off balance, her heeled feet catching on my vacant chair's legs and sending her crashing to the ground in a tangle of uncoordinated Chanel-clothed limbs. On her way down, I lifted my right knee and watched with more than a little satisfaction as her temple cracked against the unyielding bone with a harsh thud that I prayed wasn't audible through the thick metal door. I looked down and saw her lying on the floor, silent and unmoving, and realized with a detached sort of awe that I'd knocked her unconscious.

Holy crap. That had gone way better than I'd anticipated.

Using her momentary incapacitation to my advantage, I ran toward the doorway and pulled down on the lever. It didn't budge — Smash-Nose or one of Judith's other lackeys had locked it from the outside. There was an electronic intercom panel next to the door, but I didn't think that, even if I asked nicely, whoever was outside would release me. They were probably waiting for Judith's command to open the door, but I knew if enough time passed without hearing from her, one of them would come to check on their "Boss."

I wasn't about to wait around for that moment to arrive without some way of defending myself.

Turning, my eyes scanned the room, searching for a weapon of some kind, and eventually came to land on the small sofa table. I rushed forward, yanked the glass lamp free of its cord, and carried it over to the velvet window drapes, where I wrapped it fully in the heavy fabric. Lifting my arms high, I smashed the cloaked lamp down hard on the windowsill. I heard glass shatter and stepped back as I allowed the curtain to unfurl at my feet, releasing a cluster of thick, sharp fragments on the carpet.

A glance back at Judith revealed that she was beginning to stir but not yet fully conscious, whimpering in a heap on the floor. I reached forward and grabbed the largest, sharpest triangular glass shard from the pile. Using my scissors, I sawed off several thin strips of gauzy fabric from the excess material on the bottom of my dress train. I wrapped one strip around the base of my glass blade so I could grip it without cutting into my hands. Grabbing the other two strips and the frayed lamp cord, I crossed the room back to Judith's supine form.

She barely noticed as I bound her feet with ice-blue gauze and wrapped the thick electrical wire around her hands in a knot so tight she wouldn't be able to slide her fingers free. She moaned as I hooked my hands beneath her armpits, dragged her across the floor, and leaned her slumped body against the wall next to the door. With my final piece of gauze, I tied a gag around her mouth so she couldn't scream.

I heaved in a deep breath as I stood and stepped back to examine my work.

Not bad, considering my lack of resources. Now, I just needed a way out of this room.

I retrieved my glass blade from the floor and crouched before Judith, using my free hand to lightly slap one of her cheeks. She stirred awake at my touch, her eyes slivering open to lock on my face.

"You... little... bitch," she muttered through the gag, her words nearly indecipherable. She tugged against her bindings as her dull eyes cleared of fog and narrowed on me.

"Where are we?" I grabbed her chin with one fist when she tried to avert her gaze, so she was forced to meet my eyes. I pulled down her gag so she could respond. "Where are the girls? Are you keeping them here?"

She laughed, her eyes blasting me with a frigid glare. "You'll never make it out of this room. You'll never find them."

"I'll ask nicely one more time," I whispered, leaning close to her face. "If you choose not to answer, we can play another game. You answer my questions, and I won't use this." I flashed my makeshift knife at her.

"Fuck you," she bit out, laughing once again. "My men will take you down before you ever leave this ship."

Ship?

Nearly as soon as the words left her mouth, I heard it — the low sound of a fog horn, echoing out over the bay. I shoved the gag back inside her mouth and raced for the window, the sight before me making my heart stutter.

We were most definitely on a ship — a big one, judging by the height of my view.

The ocean swirled fifty feet below my vantage point, black water churning in the darkness like a huge spill of oil, stretching from the ship deck to the bank of city lights a half-mile away. I looked out across New York Harbor, the Statue of Liberty glowing like a bright beacon in the middle of the waterway, and realized I must be at a dock somewhere on the Brooklyn shoreline — perhaps in Red Hook, by the brewery I'd come to know so well, or at another port further south. A passing freighter in the middle of the sound blew again on its fog horn as it left harbor, warning arriving ships of its presence.

I inhaled sharply at the sight and raced back to Judith, crouching before her with my knife held at her throat.

"I'm done playing nice," I informed her. "Is there a guard outside this door?"

She glared at me, unmoved.

"Answer me," I hissed, pressing the blade tighter against her jugular. I could see her carotid artery pulsing beneath the skin at twice the normal rate — despite her defiance, she was afraid of me. A tense moment passed, each of us deadlocked and determined to hold our ground.

But, when all was said and done, I was the one with the knife.

"Yes," she muttered, her voice muffled by the gauze in her mouth.

"Just one?"

"Yes," she repeated.

"Good." I swallowed. "If you do what I say, I won't hurt you. Don't pretend you don't care about your life. We both know you want to see your son again."

She bobbed her head slightly in acknowledgement, and I loosened the press of my knife against her skin.

"I'm going to take out your gag and press the intercom. You're going to yell for the guard to come in. Tell him—" I broke off, my mind racing into overdrive as I fabricated a plan from thin air. "Tell him it's time to move me outside. Make it convincing, or I swear to god, I'll be the last person you ever see." I held her eyes for a beat. "And we both know, out of everyone you could envision

435

spending your last moments with, I'd be at the absolute bottom of your list."

Her reluctant nod of agreement brought a smile to my face.

"Glad we're on the same page," I told her.

I kept my eyes on her as I rose to my feet and backed up several steps to reach the upturned wooden chair. Dragging it behind me, I walked back to the portal door, stopped next to Judith and tucked my glass blade into the neckline of my gown. I knew it might slice into the fragile flesh there, but I had nowhere else to store it and I sure as hell wasn't relinquishing hold of my only weapon. With a steadying breath, I reached down and took off my high heels, throwing them across the room and out of Judith's reach.

I stared at her for a long moment before pulling the gag from her mouth. She glared back at me with an icy intensity, but remained dutifully silent. With a nod, I rose and took hold of the wooden chair with both hands, my palms sweaty as I wrapped them around the rungs.

"Now," I hissed at Judith, pressing the intercom button with my elbow.

She shot daggers at me with chilly eyes. "Miller!" she called in a shrill voice. "Get in here! It's time to move her."

Immediately I heard the sound of metal grating. My eyes followed the door's lever as it rotated open and I pressed my body close against the wall, not daring to move a muscle as the portal swung open with a heavy groan and a man's booted foot stepped through the entryway.

I allowed him to take a full step inside, his distinct facial profile immediately recognizable — Smash-Nose.

"What the hell?" he yelled catching sight of the empty room and starting forward.

Before he could make another sound or take another step, I used all the strength in my arms to heave the chair up and clip him hard across the chest. With an audible gasp he doubled over in pain, clutching at both his stomach and his nose which, if the blood pouring out of each nostril was any indication, I'd broken once more.

I didn't spare a second, jumping over his prone form and out onto a thin metal gangway on the other side of the portal. I turned and reached for the heavy door, pulling it closed and locking it into place before Smash-Nose could even regain his feet. On the outside, the latch was simple enough — shaped like a small steering wheel, it rotated clockwise and slid a deadbolt into place, barring the door.

Once it was locked, I turned and collapsed back against the cool metal, heaving deep breaths in through my nose. My eyes went wide when I saw the view of the ship sprawled out below me.

I was standing on an open-air, partially enclosed passageway on the ship's bridge platform, looking down at a vast cargo freighter roughly the length of two football fields, give or take twenty yards. The lower deck was dimly illuminated by tall light posts and stacked with shipping containers, which I'd always thought looked like LEGO pieces from afar. Up close they were huge, each towering at least eight feet high and stretching nearly twenty feet long.

A horrible thought dawned. Were they using this vessel to transport abducted girls to other cities?

I only let myself contemplate that for a short moment – I needed to find a way to call for help and get off this ship. The door I was leaning against began to vibrate with the pounding of Smash-Nose's fists, and the muffled sounds of his screams were audible even through the thick metal.

Someone was bound to hear him eventually – and when they did, I couldn't be here. I quickly turned the volume knob to mute on the outer intercom panel, so his calls wouldn't be broadcast across the ship.

Removing my knife from my dress' neckline, I saw a splatter of crimson — the glass had cut into me at some point during my escape. I ignored my wound as I took a firm hold of my blade once more and crept down the open-air passageway as silently as I could manage. The gangway's metal grates were cold against my bare feet.

Ships are never quiet the way buildings are. There's constant noise — the lapping of water against the hull far below, the grinding of metal against the wooden dock, the straining of ropes used to tether the boat to shore. It was eerie to be surrounded by so many unfamiliar sounds, enveloped in the darkness. The moon was just a faint sliver overhead, high enough in the sky for me to know that several hours had passed since I left Centennial.

I came to a halt when I reached a door and a long bank of windows. The residual light from the hanging gangway lamps illuminated the dark room enough for me to see that it was vacant. I saw the shadow of a large steering wheel in the space directly behind the row of windows — these were the captain's steering quarters.

Pushing open the swinging door, I slipped inside and waited for my eyes to adjust to the dim room. My fingers trailed across the immobile steering wheel, then skimmed down along the darkened control panel. There were so many buttons and switches, I felt instantly overwhelmed. None of them were conveniently labeled "911 EMERGENCY" or "LUX, YOU IDIOT, PRESS ME."

Damn.

My scanning eyes finally fell on a marine radio and hope stirred to life in my chest. I twisted the power knob on the transceiver box, pulled the handheld receiver from its cradle, and raised it to my mouth. Pressing the transmit button with my thumb, I spoke rapidly into the microphone, hoping someone on the other end was listening.

"Please, if you can hear this, my name is Lux Kincaid. I've been kidnapped and am being held on a container ship at a dock somewhere in New York Harbor. I can see the southern tip of Manhattan and the Statue of Liberty out the window. Send help. Please."

I repeated my message three times into the radio, but there was no response of any kind. I had no idea if I'd even broadcasted it correctly, and no time left to find out. I'd already lingered in this room too long.

Abandoning the radio, I turned and headed back for the doorway. I'd nearly reached the exit when my eyes caught on a black box labeled "FLARES" in bright red lettering. Before I could talk myself out of it, my hands were reaching for the box, pulling it down onto the floor where I crouched, and unsnapping the latches holding its thick plastic lid in place. With trembling fingers, I reached inside and pulled out what looked like a black, metal handgun with a distended barrel. It was far heftier than it looked at first glance, its weight considerable in my small hand.

There were two flare rounds nestled alongside the gun — I lifted them out as well.

I was surprised to find it wasn't constructed much differently than my father's shotgun — the barrel snapped open and I popped one of the rounds inside, easily clicking the barrel back into place once it was loaded. Now, I had a weapon — not one I knew how to use, not one that would be lethal to an attacker from a distant range, but a weapon nonetheless.

And, perhaps more importantly, a way to signal for help.

Popping the extra flare round into my cleavage, I left the steering room behind and slipped back into the corridor. I held the flare gun in one hand and my knife shard in the other as I walked down the passageway, the bank of windows to my left and the rest of the ship sprawling beneath me to my right. At the distant end of the freighter, my eyes caught on the exit I'd been seeking: a metal gangplank, sloping at a sharp angle from the raised deck at the ship's bow down to the shore dock below.

My point of escape — if I could make it through the maze of shipping containers to the opposite side of the vessel. Nearly two hundred yards and god only knew what else separated me from freedom. Ignoring the nervous clench of my stomach muscles, I continued on through the passage, my eyes peeled for a way down to the lower deck.

After a few moments, I reached the end of the narrow corridor and came to a set of metal stairs that dropped steeply to the cargo hold below. I cast my eyes downward, searching for signs of movement on the deck, but everything appeared abandoned.

Placing one foot on the top step and gathering what remained of my dress train in my knife-wielding hand, I moved with extra caution. Not only was it a long way down, should I somehow survive the fall, I'd almost certainly shoot myself with a flare or impale myself with the glass shard when I hit the bottom. I held my breath as I traversed the stairway, the burning in my chest building to a steady ache in the time it took me to reach the deck. Exhaling with a whoosh when I felt my feet hit solid ground, I looked around and tried to get my bearings.

Before me, stretching as far as I could see, were three rows of shipping containers. They towered above my head, their chipping red and yellow paint revealing heavily rusted metal beneath. I kept to the shadows as I made my way to the right side of the deck, hoping I wouldn't be spotted if there were any more guards on patrol. My heart froze in my chest when I heard the unmistakable sound of men's voices volleying through the night air as they approached the stairs I'd just come down.

I dropped into a low crouch behind a row of wooden crates, listening intently as they walked past.

"Where's Miller? We've been working our asses off getting the girls loaded and he's nowhere to be found, as usual," one man grumbled.

I heard a responding snort from his companion. "Probably whacking off in a corner somewhere. You know how excited this shit gets him."

"Well, I'm not picking up his slack anymore. Boss pays us all the same — not fair Miller does half the work for equal money."

"Maybe he's up on the bridge."

The sound of their footsteps echoed down to me as they climbed the stairway. With a quick glance overhead at their disappearing forms, I darted from the shadows into the passage between two rows of stacked containers, praying the men wouldn't look back as they ascended. I kept my senses alert for other guards as I hurried down the row, tucking my body so close to the metal boxes I felt the skin scrape off my bare shoulder. When I heard the sound of muffled voices echoing around an upcoming corner, I skidded to a halt so quickly I tripped over my own feet.

My toes failed to gain purchase on the deck and I sailed to the ground, my palms grating against the abrasive deck and instantly welling with blood. My glass knife flew from my hand and shattered instantly, reduced to a worthless crumble of shards, and the flare gun spun to a stop against a nearby container, thankfully not going off in a concentrated explosion of firepower. With a quiet yelp of pain, I scrambled to my feet and collected my gun, my ears straining to hear the noise that had set off my fall.

I waited thirty seconds in absolute silence, thinking perhaps I'd imagined the sound. I'd just decided to keep moving when I finally heard it again.

A quiet murmuring, emanating from the container to my left. Clenching my raw hands around the gun handle, I sidled forward. When I reached the front of the red steel box, I glanced around for guards but saw no one. Tiptoeing closer, I pressed an ear to the side of the container and listened.

Female voices, speaking in hushed whispers.

My stomach clenched as I shifted the gun into my left hand and reached out toward the metal door latch with my right. The voices inside fell silent as soon as the metal door rasped open. No amount of research, reading, or statistics, could've prepared me for what I saw when I pulled the hatch ajar.

There were at least fifteen girls inside the cramped space.

They stared toward the opening, their haunted eyes blinking against the sudden influx of light into their dark cell. Dirty clothes hung in rags from too-thin bodies and smudges of filth covered their exposed arms and faces. When I stepped forward, my face a mask of shock and sadness, they shrank back from me, likely fearful of the harsh treatment they'd become accustomed to whenever this door had opened in the past.

The stench of unwashed bodies was staggering — I wondered how many of these girls were sick with viral infections and malnourished from inadequate feedings. As I stepped closer, I saw past the fear in their eyes to the drug-fueled haze — their pupils were dilated, their irises glassy and unfocused.

They'd been sedated, made lethargic and compliant for easier transfer.

I thought I might vomit, turning my head to the side for a breath of fresh air and a brief reprieve from the horrors inside the container.

"Lux."

My head whipped around and my eyes searched the enclosed space, seeking the thready voice that had whispered my name. "Miri?"

"Here," she called, drawing my gaze to the corner on my left. When I saw her I rushed forward, careful not to step on the limbs of the near-unconscious girls scattered on the floor around me. Hurling myself to the ground, I wrapped my arms around Miri in a light embrace as soon as I reached her side.

"You came for me," she whispered, her eyes wide.

"You're alive," I breathed, relief evident in my tone.

"I'm so sorry, Lux, they made me call you." Miri's voice was trembling with remorse. "They threatened to kill me and my family."

"Oh, Miri, no. It's not your fault. I'm the one who's sorry — I dragged you into all of this. But we can't stay here. You have to come with me, right now. We'll go get help for the rest of them."

"I can't," she whispered, her sad eyes locked on mine. "I won't leave her."

Miri's body turned slightly, revealing the still form of a young girl lying directly beside her. There was a dangerous rattle in the prostrate girl's chest — each breath she drew was a struggle, and I feared she wouldn't last long in this dark cage without medical treatment. I felt my eyes brim with tears as I recognized the once-lustrous chestnut hair, now brittle and tangled, and the dainty features on her beautiful, bruised face.

Vera.

I reached a shaking hand out to touch her arm, my cheeks wet with traces of grief. She was clammy with fever, her skin cool to the touch. Lifting my eyes to Miri's, I wiped my face with my free hand.

"How long has she been like this?"

Miri shrugged. "Most of them are like this. They can't walk, they don't talk much," she whispered. "I'm lucky. They didn't drug me, and I haven't been here long."

"I have to go, Miri." I told her, feeling my heart tear at the prospect of leaving her and Vera now that I'd finally found them. "I'll get help. I'll come back for you."

Miri nodded. "I know you will, Lux. But... hurry."

I wrapped my arms around her once more and this time she hugged me back.

"Stay strong, Miri. I'll find you, again. I promise."

Chapter Thirty-Seven

❧❧❧

NOW

I CRIED ALL THE WAY TO THE FORWARD DECK, TEARS BLURRING my vision as my thoughts lingered on the girls. I'd closed the container when I left so the men on the bridge wouldn't spot the open door, but couldn't bring myself to bolt it again. If a guard noticed it was unlocked and was alerted to my presence on the vessel... so be it. I refused to leave those girls without even a chance at escape.

When I reached the bow and climbed the stairs to the upper deck, I was so focused on reaching the gangplank, I didn't see him until it was too late.

The Neanderthal.

He charged me with a grunt, aiming to pin my body between him and the thin, waist-high railing that wrapped the edge of the deck. He didn't see the gun in my hand. Or, if he did, he figured I wouldn't have time to fire it.

He was wrong.

It was instinctual. His life, or mine.

I lifted the gun to eye level, cocked back the pin with my thumb, and squeezed the trigger.

As kids, each Forth of July, Jamie and I would walk down to the lake, plop our butts in the sand, and eat sticky, melting popsicles as fireworks exploded in the air far above our heads. They were distant, beautiful explosions of light and color, burning into ash long before they ever returned to the ground. I remember wishing more than once during those hot summer Independence Day celebrations that they'd blast those fireworks just a little lower, so I might see their vivid sparks up close.

Tonight, I saw my childhood wish fulfilled.

The flare exploded from the end of the barrel like a compact firework, its brightness scorching my retinas and forcing my eyes closed. The harsh smell of smoke and gunpowder hung heavy around me, but it was quickly overtaken by an even more disturbing scent — the stench of singed flesh.

My eyes opened into slits when I heard the Neanderthal's scream of pain. I watched in horror as the large man clutched the gaping, smoking wound in his abdomen, stumbling backward with uncoordinated steps. The blood drained from my face when he hit the edge of the deck and toppled backward in free-fall. There was a beat of silence, followed by the loud bang of a body landing against the cargo deck far below — the grisly thud sent chills up my spine.

Soon after, I heard the sound of men yelling on the bridge and the pounding of footsteps as they raced down the rows of shipping containers toward me on the forward deck. I looked to the gang-plank on my right, which would lead me to safety, before glancing down at the spare flare round still tucked into my bloodied neckline.

I had to leave, now, before they caught me. But there was one last thing I had to do first.

Overtaken by a sudden sense of calm, I loaded the round into the still-hot barrel, cocked back the pin, and raised my arm straight into the air. The sound of the shot hurt my ears as I pulled the trigger and blasted the flare a hundred yards into the night sky, a hovering, vibrant signal of distress that would, hopefully, bring aid to the girls on this ship. It was the least I could do, if I was really going to leave them behind while I fled and sought help.

Once the round was airborne I spun around, finally ready to make my escape. Breathless, I raced toward the gangplank... and straight into a waiting set of hands that clamped down on my forearms like a vise. My eyes flew to the man's face and I felt my heart sink when I saw two startlingly green eyes staring back at me with an amused look in their depths.

"Lux," Andrew Covington whispered, his eyes sweeping down my form. "It's been a long time, my dear. And, I must say, you've looked better."

"Not nearly long enough," I grumbled, twisting in his arms as I struggled to free myself from his hold.

He laughed. "Oh, come now. Don't be a poor sport. It's so unbecoming."

"What's unbecoming is a grown man who plays lackey to his wife," I spat back at him. "How pathetic are you, Senator? When was it that you found out about your wife's extracurricular activities?"

His eyes grew flinty with anger and his grip tightened on my arms.

"During your first term? Your second?" I goaded, unable to help myself. "How emasculating was that moment, when you discovered your wife held more power than you ever would?"

"Shut up," he growled, walking me backward. "Shut your whore mouth."

I fought against him, trying to strike his hand with the empty flare gun still clutched in my fist, but he wrenched my arm in a painful twist that made my fingers spasm and unclench. The gun clattered to my feet as he pressed me up against the railing. One of his hands came up to wrap around my windpipe in a crushing chokehold. Lifting me by my neck, he cut off my air and forced me onto my tiptoes. When he leaned in closer, I felt the upper half of my body bend backward over open air and knew, if he were to push with only a little more force, I'd flip like a playground see-saw and plummet into the icy waters far below.

A fifty-foot drop.

I might survive, but I doubted I could swim to safety in this dress without swallowing half the ocean or being dragged to the sea floor.

"I should've gotten rid of you a long time ago," Andrew muttered. "You've been a thorn in my side since you were seventeen."

"Good," I rasped, kicking out with my right foot and landing a sharp blow directly between his legs. He cursed and released me. I landed hard against the deck, further injuring my already sore palms, but knowing it beat the watery alternative. Hauling my aching body into a standing position, I prepared myself for a fight.

As it turned out, I didn't need to.

Andrew had taken a single step in my direction when a figure burst from the gangplank and tackled the senator to the ground. I watched, stunned, as the two men wrestled on the deck, each movement rolling them a little closer to the edge of the platform. My eyes widened further when I saw they were nearly identical — same height, same build, same hair color. The only difference distinguishing father from son was their age gap.

Bash.

I gasped as punches rained down, their fistfight quickly escalating into an all out battle for bloodshed. Several times, I started forward to intervene but held off, knowing I might make matters worse. My fingernails bit harshly into my injured palms as I watched the senator pin Bash to the ground, his face reddening as his father's hands tightened around his neck. Seconds ticked by, each feeling like an eternity, and I scrambled into action, retrieving my fallen gun so I could knock Andrew out cold.

I froze several feet away when I saw Bash take back the upper hand. In a move so fast my eyes could barely track it, he swung his legs up abruptly, clipping his father in the chest and pitching the older man onto the hard deck surface.

I watched as Andrew rolled several feet and slipped over the edge of the platform. His legs and torso dangled midair, his fingertips the only tether holding him in place. Should he fall, he'd hit the unforgiving metal cargo deck below and suffer a fate similar to that of the Neanderthal.

"Son!" Andrew called in a desperate voice, his eyes locked on Bash. "Help me!"

Bash gained his feet, wiped his bloodied lip with the sleeve of his suit, and turned to me with worried eyes. I saw his evaluative gaze sweep my form, checking for injuries. His eyes lingered on the slice wound at my breast, the raw rope-burns around my wrists where the bindings had bit into the skin, my swollen right eye, and my bleeding palms.

"I'm fine," I whispered, stepping closer to him.

He must've agreed — not even a second later he was there, wrapping his arms around me so tightly I felt the breath slip from my lungs. His lips pressed against my temple and my head was crushed against his chest, his labored breathing and racing heartbeat pounding beneath my ear.

"Son!" Andrew called again, drawing our attention back. His face was white with the strain of holding on. "Sebastian! Please! Help me!

"Bash, he's your father," I whispered. "He's your family."

Sebastian turned his face to mine and met my eyes, his expression serious. "No, he's not. You're my family."

He grabbed my hand and walked away, his father's screams ringing out in the air behind us. Bash didn't once look back as we made our way to the gangplank and back down onto solid ground.

⚜

AS MUCH AS I MIGHT'VE WISHED IT, THE HONORABLE SENATOR Andrew Covington didn't die that day.

But he'd certainly never serve another term in office.

What I hadn't realized, in the chaos of my time on the freighter, was that the men's voices I'd heard yelling just before I sent my second flare round into the sky were not members of the crew coming after me. It was Conor and his men — a group of highly trained, covert SWAT team members — coming aboard the ship and systematically wiping out the thugs on board.

As soon as Bash and I disembarked, Conor began firing questions at me.

Who had taken me?

Had I met the Boss?

How many men were on board?

I launched into a quick summary of my abduction and my time on the ship. When I described the hold on the bridge where they'd likely find Judith and Smash-Nose, both Bash and Conor looked at me with stunned expressions.

"Judith Covington?" Conor asked, his eyes wide.

"My *mother?*" Bash's brow wrinkled in confusion.

"She's the ringleader. But that's not important right now. Listen to me — there's a container, in the middle of the cargo deck. It's red, and its door should be slightly ajar." My tone was near-frantic as I stared into Conor's eyes. "There are girls in there, Conor. They're sick and they're scared. They need medical attention. And I didn't get to search the whole ship – there might be more of them in another container."

Without another word, Conor nodded and raced away.

For the next hour, Bash and I stood on the dock with our eyes trained on the freighter, as twenty men in black fatigues and bullet proof vests ran along the upper deck and across the bridge. Their sleek black guns gleamed darkly in their hands. I told Bash more details about my ordeal, shivering as a frigid wind blew off the ocean, and he slipped his suit jacket around my shoulders to ward off the chill. He took the news of his mother's involvement in stride — aside from a few questions about what she'd said to me, he seemed more concerned with making sure I was all right.

"How did you know where to find me?" I whispered, leaning into his sturdy frame as the first wave of exhaustion hit me. Now that the rush of adrenaline was wearing off, my wounds were beginning to ache and I felt nearly dizzy with fatigue.

"When you didn't come back from the bathroom with Simon and Fae, we all knew immediately that something was wrong. We went to the curb and found Agent Greene — the man Conor assigned to watch you for the night — barking into his phone. He said he'd seen you climb into an unmarked cab."

"Miri called — she was hurt, scared. I didn't think." I shook my head. "I wasn't paying attention. I was dialing Conor..."

I felt Bash's chest heave in a sigh. "I know. It's lucky you were able to keep him on the line for a few minutes. He traced your cellphone signal to the Brooklyn Bridge — that's where it went dead."

"They tossed it out the window, into the water," I guessed.

"Probably." Bash nodded. "By that point, I'd gotten Agent Greene to bring me along as he rode to meet Conor—"

"How'd you manage that?" I tilted my face to look at him, one eyebrow raised.

Bash shrugged. "I was persuasive."

"Meaning you screamed a lot and threatened his life?" I asked.

He cracked a small smile. "Agent Greene and I rode to meet Conor. He was trying to trace the signal from the bracelet he gave you, but the pings it transmits aren't always precise. In the meantime, we drove to Red Hook and started searching the docks, but there was no sign of you anywhere. The brewery was abandoned. We got a lucky break when the Coast Guard got a message through to Conor."

My eyes widened.

"Apparently, they received a radio distress call from an unknown vessel somewhere in the harbor." Bash's smile stretched wider. "A young woman named Lux Kincaid had requested aid. She said she'd been kidnapped and gave a location that, within minutes, gave authorities enough information to track down the unregistered freighter."

I laughed incredulously, tucking my face into the crook of Bash's neck with a sigh.

"It's over," I whispered. "I'm so glad it's over."

"Me too, Freckles." He kissed the top of my head.

A commotion on the gangplank drew both of our gazes.

"Get off me! You have no right to hold me!" Judith screeched, straining against the metal handcuffs on her wrists as two agents led her onto the docks. "You can't do this! You have no evidence of my involvement."

"Actually, we have a witness who heard your full confession," Conor informed her, trailing behind the restraining agents. He smiled broadly at me when his feet landed on the dock.

Judith's head swiveled in my direction and she opened her mouth to spit another string of venomous words. Her lips froze when her eyes locked on her son, whose arms were still wrapped tight around my frame.

"Sebastian," she whispered. "Don't let them do this to me! You know I'm innocent."

Bash dropped his arms and stepped around me, walking in his mother's direction with measured strides. When he reached her, he leaned down and spoke in a voice that held no traces of love or familial loyalty.

"You did this to yourself." His tone was as cold as his words. "You're not innocent — you haven't been innocent a day in your life."

"I'm your mother!" she protested.

"Not anymore." Bash lifted his head and looked at Conor. "Take her away. I don't want Lux to have to look at her for another second."

Judith's face went pale and her arms went limp as Bash turned his back on her and walked to my side. She didn't fight the agents as they led her to a black sedan parked nearby and locked her inside.

A parade of nearly a dozen criminals soon followed, as each of her thugs was led from the ship, loaded into a waiting van, and chained to the benches inside. Smash-Nose was one of the last to emerge from the ship, his bloodied nose still seeping and his cold eyes narrowed on me with hatred.

"Bitch," he hissed as he was led past.

The agent restraining him yanked harshly on his handcuffs, and Smash-Nose fell to his knees several feet from me. "You say something, Miller?" the agent hissed.

Smash-Nose whimpered and shook his head, his eyes averted from me.

"Good." The agent pulled his prisoner to his feet and shoved him into the waiting van.

Andrew was the last off the ship — brooding in silence as he walked past, too proud to even look in our direction. That was more than fine with me; I had no desire to listen to more of his angry ramblings or promises of revenge. And, anyway, there were much more important things to focus my attention on at the moment.

Like Miri, who was rushing down the gangplank as fast as her legs could carry her.

She hit the docks and flew in my direction — all I could do was open my arms, stand still, and brace for impact.

Her arms wrapped tightly around my midsection and I could feel her labored breathing against my collarbone. The comforting weight of Sebastian's hand landed on my shoulder and I squeezed Miri tighter, my eyes locked on the gangplank over her head. They filled slowly with tears as I watched the procession of girls.

Each supported or carried by an agent, the girls were ushered off the ship and into the arms of waiting paramedics. I held my breath when Vera finally appeared, lying limp in Conor's arms. When he lowered her onto a stretcher, Miri and I rushed to her side.

"Vera," Miri breathed, leaning close to her cousin. "Can you hear me?"

The injured girl was still and silent, lying unresponsive on the cold stretcher. Tears tracked down my cheeks as I reached out to gently cup the non-battered side of her face. I bent forward, so my lips touched her ear, and saw my tears fall like raindrops onto her dirty hair.

"I don't know if you can hear me, but I have to tell you how sorry I am," I whispered, my voice hollow. "I'm sorry it took me so long, Vera. I'm so sorry."

A sob rattled in my throat as I leaned over her, and Bash rubbed a soothing hand over my back.

"You did everything you could, Lux. She knows that."

The paramedics were eager to wheel her away. I brushed a final kiss against her forehead and pulled back, allowing Bash to wrap me up in his arms. I reached out blindly for Miri, and felt her small hand slip into mine.

"Lux?" The ghost of her voice was nearly undetectable, softer than the scrape of two butterfly's wings as they beat against the air, but somehow, I heard it. So did Miri.

We turned, as one, back to the stretcher, where Vera's eyes were fluttering open. She wasn't lucid, but she was conscious — a good sign, I hoped, as I slipped my hand into hers. "I'm here," I whispered. "It's Lux."

"I'm here too," Miri added, her voice cracking with emotion.

Vera's eyes seemed to focus for a moment as she scanned from my face to Miri's. "Hi," she croaked in an uneven voice.

I felt a smile break out across my face.

"Hi," I echoed.

⚬❧

"DID YOU SEE IT?" SIMON GUSHED, THROWING OPEN THE DOOR to Sebastian's loft with Fae short on his heels.

I lifted my head from its resting place on Bash's chest. We were lying on the couch with our limbs entwined — we'd barely moved from this spot in the two days that had passed since the night on the freighter. In part, because we were both happy to be alive, unharmed, and reunited after everything that had happened.

Mostly, though, it was due to the media circus that the *Labyrinth* bust had set off.

A famous family in trouble with the law always captured the attention of gossip magazines and news outlets.

But when both parents in a rich, famous, politically-connected family were involved in a sex-trafficking ring, which was brought down by their son and his girlfriend — well, you could only imagine the press. We couldn't step outside without being bombarded by questions and photographs so, for the time being, we were stuck in our private bubble in Bash's apartment.

I pressed a kiss to his t-shirt in the spot directly over his heart and smiled. I was more than okay with our temporary confinement.

He sighed and climbed to his feet, pulling me up after him. Simon and Fae were milling about the loft like two five-year-olds hopped up on too many Pixy Stix.

"Did you see it?" Simon repeated, shoving a newspaper into my hands. My eyes fell to the printed black script, instantly recognizing the ornate block font. *The New York Times.* I allowed my gaze to drift down an inch and felt my heart stutter to a stop when I read the front-page headline.

"I HAD TO FIND THEM": ONE REPORTER'S INVESTIGATION CRACKS NYC SEX-TRAFFICKING RING WIDE OPEN

"Ohmigod," I squeaked. "Ohmigod, ohmigod, ohmigod."

"What is it?" Bash asked, plucking the paper from my trembling fingers with impatience. His eyes scanned the front page. "Oh my god," he whispered.

"I'm above the fold," I breathed, turning to him with wide eyes. "My story is in *The New York Freaking Times*! ABOVE THE FOLD!"

Bash grinned and tossed the newspaper onto the coffee table, his arms hooking around my body and lifting me into the air. I laughed down into his face as he spun me in a circle. "You are incredible," he told me, lowering my body just enough that our lips could brush. "And I am so fucking proud of you."

Our kiss was interrupted by Simon's voice.

"No, no, no. That's not what I meant at all."

Bash set me down and we both turned to face my deluded friend as he retrieved the newspaper from the coffee table. Holding it open, Simon pointed to the photograph that took up a large portion of the front page, accompanying my story. The picture had been snapped by a news photographer as he'd arrived at the scene. In the foreground, a departing ambulance was speeding for the nearest hospital with one of the injured girls inside. The background showed the freighter, illuminated by spot-lights from several news and FBI surveillance helicopters as they circled overhead. And in the center, a couple stood, locked in a comforting embrace.

The woman was dressed in a fabulous — though slightly tattered — ice blue ball gown, her harrowed eyes fixed on the ambulance as it pulled away. The man's face was shown in profile, his forehead resting on the woman's hair and his arms wound tightly around her body, as though he couldn't bear to let go.

The caption was simple enough: *Sebastian Covington, son of alleged sex-trafficking ringleaders, embraces girlfriend Lux Kincaid, whose investigation was vital to the tracking and eventual capture of the criminals. Behind them, the freighter where nearly thirty victims were held for transport.*

"It's a photo of us," I said, looking up at Simon. "I see it."

"No," he huffed. "You don't get it."

I glanced at Fae with raised brows and she grinned.

"The dress!" Simon yelled, pointing at the picture. "*My* dress! On the front page of *The New York Times!*"

I rolled my eyes and heard Bash chuckle behind me. "Oh, of course," I drawled. "How could I have missed that?"

Simon was walking in rapid circles, clutching the newspaper tightly. "This is going to change everything. Everyone will want to know what you're wearing. This really couldn't have worked out any better if I'd planned it myself."

I snorted. "I'm so glad my abduction and near death, the arrest of both of Bash's parents, and the kidnapping of twenty eight underage girls was all worth it, Si."

He looked over at me and grinned. "Oh, shut up. You know how worried I was about you."

That was true enough. After I'd left the docks, I'd been taken to a nearby hospital for treatment. Bash hadn't left my side as doctors stitched the cut on my breastbone, wrapped my damaged hands in bandages, and gave me a cold compress to bring down the swelling in my eye, though he refused to accept any aid for his own wounds. Apparently, scraped knuckles and a bloody lip weren't serious enough to merit a doctor's attention.

Psh. Men.

I'd been released from the hospital into Conor's custody and taken immediately to the FBI field office for a debriefing. They'd given me a pair of women's regulation sweatpants and a black sweatshirt that said SWAT on the back — which I immediately decided to confiscate as payment for my help with their investigation — so I didn't have to stay in my torn dress while they interviewed me in a small, grey conference room.

For nearly three hours, I'd answered their questions, speaking until my voice grew raspy and my eyes began to droop closed. Every now and then, I'd turn to look through the small window in the door and catch sight of Bash, who was pacing like a caged animal in the hallway. When Conor finally told me I could go home, it was nearly dawn.

A federal agent drove Bash and me back to his loft in SoHo, and I'd passed out only minutes into the trip. I stirred awake when I felt Bash's arms hook beneath my body and cradle me to his chest.

"Where are we?" I'd mumbled tiredly.

"Home," he'd said simply, carrying me into the elevator.

I'd smiled at his words, thinking that after the night I'd had, there could be nothing better than a warm bed with the man I loved. I couldn't wait to sink beneath his fluffy down comforter and sleep for the next three days or so.

Unfortunately, it was clear as soon as Bash opened the door to his loft that no such rest would be possible.

Simon and Fae had been inside waiting for us, their eyes glued to the muted television screen as they watched helicopter footage of the freighter. Apparently, Bash had passed off his house keys to them when he left Harding Tower and they hadn't hesitated to use them. When Bash stepped through the entryway, they'd both leapt to their feet and rushed to my side.

I had to hand it to Bash — he hadn't batted an eye when he sat down on his bed, my body still cradled in his arms, and both Fae and Simon climbed on after him. With the four of us crammed in like sardines on the king size mattress, it hadn't been the restful night's sleep I'd been envisioning. But I couldn't complain — I was surrounded by the people I loved most.

My family.

Now, looking from Simon to Fae to Bash, I grinned.

"I love you guys," I whispered.

"You better," Fae responded, smiling back at me.

"Obviously," Simon chimed in, still staring at the photo in the paper.

Bash leaned forward until his mouth brushed my earlobe. "I love you more."

Chapter Thirty-Eight

※❀※

AFTER

ASK ANY EXPERIENCED CLIMBER — NOT YOUR AVERAGE JOE, who tops the peaks and hills just beyond his backyard, but the true daredevils who attempt to conquer the Seven Summits — about his excursions and he'll say the same thing. When you're near the summit, in that precarious slope of rock and ice known by many as the Death Zone, the air is so thin you can literally feel each one of your cells screaming out for oxygen. The sun is so bright, you can actually become blinded by its endless glare off the bleached white snow. The altitude sickness affects your cognition, dizzying you to the point of disorientation and death. The pain in your limbs as they ascend higher, the burning in your joints as you force them to pull you ever-upward, only increases the closer you get to the top of the peak.

There are a thousand reasons to turn back, and precious few — perhaps only one — to keep going.

Of the many climbers who attempt to reach the summit, few

actually succeed. Two men, armed with identical skill sets, might be placed on the same mountain at the same time — and yet, in all likelihood, only one will make it to the top.

The mountain is climbable; that's been proven a hundred times over.

The conditions are perfect; a clear, sunny day with a light breeze.

The equipment is state of the art; better than any climbers in the past ever had.

So the question remains — why does one man ascend while another remains at the bottom of the peak, his skyward gaze riveted on a summit he'll never see up close?

It turns out, the answer is pretty simple: the difference lies deep within the hearts of the climbers.

Sir Edmund Hillary, the first man to successfully climb Mount Everest, said it best.

It is not the mountain we conquer, but ourselves.

Centuries before Hillary was born, a brash conqueror named Hannibal knew that same thing, as he gave the order to lead his elephant army across the Alps.

Because when you're faced with an insurmountable task, when you're on that peak, and your body has reached its absolute limit, you have to reach inside yourself and find that stubborn, reckless, insistent part of your own psyche that refuses to quit. That tiny part of your mind that's howling at you to either find a way or make one, dammit, because you can't return to the ground now. Not when you're so close to your dreams you could reach out and touch them with your fingertips.

I might not have always been one of those people. I might not have always listened to that little voice inside my head, that insisted I carry on. But I swear, as long as I live, I'll never ignore it again. Not when, on the occasions I did listen, it helped me find my way.

When Jamie was sick and we were losing the house, something deep within my soul told me to press onward.

When everyone — including me — doubted my theories about the missing girls, something made me keep searching.

And when everything was stacked against us — time, family, history, heartache — Bash and I found our way back to each other.

⚘

I DIDN'T KNOW WHAT THE FUTURE WOULD HOLD. I DIDN'T need to.

For the first time in a long time, I was so happy I didn't look down the line at what was coming for me. I lived fully in my present, and I enjoyed every minute of it.

Two weeks after the freighter raid, I'd given up the lease on my apartment in Hell's Kitchen and officially moved into the loft with Bash. It wasn't a tough transition, since I'd already been sleeping there every night and half my clothes were moved into his closet — and, anyway, it was where I wanted to be. Bash gave me a few more drawers in his dresser and there was now another color photograph brightening up his walls: a large, blown-up canvas of Jamie, Bash, and me that had been taken the summer we were all seventeen, our tanned skin and sun-bleached hair a testament to our many hours outdoors that season.

I remember that day at the lake like it was yesterday — eight years may've passed, but it remained painted bright and bold in my mind, rather than watercolored in the typical washed out hues of distant memory. We'd wheeled Jamie's chair to the edge of the dock and helped him stand, supported between Bash and me with all his weight on his right leg. A woman at the shore snapped our photo as we jumped off the edge of the dock in unison, our three forms suspended midair over the lake in the fraction of time before our feet broke through the water. In that moment, when the camera shutter clicked down, we were flying — forever frozen in our youth, with our arms stretched high above our heads as though if we reached hard enough, we might extend our flight for another few seconds or maybe never return to the earth at all.

Looking at that picture every day brought a little Jamie back into our lives and always put a smile on my face.

There were other changes, too.

The day after my story hit the front page of newspapers across the country, I walked into Jeanine's office and officially gave my two weeks notice. I wish I could say I called her a cow and stormed out in a blaze of glory, but that would be a lie. There was no grand exit — in fact, Jeanine barely looked up from her laptop as I told her I'd be leaving the post I'd held for nearly three years.

With little fanfare, I cleared out my desk and left *Luster* behind, the murmured goodbyes of my coworkers chasing me through the elevator doors and down onto the street. As I stepped out onto the curb and pulled a breath of fresh — well, fresh by city standards — air into my lungs, I felt an enormous weight slip off my shoulders.

As I'd once told a young, terrified, Swedish maid — there were other jobs, but there was only one of me. It was about time I started doing something I was truly passionate about, rather than staying somewhere I was miserable because of good health benefits and a steady paycheck. I had three interviews lined up next week at small newspapers throughout the city, for freelance positions that would no doubt pay me in peanuts. I knew I'd have to start at the bottom and work my way up the totem pole. I knew it would likely be tougher than my worst day at *Luster.* Yet, I was surprisingly okay with that. With Bash at my side and my investigation into Vera's disappearance well behind me, nothing seemed quite as scary as it had two months ago.

I wasn't the only one who quit *Luster* to chase their dreams. Simon gave his notice the same day I gave mine. He was full of plans to start his own fashion line of evening wear, spurred in no small part by the recognition he'd received since photographs of his dress had been plastered all over the internet and every major media outlet for the past few weeks. I couldn't wait to see his designs on the pages of *Vogue* — and maybe even *Luster* — someday.

Fae was, of course, mournful that both Simon and I were leaving her alone at the magazine. But I had a feeling she wouldn't be sticking around too long either. That girl was like a ticking time bomb of secrets — I couldn't help but think that someday soon, she was going to explode from the sheer pressure of keeping them all contained. Thankfully, she had two extremely overbearing friends to help put her back together if and when that happened.

Vera, Miri, and the rest of the missing girls were back with their families. Several prominent government agencies had stepped forward to ensure that the victims of the *Labyrinth* trafficking-ring would receive the best psychological and physical treatment to help them cope with what had happened and, hopefully, learn to move on. As for *Labyrinth* itself, the club was shut down pending further investigation. The freighter had been seized as evidence in the trial against Judith Ann Covington, which was set for six months from now. She'd been denied bail.

I hoped the aesthetics of her cellblock were to her taste.

Former Senator Andrew Covington was also in jail awaiting trial, as were at least twenty men in connection with the organization – including Santos and three other dirty cops. Footage recovered from Judith's personal files allowed the FBI to pinpoint exactly which government officials had taken part in those "anonymous" auctions on the fourth floor of *Labyrinth*. I'd heard at least four senators and two congressmen had already resigned from their posts and were facing federal charges.

Conor told me the FBI had an airtight case, between everything they'd found on the freighter, at *Labyrinth*, and at the Red Hook brewery. No one involved would serve less than the mandatory 20-year sentence — and Judith might serve up to three times that.

The day after I quit *Luster*, I withdrew some money from my carefully hoarded savings and bought Mrs. Patel a massive massaging recliner chair to sit in during her long hours behind the counter. It was the least I could do to repay her for saving my life. As I'd anticipated, the old woman huffed and puffed when I'd had it delivered to *Swagat* and the delivery men wheeled away her ancient, faded maroon chair. But, miraculously, as soon as she'd settled into the plush cushions of her new La-Z-Boy, her glare had disappeared and a smile — a real, actual smile — had crossed her face. She was also thrilled to discover the side cup holder made a convenient holster for her Glock.

As for Bash, well, he was Bash. He was wonderful.

And bossy and sexy and annoying and funny and so many other adjectives it would take me another seven whole years to list them all. I suppose it was simplest just to say that I loved him and he loved me, and, for the moment, we were thrilled to simply be together again.

Things had changed, for the better. I'd gotten my unexpectedly happy ending, complete with my fairytale hero. Everything was perfect. At least, it was until something came along that completely knocked me for a loop.

One change I absolutely hadn't seen coming...

❧

I AWOKE TO THE SENSATION OF A PAIR OF LIPS TRAILING ACROSS my bare stomach, leaving featherlight kisses in their wake. My eyes blinked open and I glanced down to see a familiar golden head hovering over my belly button.

"What are you doing?" I whispered, my voice cracking with sleep.

He pressed another soft kiss to my stomach.

I glanced to my left, the small glowing clock on the bedside table next to Bash's bed informing me that it was just past 5:00 a.m. "Bash?" I asked, slipping one of my hands into his hair. I watched my fingers weave through the thick strands for a moment, my bleary eyes not registering the sight before me for several long seconds.

I finally realized what was wrong — starting with the fact that there was something shiny wrapped around a very important finger on my left hand and ending with the fact that I was pretty positive it hadn't been there when I'd fallen asleep five hours ago. My hand stilled as my gaze caught on the ring.

Bash raised his head, his warm eyes cutting through the darkness to meet mine.

"What is this?" I breathed, my eyes flickering from his face to my left hand, which I held aloft as though it wasn't part of my body.

"I'm pretty sure it's your left hand," Bash said, grinning.

The lack of air passing through my constricted throat made my voice rise to a nervous squeak. "And the ring?"

"Oh, that." He laughed.

"Yes, *that*." I glared at him. "Is this a joke?"

His laughter died mid-chuckle. "Why would this be a joke?"

"There's a ring on my finger, Bash!"

"I'm aware of that," he said in a patient voice, as though I were a five-year-old who didn't quite understand what was happening. "I'm the one who put it there."

"But... what..." I trailed off, dazzled by the large rock on my finger.

"Words, Freckles. Use your words." He grinned again, his hands skimming up and down my sides in a soothing motion.

"You want to marry me?" I breathed, turning wide eyes to him.

Bash smiled. "Well, I don't make a habit of putting rings on girls I don't intend to spend the rest of my life with."

"But you didn't even ask me!" I narrowed my eyes on his grinning face. "Maybe I don't want to spend the rest of my life with you!"

His laughter rang out louder than ever and his grin widened. "Yes, you do."

"How do you know? Huh?" I teased, a euphoric smile fighting its way to the surface. "You snore. And you hog all the covers."

"Those are your criteria for not marrying me?"

Damn, I needed some stronger material. "You're always taking pictures of me without makeup on."

"Can you blame me? You're beautiful."

I huffed, but my lips were twitching dangerously. "It's five in the morning! I have morning breath! People are going to ask, 'How did you two get engaged?' and I'll have to tell them I had bed-head and bad breath," I whined playfully. "You couldn't have waited to ask me at a decent hour, huh?"

"Sorry. I couldn't wait another second."

My eyes began to water as a smile broke out across my face. "Are you sure? Like really, surely sure?"

"I've been 'really, surely sure' since I was seventeen, Lux." Bash climbed up the length of my body so we were at eye-level, his face hovering only inches above mine. "What time does City Hall open? Eight? I'm so sure about spending my life with you, we can get dressed and go right now. We'll be the first people in line."

I giggled as happy tears leaked from my eyes.

"I'm serious," Bash protested, his eyes shining. "We can drag a priest or a clerk or a captain or someone with one of those internet-marriage licensing certificates out of bed."

"You'd marry me today?" I asked, brows raised.

"Today, tomorrow, next week, next year. Any time you want." Bash leaned in and kissed the tip of my nose. His fingers interlaced with mine, and he lifted our joined hands so we could both stare at the bright diamond on my left ring finger. "When you're ready, tell me and I'll be there in a tux, waiting for you at the end of that aisle. Just say the word, Freckles."

THE END

Afterword

THE FACTS

This is a work of fiction, but the issues of human smuggling and sex trafficking across the globe are all too real. Sex trafficking is the fastest-growing criminal enterprise in the world – a $32 billion-a-year global industry. In the United States alone, each year an estimated 100,000-300,000 American children are at risk of being sold for commercial sex.

If you suspect someone is a victim of human trafficking, please don't remain silent. Call the Homeland Security Investigations Tip Line at 1-866-347-2423 or submit a tip online at www.ice.gov/tips. You can also call or text The National Human Trafficking Resource Center (NHTRC) at 1-888-373-7888 to report a tip or get more information.

Your voice could save countless lives.

SAY THE WORD PLAYLIST

Songs that inspired Say The Word

Song for You by Jesse Thomas
Boats & Birds by Gregory and The Hawk
Be Be Your Love by Rachael Yamagata
Thinking of You by Katy Perry
A Drop in the Ocean by Ron Pope
Landslide by Fleetwood Mac
I Almost Do by Taylor Swift
Human by Christina Perri
Poison & Wine by The Civil Wars
Secrets by Mariah McManus
Say Something by A Great Big World & Christina Aguilera
Shame On You by Mariah McManus
Stay by Rihanna (feat. Mikky Ekko)
Unarmed by Mariah McManus

Also by Julie Johnson

STANDALONE NOVELS:
LIKE GRAVITY
SAY THE WORD
FAITHLESS

❧

THE BOSTON LOVE STORIES:
NOT YOU IT'S ME
CROSS THE LINE
ONE GOOD REASON
TAKE YOUR TIME

❧

THE GIRL DUET:
THE MONDAY GIRL
THE SOMEDAY GIRL

UNCHARTED

About the Author

JULIE JOHNSON is a twenty-something Boston native suffering from an extreme case of Peter Pan Syndrome. When she's not writing, Julie can most often be found adding stamps to her passport, drinking too much coffee, striving to conquer her Netflix queue, and Instagram-  ming pictures of her dog. (Follow her: @author_julie)

She published her debut novel LIKE GRAVITY in August 2013, just before her senior year of college, and she's never looked back. Since, she has published five more novels, including the best-selling BOSTON LOVE STORY series. Her books have appeared on Kindle and iTunes Bestseller lists around the world, as well as in AdWeek, Publishers Weekly, and USA Today.

You can find Julie on Facebook or contact her on her website www.juliejohnsonbooks.com. Sometimes, when she can figure out how Twitter works, she tweets from @AuthorJulie. For major book news and updates, subscribe to Julie's newsletter: http://eepurl.com/bnWtHH

Connect with Julie:

www.juliejohnsonbooks.com
juliejohnsonbooks@gmail.com

Made in the USA
Monee, IL
05 June 2021

70266716R00281